Brockman, Suzanne   AF
Infamous   Brock

Large Print

	DATE DUE		
1615	7/13/13		

Infamous

**Center Point
Large Print**

Also by Suzanne Brockmann
and available from Center Point Large Print:

Dark of Night
Hot Pursuit

**This Large Print Book carries the
Seal of Approval of N.A.V.H.**

Infamous

SUZANNE BROCKMANN

CENTER POINT PUBLISHING
THORNDIKE, MAINE

This Center Point Large Print edition is published in
the year 2010 by arrangement with Ballantine Books,
an imprint of The Random House Publishing Group,
a division of Random House, Inc.

Copyright © 2010 by Suzanne Brockmann.

All rights reserved.

The text of this Large Print edition is unabridged.
In other aspects, this book may vary
from the original edition.
Printed in the United States of America
on permanent paper.
Set in 16-point Times New Roman type.

ISBN: 978-1-60285-922-7

Library of Congress Cataloging-in-Publication Data

Brockmann, Suzanne.
Infamous / Suzanne Brockmann. — Center Point large print ed.
p. cm.
ISBN 978-1-60285-922-7 (library binding : alk. paper)
1. Women college teachers—Fiction.
   2. Motion pictures—Production and direction—Fiction.
   3. Legends—Arizona—Fiction. 4. Arizona—Fiction. 5. Large type books. I. Title.
PS3552.R61455I54 2010
813´.54—dc22

2010035040

To the cast of *Looking for Billy Haines*:

Jason T. Gaffney, Jason Michael Butler,
David Covington, David Craven,
Joseph Cullinane, Apolonia Davalos,
Brandon Davidson, Annie Kerins,
Sarah Ripper, and Eric Ruben;

and to the audiences who looked for,
and found him.

$\mathcal{P}$rologue

Everyone's heard the story about Marshal Silas Quinn and the infamous gunfight at the Red Rock Saloon.

A travelogue to the American Southwest says it better than I ever could:

Like the sinking of the Titanic *or the Great Chicago Fire, like the burning of Atlanta during the Civil War or the age-old feud between the Hatfields and the McCoys, the legend of the violent showdown between Marshal Quinn and the Kelly Gang in Jubilation, Arizona, in 1898 is known to every schoolchild across this great land.*

It is the quintessential story that defines the heroic struggle of good men to tame the wild lawlessness of the Old American West, and although it has been told and retold dozens of times, the drama and tragedy never get old.

Says who?

I'd always kind of hoped that the interest in this tale would finally just fade away, but here it is, the year of our Lord 2010, and some Hollywood types are making yet another motion picture about the hoopla. This one's called *Quinn*, like the man is Cher.

Anyway, kids, here we go again. Someone obviously believes that the countless films already made—both silent and talkies—aren't already overkill. I've always treated 'em as comedies, and gotten a good chuckle from the lot.

And then there were the dime novel versions of the story. I used to read 'em aloud to my great-grandson, the pair of us laughing like damn fools at the melodrama.

"Unhand her, I say, you egregious villain, you contemptible dastard, you odious blackguard!" Quinn roared.

We'd try our damnedest, but with that mouthful of fifty-cent words, it was hard to keep a good roar going. Of course, we weren't Silas Quinn, *the lionhearted and valiant savior, friend to widows and orphans, a knight in shining armor on his dauntless white steed.*

But then again, Silas Quinn wasn't Silas Quinn either.

At least not the honorable, well-educated version of the man from the legend, with his powerful vocabulary. The Quinn I knew had never bothered to learn to read. His favorite adjective started with an *F* and was far overused. His preferred name-calling noun wasn't even close to *dastard* or *blackguard*. It started with a *C* and ended with a *sucker*.

Which is not the type of historical correction that a man wants to tell a wide-eyed six-year-old.

Particularly one whose mother cooked me dinner every night.

So we kind of skipped over that part as we compared the truth to the fiction.

The legend was what it was, or so I tried to teach the boy, same as I taught his grandfather, and father, and all of his many aunts and uncles and cousins before him. It didn't harm us. We had, without a doubt, gotten the last laugh.

It was there, that chuckle of appreciation, at every sunrise, every sunset, and every time I sat out on the front porch of my house, lost in my memories of lying in the arms of the woman I loved. . . .

But I digress.

I should probably repeat the legend here—in case it's been awhile and you need a brief refresher in the whats, the whys, and the wherefores.

Here it is, in a nutshell, again taken directly from that travelogue:

In 1898, Marshal Silas Quinn rode into the silver-mining town of Jubilation, looking to bring law and order to that wild but prospering corner of the Arizona Territory. He did so quickly, eager to send for his beautiful young wife, Melody, having decided that Jubilation would be a good place for them to call home.

But he sent for her too soon. Not long after her stagecoach rolled into town, the Kelly Gang arrived, too, accompanied by the notorious gunslinger and gambler, Jamie "the Kid" Gallagher.

Tension in Jubilation soon hit the boiling point, and Marshal Quinn courageously went up against the outlaws in the Red Rock Saloon. Outgunned seven to one, Quinn single-handedly killed five of the vicious gang members and sent two men running for the border.

But Kid Gallagher was among the survivors, much to Jubilation's misfortune. To avenge Bo Kelly's death—not because they were friends, but because Kelly owed him money—Gallagher kidnapped Melody, and left town with both the marshal's wife and the entire contents of the Jubilation Bank and Trust.

Desperate to save the woman he loved, Silas Quinn raced after them, but arrived too late. Melody was already dead at the Kid's vicious hand. Overcome with rage and grief, Quinn shot the outlaw, who died without telling a soul where he'd hidden the fortune he'd stolen.

Marshal Silas Quinn quietly lived out the remainder of his days in Jubilation, making the town safe for all who lived there. He prospered and remarried in 1899. His second wife, Agatha, bore him a daughter, but he died from what historians believe was a burst appendix shortly before the child turned six.

His final words were of his beautiful Melody, and some think that, in truth, he died of a broken heart.

And okay. All right. *Some* of that is true.

The town's name *was* Jubilation, and it was in the Arizona territory. And Silas Quinn *did* die—praise be to Jesus—some years after his second wife bore him a daughter. And yes, his first wife, Melody, *was* uncommonly beautiful, I'll grant you that, too.

But that nickname, "Kid"? Pure fiction.

Matter of fact, the entire legend's a crock of carefully manufactured horseshit. It's about as historically accurate as the Three Little Pigs, with its oversimplification of good versus evil.

And I should know, because I was there.

I'm the big, bad wolf.

That's right, my name is Jamie Gallagher—no "Kid," I never was a "Kid." In fact, I barely had a childhood. And while I'll hold to that truth that the legend never hurt any of us, enough is enough.

It's about damn time that I climb out of this pig's stewpot that I've let myself be jammed in, and help my great-grandson, A.J., set the story straight.

Chapter One

The son of a bitch was going to make her lie.

Sons of bitches, Alison Carter corrected herself, because her adorable new friend Hugh was part of this hideous charade. In fact, it was rapidly becoming crystal clear that this—her impending lie—was the young production assistant's reason for bringing her here, to this undetermined level of hell. Oh, it looked like the dusty street outside of movie star Trace Marcus's huge trailer, but it was definitely hell.

The morning sky was clear and so blue it hurt Alison's eyes. It was barely 8:30, and the desert sun was already much too hot on the back of her neck.

"Who is she?" Trace's wife demanded through her tears, her mascara making black streaks down what had once been a ridiculously pretty face. Now she just looked ridiculous, the plastic surgery she'd had leaving her looking perpetually surprised as she confronted her philandering husband. "I want to know—I *deserve* to know!"

"I hate you," Alison murmured to Hugh, who, with his tastefully messed red hair, hazel eyes, and athletically trim body, remained adorable despite his dragging her into this.

"Trace needs to be in makeup in twenty minutes," he murmured back as he pulled her closer to this snake pit of domestic non-bliss. "Ninety-seven thousand dollars an hour . . ."

That was his default answer to almost anything—his recitation of the enormous amount of money it was costing director Henry Logan's production company to bring this movie—*Quinn*—to the big screen.

And it was true that if an actor were late to the set, money would, indeed, pour from the company's veins as dozens of crew members stood around, uselessly waiting for the star to undiva his or her ass and get down to work.

So far, it had happened four different times, courtesy of Trace Marcus.

"Who is she, Tracey?" Marcus's wife asked him again. His creepy and ever-present personal assistant, Skip, mumbled something in his low-talker's voice that Alison couldn't hear, but the wife could and she snapped, "Shut up, Skippy, I wasn't asking *you*."

Alison couldn't remember Mrs. Marcus's name, but she, like her husband, had been a huge star back when she was in her late teens, early twenties.

Which really wasn't *that* long ago.

Trace had started celebrating his thirty-third birthday last night. Thirty-three, and he was in desperate need of a comeback, which playing Silas Quinn was designed to provide.

No doubt about it, this was a crazy, crazy business Alison was dipping her toe into here. And she'd always thought the academic world was a little nuts.

But here she was, standing in the dust beneath the blistering hot sun, ready to provide an alibi for a man who wasn't just a crazy actor, but was also a card-carrying moron. It was his freaking birthday. Today. A degree in rocket science wasn't needed to theorize that since it was his birthday, it was highly likely that his loving wife was going to show up here on location, to surprise him with a visit.

Instead Trace had surprised her. Eleanor. That was her name. Although it really shouldn't have been that big of a surprise for Eleanor to find her husband's trailer rocking, not after ten long years spent married to the man. He was a dog. Surely she knew that by now. He couldn't keep his pants zipped to save his life; forget about saving his marriage.

The day Trace had arrived on set, not five minutes after stepping into the much smaller trailer, which was Alison's new office, he'd hit on her—and she'd been so startled she'd laughed in his face.

Which was a mistake, because he now avoided her like the swine flu.

As the official historical consultant for this film, as the author of the latest definitive book about the shoot-out at the Red Rock Saloon, Alison had a wealth of information about the details of Silas Quinn's life. She had a file with newspaper clippings and rare photos. Pictures of Quinn with Melody, taken shortly after their wedding. Pictures of the deceptively pleasant-looking Kid Gallagher gambling in San Francisco. Pictures Trace should want to see as he worked to bring Quinn back to life in this big-budget, high-profile movie.

Alison even had an actual cigar box that the marshal had once kept upon his desk, along with the Bible that the man had carried with him for most of his too short life, even though he'd never had time to learn to read.

Filming had started, but Trace wasn't interested in seeing any of that material, because Alison had thought he was joking when he'd offered to do her on her desk, the way he'd done to Gina Gershon's character in *Last Cowboy Standing*.

And yes, the man was almost freakishly handsome with his dark hair and brown eyes, with that trademark Marcus smile. All of the excess weight he'd put on in his late twenties had finally turned into man-muscle. True, he no longer could play a scene without his shirt, but he was now the perfect size to play Silas Quinn, who'd been a full-grown, incredibly attractive bear of a man.

Still, Trace's offer had been absurd.

And maybe Alison was unused to the ways of Hollywood, coming as she had from Boston College's history department, where doing it on one's desk with a married man was usually frowned upon, independent of whether or not one was a Gina Gershon fan.

And so she'd laughed at his proposal. Loudly.

In Trace's handsome face.

She'd seen, right away, that he was affronted, and she'd immediately apologized and even thanked him—which felt beyond strange—telling him that casual sex just wasn't her thing.

Which was not a lie. It was just not usually something she had to tell a man within five minutes of meeting him.

"Let's move this inside," Hugh suggested now, talking to Skippy, who tried to herd them toward the trailer door, but Eleanor clearly liked having an audience.

"I heard him in there, fucking some slut," she told them, the crass language oddly jarring, spoken as it was in her little girl voice. She spoke loudly enough so that the growing crowd of extras and crew could hear her, too. "So I left, but then I thought, Why am I always the one running away? So I came back, but she was already gone, and now he says it wasn't him in there, that he was at a meeting—at eight o'clock in the morning when his call isn't until eleven . . . ? Like I'm supposed to believe that?"

"Trace *was* in a meeting," Hugh lied effortlessly as he tried to pull Alison even closer.

But she'd gone as far as she was willing to go. She pinched him and he released her, giving her a look that meant . . . what? That she was disappointing him? Seriously?

"See, I *was* in a meeting," Trace echoed, the slightest tinge of relief making his words rush together as he looked at Hugh and realized that they had come to rescue him. Particularly after Hugh pointed surreptitiously toward Alison. "Researching my character. With Professor, um . . ."

"Carter," Hugh helpfully filled in, because the man had apparently forgotten Alison's name. He thumbed his BlackBerry as if the star's schedule were on his personal calendar. "It was . . . Yes, at seven thirty. A.M. A breakfast meeting. In Dr. Carter's office. Which is over with the rest of the production trailers."

And now Eleanor was looking at Alison, sizing her up with her neon blue contact lens–enhanced eyes, her fading suspicion mingling with her hope and relief as Hugh kept spewing his bullcrap.

"She's tremendously busy. Dr. Carter. She needs to approve the costumes for every extra—and we've got a lot of them on set for the next few weeks. Plus she looks at every single script revision, every tweak in the dialogue. The only open time she had to talk to Trace was early this morning."

Alison stayed silent, holding her breath, praying that Eleanor didn't ask her outright about this alleged breakfast meeting—uncertain as to whether or not she'd actually go along with Hugh's bald-faced lie when pressed.

Except, really, she was already going along with the lie, just by standing there as Hugh's exhibit A.

But Eleanor turned back to Trace to ask, "Why didn't you just say so?"

"I did," he lied again, indignant now at the injustice of her accusations. What a prick. "I said, *Someone must've been in my trailer, because it wasn't me,* but you weren't listening. You were blah, blah, blah, bitching and moaning, ready to assume the worst the way you always fucking do—"

"When you left for your meeting at Dr. Carter's office," Hugh interrupted Trace, probably because he was good at reading body language, and he knew that Alison was about to reach out and smack the actor, or denounce them all for the liars that they were, "did you lock your trailer door?"

"I didn't." Trace looked properly chastised and subdued. "Did you, Skip?"

His assistant shook his baseball cap–covered head, no.

"I didn't think we had to," Trace said.

"You better lock it from now on," Hugh advised him, making a very real-seeming note in his BlackBerry. "Someone probably invited an intern in to take a look, and got a little early payback. I'm sorry about the inconvenience, and the misunderstanding," he added with an adorable smile at Eleanor, who was now in Trace's arms, apologizing, which was giving Alison heartburn. "I'll have a cleaning crew come in and . . . Have you checked to see if anything was stolen?"

Trace shook his head. "I don't think anything was." He looked at Skip, who shook his head, too. "No."

"That's good at least," Hugh said. "I'll make sure it gets cleaned and is ready for you by your break. But right now, Mr. Marcus, sir, I hate to do this to you after such an upsetting morning, but your makeup call is in ten minutes. You need to get to work."

"As do I," Alison spoke up, because she was damned if she was going to be part of this ugly conspiracy and not gain *some*thing from it. "Although, Mr. Marcus, perhaps we can schedule another breakfast meeting for tomorrow. I know how interested you are in finding out all that you can about Silas Quinn and we've barely gotten started." She turned to Hugh and gave him a tight smile. "I'll let you check our schedules and set that up for us." The *because you owe me, you little bastard,* was silent.

But understood. Hugh nodded. Message received. "Ninety-seven thousand," he started.

"Yeah, yeah," she said, as she turned away.

But this charlie foxtrot wasn't over yet.

"Dr. Carter."

Yes, that *was* Eleanor Marcus calling her name, in that Betty Boop voice that Alison had never found particularly appealing, even when the actress was a dewy-eyed teenager.

Most of the crowd had dispersed, which was good. Still, she turned back, trying to unclench her teeth enough to give the poor deceived woman a smile rather than a grimace. "Mrs. Marcus," she said, bracing herself. Trace had gone into his trailer, but Skip was still out there, watching them from behind his mirrored sunglasses.

"I'm not acting anymore," Eleanor said. "It's a choice. My choice."

It seemed like a non sequitur, a change of subject, which was a relief, but she appeared to want a response, so Alison nodded. "I'd heard that," she said. "It's a tough business."

"I hurt my back," Eleanor said, indulging in a little lying herself. Apparently it was a hobby for these people. In truth, the actress had stopped appearing in movies because, at the ancient and gnarly age of twenty-nine, she'd refused to let go of her youth—and the doctors who'd tried to make her look eighteen again had somehow botched the procedure, damaging the muscles in her face. She was still beautiful, but she now had only one expression. She'd had additional surgeries over the past five years—or so the tabloids reported—trying, and failing, to make it right.

"I'm sorry about that," Alison said as gently as she could. She backed away, gesturing back the way she and Hugh had come. "I'm melting out here. And I really need to . . ."

"I've seen pictures of Melody Quinn," Eleanor said. "She always looked so sad, so haunted—as if she knew what was coming. She was so young when she died."

Melody Quinn had always stared soberly into the camera, as did everyone who had tintypes taken at that time. *Say cheese!* wasn't a photographer's battle cry until well after the turn of the century. Until long after Melody Quinn had met her tragic end.

"I would've loved to play her," Eleanor continued. "Not now," she added with the slight movement of her lips that was now her smile. "But back when I was her age. She was only twenty-one, right?"

"She was," Alison said. "And yes, ma'am. You would've been great."

It wasn't a lie, but Eleanor rolled her eyes as if it were. "Whatever," she said, turning to go into the trailer where her skunk of a husband was showering in preparation for stepping into Silas Quinn's giant, honorable shoes.

Hugh was trying to slip away, unnoticed, but Alison quickly caught up.

"Don't you ever," she all but spat at him, her voice low but deadly, as she hurried along beside him, down the dusty street, "*ever* do that to me again."

"Ninety-seven—" he started, but she skidded to a halt, catching his arm and spinning him toward her.

"Whoa!" One of the extras, a tall, lean cowboy type, had been following them so closely, he nearly crashed into them.

But Alison ignored him as she jabbed one finger into Hugh's face, nearly sticking it up his perfect nose. "Don't. Start. I signed a contract with Logan Productions, *not* with the devil. That poor girl—"

"That poor girl," Hugh interrupted her, "was banging one of last season's American Idols, just last week, in Vegas. She knows exactly what Trace does on set without her. She just needed a plausible excuse to keep from looking too foolish. That's what we gave her."

"We? Thanks *so* much, but next time leave me out of it. Because I will not do that again. And if I were you, I wouldn't—"

"Believe it or not," Hugh said, "it's part of my job. I handle the talent."

"Well . . ." Alison sputtered. "*Ew.* Big honking *ew.* It's not part of *my* job and . . ." The cowboy was hovering. He'd backed off a bit in a show of giving them privacy, but he was clearly waiting

22

to talk to her. She spun toward him, her voice more impatient than she'd intended. "Can I help you?"

"Um," he said.

"You were told to find me for costume approval," she guessed as she scanned his clothes, adding, "Oh, no. No. Nope. The jeans are too modern—they're your own, right? They must've run out of your size."

He was tall—quite a few inches over six feet—with long legs. And while the faded jeans he was wearing looked good on him—extremely good—they wouldn't do.

"Paula!" Alison shouted. She'd spotted the intern across the street over by the Feed and Grain Store, talking with the second-unit director Frank or Fred or whatever his name was. And damnit, Hugh had taken the opportunity to escape. He'd vanished completely, so Alison turned back to tell the extra, "Even looser fitting jeans are still too snug in the crotch. Plus, I can tell you're wearing briefs, which weren't available until 1935. The things you learn from being on a movie set are amazing, aren't they? The boots are good, but you're going to have to lose the watch, and that shirt isn't . . ."

She reached out to touch the fabric of his pale blue workshirt. It was a soft cotton, but it had been stone-washed, and the pre-fade was too uniform. No cowboy in his right mind in 1898 would've bought a shirt that was already worn out.

"No," Alison said again, asking, "Who dressed you? It's all wrong. Except for the boots. And the hat. You can keep the hat." That was one very authentic-looking off-white cowboy hat he was holding loosely in his big hands. She raised her voice again. "Paula!"

"I think maybe you've mistaken me for someone else, ma'am," the man finally said in a soft voice that had a hint of a Western drawl. "I'm not an extra for this movie."

And Alison stopped examining his jeans and his shirt and looked up--he was so tall she actually had to tilt her head, which was rare—and into a face that she'd known for years.

Her mouth dropped open as she stared at him.

Wide cheekbones, narrow chin, big straight nose, elegant lips, blue, blue eyes . . .

With the exception of his hair, which was golden blond, he looked remarkably, *eerily* like the few rare pictures she'd studied of Jamie "the Kid" Gallagher.

And if he wasn't an extra . . .

That meant he was the actor they'd found to play Gallagher.

Oh, big, wonderful hip-hip-hooray. This was too good. Casting had *way* outdone themselves this time.

And sure, he wasn't perfect. He was quite a bit

24

taller than she believed Kid Gallagher had been. But he had the same slender build, with those long legs that she'd already noticed leading to narrow hips that angled upward to broad, *broad* shoulders.

He was older than Gallagher, too, by a good fifteen years, but that was okay. The makeup team could take some years off the actor's face, no problem, the same way they could darken his thick hair and make it wavier.

Alison laughed. He was perfect.

He was gazing back at her, one eyebrow slightly raised at her intense scrutiny of his face.

"Sorry for staring, but . . ." She held out her hand to him, laughing again. "I'm . . . so impressed. I'm Alison Carter. And you're our Gallagher. Congratulations and welcome to the set."

His hand felt cool against hers, despite the day's heat. He had big fingers that were rough with calluses and a palm that engulfed hers. Like many actors, this man no doubt had been forced to support himself between jobs by doing manual labor. Although after *Quinn*, that was going to change. There would be no more ditch digging, landscaping, or carpentry in this man's bright and shiny future.

"Thank you," he said. "But, um, I'm not sure—"

"Have you got a minute to come to my trailer?" she interrupted him. He'd have plenty of time to be humble later. "I've got tons of information to give you before someone else grabs you."

Before the actor could answer her, Paula jogged over, calling, "I'm sorry, Dr. Carter. How can I help you?"

"Coffee," Alison said. "Two cups—in my office, bless you, and . . ." She looked at their lovely Gallagher. "You must've just arrived on set. Have you had breakfast?" She didn't wait for him to answer. "Bring over a breakfast tray, too. Thank you, Paula."

He looked surprised and a little uncomfortable as the intern hurried away. "That's really not necessary."

"Get used to it," she told him, walking backward so that she could look at him as she led the way to the row of production trailers, one of which was her office. The resemblance was really remarkable. "It comes with the territory. Where on earth did they find you?"

"Find me?" he echoed. He had a slightly puzzled look on his face, as if she were speaking a foreign language and he was having trouble translating.

"Strange new world, huh?" she said. "I'm with you there, Alice. I fell down the same rabbit hole myself, just a few weeks ago." She rephrased her question. "Where are you from?"

"Alaska," he said.

Alison laughed. "No wonder you look shell-

26

shocked. You're a long way from home. I'm from Boston myself and every time I go outside, I feel like I'm stepping into an oven. People are going to tell you that you'll get used to the heat, but they're lying. You won't. You're going to have to drink a lot of water. And always carry a hat."

He smiled at that, and it softened his face and made at least five of those extra years disappear. "It's been a while," he said as they crossed the street and headed back behind the town's single motel, where the production trailers were hidden out of camera range, "but I've spent plenty of time in the desert. I know how to handle heat." He cleared his throat. "What I can't quite figure out is . . . how did you know who I am? Did . . . someone call you or . . . ?"

"I haven't checked messages yet this morning. Truth is, I recognized you." Alison took out her keys as she led him to the narrow door of her office, unlocking it. "It's been a particularly crazy day." She stepped back and gestured for him to go in first. "Better duck. This thing is a death trap for tall people. I can't tell you how many times I've hit my head. You'd think I'd eventually learn."

He had to both duck and angle his shoulders slightly to make it through the door and into the trailer.

It was silly for her to have let him go first, because now he stood there, at the top of the stairs, gazing at the piles of books and papers that crowded not just her desk but every available surface—including the enormous leather sofa that lined one whole side of the tiny room. The thing must've been built in there—or the trailer constructed around it—according to some actor's contract, circa 1985.

"Sorry about the mess," she said, shutting the door firmly behind her in a pathetic attempt to keep the cool air in and the scorching heat out. "And it's not really as bad as it looks, I know exactly where everything is, so let me . . . Excuse me." She squeezed past him—he was extremely solid in addition to being tall—and cleared off space on the sofa for him to sit.

"Organization is actually one of my strengths," she added, "but—and I don't know how many movie sets you've been on—but everyone who knocks on my door needs something done *immediately,* top priority, drop everything, including whatever five minutes ago's screaming priority was, so filing nearly always gets pushed to tomorrow. Sit. Please. I figure I'll get it all filed the day after we wrap."

"I haven't," he said as he lowered his big frame into the huge couch, making it look not exactly tiny, but certainly more average-sized. "Been on a movie set before."

"So it's been stage plays, then," she deduced as she moved behind her cluttered desk and sat down, too. "This must be so exciting for you."

"Um," he said, glancing around the room again. "Well . . ."

"You're probably stressed about how last minute this all is," she sympathized. "We've already started shooting, and you've got a lot of research to do in a short amount of time to get up to speed. But don't worry. I'm here to help you. It's going to be fine. You probably have a million questions, but I want to preface this part of our discussion by freely and openly confessing that I am and always have been an admirer of Silas Quinn. I've done extensive research on this man who was, in my opinion, easily the most tragically heroic figure in the history of the American West. Needless to say—but I'll say it anyway—my opinion of Kid Gallagher is neither charitable nor unbiased."

Their Gallagher was nodding. "I've read your book. You made that . . . pretty clear."

"But I don't go into much detail about Kid Gallagher's long list of crimes," she told him, happily surprised that he'd already read her book, without her having to push it on him. That was always awkward—or at least it had been with both Trace Marcus and Winter Baxter, the actress who was playing Melody. Neither of them were big readers, and their eyes had immediately glazed over when she'd pulled out the thick book. "And the list was long. Gallagher had quite a rap sheet, so to speak, starting right when he left home at age fifteen."

She used her toe to open the file cabinet that was wedged in next to her desk, and pulled out her hefty Gallagher file. "He came from Philadelphia, from a wealthy family," she continued as she handed the actor the file, which he opened immediately and began looking through—his eagerness winning him even more points in her opinion. "And although there's no record of this, I've always imagined him as one of those horrible little boys who drowned puppies and pulled the legs off insects."

He looked up at that, glancing briefly around the room before meeting her eyes, his dismay apparent.

"I know," she admitted. "There's no proof—it's just my prejudice showing. But after he left home, his family never mentioned him again. It was as if he'd never existed—as if they'd disowned him and didn't want him to come back. One theory is that he was gay and his family's rejection turned him into an outcast and it wasn't a big step from that to outlaw, but there's also no proof of that so . . . I've spoken to Henry Logan at length about the Kid's character—have you talked to him yet?"

He looked up from the file again, his dark blue eyes somber. "No. I haven't. Um . . ." He cleared his throat, glanced around the room again. "Dr. Carter—"

She cut him off again, which was probably rude, but he was a slower talker, and she had information that she knew would, immediately, relieve some of his trepidation. "I know Henry's got this reputation for being a real perfectionist when he directs his movies, but I've found him to be open to discussion. He's sincerely interested in listening to different ideas, so don't be shy about speaking up. But the one thing you should know is that he's particularly interested in making Kid Gallagher multidimensional in his film. All of the other movies about the gunfight at the Red Rock Saloon have portrayed the Kid as psychotic, which comes out as extremely one-note. But something I've heard Henry say, over and over, as we've discussed this particular character, is that no one is ever the bad guy in his own movie, or in his own life. And that was probably true of Kid Gallagher. He probably didn't see himself as a villain." She couldn't keep herself from adding, "Despite the fact that he was a bank robber, a kidnapper, and a cold-blooded killer."

Their Gallagher smiled at that. "Bank robber, kidnapper, and cold-blooded killer," he repeated, shaking his head and laughing softly. "What if I told you that you were a hundred percent wrong?"

Chapter Two

When Dr. Alison Carter laughed, her light brown eyes sparkled.

"Wow," she said. "You *are* good. Talk about not being the bad guy in your own movie. *You are a hundred percent wrong,*" she repeated, with a horrendous, over-the-top, Yankee-fied imitation of his barely-there drawl. But she wasn't mocking A.J. She was truly delighted, and it was actually pretty cute.

It was hard not to laugh along with her. Which made her smile grow even wider and warmer.

"That was fantastic," she enthused. "Henry's going to love you."

Cute was probably not a word that many people used to describe this woman. *Gorgeous* probably wasn't used very often either, although she was that, as well.

She was much taller than she'd looked in the black-and-white author photo on the back of her book, and slender to the point of almost skinny, with long arms and legs that on a less graceful woman might've made her seem like an odd, ungainly bird. Instead, she made him think of ballet dancers, of strong, athletic bodies in astonishingly beautiful motion.

Her hair wasn't the salt and pepper he'd imagined, but instead a rich, gleaming golden brown that hung to her shoulders and caught the light whenever she moved. It was almost the exact same color as her eyes—eyes that had distracted the bejeezus out of him more than once in the short time since she'd first spoken to him in the street outside the movie star's trailer.

If eyes truly were the window to the soul, hers was lively, intelligent, and passionate, with a great sense of humor.

She'd been mortified—he'd seen that in her eyes, too—that the little redheaded man had used her to help him tell his lies.

Don't you ever, ever do that to me again. . . .

It was possible that A.J. had fallen in love with her, right at that very moment, when she'd been on the verge of reaming the redhead a new one.

Which was just as bizarre as A.J.'s using the word *cute* to describe the woman. He didn't fall in love, and certainly not with strangers.

Even strangers whose books he'd read.

Strangers who were supposed to be fifty-something and grandmotherly, not thirty-something and undeniably sexy.

And as long as he was making a list of everything unusual or odd about today, he had to add that—also out of character for him, considering he was in a four-year-long dry spell—he'd fallen completely in lust with the woman, too, when she'd examined him like a piece of meat and announced that she could tell he was wearing briefs beneath his jeans.

He'd gone without sex of the non-solo variety for so long, he could only vaguely remember what it was like. Until he'd gazed into Alison Carter's highly educated eyes and gotten a vivid sense of what it would feel like to push his way between her knees as she clung to him.

And now she'd just asked him something, but he had no idea what she'd said, because he was sitting here, imagining himself having sex with her. Again. Way to go, particularly since he was in her office due to her misconception. She thought he was the actor hired to play Jamie Gallagher in this movie.

She also—obviously—thought that they were the only two people in this little room.

She was wrong about that, too, even though A.J. was the only person on the planet who could see the ghost of his great-grandfather—a ghost that had been haunting him for more than two weeks now.

And now the ghost, too, was looking at A.J. expectantly, as if waiting for him to answer Alison's question.

"I'm sorry," A.J. started, but he was saved from having to admit that he was an idiot by her phone's shrill ring.

She glanced at the clock that was above the hobbit-sized trailer door and gave him an apologetic smile. "I really have to take this. I'll try to make it quick, though. Do you mind terribly?"

"Of course not," A.J. said. He lifted the file she'd given him. "I'll just, um . . ."

She smiled again, and he realized that it was her mouth that probably kept her from being called gorgeous—at least by the rest of the world. It was too generous, too wide and not pouty enough to compete against the perceived perfection of cookie-cutter teenaged models. And yet it was her mouth that he found himself watching when he wasn't hypnotized by her eyes. She seemed to always be on the verge of smiling just a little, about to share a secret or a kiss.

"This is Alison Carter," she said into her phone, turning slightly away from him.

Meanwhile, the ghost cleared his insubstantial throat and spoke. "Turn the page."

A.J. sighed as he looked down at the file that contained the so-called historical background on Jamie Gallagher, his great-grandfather. He turned the page so that the ghost of that very same great-grandfather, who was reading over his shoulder, could see the text that A.J. had already skimmed.

"Oh," Jamie's ghost said, his words dripping with his disgust. "Nice. I was known for slitting throats so that's probably how I killed Melody. First it was that I shot her through the heart, but I guess that wasn't awful enough. Turn the next page. Come on. Let's see what else I'm guilty of, even though I've never slit a throat in my life."

A.J. closed the file. "It's all just more of the bullshit that Quinn concocted," he murmured, well aware that talking to someone that no one else could see or hear tended to raise eyebrows.

"Is there any truth in there at all?" Jamie asked.

"Not one single thing," A.J. breathed, and great—Alison glanced over. She'd overheard him talking to his imaginary friend. Perfect.

But she was still on the phone, and she turned away again to say, "But . . . No, no, no, nuh, no, Henry . . . Henry. Shh. You're paying me for my opinion, so you really need to let me speak and . . . Thank you, yes. The layout of the saloon hasn't changed, right? It hasn't, so Quinn *had* to be up on the second floor when the shooting started. There's no way he could have survived those odds otherwise."

"Quinn survived," Jamie's ghost told her, even though he knew she couldn't hear him, "because I was there. Because I wasn't one of the Kelly Gang, I was just passing through—until Quinn himself brought me into it."

For a man who'd been born nearly a hundred and thirty years ago, Jamie looked sharp. And young. He'd been ninety-one when A.J. was born, and had died the year A.J. turned ten.

He'd never seen his beloved gramps without a face full of wrinkles, but aside from the very first time the ghost had appeared to A.J., he usually chose to manifest himself this way.

As a man who was decades younger than A.J., which was weird.

Assuming that being haunted by one's great-grandfather's ghost was less weird if the spirit looked like an old man.

But Jamie—it was hard thinking of him as "Gramps" when he looked like one of A.J.'s old army drinking buddies—could apparently pick and choose how he appeared. And he chose to look much as he had back when he first rode into Jubilation all those years ago, his hair thick and black, his face unlined. He dressed, too, as the professional gambler that he'd been, in black pants, a black waistcoat, a crisp white shirt with one of those brightly embroidered vests he was so fond of, and a string tie around his neck. His black boots were polished and his chains and spurs gleamed.

And he wore a silver Colt, holstered in a gun belt, low around his hips.

Jamie slouched down now, next to A.J. on the couch, putting his feet up on Alison's desk.

"She's not exactly the wicked witch spinster professor we imagined her to be, is she?" he asked.

"Nope," A.J. answered.

"Hmm," Jamie said. "She's kind of . . . mysteriously attractive. I can't quite figure out what it is about her. I suppose, if you go for interesting-looking women . . ."

A.J. didn't say another word. He didn't shift in his seat, didn't move, barely even breathed.

And yet, somehow Jamie turned and looked at him, his blue eyes perceptive and astute as he nodded. "You see it, too. That whatever-it-is. I can tell by the way you look at her. You like her," he concluded. "Well, well, well. First day in Arizona and Mr. Ice Cube's already starting to thaw? I'll be damned. Which is not something I say lightly anymore."

A.J. just shook his head.

Jamie whistled softly through his teeth. "So . . . what's the plan? Ask her to dinner before you tell her that you're not the actor who's playing me in this movie? Save the bombshell that her book is a fictional piece of crap with nary a fact within its pages for dessert?"

A.J. laughed in despair. Yeah, that would work.

And Alison hung up her phone. "What's so funny?" she asked, eager to be let in on the joke.

"Um," he said, because she was smiling at him again, and he was an idiot.

It was idiotic that he let himself get tongue-tied, that he didn't simply ignore the way his pulse sped up when this woman met his eyes.

Because, really. What did he think was going to happen here?

Even if she got past the news that he'd come

here to explode every so-called historical "fact" that she believed about Silas Quinn, there was the little matter of Jamie.

Hi, my name's A.J and I like fresh spinach salad and slow-cooked pot roast, hikes in the mountains in the fresh morning air, classic rock, the Arts and Crafts period for architecture and furniture, the comedies of Katharine Hepburn and Spencer Tracy, and oh, yes, long walks on the beach at sunset while having heart-to-heart talks with the ghost of my long-dead great-grandfather.

There was no point in delaying any of this. There was no way to finesse this situation.

When he ponied up the truth about why he was here in Jubilation, Dr. Alison Carter was going to hate him or dismiss him. Either way, the friendly smiles and sparkling eye contact would cease.

He took a deep breath, but Alison beat him to the punch. "You know, it just occurred to me that I don't know your name."

"Showtime," Jamie said, heavy on the *sh*. "You gonna tell her your real name or make something up? I always liked Ferd McGurgle. It's not one of those names you forget, where you have to stop and think, *Now, who did I say I was again, Tom Smith or Bill Jones . . . ?*"

"Actually," A.J. said, trying his best to ignore Jamie's *help,* "you *do* know my name." He cleared his throat as she looked puzzled, that little ever-present almost-smile ready to expand across her face. He exhaled and just said it. "It's Gallagher."

"*Nicely* done." Jamie applauded. "Good segue, good choice—honesty. Much better than Ferd. I'm proud of you, kid."

But Alison was still puzzled, still about to smile, until she realized what he'd said. Her mouth dropped open, but she closed it fast. "Gallagher?" she repeated and the smile was definitely gone. "As in . . . *Gallagher?*"

"As in Austin James Gallagher," A.J. told her with a nod. "I'm A.J., for short. I was named after my great-grandfather." He lifted her file. "Jamie. He dropped the Austin after he came west. Too many people thought he was from Texas, which kind of pissed him off." He tried to make a joke. "He'd met a few Texans he didn't particularly like, so . . ."

Silence.

Yeah.

Alison was just sitting there behind her desk, gazing at him with eyes that were a whole hell of a lot less warm now.

"She's taking the news rather well," Jamie said dryly. "At least she hasn't called in the sheriff yet. You might want to tell her the rest of it, kid. This way, you get it over with all at once. Like pulling off a Band-Aid. While you're at it, come to think of it, you should tell her about me."

40

A.J. looked at him. There was not a chance in hell he was going to do that.

But Alison had found her voice. "You're not the actor the casting office found to play Jamie Gallagher."

A.J. shook his head and answered, even though she hadn't made it a question. "No, ma'am. I'm not an actor. I'm a carpenter. From Alaska."

"Then why are you here?" Alison point-blanked it with a directness that A.J. admired.

Admired and respected and, yeah, liked. A little too much. He tried to brush off the disappointment that he knew was going to pile up as he continued to talk to her, and she continued to be funny and smart.

"Well, I guess I'm here because . . ." He cleared his throat. Where and how to start? "See, I must've read about it online," he said. "The fact that Henry Logan was making this movie based on your book. It was the first I'd heard of it—your book—so I searched for it and . . . Couldn't find it. I finally ordered it direct from the publisher."

"Small press," she said. "Low print run. It's still hard to find."

A.J. nodded. "No kidding. I read there's gonna be a trade paperback reissue from a bigger publisher."

"It'll hit bookstores when the movie comes out," she said.

A.J. nodded again. "Congratulations. That's

41

great. It was, um, well written. A quick read, considering the length, and uh . . .”

"Thank you?" she said, crossing her arms and raising an eyebrow. "And you came here because you wanted to . . . tell me that? Maybe get your copy signed . . . ?"

"Not exactly." A.J. hesitated.

Next to him, Jamie started to whistle quietly, a rather tuneless rendition of one of the snippets of music the organist used to play at the college summer league baseball field in Anchorage, prompting the crowd to shout, "Let's go!"

A.J. finally spoke, just as Alison, too, leaned forward.

"I'm here because, like I said before, you got the story, the facts, completely wrong," he told her, as she said, "If you're here for your share of the millions of dollars I'm making off this book, you're in for a shock. My advance was a low five figures. And even if I *were* making a ton of money, which I'm not, every lawyer on this planet would agree. You don't even remotely own the rights to the story of a man who's been dead since 1898."

"1977," A.J. corrected her. "And no, ma'am, that is not why I'm here. Not for money, no. I'm here because . . ." He glanced at Jamie. *Because Great-grandpa's ghost wouldn't stop pestering me until I packed a bag and headed south.* No way was he telling her that. "Well, because you wrote

42

in the introduction to your book that you were striving for historical accuracy. And you seemed to mean it. And there's a whole pack of inaccuracies in your book that could use some clearing up."

"Understatement of not just one century, but two," Jamie said.

A smile had found its way back onto Alison's face. "Really."

"I thought," A.J. told her, "from what you wrote, that you'd be interested in the truth."

"A truth that has Kid Gallagher living until 1977—a full one hundred and one years after he was born?"

"That's right," A.J. said, glancing at Jamie. This was good. She seemed interested, and okay, maybe a little too amused, but at least she hadn't kicked him out on his ass into the dusty street.

"Silas Quinn shot and killed Kid Gallagher in 1898," she countered with patient authority. "It's been documented."

"Will you please ask her to stop calling me *Kid*," Jamie said plaintively, effortlessly rising and starting to pace from one end of the tiny room to the other and back again. "You might also want to point out that Quinn was a lousy shot. He couldn't hit the side of a barn, even if he was standing inside of the damn thing, firing off a cannon."

"Jamie Gallagher's death was documented only

by Silas Quinn, and by people who'd heard about it *from* Silas Quinn." A.J. sat forward, on the edge of the couch. "The marshal was pretty good at telling tall tales."

Alison laughed—a short burst of delight. "In other words, you're saying Silas Quinn was a liar."

"Silas Quinn was an asshole," Jamie interjected, "but we can go with liar for now."

"According to my great-grandfather," A.J. said evenly, trying to ignore the increasingly agitated ghost, "Quinn never caught up with him and Melody in the desert, after they left Jubilation, so yeah. That would make him a pretty big liar."

"The man was filth," Jamie said. "A ruthless, nasty, ugly piece of excrement."

Alison couldn't keep her amusement off her face as she stood up, unaware that she was neatly blocking Jamie's path. "So I'm supposed to take the word of a man who kidnapped and murdered another man's wife? Over the American West's most well-known hero?"

"A walking turd, he was," Jamie said, pulling up short to avoid going directly through her. "Conniving and cruel. Plus, he smelled bad. Didn't bathe often enough." He examined Alison's face from his up-close vantage point, then glanced back at A.J. "She *is* oddly attractive for such a tall woman, isn't she?"

"Yes," A.J. said, answering both of them. "You have to wonder about the fact that no one besides

44

Quinn ever saw Jamie's body. Or Melody's, for that matter."

"Because there were no bodies," Jamie said. "She's a little too skinny, but those legs must be a mile long. Gotta love that, especially when she wraps them around—"

"Don't," A.J. stopped him, unwilling to hear anything having to do with sex come out of his gramps's mouth. But of course, now Alison was looking at him oddly, so he quickly added, "Get me wrong. I appreciate the amount of research that you've obviously done, but much of what you included in your book can be traced back to a single source—Quinn himself. I know he said he buried them both up where he said he killed Jamie."

"It was near the Painted Desert, where he caught up with them," Alison said, unaware that Jamie had given her physical appearance a hearty thumbs-up. "It was summer. There was no way he could bring the bodies all the way back. Not in that heat."

"Not to Jubilation," A.J. said, resisting the urge to tell the ghost, who was still too close to her, to back off. "You're right, that would've been too difficult. But there were other towns nearby. At a time when a strategy for keeping men from breaking the law was to drag the bodies of outlaws into town behind your horse . . . ? A time when lawmen would display the men they'd killed, like heads on a pike on a castle wall, as a warning to stay in line . . . ? When newspapers would pay good money to snap a picture of a dead outlaw like Billy the Kid . . . ?"

"Quinn was heartbroken," she countered. "He stayed in the desert for months. His wife was dead—"

"Nope," A.J. said. "You got that wrong, too. Great-grandma certainly wasn't anywhere close to dead."

"Nice!" Alison laughed. "I didn't see *that* one coming. Although I probably should have."

"It's true."

"Let me see if I've got this straight. You're saying that Melody Quinn left her famous, important husband and ran off with some two-bit, vicious gunfighter." Her sarcasm made it clear she was highly skeptical of A.J.'s claim. But he had to give her credit for hearing him out.

"Vicious," Jamie said. "That's a good one. He was a vicious, conniving, stinking, walking turd. Thank you, darlin'." He blew her a kiss and disappeared, only to rematerialize on the other side of her.

"Jesus," A.J. said, because he still hadn't gotten used to Jamie popping in and out like that. He still couldn't believe his eyes—if it truly were his eyes that needed to be believed, and not his brain that was responsible for sending him hallucinations of the old man he'd adored back when he was a child and life was so much less complicated.

And great, now Alison was looking at him as if he'd just shouted *Jesus* in the middle of her office, which he had, and there was nothing to do about it but plunge onward. "Yes, Jesus, yes," he said, which sounded even more stupid than he'd thought it would. "She ran. As fast as she could. Although *escaped* might be a better word."

"*Escaped* is a much better word," Jamie said.

"Ah," Alison said, leaning back so she was half sitting on the very edge of her desk, arms crossed in front of her. "And that must've been . . . because Silas Quinn was, what? Abusing her?"

She clearly didn't believe a word of it, but at least she was willing to discuss the possibility. It was a start.

A.J. nodded. "Yes, again. Quinn absolutely abused her, both physically and emotionally. She was planning to leave him, even before she met Jamie."

Alison didn't speak, didn't nod, didn't react. She just calmly and silently—and thoughtfully, with a serious chunk of this-is-too-funny in her eyes— looked down at him, her long, blue jean–clad legs out in front of her, her purple T-shirt stretching slightly against the lithe, trim, yet very feminine curves of her body.

A.J. waited, gazing back up at her, as Jamie

47

started pacing again at the edge of his peripheral vision.

Alison moved first, spoke first. "And that's it?" she asked, pushing herself off her desk so that she was standing in front of him.

A.J. blinked. But before he could open his mouth to respond—assuming he had the slightest idea how to respond to *And that's it?*—she continued.

"You walk up to me and say, *Excuse me, Dr. Carter, may I have a moment of your time . . .* Well, actually, I think you said, *Um,* but I'm almost positive what you meant to say was *Excuse me, Dr. Carter, may I have a moment, because everything you wrote in your book, which you spent close to a decade of your life meticulously researching and documenting, is wrong,* and you . . . just expect me to believe you?" She smiled at him, genuinely amused.

"I know it can't be the easiest thing to hear"— A.J. found himself smiling, too—"but it happens to be true."

"Okay," Alison said. "If it's true, where's your proof? If you're talking about changing history, you better have something that proves what you're saying."

A.J. held out his hands. "I'm proof," he said. "If Jamie had died in 1898, I wouldn't be sitting here today. My grandfather, Adam Gallagher, was Jamie and Melody's youngest son. He wasn't born until 1920, so—"

"Did you happen to bring along Grandpa's birth certificate?" Alison asked.

A.J. glanced at Jamie, who'd stopped pacing and was leaning against the frame of a door that led into a back room—probably a bathroom. "Well," A.J. said. "No."

"Well"—this time her imitation of him was less friendly—"why don't you go get it and bring it back, and *then* we'll talk," she told him. "It's been surreal, but it's time for me to get back to work."

A.J. stood up, too, pushing his jeans slightly down his thighs. "He doesn't have a birth certificate. 1920, in the Territory of Alaska? He was born at home, there was no official record."

"I see." She didn't sound surprised. "I don't suppose you have anything else to back up your story?"

She stood there, waiting, calmly confident both in her research and in her book, smiling slightly because she knew what his answer was going to be.

No.

"I'm willing to do a DNA test," he told her.

"Not real useful," she pointed out, as she moved toward the door, to open it and usher him out, "without some of Kid Gallagher's DNA."

"Argh," Jamie said. "Will you *please*—"

"He was never called *Kid,*" A.J. interrupted him, holding his ground against Alison's attempt to show him the door. "That was just a dime

49

novel embellishment. He hates it—hated it. The nickname."

Her hand stilled on the doorknob. "You actually knew him?"

A.J. nodded. "He lived with us at the end of his life," he told her. "My mother, my sister Bev, and me. From the time I was three until . . . Well, when I was ten, he just . . . died. In his sleep. He just went to bed one night, he seemed fine, it was just another day, but . . ." He had to clear his throat, clench his teeth. "He didn't wake up." He didn't look over at Jamie. He couldn't. But he knew the ghost was watching him.

It had been devastating. He had been a kind of a weird kid, a loner who didn't easily make friends with the other boys at school. Jamie had filled that role, been his constant companion, his best friend, except, just like that, he was gone.

Which was why, according to A.J.'s mother, his brain had conjured Jamie up, even all these years later. Assuming that she was right and A.J. was hallucinating, as opposed to Jamie's actually being a spirit from beyond.

Haunted or crazy.

A.J. was definitely one or the other, and he wasn't quite sure which he wished was true. Hell of a choice to have to make.

"That must've been hard," Alison said quietly. "I mean, assuming you're not making this up."

"I'm not," A.J. said.

"I didn't do it on purpose." Jamie's voice was rough. He had to clear his throat, too. "You know that, right?"

"Yeah," A.J. said, answering him—and Alison, too. It *had* been incredibly hard. "And I actually do have some of Jamie's DNA. He cut his hand in my grandfather's—Adam's—carpenter shop, which is my shop now. There was a leather apron that got stained—it's not the kind of thing you can easily wash out. It's still hanging on the wall. But of course there's no way to prove that the blood was Jamie's," he added before Alison could throw that monkey wrench into the mix herself.

"If we want to prove that my story's true," A.J. continued, "we need to find a sample of Melody's DNA. I figure that, plus holding up a picture of Jamie next to me. . . ."

"Well, you *do* look like him," Alison admitted. "I'll give you that. But . . ." She shook her head. "I'm assuming this is the point where you announce that you have Quinn's locket—the one that held a lock of Melody's hair . . . ?"

According to the legend, that locket was one of the things Quinn allegedly buried deep within one of his many silver mines after Melody was killed. He'd packed up a bunch of her belongings in a tin box, and laid it to rest. Or so he'd claimed.

"I don't have it," A.J. told her. "I was hoping you did."

But Alison was already shaking her head. "It's

long gone," she said. "And you know it. You read my book."

He shrugged. "I figured that since Quinn had lied about Jamie's and Melody's deaths, he might've lied about burying that locket, too. You said in your book that you had access to Quinn's belongings, that his descendants, the Sylvesters, had an attic filled with boxes—"

"I've been through them," Alison interrupted him. "Thoroughly. No locket."

"You mentioned that Quinn had kept Melody's clothes in a locked trunk," A.J. reminded her. "It is possible that there might be a strand of her hair or maybe a pair of shoes with some . . ." What? Dead skin? Toenails? Dried blood from a blister?

But Alison was giving him another of those headshakes. "Quinn's daughter, who was also named Melody—"

"Which is fricking creepy, if you ask me," Jamie interjected.

"—let *her* daughters use those clothes to play dress up."

And so much for *that* idea.

"Naming your daughter after your allegedly dead first wife?" Jamie was disgusted. "I wonder what wife number two—what's her name, Agatha—thought about *that*. You know, I don't know if I ever told you this, kid, but I still think *she* was responsible for Quinn's demise. Intense stomach pains, yeah, it could've been his appendix, but it also could've been poison. I think Agatha caught ol' Silas eyeing their little girl, and I think she put a stop to that, right quick."

Jamie hadn't ever told him that. Not back when A.J. was ten. He wouldn't have understood it, anyway. A father contemplating having sex with his own daughter, let alone battering and beating his wife . . . ?

"Maybe that's the way to go," A.J. said aloud, before he realized he was talking to Jamie. He turned to face Alison, tried to make it look like he'd been speaking to her from the start. "Agatha Quinn. You said in your book that you didn't spend much time on her—research-wise. If Quinn abused Melody—my great-grandmother—then it's likely he did the same to his second wife, isn't it? Maybe we could find proof if we went through her things—her clothes, her papers, I don't know . . ."

Alison sighed. "Look, A.J. If your name really is A.J."

Ouch.

"After Quinn died," she continued, "Agatha took Melody-the-second, and moved to Tucson where, after *she* died, Melody's house burned down. Silas's trunks were safe because Agatha had left them here, in Jubilation." She paused. "Which does sound a little weird when I say it out loud. Why did Agatha leave everything behind? Of course, you didn't exactly hire a van when you moved across the territory back in 1906. You boarded a train or took a horse and wagon. Still, to leave *every*thing of Silas's . . ."

"Where did Agatha come from?" A.J. asked. "Maybe she had sisters or friends."

"That she might've written letters to," Alison finished for him. "No, I haven't found any record of that. Silas Quinn's descendants—Neil Sylvester is the person I've been working with. He admitted that they don't even know Agatha's maiden name." She finally opened her door. "As fascinating as this has been, I'm going to have to stick with the substantiated facts, and leave the hearsay, rumor, and gossip out, no matter how . . ." She paused, meeting his gaze steadily, and smiling. "Intriguing it seems."

His inner idiot's mouth went dry and probably would've started him stammering again, if she hadn't had more to say.

"I really do need to get back to work," she continued, "so if you don't mind . . . ?"

She held out her hand for the file he was still holding, and he gave it to her as he headed past her, toward that little door. But then, on a whim, he also pulled his wallet out of the back pocket of his jeans and handed that to her, as well.

He'd surprised her. Good, that made two of them. Three, counting Jamie, whose eyebrows were up beneath his hair.

"My name really is A.J. Gallagher," he said. "Feel free to copy the contents—my driver's license and credit cards and what-all—and substantiate it."

Alison blinked at him, and before she could find her voice and tell him that it didn't matter, she wasn't going to believe anything ill of her beloved hero Silas Quinn, A.J. went down the steps and out the door into the heat of the Arizona morning.

"Smooth," Jamie said as he followed him, his boots not kicking up any dust in the motel driveway, the way A.J.'s did. "Now you have a reason to go back and see her again."

"Yes, sir," A.J. agreed. "That I do."

June 18, 1898
Dear Diary,

One day from my destination. Another silver mining town. Another breeding ground for violence and death. Maybe this time, mine.

The countryside I see from the window is desolate, empty. No water, no shelter. If I leave the stagecoach, there is no hope of survival.

My traveling companions speak often of the beauty of the vast openness, the great freedom of the western sky. But I feel trapped as surely as if I were in the smallest prison cell.

He is waiting for me.

Chapter Three

"You're no help at all," Alison told Hugh, who was using her office trailer as a hiding place.

Kent from accounting was on the set today, aka Kent-that-bastard-from-accounting, who had led Hugh to believe that their impetuous St. Patrick's Day hookup had been the start of a richly meaningful and long-term relationship instead of the cheap and easy one-nighter that Kent had truly been after. At least that was Hugh's story.

The professional liar had been lied to, and no doubt about it, karma was a bitch.

Hugh didn't see it as karma, though, which might've been part of the problem. But it was more than his desire to avoid an awkward encounter that had brought him here to her office. Alison believed that the production assistant's heart had actually been broken. He didn't say as much—he wouldn't or maybe couldn't, his stoic and pragmatic midwestern salt-of-the-earth upbringing dominating his gay gene. But Alison could tell the wound was a deep one, mostly from the way he didn't seem to want to complain about or even badmouth Kent, aside from that one heartfelt *bastard*. He just kept changing the subject, with a flash of hurt on his perfect face.

What would he say, she wondered, if she sat

down next to him, patted his hand, and said, *Sweetie, you know it's really okay if you cry.*

The fact that her adorable buddy Hugh actually had a heart to break would've been the surprise of the day had one alleged A.J. Gallagher not walked into her office and her life a few hours earlier.

"I'm just saying," Hugh said now, feet up on the very same couch that A.J. had been sitting on as he'd given her those slow smiles that had made her grin back at him foolishly, "that if I were going to come in here to try to pull some kind of con, I'd have a worn-out library card in my fake name, too."

"He's from this tiny town that's actually called Heaven, in Alaska," Alison told him, flipping through the handful of credit and ID cards belonging to the man who, according to an extremely official-looking Alaskan driver's license, was indeed named Austin James Gallagher. Which didn't mean a thing. The best forgeries looked authentic. "I MapQuested it, and it's real. Heaven, Alaska, can you believe it?" She didn't wait for him to answer. "I googled A.J., too, and there's, like, twenty other Gallaghers in town, not to mention—" she consulted her list "—a Dr. Rose Gallagher—I think she's A.J.'s mother; a Gallagher's Bar and Grill, Gallagher's Hardware, and Gallagher and Sons Carpentry and Furniture Design. The furniture place and the doctor both have websites. Everything seems legit. The local paper had birth and death announcements for dozens of Gallaghers, going back as far as I could access. I found A.J.'s—it matched the date on his driver's license. And—get this—I also found his father's death announcement." She'd printed out the obituary. "Marine Sergeant Ryan Austin Gallagher, loving husband of Rose Hawkes Gallagher, father of Beverly and A.J., son of Adam and Celeste Gallagher, killed in Vietnam in 1970— four days before A.J.'s third birthday, which had to suck. Among surviving family members listed was Ryan's grandfather, J. Gallagher."

"*J* could be Joseph," Hugh said. "Or John. Jack. Jerry."

"And it could be James," Alison said.

"So . . . are you saying you believe him?"

"I'm saying it's kinda hard to dispute forty years of newspaper records."

"Maybe when President Obama traveled through time to plant his birth announcement in the paper in Hawaii, he stopped in Alaska and—"

"My point exactly," Alison said, back to looking at the battered library card, and some kind of laminated military ID that seemed to imply that A.J. had been in the army but had been discharged years ago. An ACLU membership card and a little paper card with five talking points to "tell your neighbors" why off-shore drilling for oil was environmentally a bad idea. His social security card—she'd never met anyone before who actually carried that—was shoved into a separate slot, along with a bank ATM card, and what looked to be a shiny new Visa card.

He was also carrying two hundred and thirty dollars in cash.

She tried to imagine just casually handing a stranger her wallet filled with that much money and personal information. But she couldn't do it.

She also couldn't imagine Silas Quinn lying about Melody and Kid Gallagher's deaths. The marshal's honesty was legendary.

"I think maybe A.J. *thinks* he's telling the truth," she told Hugh. "And yeah, I know, you think he's here to con me. I haven't seen the actual newspapers, I've only seen the Internet microfiche—although I'm not sure how that could be tampered with. Clearly a trip to Alaska is in order. But . . . Here's what I'm thinking: What if A.J. grew up being told that Great-grandpa was Kid Gallagher and Great-grandma was Melody Quinn, when in fact it was just a family legend or, I don't know, some ridiculous joke. They had the same last name as this notorious outlaw. Maybe it was a pretense that young, fatherless A.J. took too seriously."

"You like this guy," Hugh deduced. "You don't want him to be a con man. And that's step one in a con. Make the mark like you. Check."

"I *do* like him," Alison realized. "I don't really know why."

"I do," Hugh said. "He's extremely hot."

"Right," Alison said. "And you know me when it comes to hot guys. I can't resist 'em—no, wait, that would be *you.*"

"Deny, deny, but I saw the way you looked at him."

"Whatever you *think* you saw," Alison said, "in the fraction of a second that you saw it—before you ran away like a frightened little girl because you knew I was going to kick your ass—was me checking to make sure he was correctly dressed to be an extra in our multimillion-dollar movie. Which he wasn't."

"I don't know, Al," Hugh said. "I think you just instinctively connected with him. I think he's your type."

She had to laugh. "He's about the farthest thing from my type on the planet," she told Hugh. "I mean, can't you just picture me with some cowboy? He also actually called me *ma'am,* which is a strong signal that I'm not his type either. Which is a good thing."

"Is it?" Hugh asked. "A good thing . . . ?"

"Yes." Alison tried to sound absolute. "Because as crazy as his story is . . . ?" She looked up and sighed. "I *am* gonna have to go up to Alaska to check this out. I can't not, you know? And I've got to be impartial. Or as impartial as I can be about the idea that Silas Quinn was lying about Kid Gallagher's and Melody's deaths, which, if

60

he was, means that all of his other claims—about the shootout and the bank robbery—are therefore also suspect, which I just find really hard to swallow." She paused. "Except . . ."

Hugh turned to look at her. "What?" he said.

Alison shook her head. "Nothing. No."

"Sure sounded to me like something was cooking in that giant head of yours."

"I don't have a giant head. You just have an adorably tiny one."

"Except what?" Hugh persisted. "You know you want to tell me. You've said it yourself—things get more clear when you let yourself think aloud. So, think aloud, babe."

"That's Dr. Babe to you, Junior Mint," Alison said, and then sighed. Hugh was right. She did like to think aloud. "Okay, look. This by no means implies that I'm doubting Marshal Quinn's impeccable word, but ever since A.J. came in here, suggesting that Melody was the victim of domestic violence, I haven't been able to stop thinking about a letter that was written by a local woman to her sister in Denver." She moved the piles of papers and files around on her desk, like a giant game of three-card monty, searching for the right stack and . . . Got it. "Someone sent it to Henry just a few weeks ago, the original 1898 letter, just stuck in a regular envelope, like, *Hello, I know you're about to make this movie and thought you'd be interested in seeing this*." She handed the photocopy to Hugh. "I sent out the original to be tested for the ink and paper content, but we're ninety-nine percent sure it's the real deal. It was written by Mrs. Penny Eversfield, who was the wife of the man who owned Jubilation's general store. She and her sister Hortense were voracious pen pals, and Horry, as she was lovingly called—"

"Seriously?" Hugh looked up. "That's how you pronounce it?"

"Oh, yes," Alison told him. "Horry saved all of her sister's letters. There were hundreds—Penny only died in 1920. Her great-niece Lorraine has, in turn, kept them all. She's getting on in years herself, Lorraine is, and she wants to donate them to the Silas Quinn museum that Neil Sylvester is opening here in town."

"Dearest Horry," Hugh read aloud. *"Once again, the summer heat is upon us, and once again the money I had saved to come visit you and dear Papa must be spent, this time to buy a wedding veil for Mr. Eversfield's eldest and most spoiled daughter, Mary. It had best be a thick one, or the groom may well run away.* Oh, zing, Penny."

"The bit about Melody is at the end—middle of the second page," Alison told him, and he shuffled the pages. "It in part clears up a mystery that no one could ever explain. Melody Quinn arrived in Jubilation in early June, yet the official welcoming ball, held by the town in her honor, didn't happen until early August. And yes, the date got pushed even later, because the marshal was injured in the shootout at the Red Rock, but the original date of the dance was late July. Which seemed odd. But apparently, shortly after she arrived, Melody fell off her horse and got badly hurt."

"Mrs. Quinn was confined to her bed when I arrived," Hugh read, *"her eyes blackened and her face bruised and bloodied, clearly in pain from a recent, violent 'accident.' "* He looked up. "She put the word *accident* in quotes."

"Yeah," Alison said, drawing the word out. "That's what I haven't been able to stop thinking about. Keep reading."

"She told me she'd been thrown from her horse—"

"She told me," Alison repeated. "Why write that? Why not just write, *She'd been thrown from her horse?"* She laughed as she rolled her eyes. "Of course now I'm finding sinister meaning in everything. According to Silas's reports, Melody wasn't an accomplished rider, so it's entirely possible that she *was* thrown from a horse."

"I stayed with her for only a short time that afternoon," Hugh continued reading, *"and left as quickly as I could when the marshal arrived home.* That sounds sinister to me. Like Penny was afraid of him."

"Or just well aware that, after all those months apart, the marshal might've wanted some alone time with his wife." But as Alison gave voice to the excuse, it felt like just that—an excuse. Alone time with a wife who'd been *bruised and bloodied* from a bad fall . . . ?

"Maybe you'll get more answers in the other letters," Hugh suggested, sitting up and giving her back the photocopy.

"Maybe." Alison wasn't convinced. "Lorraine's sending them—they should arrive in a few days."

"At the very least," Hugh pointed out, "you'll be able to use them for the new book."

"And then there's that," Alison agreed. Her next opus—and it was turning into an enormous monster of a project—focused on the hardship of day-to-day life for American women in the Old West. Specifically in Jubilation, Arizona.

Hugh's phone beeped and he pulled it from his pocket to check it. "Text message," he announced, as he stood up and headed for the door, "from Lana the caterer. Elvis has left the building." He turned to look back at Alison. "Thanks for letting me hide in here."

"I think the next time Kent shows up, you should stay out there," she told him. "Sing him a verse or two of 'I Will Survive.' "

"Hey, hey," Hugh said, as he opened up her trailer door. "That's just it, though. I'm not sure I

will, you know? Survive. Seeing him again . . ."
He shook his head.

"If you want, I could probably get Trace's thug, I mean, assistant Skippy to beat him up for you," Alison called after him.

But he was gone.

And she was back to staring at A.J. Gallagher's driver's license.

She stood up, too. It was time to go find the man, and give him back his wallet.

But first, just to be thorough, she was going to photocopy the contents.

June 23, 1898
Dear Diary,

A visitor. One with an enormously unfashionable hat.

She didn't question my vague explanation—I fell from my horse. Clumsy me.

I could see the fading bruise around her own eye, and realized I have an ally.

An ally. I write the word and it makes me laugh, makes my split lip burn. What good is it to be allied to a timid and frightened mouse? No, there are no allies for me here.

I am alone in this hell.

Even God has forsaken me.

A.J. seemed to want to be alone for a bit, so I wandered the streets of Jubilation. Not much had changed in the town since I'd left in a hurry, all those years ago. And what *had* changed was being transformed by the movie crew back into what it had once been.

Within reason, of course.

Sure, there was a gas station now. And a Circle K convenience store. And a single-story motel, built with the misguided and over-the-top architectural angles and colors popular in the 1950s which was, ironically, the *last* time a major motion picture had been made about Silas Quinn and me and the shootout at the Red Rock. In faded orange and turquoise, the neon sign out front of the place displayed the outline of the hat and face of a sneering cowboy with a cigarette in his mouth and the words OUTLAW INN in a loopy, electric cursive.

It was, of course, supposed to be me. It would have made me laugh, but the reminder that I used to smoke still bothered me tremendously.

As I walked on, I saw that the attack of the 1950s urban sprawl was confined, thank God, back behind Main Street. The Outlaw Inn was next to a rather grim-looking two-unit strip mall with a shop advertising "Palms Read," which was next to an establishment where you could pawn your watch, cash your paycheck, and get tattooed and pierced all at the same time.

Combining that with an exorbitantly expensive half-sized box of Lorna Doones and the ice cold but metallic-tasting canned beer you could pick up at the Circle K, Jubilation truly had become an oasis of modern convenience.

That Circle K, as pricy as it was, was the only place in miles that sold groceries and/or food-like grocery substitutes, as A.J. called the chips and Cheetos he'd downed by the cubic ton as a child but now spurned.

The old general store, which back in the day had been owned by a real ornery sonuvabitch named Richard Eversfield, had sold a variety of supplies. But even though it was still standing, it was now a museum.

Or rather a fact-defying house of worship where tourists from Indianapolis and Des Moines could kneel at the altar of the god Silas Quinn.

Part of the Red Rock Saloon had been transformed into a museum, too, although the main room still served shots of whiskey and less-than-generous-sized glasses of beer.

A hand-lettered sign proclaimed that five dollars, paid to the bartender, would gain you admittance behind the curtain to the back room, which held THE ACTUAL BOOTS WORN BY THE VILLAIN KID GALLAGHER AT THE TIME OF HIS DEATH.

The caps are theirs, not mine.

I slipped past the curtain without paying—a benefit that came with being visible only to my great-grandson—and went into the back room that had held the stage where the local ladies of the evening had put on shows (and I use the term loosely, because none of 'em had all that much talent beyond the obvious).

The movie folks were crawling all over the place, carefully packing and inventorying all of the "artifacts" that hung on the walls in the once festive room.

They hadn't gotten to the glass display cases yet, and I strolled past them, squinting to read the handwritten explanations that were pinned near each item. A chamber pot. A spittoon. Both believed to have been used by the great Silas Quinn when he crapped and/or hacked.

And there, in a case of honor in the center of the room, were, indeed, my boots. The black ones that I'd abandoned, in order to make room in my saddle bag for more food and water.

The once fine, tooled leather was dull and cracked, the silver tarnished.

I hadn't died in them, but I *had* been wearing them the first time I saw Mel. My life had irrevocably changed in that single moment, but it was more like a rebirth than a death. Although one could argue that in order to be reborn, a part of you has to die.

A pair of young ladies carrying boxes nearly went right through me. As I danced out of their way, I spotted another sign, proclaiming ENTER HERE. It was at the door to the tiny room that had once been Big Sal's handjob factory, where a mere five cents would get you a less satisfying variation on the theme of what you'd receive by taking one of the younger, prettier, and less contagious girls to her far more ornate quarters upstairs.

I went in and saw that it had been transformed into a small theater. There were heavy shades over the single window and about six or seven folding chairs set up in front of an old TV, upon which played a continuous video loop of an ancient and faded documentary about the notorious gun battle that had raged out in the saloon on that summer morning in 1898.

It wasn't—let's face it—even a fraction as entertaining as Big Sal had been even after she caught the pox and knew that her future held a slow slide into madness.

I went out through the back door—literally *through* it, seeing as how I no longer needed to open or close the damn thing—and into the narrow alleyway between the saloon and the marshal's office.

It was not a mistake that Quinn's and the Red Rock's back doors were in such close proximity. Quinn owned the saloon, owned Big Sal and all of the girls who worked upstairs. And whenever he was in the mood for a little afternoon delight, to quote a song that A.J.'s sister Bev had loved but me and Age had hated, he'd just knock three times on Sal's back door. She'd clear out and give a whistle for Nancy or Irmine or sometimes the pair of 'em together, to come down and entertain the good marshal.

And this I know not just because Big Sal told me so, but because I saw it happen.

Not from inside the room, of course. I was flesh and blood back then and walls thwarted me. But I sat at the bar—that curtain wasn't up in those days—and watched Sal leave and the girls go in and that door shut. I meandered back to the alley where—sure enough—Quinn came out some long minutes later, buttoning the front of his trousers, which was a clue that he hadn't been in there reading those girls Bible verses.

But I digress.

As I wandered through Jubilation, I saw that the marshal's office and the town stables where the blacksmith had done his business were just as they'd been, too. Most of the town had been preserved, apparently, by Quinn's descendants, the Sylvesters, who'd realized in the 1950s that this ghost town that they still owned could become a tourist attraction.

It never quite did—it was too far off the beaten track.

But the latest Sylvester—Neil was this one's name—was still trying to hit the mother lode. There was a sign on the outskirts of town that announced the arrival of a whole parcel of

70

modern hotels, plus a Food Lion and a Target. Building would commence as soon as the movie had wrapped, and the hotels and stores would soon stand ready for the hordes of tourists, inspired to make a pilgrimage to Jubilation by Trace Marcus's nuanced performance as that greatest of American heroes, Silas Quinn.

I spat on the dusty ground—or I would have if I could have. But not being able to spit was okay with me, because just as I didn't have spit to spray around, I also didn't have thirst.

Which, along with being able to sneak into museums without paying, was one of the relatively good things about being a ghost, and actually, if you want to know the truth, I'm partial to the word *spirit*. *Ghost* makes me think of chains and moaning and Christmas Past and haunted houses.

And although the kid swears up and down that I'm haunting him, it's not like that at all.

But wait. I'm getting in front of myself again.

Point one: Another of the good things about being a *spirit* is that you can walk around in the blazing Arizona sunshine without a hat and never break a sweat or need refreshment of any kind.

Point two: If I *were* haunting A.J., he'd damn well know it. I think of my time here with him as a friendly visit, a trip down memory lane. A.J.'s helping me, and I'm helping him, even though he doesn't know it yet, and even though I'm not sure exactly *how* I'm helping him, aside from the obvious—that I've finally gotten him to emerge from that isolated and lonely workshop where he builds furniture, day in and day out.

The furniture's beautiful, true, but his life is slowly slipping away from him. It's time for him to live it.

I don't possess a real clear master plan as to how I'm going to make that happen, but I'll figure something out.

See, I've gone nimbly through 101 years of life, plus all of those additional years of afterlife, by the seat of my pants.

Why stop now?

Inspiration will strike when it's good and ready. There's no need to try and force it. Besides, the kid's a think-things-through-er. He's not big on impetuous spur-of-the-moment decisions. I figure at the rate he's moving—and I do believe that crunching between my teeth comes from eating the dust of both a tortoise *and* a snail—I've got another four months, which is the entire remaining length of this movie shoot, to figure out what to do next.

Maybe I'll talk him into taking a trip to London. Or a cruise up the Nile.

Anything to keep him from locking himself back into his workshop in Alaska. For years now, he's been living in some kind of self-imposed purgatory. It's not hell, but it sure isn't heaven.

The boy deserves better than that.

Although he's not a boy anymore. Hasn't been in a long time.

I found him sitting in his truck with his AC running, checking the messages on his cell phone, looking none too pleased at the fact that his mother, Dr. Rose, had called him five different times since they'd spoken last, which was just yesterday evening.

As I slid into the seat next to him, he didn't look too happy to see me, either. He never does these days.

"When you were ten years old, you thought I was the King of Alaska," I reminded him.

He was grumpy. "I'm not ten anymore."

"And yet," I said, "I remain the King of Alaska."

That made him laugh, although to be honest, it was more of an exasperated exhale.

"So," I said, slapping my hands together with a crack that made the kid drop his cellular phone, "you figure out what you're going to do about Alison Carter?"

"I'm going to figure out a way to tell her your story," A.J. told me grimly, as he awkwardly retrieved the phone from the floor mat beneath his feet, "and then I'm going to figure out a way to prove it."

I shook my head. "That's not what I meant, kid, and you know it. You've been living like a monk

73

for way too long. And I saw the way this girl was looking at you."

"First of all," he said, "she's a woman, not a girl, thank you very much."

"You're very welcome," I told him. "But to me, anyone under seventy-five is a girl."

"It's disrespectful," he informed me. "Times have changed."

"Fair enough," I said. "But times haven't changed so much that I don't recognize when a girl—excuse me—when a *woman* sizes up a man, and not just in terms of whether he'd be a charming and intelligent dinner date, but also whether or not he'd be a good partner in the non-slumber activities that go on in healthy and happy folks' beds."

"We are, not now, not ever, talking about sex," A.J. said flatly.

I had to laugh. "We're both grown men," I pointed out. "I don't see what the big deal—"

"Do it," he said, "and I will walk over to the church, wake up the priest, and demand that he perform an exorcism. On the spot."

"Well, now, *that* won't work," I scoffed. "I'm not a demon. Not even close."

"Yeah, well, I'm willing to try it," he said. "So go on. Make my day."

A.J. didn't look much like Dirty Harry. In fact, he was pretty much the opposite of Clint. He was the kind of man who couldn't look threatening or dangerous without a huge amount of effort. I'd always had that problem, too. Particularly when I was younger. But he *did* look determined, and I knew that he wasn't kidding.

I also have to confess that my feelings were a little hurt. "Gee," I said. "And here I'd thought you'd enjoy having me around again."

"There were times when I truly needed you, Gramps," the kid said quietly. "Why didn't you show up then?"

Because there were things that you needed to learn on your own, I started to say, but only got as far as "Because—"

"Because you're not really here," he said. "It's really just me, sitting in my truck, talking to myself—Jesus!"

He jumped and I jumped, too—because Alison Carter was knocking on his window.

"Sorry," she said, as he powered it down. "I didn't mean to sneak up on you or . . ."

She was looking in the cab, looking right through me, and I knew that she was curious because she'd seen A.J. talking to me. Which, to her, looked an awful lot like A.J. was talking to himself.

"Say, *I gotta run, Mom, I'll call you later,*" I instructed the kid, "and then pretend to hang up your phone."

Instead he ignored me. "I was just, um, thinking aloud," he told Alison.

75

She smiled. "I do that, too. Just . . . usually not when I'm alone."

"Ah, but, that's the best time to do it," he countered with a return smile and a heavy serving of that blue-eyed, angel-faced honesty that he'd always done so well, even back when he was small.

Especially back when he was small.

She handed him his wallet through the window. "I wanted to give that back to you. I figured you'd need it to buy yourself dinner."

"Invitation, invitation," I said. *"Any chance I can buy* you *dinner, too?"*

"Thanks." A.J., the fool, was steadfastly ignoring me. "Hey, you wouldn't happen to know if the crew's hiring carpenters?"

"Oh," Alison said. "No, I don't think so. Everyone's union, so . . . But we *are* still looking for extras. Of course, the pay isn't that great. A hundred dollars a day."

"A hundred bucks for standing around?" A.J. asked, bemused.

"In the hot sun," she pointed out. "We have an air-conditioned tent for the extras, between shots. The stars have their trailers."

"You, um, don't mind?" A.J. interrupted. "If I, you know, stick around for a while . . . ?"

"Actually, I'd like it if you did," she said, with that directness that I found so appealing. "Very much. I'd like to talk to you more about your great-grandfather."

"You would?" A.J. was as surprised as I was.

But she was quick to add, "I'm not saying I believe you're related to Kid Gallagher—"

"For the *love,*" I said, "of *God* . . ."

"Jamie," A.J. interrupted her. "Not Kid. Jamie."

"Right," she said. "Sorry. I just . . . You seem to be who you say you are, and it's possible that your great-grandfather knew Jamie Gallagher—maybe even took that money that he stole from the Jubliation Bank and Trust—"

"He didn't steal any money," A.J. interrupted her.

"Maybe not in your version of the story," Alison pointed out, "which I definitely want to hear. But, just for the record? In the version of the story that I know, Kid Gallagher, not Jamie but Kid, cleaned out the bank before kidnapping and killing Melody Quinn. It's entirely possible, in fact, it's *likely* that he had a cohort. If that cohort survived, he might've taken the money, gone to Alaska, built a new life for himself. You know, with a new name . . . ?"

"The name of a wanted man?"

"The name of a dead man," Alison countered, "who later—much later as the story spread— became known as the man who killed Melody Quinn."

A.J. glanced at me.

"She's willing to hear our story," I said, taking that look as an invitation to give an opinion. "I think you should do the extra-actor thing. Stick around Jubilation for a while. Maybe even get laid. Damnit, *I* apparently think aloud, too."

"I gotta go," Alison said. "I've got a dinner thing tonight and a lot of work to do before then. The real actor who's playing Gallagher is coming in this afternoon and . . . You know, if you're serious about signing on as an extra, go see Lucy in the main production trailer. She'll tell you where to go for a costume fitting. And don't let them scrimp. Make sure you get boxers or you'll end up going commando. I don't want any briefs underneath those jeans. And don't try to cheat—I *can* tell when you're wearing them, and they *will* come off."

And with that she flashed another of those beautiful smiles and hurried away.

A.J. closed his window. "Don't say anything," he told me. "Not one word."

I stayed silent for maybe fifteen seconds, then figured what the hell. "I just . . . love you and want you to be happy," I told him. "Is that so wrong? And that girl—woman—has your immediate happiness written all over her interesting face."

He laughed as he shook his head no, but he didn't look at me. Instead he looked steadily out the window. "I love you too, Gramps," he said. "But please, just . . . don't."

"I'm also really here," I told him, bringing our

conversation back to where we were before Alison interrupted. "Your mother, as much as I love her, too, is dead wrong about that one."

"You are really here," A.J. agreed. "One way or the other, you're here and I've gotta deal with it." He finally looked up. "Dr. Carter wants to hear your story, so I'll tell her your story. And then I'll go home. You can go with me or you can stay here in Jubilation—it's up to you."

"Your mother *is* wrong," I told him again, and he nodded but I knew he didn't believe me.

Chapter Four

A.J. Gallagher was sticking around.

Alison felt inordinately pleased about that, particularly about her theory that Kid Gallagher had had an accomplice. Maybe a cousin or even a brother—which would explain the almost uncanny resemblance between A.J. and her pictures of the ridiculously handsome Kid.

Jonathan White, the actor who was playing the Kid in the movie, was much smaller and, although handsome, was no Jamie or A.J. Gallagher. He'd dropped by, not to talk, but to pick up a copy of her file. His assistant, Bonnie, lingered to explain that Jon's method of preparing for a role demanded privacy and isolation. If he had any questions about her notes or research, she—Bonnie—would be in touch.

So that happened. Which left Alison with several hours of time to flesh out her theory.

And, as she dug through her computer files, she found exactly what she was looking for. A note she'd made on one of her first trips to Philly, where Kid Gallagher had been born. It said that his older brother, Caldwell, nicknamed Wells, not only had the same middle name, James, but had mysteriously died—*allegedly* died—the very same day that the fifteen-year-old Kid had left his blue-blooded, old-money family behind and struck out on his own, heading west.

Try as she might, Alison had never found any record of Caldwell's cause of death. There was also no record of his burial place, which was equally odd. All of the other Philadelphia Gallaghers—except for Austin, aka Kid—were buried together in a peaceful, well-kept cemetery in Germantown.

Caldwell James Gallagher was three years older than his outlaw brother, and was known for his artistic and musical talents and . . .

Her trailer rocked on its wheels, as if someone had run full force into it—Wile E. Coyote–style.

"No, no, don't—*don't! Please!* I'll have the money for him next week, I swear!"

That sounded like Trace Marcus's voice, and sure enough, as Alison went to the window and pulled back the curtain, she could see that it was, indeed, the actor. Two men had pinned him to the side of her trailer.

They looked as if they'd come straight from central casting. *Hi, can you send down a cross between Stan and Ollie and two of the thugs from* Reservoir Dogs?

One was tall and built like a refrigerator, the other was shorter but almost as stocky. The shorter man was dressed in urban casual—jeans that defied gravity, and a T-shirt that bore a skull and crossbones. He had densely colorful tattoos that ran down both arms all the way to his wrists and up his neck toward a head that was carefully clean-shaven. Blue eyes, Fu Manchu mustache, and a soul patch completed the look.

He had one arm pushed up beneath Trace's quivering chin, his other hand grasping the actor's hair.

"Ow!" Trace said. "Ow, ow! Please!"

Tall guy was more conservatively dressed. Darker jeans, plain black shirt. He stood nearby and watched, his craggy face expressionless. Brown eyes, long brown hair pulled back into a ponytail, he had a deep scar beneath one eye—as if someone, years ago, had tried to blind him and missed.

Alison let the curtain fall back into place as she scrambled for her phone, calling security as she also locked her door. Then, she quickly accessed her phone list to search for Skip's direct number.

His last name was Smith. She dialed him quickly.

He answered on the first ring. " 'Lo." Or maybe that was a "Yo."

"This is Alison Carter," she told him. "I've just called security because a pair of men—neither of whom I recognize—seem to be shaking down Trace Marcus right outside my trailer."

"Fuck," he said, adding, "Stay where you are," before he hung up on her.

Presumably—hopefully—to come to the aid of the man he was supposed to be bodyguarding. Or babysitting. Alison wasn't quite sure which.

She went back to the window, but they were gone. All of them—Trace, too. Maybe they'd seen the movement of the curtain.

She heard a backfire and then a squeal of tires, as if a car that had been parked on the other side of the production assistants' trailer peeled away. Hopefully Trace Marcus wasn't in it.

She chewed on her lip, uncertain as to what to do. The horrible, uncharitable part of her was secretly hoping not that Trace had been kidnapped—that would be too awful—but that maybe the little angry man had broken his arm or even just a few fingers, and that the part of Silas Quinn would need to be recast. All of the unnecessary drama on the set circulated around Trace Marcus. It was true, the man was a decent enough actor, but he wasn't as great as he thought he was, and there were dozens of other

82

Hollywood stars who could've played Silas Quinn with just as much conviction.

Skippy—which was a stupid name for a bodyguard—had told her to stay where she was. But even if she stepped out of her trailer, she'd still be where she was, wouldn't she? Or close enough . . .

Alison looked out all of the windows on both sides of her trailer. No one was out there—most of the cast and crew were up in the mountains today, out by the entrance to one of the mines, setting up what was going to be a sunrise shot, which they'd all wake up hours and *hours* before dawn to capture.

But then she saw the security team arrive via electric golf cart—a pair of overweight rent-a-cops in uncomfortable-looking uniforms. They didn't get out of their cart, they just slowed as they went past, maneuvering to get back behind her trailer.

She watched from the window, intending to go out and join them, when Skip Smith jogged over. So she kept watching.

He spoke to them and he was far more animated than she'd ever seen him. He glanced over at her trailer and although he didn't wave, it was clear that he saw her at the window. He spoke to the security guards at some length, and they all laughed at something he said. Then he stepped back, gesturing for the cart to proceed, which it did, driving away as if nothing had happened. And Skip, again turning to look directly at her, came toward her trailer.

Alison met him outside. He was a heavy smoker and she didn't want him exhaling or even just bringing his ashtray-smelling clothes into her personal work space.

"Whoever they were—and Marcus made up some bullshit," Skip told her, no ceremony, no greeting, "they must've realized you were watching, because they let him go and ran."

"Is he okay?" Alison asked.

The man shrugged, his expression hard to read behind those mirrored sunglasses. "Seems a little shaken. He says he was rehearsing a scene."

"If he was," Alison told Skip, "it wasn't from this movie."

"You . . . overheard him?"

She nodded. "He said, *Don't,*" she reported. "Like, *Don't hurt me.* And something about money. That he'd have it next week."

Skip nodded. "Great. The man is a retard. I let him out of my sight for two goddamn minutes . . ." He reached for a cigarette, lighting it up without even asking if she minded.

"Skip," Alison chose her words carefully as she took a step back. "I know Trace has had substance abuse issues in the past, and I also know you've been with him for a long time, and because of that, you must feel a certain amount of loyalty—"

84

He made a raspberry sound. "Screw loyalty," he said. "Right now Hank Logan pays my salary. My job is to make sure Marcus shows up on time with his freaking lines learned—which is a pain in the balls, because like I said, he's a retard. I'm also in charge of making sure that he tests negative whenever they spring a drug test on him. It's been a year since he's popped a positive, FYI. But he's heavily in debt. Has been for years. It sounds like that's maybe catching up with him."

"That's good," Alison said. "About the drug tests, I mean. Not so good about the debt." She paused. "I think it's important that Henry Logan knows about this latest incident."

"Oh, believe me," Skip told her, "it'll be in my daily report. I'll make sure he knows."

"Good," she said. "That's . . . I hate to bother Henry, but . . . I'm really sorry you have to deal with this. It's been a heckuva day, with Eleanor's visit this morning."

"Yeah," he said. "Right. Jesus, was that this morning? It's been a *fucking* heck of a day."

"Thanks for getting here so quickly," Alison told him with a nod that was meant to be a conversation ender.

But he had another question for her. "Miss Carter. The men that you saw with Marcus . . . Do you think you'd be able to give, you know, an accurate description?"

She nodded. "Absolutely. I got a good look at

both of them." She gave him a brief rundown. Short guy, tall guy.

He nodded, taking one last long drag on his cigarette before dropping it into the street and grinding it out with the toe of his boot. "Good to know," he told her. "Excuse me."

He pulled out his cell phone and started to dial, even as he walked away.

A.J. phoned home.

One of the conditions that his mother had set, as he'd loaded his truck for the ferry ride to Seattle, was that he take a cell phone that she'd bought him.

He hadn't needed one before this, even though she'd been trying to push the damn thing on him for years.

"But I need to be able to reach you," she would say.

"You know where I live," he'd answer. "You know where I work. If I'm gone, I'm camping, and if I'm camping, it's because I don't want to answer the phone, so I wouldn't take it with me even if I had one."

But this time? He'd taken the phone when she'd offered it. And even that didn't alleviate the worry that was ever-present in her eyes after he'd dropped the Gramps bomb on her.

That had been one hell of a hard conversation. He'd actually scheduled an appointment, and gone into her doctor's office in town, to talk to her. *So, Mom. You know how some people hear voices? Well, I both hear and see Gramps. In fact, he's here right now. He says to tell you he likes your haircut. I'm not sure what to do, but I figured the first step was to maybe do a CAT scan to make sure I don't have a tumor pressing on a part of my brain that would make me hallucinate.*

"A.J.," she said now, in lieu of hello. The fact that his name and number showed up on her phone's little screen before she even answered was something he found disconcerting. Dr. Rose Gallagher seemed omniscient enough as it was. "How are you?"

"Hi, Mom," he said. "I'm fine. How are you?"

"Are you still seeing . . . ?"

"Yep," A.J. said. "Jamie's sitting right here, next to me."

"Let's freak her out, okay?" Jamie said, mischief glinting in his eyes as he popped away—which worked more to freak A.J. out.

"Well, he was," A.J. amended himself. "He's gone now."

"You'll be glad to hear that the CAT scan came back normal," his mother told him briskly. She'd referred him to a colleague who'd agreed that they should run an array of tests, and he'd given his mother permission to discuss the results with the other doctor. It seemed silly not to, since he was just going to tell her everything anyway.

87

Otherwise, what good was it, having a doctor in the family? "Your bloodwork looks good, too. You're healthy."

"Healthy but crazy," he said. In his mother's opinion, the idea that Jamie's ghost had actually returned to earth was not a possibility. "Great."

"You *wanted* a brain tumor?" she asked.

"I wanted an explanation," A.J. said evenly. "Besides, you know . . ." He choked the acronym out. "PTSD."

"It's nothing to be ashamed of," his mother told him fiercely, as if she might sternly scold him if he disagreed.

So he didn't disagree. At least not aloud.

"Have you found a meeting?" she asked.

"There's a church in town," he told her. "If there's a church, there's a meeting."

"Not always," she started, but he cut her off.

"Mom," he said. "I'm okay. I've been doing this a long time. I'm not going to drink. And if Jamie starts telling me to kill people, I'm not going to do that, either."

"Not even remotely funny," she said tightly.

A.J. sighed. "Sorry."

"I think you should come home."

"I know you do," A.J. told his mother. "But the history professor's . . . She's open-minded, Mom. She wants to hear Jamie's story, so . . . I'm going to stay as long as I need to, to tell her and . . . maybe even try to find some proof." He changed

88

the subject before she could try to change his mind. "Can I ask you a question?" He didn't wait for her to respond. "Did Gramps ever talk to you about Silas Quinn's second wife? Agatha something."

"The one he thought must've poisoned Quinn?" she asked.

"Yeah," A.J. said. "Huh. He just told me about that. Just. And he wouldn't've told me what he told me—that Agatha thought Quinn was on the verge of sexually abusing their daughter—back when I was ten."

"No," his mother agreed, "but that doesn't mean you didn't overhear things that were too grown-up for you to understand when you were supposed to be in bed."

His mother had an explanation for everything.

"Hey."

A.J. turned to see that Jamie was back. "She's grabbing a sandwich—turkey and Swiss on pumpernickel, she's wearing a black blouse with those turquoise earrings that she loves, and—drumroll, please—Julie's at the reception desk."

"If finding the oil tank didn't convince her," he told Jamie, "this won't do it, either."

Right before they'd left Alaska, Rose had asked A.J. to please stop by the house. She still lived in Jamie's house, where she and Bev and A.J. had eventually moved to quote unquote *take care of Gramps*. Of course, at first anyway, it had been Gramps who'd taken care of them.

It was a smallish house, but one that was filled with good memories and laughter—Jamie and Melody had raised much of their family there.

And buried somewhere in the big backyard, Rose had told A.J. the day before he'd headed south, was an old oil tank, long unused. It needed to be removed before the contents started leaking, but all the experts she'd hired to find the thing had come up empty-handed.

She'd stood out on her back porch, arms folded regally across her chest as she told him this.

And he'd realized what she wanted. She wanted him to ask Jamie's ghost where that oil tank was buried.

"He's not sure he wants to tell you," A.J. had informed her. "Seeing as how you don't think he's real."

"Don't be a pill, kid." Jamie had been far more relaxed about it. "I'm happy to tell her. Hell, maybe it'll help convince her—and you—that I'm not a growth on your brain."

It didn't convince her. Despite the fact that the tank had been precisely where Jamie, via A.J., told Rose it would be.

His mother's theory was that its location was something Jamie had told A.J. when he was small—a distant memory that had been awakened.

A.J.'s sister, Bev, though, was happily convinced that their gramps was back. And because Bev knew that A.J. was being "visited," which was what she called it, the entire rest of the town now knew it, too.

Bev had left him a cheerful voicemail message, telling him that everyone made a point to ask about both of them. *How's A.J.? Tell him to say hey to Jamie for me. . . .* It didn't seem to make too much of a difference whether A.J. was haunted or crazy. They all took it in stride. With the exception of A.J.'s mother.

"Is he back?" she asked now, her voice tinny through the speaker of his cell phone. "What's he telling you?"

"That you're wearing the earrings Jamie and I gave you for Christmas, you're having lunch at your desk, and that Ariana's AWOL, so cousin Julie's filling in again."

His mother was silent.

"Jamie says he can move from one place to another with no travel time," A.J. explained. "He just thinks himself there, and . . . There he is."

"Convenient," she said.

"Very," A.J. agreed.

"Hang on," Jamie said. "I'll go and tell you which files she has in front of her, which page the book she's reading is open to. We're going to make her believe us this time, kid. I'll be right back." He popped out again.

"A.J.," his mother said, but then she stopped. He could tell that she'd covered the phone, but still could hear her saying, probably to Julie, "I'll be right there." The hand was removed. "I've got evening hours tonight. Will you call me tomorrow?"

"Yes, ma'am," he said. "And if I don't call you . . ."

"I'll call you," she finished for him. "Because I think I can get you the proof that you need. For this history person. If that's what it takes to get you back home."

"You have proof?" A.J. asked. "Written, documented proof . . . ?"

"Your great-grandmother kept diaries," Rose informed him.

"Really?" A.J. was bemused. "And you couldn't have told me this last week . . . ?"

"I didn't think you'd be able to get anyone to listen to you," she said honestly. "And . . . there's a reason you didn't know about the diaries. They contain a lot of personal information. It's been a tradition to pass the diaries down only to the women in this family and . . ." She broke off again, again speaking, no doubt to Julie, her words muffled. "I'm on my way." Unmuffled, "Kyle Notterly fell off his bike and needs stitches. I'll talk to you tomorrow."

"Wait," A.J. said. "Could you call me tonight?"

"It'll be late," she informed him.

"I'll be up," he said.

"Not sleeping again?" she asked.

"I'm fine," A.J. said again, shaking his head at his mother's inability to see the glass as anything but half-empty. "I'll talk to you later."

He hung up his phone with a snap, and sat in his truck for a moment, wondering where Jamie was—eager to ask him about those diaries. Although how would Dr. Carter know that they were really written by Melody? Maybe there was a sample of her handwriting somewhere, on something that *was* documented. A church certificate she'd signed when she'd married Quinn . . .

Maybe this was going to be easier than he'd thought.

He turned off his truck and climbed out. Time to find that main production trailer and make sure whoever was costuming the extras gave him boxers. Or else Alison would make him go commando.

Which—although he'd never admit it to Jamie—had a certain undeniable appeal.

For one hair-raising moment, I thought I was in hell.

And then I thought that somehow, in the short time that I'd been gone, A.J. had been in a horrible car accident.

But then I realized that there was only one

vehicle burning, and it wasn't his truck. In fact, the kid's truck wasn't the only thing of note that was nowhere to be found.

The entire town of Jubilation was off the map.

Of course, I then realized that *it* wasn't gone—I was.

Somehow I'd gone off course. I'd thought myself up to Alaska, to Rose's office, and found out that she was reading an old favorite, *The Small Town Physician's Guide to Mental Disorders*. It was open to page 358. Schizophrenia.

Not exactly the kind of thing I wanted to tell A.J. when he was already in a dark mood, so I'd decided to save my latest prove-the-ghost-is-real effort for another day.

Which is when I thought myself back to A.J.— and found myself here, instead.

There was a dead man in that car. I don't know how I knew it, but I did.

You don't get a rule book or an orientation seminar when you return to the world of the living. You just know what you need to know.

One could argue that an instruction manual or at the very least a mission statement could be useful on the journey, but it was not a stretch for me to have to go on faith, so most of the time I got by all right.

When A.J. had asked me how I did what he called *that popping in and popping out bullcrap,*

I told him that I just thought about where I wanted to be, and I'd go where I was meant to go.

But this time, something wasn't working right, because I sure as hell didn't want to be here.

I didn't know the dead man, who no longer had a face. But the rest of him was as ornately tattooed as a circus sideshow freak.

Another fellow—tall and dressed in black—was standing back, next to some kind of gas can and a hiker's backpack. I didn't recognize him, either. He watched the flames and smoke rise into the cloudless afternoon sky as he spoke on a phone that looked far fancier than the one Rose had given A.J.

"Wayne's head exploded all over the backseat," he told whoever he was talking to. "I'm torching the car right now. I don't know what kind of ordnance that was, but you gotta get me more. It was a mess, but the message was received. The fuckwad crapped his pants *and* pissed himself." He laughed. "Yeah. Both at once. He'll get the money. It'll be the first thing he takes out of his next paycheck. Count on it."

It was all magic to me—telephones that you could carry around with you and talk to other people, out in the middle of nowhere, like Kirk with his communicator having a conversation with Scotty back on the *Enterprise*.

The future had truly arrived, but this man, with his long brown hair coming out from its ponytail, and his face sprayed with poor, dead Wayne's blood, wasn't any kind of hero from outer space.

As I stood there watching him, he tucked that phone between his shoulder and his ear while he took off his shoes and his socks and his black shirt and dark-colored denims, stripping down to a pair of teal blue briefs.

No doubt his clothes were covered in evidence. Killing a man, even with a gun, is powerfully dirty work.

"It's not a big deal that she saw us with him," he said to whomever was on the other end of that phone, adding, "No, no—would you relax? There's going to be nothing to find. Wayne'll be a cinder before the car is found. *If* it's found. I'm on the fucking dark side of the moon. And like I said, his head evaporated. His teeth are gone, and the fire'll take care of fingerprints. Hold on."

He put the phone down as he used his shirt to wipe his face, wipe his hands. Then he opened his pack and pulled out a bottle of water and a small towel and used that to wash up, too. He tossed it all—clothes, bottle, towel—into the inferno before picking up the phone.

"I'm back," he said, then listened to whatever his co-conspirator in a first-degree murder was telling him. He sighed heavily before saying, "If that happens, then yeah. We'll kill her, too. Does that make you happy?"

I stepped closer to him, because now they were

talking about killing *her*. Killing who? I wanted to know.

But I couldn't hear more than a buzz as the other fellow spoke, then, "Yeah, don't worry, we'll make it look like an accident. Look, Jesus, it's not a problem, Loco, so don't turn it into one. I'll call you when I get to Tucson. All right? All right. Be cool. Talk later."

With that, he hung up the phone and threw it, too, into the fire.

And walked right through me.

"Jesus!" We both said the same thing, at the same time.

I'd moved even closer in my attempt to hear who this Loco was, still trying to hear his end of the conversation, hoping at least for the dead man's last name—or better yet Mr. Tall-with-a-Ponytail's name.

Instead, I'd gotten the unpleasant sensation of temporarily cohabitating the same square footage of earth with him.

I could see where it might be nice to do that with a lover who'd been left behind. It felt both hot and cold—at least it did to me. And it tingled and buzzed.

No doubt it had felt as freakishly bizarre to Wayne's executioner, because he jumped and said, "What the hell . . . ?"

And then he swatted the air around him, but I was well out of reach by then.

In fact, I didn't dally. I headed back toward Jubilation, homing in on A.J., but taking a slower, more conventional route this time.

You might call it flying, but it's not quite, because I don't have a body to use to ride air currents and sail above the ground. It's more like taking the astral projection scenic route, with the Arizona desert unfolding beneath me.

I paid attention, counting the miles that passed, somehow knowing when they did, aware of the direction that I traveled with a sense of absolute knowledge that would've come in handy back when I was alive.

I arrived in Jubilation just as A.J. was stepping out of a trailer, with what must've been his costume for tomorrow's shoot covered with plastic and on a hanger.

He glanced at me as I came in for a landing, but he didn't break stride, so I hustled to keep up.

"Forty-seven miles outside of town," I informed him, "due northeast, a car is on fire, with a murdered man named Wayne inside. Lotta tattoos, relatively short of stature, and much shorter now with his head blown to hell. The killer is a tall man, about six foot four, long brown hair in a ponytail, scar beneath his left eye. He was talking on the phone to someone he called Loco."

A.J. stopped walking and looked at me. "Are you kidding me?" he said. "Now we're going to be caped crusaders and fight crime?"

"Hell, no," I said, laughing at the idea, but sobering up real fast. "No, no, son, that's not why I told you—in fact, I don't want you near that man, he's a bad one, he was talking about killing again, which is why I want him caught. All I need you to do is dial nine-one-one for me and report the fire, and the fact that the man in the car is named Wayne. You don't need to tell 'em who you are. It can—it *should* be an anonymous tip." I pointed down the street. "There's a pay phone outside the Circle K. You can do it from there."

Chapter Five

Hugh finally pulled up outside of Alison's apartment at ten to four in the morning. She'd been waiting out front in the darkness, tapping her foot, her production bag over her shoulder, cup of coffee in hand.

"You're late," she told him as she climbed in on the passenger side of his Jeep, "which means I'm late." She closed the door behind her. "I'm in—go!"

Gears ground and the Jeep lurched, and because Alison was juggling her coffee with the seatbelt that she hadn't yet managed to fasten, she spilled nearly the entire supersized cup of hot liquid down the front of her shirt when the stupid, stupid lid came off.

"Ow!" she said. "Hot, hot! Shit! *Shit!*"

Hugh braked to a stop, and grabbed a squeeze bottle of water that was sitting in the cup holder—where she should have set her coffee down when she'd first gotten in—and sprayed her.

But the top of his bottle apparently wasn't on securely either. It popped off and she was hit, first in the face and then in the chest by a stream of icy cold water. It came simultaneously with Hugh's heartfelt apology and laughter. "Oh, no, I'm so sorry!"

She was drenched, but at least she was no longer in pain. She wiped her face as he continued to laugh. "Sorry!"

"Drive," she ordered him.

He put the Jeep back in gear, still snickering, but hesitated. "I think you might want to go back inside and change."

"What I want," Alison told him curtly, "is to not be late. *Drive.*"

He hit the accelerator.

She looked down at herself, surveying the damage, and realized the impetus behind his suggestion. Because her tank top was white, it was now transparent. "Oh, *shit,*" she said.

"You want me to turn around?" Hugh asked.

"No," she said, digging in her bag. She'd brought a spare cotton button-down shirt, just in case one of the extras needed a change. While it was true that both the head of costuming and the extras wrangler would be on hand, she'd learned it took far less time simply to carry a shirt or two with her.

It was long-sleeved and about the size of a two-man tent, but she pulled it on, exasperated. She always wore overshirts to protect herself against sunburn during the daylight hours. This predawn shoot had been her one chance to be both outside and cool despite the temperatures in the mid-eighties. But it was clearly not to be.

Now to handle her second problem: What to do about her lack of caffeine. "Has craft services been moved up to this location?" she asked.

Hugh looked at her as if she were a moron.

"Stupid question?" she asked as she reviewed the schedule.

"Very. The coffeemaker's got its own generator," Hugh assured her. "I don't think Henry's slept in four days, and without coffee to mainline, he'd be weeping and babbling."

"Good to know," she said, as she pulled her schedule from her bag and reviewed it.

This morning they were filming part of the scene in *Quinn* where Kid Gallagher, after winning the deed to another man's mine in a poker game, shot the man in cold blood, then heartlessly threw his widow and young children off the property in the middle of the night.

They were filming the final shot of this scene first, taking advantage of the promise of a colorful sunrise. Later tonight they'd film the first part of the scene—the harsh predawn confrontation between the Kid and the distraught miner's wife.

A movie's scenes were usually shot out of order. Somehow the actors coped, but Alison found it disconcerting. She wasn't sure she'd ever get used to it.

"I didn't sleep much last night either." Hugh glanced at her as he downshifted to make the climb up the trail and into the mountains. "I got an email from Kent. He was sorry he missed me yesterday, and hopes I'm well."

"He has a lot of nerve." Alison looked up from her notes. "You okay?"

"Yeah," Hugh said, even though he shook his head. "But I spent the entire night composing the perfect email back to him. Which I ended up not sending because the real perfect response for this situation is silence."

He was quoting her own words back to her, words she'd said to him just a few days ago, and she smiled. "Ah, grasshopper. You have learned well. My job here is done."

He pulled to a stop in the parking area that was not quite at the end of the rutted dirt road. Their headlights illuminated what looked like a wagon trail, going even farther up into the hills.

"We're supposed to walk it, from here," Hugh told her, reaching into the back to grab a pair of flashlights, one of which he handed to her.

"Although, you got the memo, right? With the warning that snakes like to move around before the sun comes up . . . ?"

"Snakes?" Alison repeated, and the word came out a little bit louder than she'd intended. She said it again, more softly this time, but no less intensely. *"Snakes?"* She'd opened the car door but now froze, her right foot in the air as she peered out at the ground. "No, I didn't get the memo—I'm wearing sandals. Why didn't I get that memo?"

"That's not good. You can't wear sandals out here." Hugh went around to the back of the Jeep and rummaged around. "Luckily, I have an extra pair of boots."

He pulled them out and brought them over to her. "Luckily?" she echoed.

They were big and black and rubber—the kind of boots you might be wearing as you came in the kitchen door, shaking rain off your slicker and saying, *Grab the younguns, Ma. Crick's a-rising.*

Alison's cell rang. "Why didn't I get that memo?" she again asked Hugh, who shrugged as she dug for her phone in her bag. It was the intern, Paula, calling, so she opened the phone. "Paula. Perhaps *you* know why I didn't get the memo *about the snakes!*"

"I am so sorry," Paula said, which was her constant refrain, as Hugh mimed the message that he needed to get moving up the trail. He vanished into the night, the little bastard. "I don't know, but I will certainly look into it for you. In the meantime, please God, tell me you brought an extra shirt."

"I did," Alison said, "but I'm going to need—"

Paula steamrolled over her. "Praise God, but where *are* you?"

"In the parking lot by the trail," Alison said. "Will you bring me a—"

"Fabulous. I'll meet you halfway," Paula said and hung up her phone.

"—replacement? Shit!" Alison said as she jammed her phone back into her bag and started to pull those stupid boots on. But wait a minute. Weren't you supposed to check boots for scorpions in the southwest? She used the flashlight Hugh had given her to peer into each boot, turning it upside down and shaking it before she cautiously reached a hand in. They were empty. They were also big enough so that she didn't have to take off her sandals before she pulled them on.

They came up to her knees which, with the overshirt that hung down past her shorts, was quite the fashion statement.

She shouldered her bag and aimed her flashlight up the trail.

She could see the bright glow of lights far, far up ahead and shuffled toward it, vowing to step on any snake that she encountered.

She'd had no idea she'd be starting the day with a hike in oversized wading boots.

And then there Paula was—the light from her flashlight bobbing down the trail. "Dr. Carter?"

"It's me," Alison said as she took off the overshirt and held it out to the younger woman. "You wouldn't happen to have a shirt you could trade for this, would you? I kind of spilled my coffee in the car—"

"I don't," Paula said. "But don't worry about a coffee stain. It's par for the course."

"It's not the stain I'm worried about," Alison said, but of course Paula couldn't see her in the darkness.

She was already hurrying away, running back up the trail, faster than Alison could manage in her boots. "I'll certainly make sure you have something to cover you by the time the sun comes up."

"I could use it a little earlier, please," Alison called after her. "Like, right away . . . ?"

"I'll put it on my to-do list," Paula called back. "FYI, there's sunscreen on the table near the coffee."

"I don't need sunscreen, I need a shirt that's not transparent," Alison called back, but she was gone.

So okay. She tried to wring herself out a little bit more, but it was hopeless. The bra she was wearing had seemed sturdy enough—before it got doused. She was going to have to stand with her arms folded across her chest, and although she could manage to cover her nipples, the position, by its nature, pushed her breasts together and made her into the queen of cleavage.

Her best hope lay in staying in the shadows and trying to remain invisible until her shirt dried.

Which it would do rather quickly in this heat. But it just wasn't happening fast enough.

Alison finally made it up to the entrance of the mine where they were filming this morning. There were dozens of played-out silver mines in this area, dotting the hillsides, most of them bearing signs that warned, *DANGER! STRUCTURALLY UNSOUND! DO NOT ENTER!* The warnings about a possible cave-in had been removed from this one, though, and the clearing in front of it was brightly lit with spotlights and huge reflectors. Dozens of crew members were busy at work wherever she looked, and no one was paying any attention to her.

Maybe she could pull this invisibility thing off.

Henry Logan sat up in a huge crane with the cinematographer, rehearsing the shot. According to Alison's notes, the camera would start out focused on a woman and two small children, who were huddled in the dirt outside of a tiny cabin that the set construction crew had built near the mine entrance. The camera would slowly lift, courtesy of the crane's enormous arm, and zoom

106

out to reveal the beautiful desolation of the surrounding countryside and the very first rays of light from the sunrise peeking over the hills to the east.

"How's it look, Carter?" Henry shouted down at her as he gestured toward the set.

So much for being invisible.

"It seems okay from here," Alison called back, gritting her teeth and moving into the lit area to get a closer look as she kept her arms crossed in front of her. Her shirt *was* going to dry—and soon. She held on to that thought like a mantra. But until it did, she'd just have to hope that it didn't turn into a thing.

The mine entrance had been shored up so that it looked like a working mine rather than the deathtrap that it was. And a tiny cabin had been constructed on the exact spot where the original mine owner's cabin had stood. She stepped even closer, making sure there were no telltale signs of the twenty-first century in the shot.

A Sears brand hammer left behind or a neon green measuring tape.

She'd found both of those things last week, on the boardwalk back in town.

But here, everything was perfect—even the costumes on the woman and children. The kids had given their iPhones and Gameboys to their mothers, who were patiently standing back behind the camera.

"Carter!" Henry yelled. "Get out of my shot!"

Alison jumped and quickly moved off to the side. But damnit, she'd uncrossed her arms. It was just for a mere fraction of a second, but that was all it took.

"Thanks," the director called, his face hidden behind the camera. "By the way, congratulations on winning the wet T-shirt contest."

And so now, it would be a thing.

All over the set, eyes turned toward her in amusement.

Inwardly, she cringed. Still, she managed to smile, arms again in front of her. "I'd like to thank the judges," she said, loudly enough for them all to hear her, "and let them know that I will work diligently in support of world peace and gay marriage."

A smattering of good-natured applause and whistling broke out as she ducked back into the shadows.

"The boots really make it work," Logan said. "Very misguided dominatrix."

Alison had to laugh at that. "Very," she agreed.

But then, just like that, it was over, as he raised his voice and called, "Hugh! What's our time?"

"Sunrise in fourteen minutes," Hugh shouted back.

"Places, people!" someone yelled. "Let's rehearse this shot."

"Extras!" called Jane from continuity, running

across the set with a digital camera in her hand. "Mark where you're standing!"

Extras? There were extras in this shot? Alison hadn't checked the costumes of anyone besides the principals. She took off after Jane.

But then she saw him and stopped short.

A.J. Gallagher.

He was across the set with two other extras, near the scrub brush line, blending into the darkness.

And looking directly at her from beneath the brim of his cowboy hat.

Even his hat, which had been a bright off-white in the sunlight, seemed muted in the darkness. Like the men beside him, he was dressed in authentic 1890s cowboy wear—faded and dusty dark-colored pants, a shirt that was no longer pure white, and a ragged brown vest.

He'd rolled his sleeves up as far as he possibly could because of the heat, and his arms were muscular and powerful looking. Where on earth had she gotten the impression that he was slender, almost skinny? He was lean, yes, but not skinny. Not at all.

He wore a gun belt around his hips, complete with a very deadly-looking prop gun.

No doubt about it, he looked incredibly authentic and absolutely at home in the costume he was wearing. In fact, he looked as if he'd stepped out of a time machine, with that familiar face and those Gallagher blue eyes.

And great. The last time she'd spoken to him—through the window of his truck yesterday afternoon—she'd actually teased him about having to go commando. And yes. She'd admit it. She'd been flirting. Which was stupid, but his smile was just so sweet. And now here she was, looking as if she were two margaritas away from a *Girls Gone Wild* video. Wasn't *this* just perfect?

Arms crossed, she strode toward A.J. and the other extras as purposefully and as businesslike as she could manage in her boots and cleavage. She'd do her job, be cool and impersonal, keep her distance.

No flirting, no wrong messages sent.

As she drew closer, A.J. glanced down at the ground, at the worn-out toes of his boots. The brim of his hat hid his face, as if up close he was suddenly shy, or maybe embarrassed by what his eyes might reveal. It was a gesture both respectfully sweet and utterly charming.

From a man who claimed to be a descendant of the notorious outlaw and murderer Kid Gallagher.

"Okay, everyone," Alison said briskly to all three extras. "Wedding rings and watches—are they all off? Let's see wrists and left hands."

One of the men, Marty, had a pale stripe where his wedding band had been. "Make up!" Alison shouted, telling him, "Get that covered up. Come on, Marty, you should know better."

110

"I didn't think it would show," Marty said as he turned to meet the makeup boy.

Alison looked at A.J., who had big hands with strong yet graceful fingers.

"No ring," he told her. "Not married. Do you have any time to talk, maybe later?"

"Early this afternoon," she said, as she stepped slightly back and scanned each of the three men, looking for anything out of place that continuity might've missed. "Catch me after the shot, I'll check my schedule and find you some time."

"Thanks," A.J. said, wisely leaving it at that, which she appreciated, because—

"Hey, wait a minute," she asked the third man, "are you actually *smoking?*"

"Henry said it was okay to have a cigarette during this scene," the raggedy-looking extra said a touch defensively.

"They didn't have filter tips back in 1898. You would have rolled your own from a pouch of tobacco," she told him. "Come on, put that thing out."

"We're only in the background," the man protested. "No one's gonna see me, let alone my cigarette's filter."

"And what if," Alison said, "Henry Logan, in a burst of creativity, decides that instead of pulling the camera back, he's going to zoom in for a close-up of your face? And what if it's brilliant? What if it's the shot that's going to win him the

Oscar? Do *you* want to be the one to tell him he can't use that shot because you're smoking a twenty-first-century cigarette with a filter?"

Sullenly, with an exasperated exhale and an eyeroll, the man stubbed out his cigarette.

"Thank you," Alison said. She turned to find A.J. watching her, a smile softening the lines of his face. God, he was a good-looking man—and doubly so when he smiled.

He bent down and picked up the now cold cigarette butt.

"Better not leave that lying here," he said with that slight twang of his western drawl. "What if Henry Logan decides to zoom in on my boots?"

Alison laughed. "Are you making fun of me?" she demanded.

His smile deepened, revealing a dimple in his cheek. "Yes, ma'am," he said. "Because you know as well as I do that Logan is no more likely to zoom in to a close-up of Mr. Flynn here, than he is to zoom in to a close-up of my boots—as attractive as they are." He admired his boots for a moment, then looked back at her. "Logan's pulling back to get a wide-angle shot of the sunrise. From that camera angle, we're going to be nothing more than shadows that move across the clearing to help the lady and kids back toward town. Matter of fact, I'm a double for an actor who's got lines in the altercation scene—between

112

Gallagher and the widow—that they're going to be shooting tonight."

"Huh," she said. "I thought this was your first time on a movie set."

"It is," A.J. said. "But I've seen a lot of movies, plus I learn pretty fast."

"Places in five minutes!" someone shouted.

"Better move behind the camera," A.J. told Alison. "I'm no expert, but even I know they didn't have outfits like the one you're wearing back in 1898."

The devil in her made her say, "Yeah, women definitely didn't wear boots like these back then," as she backed away.

He laughed, but there was a flash of heat in his eyes. He tipped his hat down across his face again, as if to hide it from her. But he couldn't resist another look as she walked away, peeking out at her from under the wide brim.

She knew, because she hadn't been able to resist looking back at him, too. What *was* it about this guy?

He was smart, he was funny, he was handsome, and he didn't hide the fact that he found her attractive.

"Hey, if you want to borrow it," he called after her, "I've got a spare shirt in my bag. It's the blue gym bag with my name on it, in the extras tent. Help yourself."

Plus, he was generous and kind.

"Bless you," Alison said. "Thank you."

He smiled. "My pleasure." And he ducked his head again as if afraid to let her see how happy it was making him—his being able to help her this way.

It was, quite frankly, unbelievably sexy, and as he looked at her again, she turned and ran.

June 24, 1898
Dear Diary,

He wants a child.

What in God's name would he do with a child?

This is why he was so very angry when I first arrived. And here I'd thought he'd realized that I had lied. But I was wrong. My punishment came not from my pretending to be in the family way to keep him from harming me, but from what he sees as my failure—my "losing" the babe through miscarriage.

The doctor fears him, and although I am still sorely battered from my "accident," he says I am finally well enough to conceive.

And I am lost, with no way out.

For I would never, ever, willingly bring a child into his world. Not to save myself a brutal beating, or even to prevent my certain death.

But I see it coming. I see my future.

And I am in despair.

Chapter Six

After the endless hours of setup and preparation, the sequence took maybe forty-five seconds.

Henry Logan filmed the same shot three different times, although it was only during the first take that the camera caught the exact instant of the sunrise.

The actors playing the miner's widow and children had gone back into town, but the crew was busy all over again, setting up another scene that took place here at the mine entrance—a daytime scene in which Silas Quinn came looking for Kid Gallagher.

Trace Marcus had arrived—his Jeep was allowed all the way up to the entrance. He was in the small tent that was being used by whoever needed it—the same tent that Alison had gone into, to dig A.J.'s shirt out of his bag.

Henry Logan had gone into the tent, too, and Alison knew he was warning the actor about the mine shaft. The scene they were about to film ended with Silas going into the mine to search for Gallagher.

She may not have received the memo about the snakes, but she *had* gotten the very clear warning about the decaying old mines. The warning was not just for this one, but for the entire area. Most of the old structures were in poor condition and in very real danger of cave-in or collapse. Some still contained caches of explosives—decaying TNT that was extremely volatile and dangerous. Henry was reminding Trace to go no more than a few feet inside, even though this mine didn't plunge straight down into the earth. It actually ran along the hill line, close to the surface for quite some distance and thus was deemed relatively safe.

Relatively, because the rock and earth walls were shored up by timber that was long rotted.

It was hard to imagine Trace taking any kind of risk and actually going too far into the mine, but actors could be funny that way, in the heat of the moment.

All of the interior shots of the mine were going to be filmed on a soundstage, back in California, after the weather in Jubilation got too hot.

"Need to stick around?"

Alison turned to see A.J. standing behind her, his bag in hand.

"Or can I offer you a ride back into town?" he asked.

"Oh," she said. "No. Thanks. I'm, um, almost done. But not quite. I don't want to make you wait."

"I don't mind," he said.

"But, see, I can't tell you absolutely if it's going to be five minutes or three hours," Alison admitted. She lowered her voice. "I have to approve Silas's costume, but in order for me to do that, he's got to come out of the tent. Which he won't do until he's ready."

Once she gave her approval, she could leave the painstaking and endless responsibility of checking the actor before each take in the very capable hands of the team from continuity.

"Can't you go in there?" A.J. asked.

"I can," Alison said, "but I don't want to. Fewer mistakes happen when the actor comes onto the set. I don't want to give approval and then have him walk out here with his iPod earphones hanging out of his pocket, or a pack of Tic Tacs in his hand."

"Does that happen often?" he asked.

"More often than it should," she said, and then realized that he was standing there in just a snug-fitting T-shirt and jeans, having changed out of his costume. She started to unbutton the shirt he'd lent her, unfastening the tails she'd tied together in front. "I should give this back to you."

"Oh," he said. "No, I'm fine. I don't need it— besides, it . . . looks good on you."

"Then you should go ahead without me," Alison told him. "I don't want to be responsible for putting the extra from Alaska into the hospital with sunstroke."

"When I was in the army, I spent nearly a year in the Middle East," he told her. "Saudi Arabia, Kuwait, and Iraq. First Gulf War," he added, no doubt when he saw her trying to do the math. "Not this one."

"I saw your military ID," she said. "But I had no idea. You're lucky you didn't get called back up."

"Yeah," A.J. said. "I didn't get called for . . . well, for a lot of different reasons. Bottom line, though, I know what real heat is, and I'm well aware of my limits and . . . I'm fine."

"Still," she said, glancing over to the tent from which Trace Marcus still hadn't emerged. Skip Smith had come outside for a cigarette, and he nodded as she met his gaze. She nodded, too, before pulling her attention back to A.J. "You're probably dying for a shower."

"I'm happy to wait," he said, and then deftly changed the subject so they didn't have to stand here arguing about it, smart man that he was. "It must be a kick for you—to be here in Arizona, where it all happened. Jubilation and the Red Rock Saloon . . . It's amazing that it's all still standing."

"Yeah," Alison said. "You know, Jubilation was abandoned for years, shortly after Silas Quinn died. The silver was played out, and it was a total ghost town."

"I didn't know that," he said.

"Quinn's family, the Sylvesters, still owned it," she told him. "But they weren't living here. There were a few squatters—hermits and madmen—

118

who were trying to get the last of the silver from all the abandoned mines, and I think they kept the tourists and looters at bay. So when Neil Sylvester's father came back in the 1950s, it was all just here, waiting for him. He checked to make sure the buildings weren't going to fall down on him, did a few repairs, hired a manager to run the saloon, hired a couple of tour guides, built that motel, and boom, he was in business."

A.J. nodded, looking over at the old mine entrance. "Really?" he said.

"Well, it wasn't *much* of a business," Alison conceded.

And he looked slightly perturbed as he said, "No, I didn't mean—" He cut himself off and started again. "I'm sure he did fine. I just, um . . . Did you know that this is the actual mine? The one that belonged to my great-grandfather."

"Gallagher's Claim," Alison said, nodding. "At least, that's what we believe, with the inexact information and maps that we have."

"It's the one," A.J. said, definite. "But it didn't happen this way. I mean, not the way that it's written in this script. Jamie didn't incite the confrontation with the miner. He didn't force a drunk to draw, and he certainly didn't throw any women and children out of their home."

"This scene," Alison pointed out, "is from Silas Quinn's eyewitness report. A direct recounting—"

"Which was never confirmed by a second

119

source," A.J. pointed out rather gently. "Truth is, Quinn wasn't there."

"Okay," Alison said, folding her arms across her chest. "Hit me with your version. Jamie *didn't* win this mine in a poker game with a man who was too drunk to stand up, let alone to 'know when to fold 'em,' or when not to face down a notorious gunslinger's quick draw."

"No," A.J. said. "That part's true. Jamie won the mine in a game from a miner who was drunk. But by the time it came into Jamie's possession, the silver in this vein was played out. Jamie accepted what was a worthless deed, in an attempt to avoid trouble."

"At the very least," Alison argued, "it was land, with a cabin."

"Land with no water isn't worth much out here." He was silent for a moment, staring into the air next to her, as if listening to the sound of the wind. "The cabin was more like a lean-to," he added. "It barely had a roof, and the floor was dirt. Jamie didn't live there—he stayed at the Jubilation Hotel. It's not there anymore—they had a fire a few years later—but it was just a few buildings down from the Red Rock Saloon. Hotels—the fancier the better—were more his style.

"The man from whom he won the mine," he continued, "was named Barnum Ruggers—Sorry, Barnum T. Ruggers. Don't want to confuse him with all of the other Barnum Ruggers now, do we?" He laughed. "He was a liar and a thief, who was wanted in Kansas and Oklahoma for horse-rustling. He wasn't exactly a family man. No wife, no kids. Although he was a frequent customer of someone named Big Sal who worked at the Red Rock, and . . . Okay, I didn't need to know that and . . ." He shot Alison an apologetic smile. "Sorry, um . . . Anyway, after the poker game, Ruggers tried to backshoot Jamie, but he was drunk, so he missed.

"Jamie could've killed him right then and there, in self-defense, but he didn't. Instead he waited until the man sobered up and then took him on, face-to-face. And yeah, he drew first—he was fast—and he killed the man. He had to. That was the way it worked back then. Ruggers had a kid brother, Cal, who was just sixteen, but he was a mean SOB, too. Jamie ran him out of town, didn't even give him a chance to pack up his things from his cabin—which is probably the basis for Quinn's fiction about Jamie evicting the wife and kids in the dark of night."

It was a good story. But . . . "You remember all those details," Alison asked, "from conversations you had with your great-grandfather back when you were *ten?*"

"Yeah," A.J. said. "I do. He told me his stories over and over. And his nearly getting shot in the back was one he liked to tell. I think he knew how

121

close he'd come to dying that day, and the memories stayed with him, crystal clear, even all those years later. Killing, even a bastard like Ruggers, didn't set well with him, either. It weighed on him—the lives he took. But not as much as the lives he didn't take—namely Quinn's."

"Hmm," she said.

He smiled at that. "I know how hard this is for you to believe, and I can't tell you how much I respect your willingness to listen, I truly do."

"But," she said, because she heard it coming.

"But Silas Quinn wasn't the hero that he made himself out to be," A.J. said. "And if you think about it? Almost every account of his so-called heroic deeds can be traced back to a story he himself told first."

"But everything *you* know," Alison pointed out, "also can be traced back to a single source—which was your great-grandfather."

"Not so," A.J. countered. "I spoke to my mother on the phone last night. I didn't get a chance to talk for very long because she'd had a hard day and she was tired, but I'm going to be speaking to her again later today. She, um, kind of dropped a bomb on me. I didn't know this before last night, but it turns out Melody kept diaries, starting back before she married Silas Quinn."

"Melody Quinn kept diaries?" Oh, if only that were true. What a resource that would be—a glimpse into the heart and mind of the woman who was the Jackie O of her time.

"Melody Gallagher," A.J. gently corrected her. "And yes, ma'am. Apparently she did."

"I'm going to want to see them," Alison told him.

"I thought you probably would," he said. "Considering they'll be that documented proof you were looking for."

"Assuming we can verify, without a doubt, that they were written by Melody Quinn," she warned him.

"Of course," he said, and hesitated. And here it came. Whatever excuse he was going to come up with for why she couldn't see these alleged diaries. "There's just a . . . well, a small— smallish—problem."

"A smallish problem," she repeated. Of course there was a problem. "They're lost," she guessed.

And sure enough, A.J. nodded, but then shook his head. "More like misplaced," he told her. "But there're not that many places they could be. My mother's or maybe my sister Bev's attic . . . Or maybe Aunt Betty has them. Or Julie, my cousin . . ."

He looked at her, and Alison could see that he knew she'd taken a mental step back from him.

"To be honest, I've never seen them," he said quietly. "Never read them. I'm going purely on what my mother told me last night. And I can't promise you that she didn't fabricate her story about these diaries completely—in an effort to get me to come home. I haven't had a chance yet to call my sister, but I can tell you this—if Bev says the diaries are real, they're real. Then it's just a matter of finding them."

Alison looked at him as he stood there in the morning sunlight, a picture of both honesty and sincerity. It was rolled up in that tall, blond, and handsome package, with those steady blue eyes and that knee-melting smile.

If he'd been just an extra, an actor looking to make contacts and work on a Henry Logan picture, she might've invited him to lunch. And then dinner. And eventually breakfast.

Yes, he was attractive—so much so that she could imagine having an on-set relationship with him. It would be like going away to camp and having a summer romance—or so Hugh had told her. Single cast and crew members frequently hooked up for the duration, then went their separate ways when the movie was wrapped.

It was no big thing.

But it *would* be a big thing, if even part of his story turned out to be true. She couldn't sleep with her source of information. It would add a coat of sleaze to any new truths that she did discover, and it would help others discount them.

She wasn't the only person who believed Silas Quinn was a true American hero, and there would be a huge amount of resistance to any change in this well-known legend.

Alison took another step back from A.J., this one physical. "Suppose they are real," she suggested. "The diaries. What if your mother kept them from you because they paint a less-than-flattering picture of your great-grandfather? What if they prove not your story but Silas Quinn's—that Melody *was* abducted by Gallagher. When was the last entry allegedly written?"

"I don't know," A.J. said. "Maybe you should talk to my mother." He laughed. "Yeah. Or maybe you shouldn't. She's, um . . ." He took out his phone and looked at it. "I don't have good cell coverage out here, but let me call my sister when I get back to town. She might be the one for you to talk to. I'm pretty sure she's read them. My mother said it was a family tradition to pass them around among the women."

"Why don't you go and do that," Alison suggested. "I'll meet you in my office, later." She checked her watch. "Say . . . one o'clock?"

A.J. nodded. "I'll be there." He turned to leave, but then turned back. "I know there were parts of the story that my great-grandfather didn't tell me," he said. "I was ten. I'm sure he left out a lot of the violence. And the sex. I know that when Melody came to him, in Jubilation, to ask him to help her escape, she offered him sex. Of course, in his G-rated version of the story, he said he turned

125

her down, but . . . Since I'm not ten anymore, I no longer find that so easy to swallow.

"I'm not afraid of the truth, Dr. Carter," he continued. "I'm well aware that my gramps was human. He was far from perfect, as most men are. Kinda makes Quinn's 'documented' perfection a little suspect, don't you think?"

He didn't wait for her to answer. He just tipped his hat, which was charming.

"One o'clock in your office," he said. "You can return the shirt then."

The FBI had come to town, a man and a woman in dark suits and sunglasses trying to look inconspicuous as they checked out the pay phone in front of the Circle K, where I'd pressured A.J. to make that anonymous call.

I'd been dead for decades, but even I recognized how ridiculous it would be for a couple in those clothes, with that car, not to have a cell phone and thus have to use the public one. In fact, they looked the type—early thirties and plugged in— to have cutting-edge technology. Maybe a satellite receiver wired right into their fillings.

My point being that they weren't getting the job done when it came to inconspicuous. Not even close.

I was not the only one who slowed down to give them a second look. I recognized Henry Logan's redheaded assistant, Hugh, in his Jeep, giving them a once-over. And Lucy from continuity. And that AD fellow—the one whose sole job seemed to be to shout every now and then. "Settle!" And "Action!" And "Cut!"

I even saw Alison, catching a ride with the intern named Paula, her head thrown back in laughter. I raised my hand to wave before I remembered that she couldn't see me. Which was just as well.

After that I lost track—there were so many people coming and going, up and back, from that old mine that still bore my name. Gallagher's Claim.

As if I'd ever pulled enough silver out of that damn thing to make Mel more than the slenderest of rings.

But I'd tacked that sign up there to remind folks that I'd killed a man who'd tried to kill me after I'd won that worthless piece of crap land, fair and square. It was an announcement to all: I was a gambler by profession. I'd made that clear and anyone who played cards with me knew that going in, drunk or sober. I played to win, and would keep what I'd won, and I'd kill anyone who came after me.

I'd killed plenty of times, back in those days, but I'd never killed a man merely to send a message. Sometimes, though, I'd killed to keep myself from getting killed, *and* to send a message.

But nothing like what happened to headless

Wayne, whose death, according to his tall killer with the ponytail, had made some nameless and unknown-to-me person crap his pants.

I was tempted to dumpster-dive throughout Jubilation, see if I found any crap-filled, urine-doused trousers, and see if I couldn't figure out to whom they'd belonged.

I'd considered the possibility that Wayne had been killed back in L.A. or maybe Tucson. But there were closer stretches of desert near both of those cities. And having spent time in the unpleasant company of the recently deceased, it's hard to believe that anyone would've gone farther than he'd absolutely had to with Wayne's brains on the back windshield of that car.

I'd also spent a lot of time last night pondering whether or not this Loco person that the tall killer with the ponytail had been talking to was right here, beneath our noses, on this movie set. And who was the woman they were maybe going to target next?

It was making me fret, thinking someone's life was in danger. Still, I was careful not to spend too much time bouncing my ideas off of A.J. since his "caped crusader" crack had made me aware that even though bullets could and would go right through me, A.J. had no such superpowers.

Part of the reason I'd come back was to change the kid's life, not get his ass killed.

I was glad now that I'd been adamant about him

using the bottom edge of his shirt to wipe both the push buttons and the receiver of that pay phone after he'd made that call. He'd rolled his eyes, but he'd left no prints behind.

Thank God.

Because my making him make that call had created waves and conjured up the obtrusive twins.

Which was a rather interesting turn of events—the fact that the investigation into poor headless Wayne's murder wasn't being run by the local or even the state guys. No, someone, for some reason, had called in the feds on this one.

I drifted close, hoping to overhear some private detail as they muttered to themselves.

Turns out they were arguing because the female agent had, apparently, gotten a little too friendly with the male agent's brother.

"Don't worry, Rob," the woman said tartly. "I didn't go into this thinking John was any less relationship-challenged than you are. I was just looking for a little help relaxing, a little fun."

"With my brother?" Rob said incredulously. "He's an idiot."

Idiocy must've run in the family, because she was standing there, her body language screaming that she was crazy about him, not his stupid brother, but he didn't see it.

"You can do far better than him, Lombardi," Rob continued. "Trust me on that one. Next time you want some fun, I'll hook you up with my friend, Donny."

It was then that I felt it. A.J. reaching out to me with his mind. *Jamie, where are you?*

That was new.

Of course it was hard to say if it was something that he'd just figured out how to do, or if he'd never particularly wanted me around before this.

Either way, I realized I should at least pop in, see what he needed, and let him know that my time was probably best spent eavesdropping on Rob and Ms. Lombardi, because sooner or later they were going to start talking about headless Wayne and the murder investigation.

So I sent myself to A.J.—and found myself instead on the sidewalk in front of one of Tucson's police stations where, lo and behold, Wayne's tall and ponytailed killer was coming out of the door, dialing his cell phone.

He was dressed in far nicer clothes than the blood-covered outfit he'd been wearing yesterday. A dark suit, dark shirt, dark tie. He dressed the way I imagined the devil would— assuming Satan wasn't just a myth concocted to scare naughty children into good behavior.

He didn't look happy, and I found out why when I moved closer, as he put his phone to his ear.

"I've just been released," he told whoever was on the other end, his voice grim as he headed down the street. I had to double-time it to keep up.

"They picked me up. I don't know how the hell they knew, but they found Wayne's body—and they knew it was him. I swore up and down that I hadn't seen Wayne in months—not since he went to Pelican Bay. But if your witness puts me with him yesterday, I'm fucked. And if I'm fucked, you're fucked, do you understand me?"

He was silent then, listening, and I crept cautiously closer, not wanting to touch the man and get that same bizarre hot/cold shock that I'd gotten yesterday. But as I shuffled along next to him, all I could hear was the electronic buzz of that other voice, going into whatever phone he was talking on, bouncing up to some satellite tens of thousands of miles above the earth, and then back down to Tall-with-Ponytail's phone and into the man's ear.

"No, I don't think she has," he said, his voice doing the same in reverse and into Loco's ear—and it had to be Loco he was talking to, "or I wouldn't've been cut free."

Jamie, where are you . . . ?

I could feel A.J. out there, pulling me, but I didn't want to go. I was about to get some answers.

The killer listened some more, looking mighty peeved at whatever Loco was telling him. "No," he said. "Hell, no, asshole. You don't think that's going to raise eyebrows? That's not an accident— Jesus, you're incompetent. Just fucking sit tight.

131

Don't help again, you hear me?" Pause. "No, I'm not. It's not going to be me. I'm not going anywhere near Jubilation if I can help it."

"Hah!" I shouted aloud, and then quickly shut up, because he was still talking.

"I'm going to send someone. . . ." He made a disgusted sound. "I don't know who it's going to be, but even if I did, you don't need to know anything more than the fact that he'll do what he needs to do, you understand? You just keep your boy in line." He shut his phone. "Fucking assholes, both of them."

He dialed his phone again and waited. "Gene," he said. "It's me. I got a job for you. Meet me in two hours. Don't be late."

And with that he hung up.

JAMIE, WHERE ARE YOU . . . !?

Crap-hell. A.J. needed me, but I was afraid that once I jumped away from this man, I wouldn't be able to find my way back.

And now I was thinking to hell with Rob and his FBI partner. I now wanted, desperately, to sit in on that meeting with Gene, whoever he was. Because I suspected that if I could be a fly on the wall—and I surely could be the equivalent of that—I would find out the name of this woman, this witness to Wayne's murder, whose life was still in danger.

Although, chances are she already knew that. And if she'd seen Wayne's murder, but hadn't yet called the police, wasn't she then responsible for her own impending demise?

GRAMPS!

I closed my eyes and went—not completely positive I'd find A.J. since that was two times now that I'd tried to join him and had ended up with Tall Ponytail Man instead.

But three was apparently a charm, because I popped in directly in front of my great-grandson. He had to stop short to keep from walking right through me as he paced back and forth in front of the row of little houses on River Street—which had been named optimistically, back in the early 1890s, after a heavy rain when an arroyo flooded. As far as I knew, that "river" hadn't run since.

"Where," A.J. said, "the fuck have you been?"

He normally doesn't use that kind of language—or at least he's tended not to in the recent past. But the kid spent a serious chunk of his formative years in the army, and he could let go a blue streak with the best of 'em.

"I was doing that caped crusader thing," I admitted. "My killer's been let out of jail. Apparently they don't have enough evidence to hold him." I could see that the kid was both frustrated and upset, and really wasn't listening to what I was saying. "What's going on?"

"Alison's missing," he told me. "She was supposed to meet me at her office at one o'clock."

I could see from the watch he wore around his wrist that it was barely 2:15.

"Son, she's not missing," I tried to say as gently as I could, "she's just standing you up. It happens—"

"No." A.J. was adamant. "Hugh can't find her either. He was sure she left the mine hours ago, but no one's seen her since. She didn't have a hat, and with the sun as hot as it is—"

"Whoa," I said, holding up a hand.

But his brain and mouth were on a fear-induced stampede and he didn't stop. "—if she somehow left the trail or fell or fainted from the heat—"

"*I've* seen her since," I said, interrupting him and then repeating myself because he still wasn't listening. "I saw her, A.J. She was driving back from the mine with that little intern. Paula. Maybe you should check with her." I looked around. Why were we here? "Or you might want to hang out over at her trailer, just in case she was late. She does have an important job. Maybe something came up."

"This is where she lives," he told me, pointing to the little house that, back in the early 1890s, a young miner named Frank Fortiblanc had adorned with gingerbread trim. He'd slaved over that thing, cutting the wood by hand, painting it in bright, pretty colors that made him a bit of a local joke—until he stole the heart of beautiful Esther McCormick, who'd come to town in a gospel wagon with her parents, to preach against drinking and whoring and killing and sinning. She'd married him without her father's permission and brought music and laughter to Frank's life, until she died two years later in childbirth.

I met Frank and his son a few times, back in '98. Unlike some men, who might've let their grief destroy them, he'd stepped up to the challenge, and raised that child that Essie had died delivering into this world. And he did it as carefully and patiently and lovingly as he'd transformed his house into a thing of beauty.

I'd thought of him often and prayed for his strength, that awful winter of 1944.

But I digress.

"Hugh went to find the landlord," A.J. was telling me. "To get the spare key. Sheriff's office won't start a search until we've checked to make sure she's not in there, asleep."

"Well, there you go," I said. "She was up awfully early. Maybe she figured she'd put her head down for a few minutes before your meeting. If she was on set, she probably turned her phone off and forgot to turn it back on. Have you tried hammering on the door?"

"Hugh said he knocked," A.J. reported.

"Hugh probably weighs in at one-thirty, soaking wet," I pointed. "But never mind. I'm here now, and I don't need a key."

And with that, I stepped through the wall and

into Frank Fortiblanc's old house. The front parlor had been transformed into a kitchen and, unlike most of the buildings in Jubilation, it had been given an additional update, post-1950. Someone had actually installed built-in cabinets and Formica counters. The Frigidaire and stove were both a faded yet awful shade of green.

Alison had brought one of those microwave things with her and, because she was tall, had stuck it up on top of the refrigerator. It beeped at me, and I saw that some kind of burrito was still inside—as if she'd made herself lunch but forgotten to eat it.

And I just knew I was going to find her sprawled out on her sofa. But her living room—a cheap-wood-paneled cave of a room with a bookcase that, among all the knickknacks, had only one book on it, the Bible—was empty. Okay then, that meant she was going to be fast asleep in her bed, but when I peeked into the bedroom, she wasn't in there, either. The second bedroom—a little lean-to that Frank had added on when his boy got old enough to want some privacy—held only a chair and a desk, upon which Alison's portable computer was out and open. The thing was quiet—no flashing icons or dizzying fields of stars zooming across the screen.

But a glass of what looked like iced tea—sans the ice—was on a soaking wet coaster near that computer.

I was still a novice at the caped crusader super-sleuth thing, but it didn't take a degree from the Sherlock Holmes Detective School to see exactly what had happened here. Alison had come home, put her lunch in the zapper, poured herself a beverage, turned on her computer and . . .

Vanished off the face of the planet.

I was starting to get paranoid myself and wonder if maybe Alison was the woman that Loco and my killer were looking to disappear on a permanent basis, when I realized there was still one room that I hadn't checked.

The bathroom.

The door was shut, and I didn't do more than poke my head through it when I saw her. Naked, through the glass of the shower stall, curled up on the tile floor.

A.J. was right. She must've slipped and fallen, and I rocketed out of the house to tell him so.

I didn't get more than a few words out before he ripped off his T-shirt, wrapped it around his hand, and punched his way with a shattering crash through the lowest of the big glass panels in the front door.

Alison awoke to the sound of breaking glass.

She sat up, disoriented, her heart in her throat, but it wasn't the shower stall glass that had broken. It was still intact—acting as both her protective shield and her prison.

The biggest snake she'd ever seen in her life was no longer out in the middle of the bathroom floor. She panicked for one brief moment, scooting back against the wall, shifting to make sure it hadn't somehow gotten past the glass. But she was safe. She was alone in there.

Until the bathroom door opened with such force that it crashed against the wall.

Alison screamed in surprise, and then screamed again because she was naked, and that was definitely A.J. Gallagher, shirtless, as he stormed his way into her bathroom.

He grabbed the towel from the rack and, as he opened the shower door, he used it to cover her, which was nice. But he kneeled down beside her as he asked her, "Are you all right? Did you hit your head when you fell?" which wasn't so nice.

And this time she didn't so much scream as shout, "Snake!" as she grabbed him by his arm and his shoulder and tried to pull him into the tiny space with her, as she heard the snake's rattle before she saw it. And there it was—between the toilet and the sink, already in a coil, ready to strike.

But A.J. was kneeling half inside the shower, half out, and there was no way he could get both of his long legs inside the stall and shut the door behind him in the fraction of a second before the snake attacked.

"Kick it!" Alison shouted as she saw he was

wearing his thick leather cowboy boots. "Kick the shit out of it!"

And he shifted to do just that, except it was going to be a disaster, because that snake was huge. It could leap three feet, easily, and if it hit A.J. up past the tops of his boots, those sharp teeth—the ones that Alison had spent well over an hour staring at as the ugly thing hissed at her through the shower door—would slice right through his jeans.

But the snake didn't strike. Instead it flinched and almost seemed to spasm as it uncoiled, as if it had been hit with an electric current and was temporarily stunned. A.J.'s kick pushed it over to the bathroom door where it quickly regained its senses and sprang back into a coil.

"Do *what?*" A.J. shouted, but she hadn't done more than squeak in alarm. "How?" he asked— was he talking to her?—as the snake once again went from coiled and dangerous to flopping about. *"Really?"*

"I didn't say anything," Alison said, as A.J. scrambled to his feet and pushed the shower door shut with himself on the snake side of it. "Why is it doing that? What did you do to it?"

A.J. didn't answer, not at first, his full attention on the snake, which meanwhile had scrambled itself back into its attack position. Whatever A.J. had done to it with that kick, the serpent was good and mad now.

But then A.J. said, "I am," and "Do it! *Do* it, *now!*"

"Do what?" Alison asked, adding, "Oh, my *God!*" as the snake again spasmed, only this time, when it did, A.J. charged toward it. He pinned it beneath his left boot as he raised his right foot.

"Don't look," he shouted as he brought his boot down hard. "Agh!" His shout obscured the sound of the snake's demise.

Alison didn't not look—she was too concerned for A.J.'s safety and well-being. But there wasn't much to see besides the snake's tail, still twitching, its rattle still making that ominous sound.

"Jesus," he breathed, or at least it sounded as if that was what he'd said. "Are you real?"

"A.J." she asked. "Is it . . . ?"

"Dead. It is." He turned just slightly, not enough to see her, in case she didn't have that towel secured around her yet—which she didn't. He was breathing hard, and he exhaled forcefully a few times as if he was trying to regain his equilibrium. "Are you okay?"

"I am," she said, tucking the end of the towel beneath her arm and pushing open the shower door. "Are you?"

"Yeah," he said.

But then she realized that there were streaks of blood on the towel he'd handed her. "Are you bleeding?" she asked.

"No, I'm pretty sure that's the snake," he started, but then said, "What? Oh, wow. Yeah, I guess . . . I guess I am. It's not bad. Don't come too close," he warned her. "I don't know much about snakes and whether or not . . ."

He paused, then said, "Actually I *do* know about rattlesnakes. I just, um, remembered. My great-grandfather is, um, *was* familiar with, um . . ." He cleared his throat. "The venom *is* still potent—great. We need to be careful how we clean this up. Plus, you probably shouldn't go into your kitchen with bare feet. See, you were missing, and we didn't know where you were, so Hugh went to try to find a spare key, but then he didn't come back, so . . . I kind of broke the window in the door, which is how this happened."

He held up his left hand, which had a nasty-looking gash on the edge of his palm, beneath his pinkie finger. "I broke the glass with my right hand—wrapped in my shirt, which is why I'm, um . . ." He gestured self-consciously to his bare chest. "Anyway, after that, I reached in to unlock the bolt with my left hand and . . . I wasn't careful enough. If you could just get me a rag or something so I don't bleed all over your house . . . I don't want to tromp around in these boots, until I get 'em cleaned up and . . ."

Alison reached into the bathroom closet, and yeah, okay, she didn't just reach right in, the way she would've done just a few hours ago. First she checked for snakes. But seeing and hearing none, she grabbed a towel and gave it a quick shake before holding it out to A.J.

"Oh," he said, "no, I don't want to ruin another of your towels."

"Please," she said. "Take it." She didn't wait for him to argue, she just wrapped it around his bleeding hand.

"Careful of the boots," he said, and she took a step back. "Why don't you get, you know, some, uh, clothes on, while I go and hose off my boots outside?"

Ah, yes. That was right. A.J. had seen her naked. Way to establish a good professional working relationship with the man.

"Don't be embarrassed," he said softly, as if he were somehow able to read her mind. "I didn't see much."

He was a lousy liar—although his approach certainly was one way to play it. Pretend it hadn't happened.

"Watch where you step," he added, "and don't forget that there's glass on the floor in the kitchen."

"Sir, yes, sir," Alison said, as she turned to head into her bedroom to find the clothes that she'd rather desperately wanted to put on for the past two hours, while she'd been trapped in the snake's human zoo. But then she turned back, because it needed saying. "Thank you."

A.J. nodded. "I'm just glad you're all right."

"Me, too," she said. "I mean, that *you're* all right." She stopped herself. "Okay, you know what? This is just too awkward and weird. A) I know you saw me naked and it's just not that big of a deal. I mean, I'm relatively fit, right? A little under endowed on top maybe, and certainly no Winter Baxter or Eleanor Marcus, but—" She cut herself off as she held up her hand to keep him from speaking, too. "Don't say anything, because now it's going to be even more awkward, like I'm fishing for a compliment, so you have to say something nice or positive, which, even if you mean it sincerely, I'm going to assume is a load of crap. So just, rewind everything I just said and let's go back to the you-pretending-you-didn't-see-anything strategy. That way we can focus on B), which is I have never seen *anything* as bizarre as that in my entire life, and I still don't have a clue what just happened here."

A.J. stood there, just watching her, and she realized he was waiting for her to clear him to speak.

"Please," she said. "Explain. What just happened here?"

He glanced down at the remains of the snake before looking back at her. "I'm not really sure myself," he said. "It happened so fast. What, um, did *you* see?"

"The world's biggest rattlesnake," she said,

"about to strike, but then having some kind of weird seizure? Can snakes even *get* seizures?"

"You saw that, too," he said. "Huh. I mean, yeah, that *was* pretty weird. I wonder if they can. Get seizures, or I don't know, maybe . . . it had . . . rabies?"

Rabies? Was he kidding? "Snakes don't get rabies," Alison said. "It's a mammal thing."

"Then, I don't know," he said. "Maybe when I, um, kicked it, I crushed some kind of nerve. I kicked it pretty hard."

"Except didn't it do its first weird twitchy thing *before* you kicked it?"

"Did it?" he asked. "It's all kind of a blur."

It *did* happen fast. Still, Alison shook her head. "It did its weird thing first. I was sure it was going to bite you, but then it didn't, and *that* was when you kicked it." She felt her eyes fill with tears. Oh, good. *Now* she was going to fall apart. She turned away because there was no need for him to see her emotionally naked, too. "Excuse me," she said. "I'll just . . ." And she escaped into her bedroom.

Chapter Seven

A.J. hosed off his boots and the bottom of his jeans, wiped up the snake, swept up the glass, walked around the outside of the house to try to figure out how the snake had gotten in in the first place, and found a piece of plywood to temporarily cover the window he'd broken in the door—all before Alison came back out of her room.

"Sorry," she said. "Henry called." She was wearing her usual Bermuda shorts, this time with a golden brown T-shirt that matched her eyes and hugged her extremely fit body.

That was the word she'd used to describe herself—*fit*. A.J. would've used other words. Like *holy shit* and *sweet baby Jesus*.

A) If it were up to me, Alison, you'd never wear clothes again. Nor, for that matter, would I. . . .

Things not to say.

Particularly when she wanted explanations he couldn't provide. *Well, see, what happened in your bathroom was that the ghost of my great-grandfather, you know, Jamie Gallagher? The man that you call "Kid" even though that never was his nickname . . . ? See, he threw himself between me and that snake.*

He wasn't sure if it would do any good, because he has no power over earthly beings or even inanimate objects. He passes right through them. But he'd noticed yesterday, when he bumped into some guy who'd just killed some other guy named Wayne—which is a whole nother story . . . But he found out that occupying the same space as another being creates this strange sensation and odd energy.

*Turns out it worked to freak out the rattler,
which was a damn good thing, or I could well be
dying, right now, on your bathroom floor.*

*So. To summarize. Jamie threw himself at that
snake, got the reaction he got, so he did it again.
And then, he told me how to kill the damn thing—
to crush its head. Which I did, right after he
stunned it one more time.*

*Although my mother would say that I must've
read some book somewhere that told me how to
kill a snake, and that Jamie didn't really help—I
just imagined it.*

*And I know that snakes don't get rabies. I said
that because I didn't know what to say, not just
because I'm an idiot, but because I was a little
overwhelmed by everything that had just
happened—including seeing you naked.*

Yeah, A.J. wasn't about to say all that. At least
not any time soon. If he did, he was sure as hell
never seeing her naked again. And his doing so
had moved up, quite a bit, on his list of priorities.

"Oh," Alison said as she looked around. "That
was fast."

She was carrying the shirt she'd borrowed from
him earlier, a dustpan, and a brush.

"You should've left her something to clean,"
Jamie said from his perch on the kitchen counter.
"When women are shaken up, they need
something to do. And she *was* badly shaken by
that, although you won't get her to admit it.

Because I think the thing that shook her up the most was you nearly getting yourself snakebit. I'm pretty sure she's fond of you, kid."

A.J. shot him a silent look because he'd already said enough to the ghost in front of Alison. He wasn't going to give her any other reason to suspect he was crazy. Which he quite possibly wasn't.

Because she'd seen that snake flail and twitch, too.

He'd like to hear his mother explain *that.*

Of course, maybe he'd moved that snake with the force of his mind—simply by wanting it badly enough.

Although, if he truly had that kind of power, then—just from the sheer force of his wanting—Alison was going to put down that dustpan and walk over to him and wrap her arms around him.

Which she didn't do. She did, however, set down the dustpan and hand him his shirt. Which A.J. gratefully pulled on. He'd shaken out his T-shirt a few times, but it still glittered with tiny specks of glass. He was going to need to visit the town Laundromat and wash it. Hopefully there was a town Laundromat.

This other shirt—long-sleeved and pale blue cotton—smelled like Alison, which was nice. He managed to resist the temptation to bring the sleeve up to his nose and breathe in her sweet scent. That could have read as creepy, and his being snake-killer-guy, who broke into her house and burst into her bathroom uninvited, was creepy enough.

"What's your squeamishness rating?" he asked her instead, as he buttoned it and rolled up the sleeves, careful not to bleed on it with his injured hand.

"I'm good with relatively minor injuries," Alison said, knowing right away to what he was referring. She motioned to his hand. "You need me to look at that?"

"I think there still might be a piece of glass in there," he confessed. "But I'm left-handed, so it's hard for me to—"

"Sit." Alison motioned to the chair at the near end of her kitchen table. She turned on the overhead light and sat down next to him. "Let me see."

A.J. held out his hand, and as she took it, she inhaled through her teeth.

"It's not that bad," he said. And in a sick and twisted way, whatever pain he was feeling was worth it, because she was holding his hand in both of hers, her long fingers cool against his skin.

"I can see the glass," she said. "But I should get tweezers." She looked up, directly into his eyes. "I'm so sorry. I didn't realize, when I wrapped that towel around you . . . That must've hurt."

"Yeah, that was kind of how I knew something

was still in there," he told her. "It's okay. You didn't know."

"You didn't scream," she pointed out, still holding his hand, holding his gaze. "How could I know that it hurt, if you're too busy being stoic and manly to scream?"

"I try to save the bulk of my screaming for when I'm killing giant snakes," he told her. "Although a giant squid could probably get a rise out of me."

Alison laughed. "Not a lot of giant squid in Arizona."

A.J. nodded. "That would make it even scarier, don't you think? Giant squid attacks from behind the desert scrub . . . ?"

And time seemed to hang as they just sat there, smiling at each other. Until, that is, A.J. cleared his throat, and sat back.

"Oh, come on," Jamie said, exasperation thick in his voice.

Alison let go of his hand, rising out of her chair. "I'll get those tweezers."

Jamie slid down off the counter. "For the love of God, son," he said. "Are you waiting for an engraved invitation?"

"Don't you need to be off fighting crime and righting wrongs?" A.J. asked, keeping his voice low. "Somewhere that isn't here?"

"Dr. Alison Carter requests the presence of Austin James Gallagher, the Second, in her kitchen, after a soul-shaking, near-death experience, for a liplock in which she will kiss the jumping bejeezus out of him. No need to RSVP."

"She doesn't want to do that," A.J. murmured.

"Yes," Jamie said. "She most certainly does. She was trapped in her bathroom for hours with that snake, and you don't even pat her hand, let alone give her a comforting hug? And okay. All right. I get the fact that you were being careful, when you thought you might be certifiable, but now that, thanks to that snake, may he rest in peace, I've managed to convince you that I'm truly here, that's it's really me, Jamie, your old gramps. . . . Right? So I just don't get what's holding you back. In fact, now I'm starting to think you're just chickenshit."

"I am not," A.J. said. Not chickenshit nor entirely convinced that Jamie was real. He had been, yes, in the moment. But now the doubt was back. His mother would've insisted that there was some scientific explanation for the snake's behavior. But he didn't say any of that aloud because that was, of course, right when Alison came back into the kitchen.

"You're not what?" she asked.

"Sure," he said, clearing his throat to give himself time to think. "I'm, um, still not sure how the snake got in."

"Well," she said, sitting down and taking his hand again. "I'm calling the local pest control company. Let them figure it out and spray eagle urine or whatever they need to spray to keep it from happening again."

"Eagle urine?" A.J. repeated just as Jamie did, too.

"Yeah, don't eagles eat snakes?" Alison asked. "Wildlife tends to stay away from the wildlife that eats them, right? And while I prefer organic, natural solutions like eagle urine, after staring into that snake's evil eyes for all those hours, I just might be okay with the boys from Snakes Begone Incorporated spraying toxic waste around the outside of the house, if that's what it takes." She looked up from his hand. "And yes, probably not, but still." She held up the tweezers. "I sterilized this with a match while I was in the bathroom." She paused and one elegant eyebrow went up as she added, "While you were out here. Talking to yourself."

Oh, good.

"I, um, do that a lot," A.J. told her, purposely not looking anywhere near Jamie.

"It's a little weird," she said, "but not too weird. A guy who looks like you? It's quirky and even charming. But dye your hair chartreuse, gain four hundred pounds, tattoo your entire face, and stop bathing . . . ? Different story, pal."

A.J. had to laugh. "I'll take that under advisement. I just . . . I'm alone a lot up in Alaska—"

Jamie moved directly into A.J.'s line of sight.

151

"Why don't you just tell her the truth," he said, right when Alison said, "This might hurt."

"Come on, kid," Jamie implored him as, yes, her probing *did* hurt.

A.J. gritted his teeth but managed to force a smile as Alison looked up at him.

"You okay?" she asked.

He nodded.

"You know I'm real," Jamie continued, "so just tell her about me, get it out of the way. Yeah, she'll be freaked out at first, but I've figured out how we can prove it to her—"

"Got it!" Alison said triumphantly. She stood up, cupping her hand under the nearly invisible splinter of glass, washing it down the drain of the kitchen sink.

When her back was to him, A.J. took the opportunity to shake his head at Jamie. No. He wasn't going to do that. Not yet. Not here. Not now.

Not until he gave it a whole hell of a lot more thought.

Because what if she was like his mother?

And what if his mother was right?

Alison rinsed the tweezers and washed her hands, raising her voice to be heard over the running water. "I don't have the kind of bandages you're going to need, but there's an extensive first-aid station in the main production trailer." She shut off the water and turned to face him, drying her hands on a towel. "I think they have some of those flexible fabric ones—you know, so that you can bend your hand? But I'm going to need you to be really careful, if you do any extra work, to take it off during the shot. When are you working next?"

"Tomorrow morning," he said.

She nodded. "I'll be there," she said. "I'll remember to watch for it." She glanced over at the clock on the microwave and took a deep breath. "I hate to snake and run, but I have a production meeting."

"Oh," A.J. said. He'd thought she had the afternoon free.

She followed his train of thought. "We'll have to reschedule," she said. "Our meeting. I've really only got my lunch and dinner times free. I've kind of used up lunch, and dinner's already filled."

"I didn't realize that," A.J. said, standing up and pushing the chair he'd been sitting in back under the table. "That you were using your downtime to . . ."

She waved it off. "It's fine," she said as she crossed back to the table and started rummaging in a bag that was on one of the other chairs. She pulled out a clipboard, with what looked like a calendar attached. "It's . . . interesting. Your story is . . . Well, there's this new letter that just surfaced, from a local woman who met Melody right after she arrived in Jubilation. I didn't know

153

about it when I wrote my book, but . . . It raises some questions. And of course, if those diaries are real . . ."

"I still haven't reached my sister," A.J. told her.

"Ask her who wrote the letter," Jamie said.

"Keep trying," Alison said, flipping through the pages and checking her schedule. Unlike most of the crew, she apparently didn't keep track of her life on an electronic device. "How's tomorrow evening?" She looked up. "I've got a break from seven to eight-thirty."

"Does that give you enough time to eat?" A.J. asked.

"Ask her." Jamie was focused on the letter. "Better yet, ask her if you can see it."

"We can meet at the caterer's tent," Alison spoke over Jamie, of course, because she couldn't hear him. "Grab a tray and bring it over to my office. Eat while we talk. I'll try to remember to clear us some desk space."

"Almost like a dinner date," Jamie pointed out.

"That sounds great," A.J. said, resisting the temptation to hush the ghost.

"Letter," Jamie persisted as Alison found a pen and wrote A.J.'s name next to 7:00 on her calendar. "Ask her if it mentions Mel's black eye. She still had a trace of the bruise when I met her, nearly a month later, so it must've been a doozy when Quinn first hit her."

A.J. sighed. "This letter," he asked Alison. "Did

154

it mention that Melody was injured, maybe? A black eye, or . . . ?"

Alison tipped her head to look at him. "As a matter of fact, yes, it does. She fell off her horse."

Jamie snorted. "Mel? Never. She could outride me—sidesaddle. You know how hard it is to ride sidesaddle? In a skirt? You should try it sometime—"

A.J. spoke over him. "She was an experienced rider."

"Not according to Quinn."

"I know I'm starting to sound like a broken record, but the whole story's according to Quinn."

"*Melody* said she fell off her horse."

"Fell off her horse," A.J. said. "Tripped and fell down. *Clumsy me, I ran into a door. . . .*"

Alison nodded somberly. "Yeah," she said. "I hear you. Although, really, A.J., sometimes an accident's just an accident."

"Who wrote the letter?" Jamie asked again, and A.J. repeated his question.

"A Mrs. Penelope Eversfield," Alison reported.

"The general store owner's wife," Jamie said, along with her, adding, "Second wife. Ol' Dick Eversfield. He was a mean SOB and Quinn was in his pocket. Dick paid extra so that if there was trouble in town, Quinn and his men would protect the store first. After Quinn's private interests, of course."

"Apparently she wrote hundreds of letters to a

155

sister in Denver," Alison told A.J. He was getting good at listening to both of them talking at once. "I haven't had a chance to read any of the others, but the woman who owns them is sending them. Which is really exciting." Her eyes sparkled, but then she mocked herself. "And yes, I know I'm a total history nerd. Letters—whee!"

A.J. laughed. "I think it's great," he said. "Being able to see Jubilation through someone else's eyes . . ."

"You are starting to sound like a broken record," Alison told him. She glanced at the clock again.

"You need to get ready to go," A.J. said, heading for the door. "I'll see you tomorrow night."

But she stopped him with a hand on his arm. "Thank you," she said again. "Can I just . . . ?" She moved toward him, into what might've turned into an awkwardly loose embrace.

But A.J. saw it coming and he stepped into it, wrapping his arms around her and pulling her close, remembering Jamie's words about his failure to deliver a comforting hug. But she'd been in bare feet and he'd been standing in a puddle of dead snake.

But he wasn't anymore, and he tried his best to be brotherly or paternal, to make this be about comfort instead of his wanting like hell to grab her ass.

She slipped her own arms around his waist and pressed her face into his shoulder, and there he stood, trying not to think too much about how smooth and soft her skin had looked when he'd burst through that bathroom door. He tried not to think about what he wanted, but instead to enjoy and appreciate this simple moment for what it was.

A little shared comfort after a bad scare.

"Kiss her," Jamie murmured. "Come on, kid."

A.J. shook his head and closed his eyes, trying to block Jamie out.

But then Alison laughed, her head still down, her voice muffled as she said, "Okay. So this was a mistake. I know I'm completely unable to think about anything besides the fact that you saw me naked, and I'm not sure what's worse—" she lifted her head to smile up at him with amusement, except her eyes revealed that she was also feeling a little vulnerable "—the idea that you're thinking about it, too, or that you're maybe not thinking about it at all and—"

A.J. didn't need any additional prompting. He kissed her, and he felt more than heard or saw Jamie vanish.

He felt Alison's surprise, too, and for several oh-crap-filled fractions of a second, he worried that he'd read her wrong, that he'd listened to Jamie's nonsense when he shouldn't have.

But then her surprise turned to something else— something not just warm and welcoming, but also urgent.

And then she was kissing him back with that mouth that was both softly pliant and sweetly demanding. Her arms were tight around his waist, her hands against his back as she pressed herself against him, as he pulled her even closer—God, the woman was fire in his arms.

A.J. couldn't help but think that had he done this while she'd had nothing more than that towel on, it would've fallen to the floor at their feet by now, and her skin would be warm beneath his fingers.

Still, this was good, it was better than good, it was great, because now wasn't the time to do more than kiss her. She had to go to her meeting, and he had to tell her . . . Something.

I might be crazy.

I see dead people, but that was not quite true. He actually saw dead *person.* Singular.

But then she slipped her hand up beneath the edge of his shirt, her fingers cool and soft against his bare back, and he knew he had no strength, no willpower, no resistance.

No integrity, and absolutely no honor, either, because if she started to tug him toward her bedroom, he would follow. Hell, if she started unfastening his pants, he'd have sex with her, right here, in her kitchen, pushing himself hard inside of her with most of their clothes still on, while she half-sat, half-leaned up on the counter. No explanations, no warnings, no *Before we do this, there's something you should probably know about me . . .*

And that should have made him feel bad, but he was too busy feeling unbelievably good as she kissed him even harder, deeper, longer, as her hand swept up his back, as he felt the softness of her breasts against his chest, as his own hand slid down, down, until, God, he was cupping her incredible ass and pressing her hips more tightly against him, and still, all she wanted, too, was more.

"Hey, Al, are you—whoops—sorry!" It was Hugh. He'd finally found the key and he'd used it to open the door. "I guess A.J. found you."

Alison had pushed away from A.J., who immediately let her go.

"Hey," she said weakly. "Hugh! We were just . . ."

She looked at A.J. and he saw on her face everything that he was feeling. Confusion, desire, embarrassment—and wonder. A whole hell of a lot of wonder. *Like, Did that actually just happen and could it really have been that incredible . . . ?*

"Getting ready to go," A.J. finished for her. "Dr. Carter has a meeting and I, uh, have to, um, let her go to that meeting. As much as I'd rather . . . not."

He took his hat from where he'd set it on the kitchen table, and nodded to Alison as he stepped around Hugh and opened the door. "Have a nice evening. I'll see you tomorrow."

"Okay," A.J. heard Hugh say as he went down

159

the steps and out into the dusty street. "*Now* I know why he was in such a screaming hurry to find you. Damn, girlfriend . . ."

A.J. didn't hear what Alison said in reply, but then he heard Hugh, loud and clear. "*A rattlesnake* was inside your *house?*"

I had had a bitch of a day.

Even though spirits didn't feel exhaustion, I was frustrated by the fruitlessness of my afternoon-long search for the tall, ponytailed killer-of-Wayne. When I'd found neither him nor his mysterious murder-mate, Gene, in the various lowlife bars and pool halls of Tucson, I changed tack and returned to Jubilation. Where I searched for FBI Rob and his partner, Agent Lombardi.

They should have been easier to find—I knew what their car looked like. But I found neither it nor them.

I did find Alison, sitting in on a meeting in the production trailer. She was arguing with the baseball-cap-clad director about the logistics of the shoot-out in the saloon.

"Silas Quinn doesn't mention reloading," she was saying stubbornly. "Come on, Henry, I know *Red Rock* and all the other movies made it seem as if the gunfight went on for hours, but it didn't. These things happened fast. The Kellys all had six-guns—revolvers with six bullets—as did Quinn. Think about it. He had to have been a remarkable shot to kill as many of them as he did."

"He was atrociously bad," I said, but of course, she didn't hear me.

"If he weren't an amazing marksman, if he hadn't immediately taken most of the Kellys out, he would have been hit by a virtual wall of bullets," she continued. "Seven gang members, seven guns. Some had one on each hip."

"What if Quinn had a shotgun?" one of the production assistants suggested. "He could have just walked up and boom, one barrel takes out half of 'em, boom, the next finishes the rest of 'em off. . . ."

Henry laughed. "I kind of like that image."

"But he doesn't say he had a shotgun," Alison argued. "It wouldn't be historically accurate."

"The way the story's currently told, it's completely fiction," I said, "so it doesn't much matter."

"He doesn't say he used his revolver during the shootout, either," Henry pointed out. "Maybe he left that detail out on purpose."

"But he always had his revolver," Alison said. "Always. That's why he didn't mention it. If he were suddenly carrying a shotgun? That would be different. He would have mentioned it."

If a blue orangutan had been sitting at the bar at the Red Rock that evening, Quinn wouldn't have mentioned it, because none of his account was

161

even remotely true. But I wasn't able to appear to these people and set them straight. A.J. was going to have to do that.

"Maybe," Henry said. "Maybe not. It certainly provides a new twist on the legend—the shotgun idea. And it answers the question about how he could have killed so many of them so quickly, while being barely wounded himself."

Alison was shaking her head. "The way I see it," she said, "and a far more fascinating aspect to the legend, is that it's all about the randomness. Where was Kid Gallagher standing, that he wasn't one of the gang members immediately killed by Quinn? Did he get up, I don't know, to go to the bathroom or to get another drink? Why, with so many of the Kellys dead, did *he* survive? What did he do differently? Quinn doesn't go into detail of who was sitting or standing where."

"What we should do," the redheaded kid sat forward to say, "is find some sharpshooters and stage a reenactment, like with paintballs."

"No way are we using paintballs in the actual Red Rock Saloon," Alison said. "But . . . We could maybe use some kind of, I don't know, laser system . . . ?"

"Do it," Henry ordered. "Set it up."

"Me?" Alison asked.

"A.J. will help you," I told her, and then I realized that since she was here, in this meeting, then she wasn't still with Age, which was kind of a shame.

I'd been hesitating to jump to him, for fear—well, no, more like for *hope* that I'd pop in on something private. And by that I don't mean that I *hoped* I'd pop in when they were . . . You know what I mean. My hope was that they were getting to know each other, not that I'd witness it.

So I jumped to A.J. now, thinking maybe I'd be rerouted to Tucson, but instead, I ended up waking him from a nap as he sat in his truck with his AC blasting.

The sun hadn't yet set, and until the night cooled the desert down, crawling into that little tent he'd pitched on the outskirts of town would be like crawling into an Easy-Bake Oven.

Having made camp myself, plenty of times, in the Arizona desert, I knew that he was wishing rather desperately that the motel hadn't been sold out. Or that he'd accepted the production staff's offer to rent him a trailer, before they'd run out. But it was what it was, and he wasn't going to complain. At least not near as loudly as I would've.

And I have to confess, I was a little snotty to him after I asked, "Sorry, are you sleeping?" and he said, "Not anymore."

"Well, if I'm not real," I said, "then I couldn't've just woken you up, could I have?"

"That's right," he agreed with his eyes closed

again. "And that's nothing new. I wake myself up all the time."

"You didn't used to," I said. "Back when you were a boy, you slept like a baby."

He sighed. And turned to look at me. "What can I do for you?" he asked.

"Alison needs a sharpshooter or seven," I told him.

"What for?" he asked and I explained what I'd overheard.

"You still handy with a gun?" I asked.

"It's been awhile," he said. "A long time."

Back when he was a tyke, I'd taught him how to shoot and how to properly handle a deadly weapon. He was good at hitting stationary targets—a natural, you know?

Of course, I'd shown him my fast draw, too, although at ninety-plus, I'd slowed way down. He'd gotten the hang of that, too, rather quickly, which is why I'd teasingly called him "Kid."

"It's important that we help Alison find someone who can do this," I told A.J. "When she sees how ridiculously implausible Quinn's version of the shoot-out is, well, that's going to make her wonder what else he lied about."

"What if she doesn't want our help?" he asked.

I laughed. "Kid, I saw her kissing you. Trust me, she wants your help." I glanced at him. "Any innuendo in that statement is purely unintentional."

"Have you ever done anything unintentional?" he asked me wryly.

"Sure," I said. "Plenty of times. I just can't think of any right now. So come on. Wake it on up. Let's get your full amount of synapses firing. When are you seeing her again?"

"Alison?" A.J. asked.

"No," I said. "The *other* girl you were soul-kissing in her kitchen. Yes, Alison."

He sighed. "Look, I'm not sure yet what that was, but . . ."

"It was the engraved invitation you were looking for," I said, "but all right. You don't know what it is when a woman all but throws herself into your arms. Maybe it was an accident. Maybe she slipped. You can ask her. You *are* going to see her again, aren't you? Some time tonight?"

A.J. shook his head no. "She had plans."

"Well, son," I said. "This is your lucky day. I took a look at her schedule. She's meeting what's her name, Summer or Autumn—the actress playing Mel—at that roadhouse, that honky-tonk. What's it called? I guess it doesn't need a name, it's the only watering hole in town that's not an exorbitantly priced museum. You know the place. It's on the corner of Main Street and Mexicali. She'll be there at eight."

A.J. opened his mouth to speak, but I cut him off.

"Now, I know you don't want to go in there," I

told him. "I get that. I respect that. I agree with that decision. But you *can* run into her on the sidewalk out front, am I right or am I right?"

He didn't look as thrilled as I was at my plan. "It's been a long time since I've handled a firearm," he said, harking back to that. "I'm not sure I'm going to be able to help her."

"But you know someone who can," I pointed out. "Your friend. What's his name. The one your mother keeps trying to get you to call. Greg."

"Craig Lutz?" A.J. was surprised. He laughed. "You agree with my mother, and think I should call Lutz. *That's* a twist I didn't expect."

Before we'd left Alaska, the kid's mother, Rose, had tried to convince him to call this friend of his, Craig Lutz. Craig had served with A.J. over in Iraq, and had been through some of the same things A.J. had. The idea being that a man might not want to talk about the horrors of war with his family, and he might not even want to talk about it with those very friends he'd served with, but that he *would* get some relief by spending time with them—knowing that they'd been there, that they *knew*.

This Craig was apparently some kind of fancy commando-type—special forces or special operations—I never could get them straight. And I never did quite understand how A.J., who was regular army, got to know the man in the first place. But war isn't always neatly organized and tidily set up, so somehow they'd ended up in the same village, working for the same goal.

And in the time they'd spent together, they'd become close friends.

"You know why my mother wanted me to call Lutz, don't you?" A.J. asked me now.

I did know. She'd mentioned her reasons in that prior conversation. Something about the importance of A.J. having friends who weren't invisible. But I went beneath that immediate and superficial reason, and dug down to the good woman's true, loving-mother's motivation. "Because she's watched you become more and more isolated over the years. It takes one to know one—she's done it herself. And she doesn't want you ending up as alone and lonely as she is."

A.J. brushed that away. "She thinks if I have a real friend to talk to, then I won't need you. She thinks you'll just vanish. Problem gone. Mental illness cured."

"She doesn't know what she's talking about."

"Except," A.J. pointed out, "when she says to call Lutz."

"It is possible for a person to be partly right. You know, she lost a lot when your father died," I reminded him. "She's learned to view the world through a much harsher lens."

"I lost a lot, too," A.J. countered, but then he turned to look at me. "Those stories you used to tell me—about my father. Were they true?"

"They were," I said. There was never a need for embellishment, at least as far as Ryan Austin Gallagher had been concerned.

Ryan was a one. You know the type. Straight A's in school, but damned if a week never went by when he didn't cut classes at least once. He was always in trouble of some kind, and always using his smile to get himself out of it. And, often as not, succeeding.

Rose Hawkes was the smartest girl in the school. She also happened to be the prettiest, but no one could see past her spectacles and the hand-me-downs she used to wear. No one but Ryan.

I'm not sure exactly how and where they met, but they did meet. I remember the first time he brought her home for dinner. She was the first and only girl to whom he'd ever offered that invitation. I was over that night, and I remember it well.

She told me she was studying to be a doctor. She had this way of looking at you that was real direct, real honest. I liked her right away.

I knew she'd be able to handle Ryan's bullcrap, and I also knew that ol' lightning bolt had struck him full force, despite the fact that he was just a kid.

Damn, what was he? Seventeen. He was just seventeen years old, just a baby. But like I said, he was a smart kid, and once he decided that he wanted

Rose Hawkes, he was gonna have Rose Hawkes.

The only problem was, Rose had Plans. She was going to medical school, and there was no medical school in Heaven. Hell, at the time, there wasn't even a medical school in Fairbanks.

She'd been accepted at a school back east, in Boston. Pre-med. She'd received a full scholarship. She was leaving a few weeks after graduation, in the middle of July.

Ryan was heartbroken. He asked her to stay. He bought her an engagement ring, asked her to change her mind. He wept, he railed, he begged, he pleaded, and he prayed.

And when mid-July rolled around, we weren't throwing Rose a farewell party, we were throwing Rose and Ryan a wedding feast.

I didn't quite get it, but Rose seemed happy. She loved Ryan, that much was clear. And he adored her.

A year after they were married, Beverly was born. A few years later, A.J. arrived. He was also a one, just like his dad. I could see it, right from the start. But I'm not telling his story right now, I'm talking about Rose.

Rose didn't have her college education or her medical degree, but she had two of the sweetest, healthiest babies in all of Heaven, and she had Ryan, who loved her deeply. Life was great.

And then Ryan got drafted. He got called up to serve in a faraway place called Vietnam.

So Ryan kissed Rose and Bev and A.J. good-bye, and he got on a ship and went to Vietnam, where he died.

When the telegram arrived, Rose went into shock. She was like some kind of zombie, just going through the motions of taking care of her children. It went on like that literally for years.

It was as if a part of her had died with Ryan.

Hell, I knew what that felt like. Part of me had died with Mel back in 1944.

It took me awhile—and a case of a mysterious "flu," which kept me bound to a bed for a few weeks and made Rose and the kids move in, to take care of me. But I finally cajoled and insulted the girl into taking college courses by mail. Don't be a ninny, I used to say when she talked about getting a job down at the grocery store. You don't want to be a grocer, you want to be a doctor. And slowly but surely, and then faster and faster, she started to work toward her degree. Because life goes on.

She got it, too. Bev and A.J. and Adam and I whooped and hollered when she hung that college diploma on the living room wall, and when she passed her MCATs with flying colors.

Her plans were on the verge of coming true, but I knew from the look in her eyes that her plans had changed years ago. I knew that she would have gladly given that diploma away if she could've had our Ryan back.

But life does go on.

And after I'd passed, after Bev had had her adventure with Charlie, after A.J. left home to join the army, Rose became a doctor.

I confess I had high hopes that, as time went on, Rose would also let herself fall in love again. I had hopes that she would find someone to fill the hole that Ryan's dying had cut into her heart.

I was sorely disappointed when I returned to Heaven and found her living all alone in that big old house that Mel and I used to share.

She was still smart, still beautiful, and still lonely as hell.

"Call Craig," I told A.J. now. "It's a three-birds-with-one-stone thing. You maybe help Alison, you get to make your mother happy, *and* you reconnect with a man you used to call friend."

"I don't think my mother's going to be happy," A.J. pointed out, "unless my calling Lutz makes you disappear."

Chapter Eight

While A.J. was still several blocks away—too far to shout a greeting—he saw Alison and another woman go into the sleazy-looking little roadhouse on the corner of Main Street and Mexicali.

It was crazy the way his heart did gymnastics at just that distant glimpse of her. And not just his heart. His dick was warming up and stretching, too. It definitely wanted to be part of the workout.

He was early, as planned, but she'd beaten him over here. And now if he wanted to see her— which he suddenly desperately did—he was going to have to go inside.

When the door opened, music and laughter spilled out onto the hard gravel of the parking lot. It was only 7:30 at night, but a country band was already playing full volume and the little honky-tonk was packed.

The sky and the building seemed to glow with the rosy hues of the desert twilight. It softened the piles of scrap metal and old tires that surrounded the place like ornamental shrubbery and even made the crumbling adobe of the dingy roadhouse a pretty shade of pink.

The roadhouse door opened again as more members of the movie's production staff went inside, and the muffled music again became sharper. A pedal steel guitar solo cut through the darkening heat, clear and sweet, before the door closed again.

A.J. could almost smell the thick cigarette smoke that he knew hung heavily in the air. He could almost taste the golden flavor of the whiskey, sliding down his throat, warm and welcoming. . . .

A throat he now cleared as he turned to look at Jamie, who was standing beside him.

"Well, hell," Jamie said. "Who knew she'd be early?"

"It's no big deal," A.J. said. "I'll just . . ." He cleared his throat again. "Go in." He'd get a cola so he had something to hold on to. And then, maybe—if he was lucky—he could put down the drink and hold on to Alison.

"Bad idea, kid," Jamie said. "Just slow down a bit. Let's regroup. Figure out our plan B. Don't move, okay?"

As Jamie popped away, A.J. looked back at the roadhouse, listening to the throbbing, low beat of the kick drum and bass guitar.

The ghost reappeared almost immediately. "There's a back door," he reported, "but the back parking lot is badly lit. I seriously believe that when Alison leaves she's gonna exit through this entrance here."

"So your plan B is to sit and wait for her to come back out?" A.J. asked.

"Seems as good a plan as any." Jamie shrugged. "Or you could wait for her over at her house—on her front steps."

A.J. sighed. "Yeah, that'll go over well."

"What's to not go over? She gets home, you stand up and back off a bit because you're a gentleman. You tell her that you couldn't stop thinking about her so you dropped by because you wanted to say good night."

"Which she'll interpret—correctly—as a booty call."

"No, she won't," Jamie scoffed.

A.J.'s head suddenly ached—or maybe he just suddenly became aware that he was carrying around one big pain-in-the-ass headache. He was tired, too—it had been a long day. And—bonus!—he was sweating. Even though the sun had faded almost entirely from the sky, the air was still thick and hot, the temperature still in the eighties.

"She'll think it's romantic," Jamie continued. "And okay, yeah, maybe she *will* think it's about sex, but she'll realize she was wrong when you bid her good evening and walk away."

Two of the other extras—Flynn and Marty—were sharing a motel room, and they were fine with A.J. stopping in to use the shower. Once a day. More than that, though, would be an imposition.

Problem was, this was three-shower weather and by the end of the day he was pretty damn ripe.

God, but he missed Alaska. He missed the long, endless summer days and the fresh bite of the cool northern air. He missed the peaceful solitude of his isolated cabin and workshop—a complete one-eighty from the bustle and noise of this movie set.

And as long as he was missing things, he missed the soothing feel of the wood against his hands as he crafted it into furniture—beautiful furniture, that would last well beyond a single lifetime. But most of all, he missed his sense of . . . not quite contentment—he doubted he'd ever feel truly content—but he *had* felt acceptance. Before Jamie had returned, before they'd taken this insane road trip and arrived here in Jubilation, A.J.'d accepted that his life—the rest of it anyway—was destined to be a quiet one. He'd accepted it, because he knew that, just as things had once been a whole hell of a lot worse, it wouldn't take much for him to get tossed back there, for his life to become much worse again.

The certainty of his acceptance of his current quiet life brought with it a huge amount of safety.

For example, he would never find himself, while up in Alaska, standing in front of a bar and seriously considering going inside.

All because he'd kissed some random woman and now wanted more, even though he knew it would lead absolutely nowhere.

"What if I don't?" A.J. asked Jamie as the sky darkened even more and the first stars appeared. He turned to look at the ghost. "Tell her good night and walk away."

For once, Jamie wasn't flip or funny. For once, he paused before answering, as if he were really considering A.J.'s words.

"Well," he said. "I guess it all depends on what you're really looking for. If it's a quick slap and tickle—a booty call—then, by all means, take it if it's offered. But if you want something more substantial? Then walking away, as hard as it might seem, will get you farther in the long run."

Something more substantial.

The way Jamie said it, it actually sounded reasonable. Attainable. Not just possible but likely to happen.

But it wasn't.

According to Bev, his sister, who was a social worker and knew a thing or two about human nature, it made sense that A.J. would only be attracted to women that he absolutely knew he couldn't have.

Through the years, Bev had gently suggested that A.J. was commitment-averse because he was frightened by the idea of having to open himself up and share his secrets with anyone.

She got that right. The past was the past, and it was going to stay in the past—unmentioned, unacknowledged, unable to hurt him anymore.

He'd done the veterans' support group thing, he'd done the therapy, he'd done as many steps as he could handle, and he'd come quite far in the ten years since he'd wandered the streets of Los Angeles, too drunk to care that he'd lost his job, his truck, his home. . . .

And that alone was something that he couldn't imagine telling even the most intimate of lovers. *Yeah, back when I was homeless* . . . That would go over well with a woman like Alison.

Yet, at the same time, A.J. couldn't imagine ever

making a lifetime commitment to someone who didn't know all the terrible things he'd seen and done.

Hence his lack of attraction to anyone with whom he might forge a relationship that was *more substantial* than a relatively short-term sexual encounter.

And to be honest—at least with himself—for years now, even the sex seemed too much. Too close. Too personal. Too risky.

About two years back, Bev had tried setting him up with a vast variety of beautiful, smart, funny, successful women. Blind-date-of-the-week, was how she'd jokingly referred to it, even though the entire operation had been deadly serious.

But out of all the women Bev had introduced to A.J., there was only one to whom he found himself attracted. She was the older sister of date number seven.

And she'd been happily married.

In a similar way, Alison Carter was attached to her career. It seemed clear to A.J. that she was living the life she wanted, and any space she made for a lover would be only temporary.

With that in mind, he should go, as Jamie put it, for the slap and tickle.

And he should feel no guilt, whatsoever, for secrets left untold.

"Where'd you go, boy?" Jamie asked quietly. "What's cooking inside of that head of yours?"

But A.J. forced a smile. "Let's wait for her at her house."

"I changed my mind," Jamie told him. "Now I'm thinking that might not be a real good idea."

A.J. looked at him in disbelief. "*Now* you're thinking that?"

"It's kind of clear you just decided that this *is* a booty call."

This was too much. "How many hours ago was it that you were telling me I should get laid?"

"That was before I saw how you look at her."

"Enlighten me." A.J. crossed his arms. "How, exactly, do I look at her?"

"Like she's the one," Jamie replied evenly. "You look at her in the same way that your father looked at your mother."

"And look at how well that worked out for *her*."

Now Jamie was starting to get mad, too. "Life can be a real pisser of a bitch," he said. "You know that as well as I do. But you learn to accept what you get, and if you're lucky, you'll get decades. If you're not, you don't. Rose and Ryan were unlucky, but at least they had the time that they had, as short as it was. And at least they had Bev and they had you."

"Oh, I'm a real gift," A.J. said hotly.

"You are," Jamie shot back. "And not just to your mother. You were *my* gift, too. You brought me joy, A.J., at a time in my life when I thought the joy was through. And together, with your sister, we made your mother laugh again."

"I'm sure as shit not making her laugh now!"

"She'll get over it," Jamie said.

"The way she got over my father's death? The way she got over *yours?* You weren't around to live through *that.* Believe me, it sucked." He'd spent months, terrified that his mother was going to spiral back down into the deep depression that had nearly broken her years earlier. She hadn't, but A.J.'s fear had been real, just the same. He pulled off his hat, and ran his hands through his hair. God, would this heat ever abate? "If I really want to be 'her gift,' if I want to bring her any kind of real fucking joy, I should just go home and let her check me into whatever facility she thinks will help me."

"You're. Not. Crazy," Jamie said. "Will you just goddamn stop with that already?" He turned, his frustration and anger evident in the sharpness of his movement as he pointed at the roadhouse. "Have you ever been inside of that honky-tonk?"

A.J. shook his head, suddenly exhausted. "No. I told you—"

"Have you ever talked to anyone who's even been inside of it?"

What? "Of course I have," A.J. said. "Alison's in there right now."

"But have you talked to her or anyone else

about it? What it looks like inside? That sort of thing?"

"No," A.J. said. "Why would I?"

"Wait here."

Jamie vanished, leaving A.J. alone in the darkness. Alone with his thoughts.

Which included a boatload of swearing and a burning thirst for a shot of something with a hell of a kick, mostly because he knew that if he had a drink or two, he wouldn't give a damn. Not about anything. And he'd get what he wanted—Alison, right now, tonight—because his honor and integrity would vanish with his nearly ten years of hard-won sobriety.

He'd be charming and funny—he had that down—and he'd sweep her off her feet. And the sex would feel so fucking good with the warm buzz of whiskey or tequila in his blood and he'd think, no, he'd *know* that this time, it would be different. That he could handle it. That he could ration the alcohol, and it would be okay, because he wouldn't have to ration the sex. And it would work for four or five days, or maybe even a week, but by then the demon would have its claws in him so deeply that he'd break his rules because he'd need more and more—another drink, and another drink, and then a whole goddamn bottle, and he'd be puking on the bathroom floor or maybe even right in the bed, which was neither charming nor funny.

And Alison would jettison him, and the sex would stop, but he wouldn't care as long as he could get another drink, and another drink, and another drink—

A.J. sat down on the curb, across the street from that bar, and put his head between his knees and breathed.

This was all he had to do, right here, right now. In this moment. He had to breathe. Just breathe. One heartbeat at a time.

He'd come out of the darkness by surrendering control and simplifying his rules. No drinking. None at all. No hanging out in bars. No temptation. And he'd made it as easy as he possibly could. He didn't have to not drink tomorrow or next year or five years from now. He never had to think that far ahead. All he had to do was not drink in this one moment.

So he breathed—just breathed. He was okay, and he was going to stay okay. At least for right now.

"The band has eight members, one of them's a girl," Jamie reported as he popped back in. "Whoa, you okay, kid?"

"Yeah," A.J. said, lifting his head to look at the ghost. "I just got a little dizzy."

Jamie sat down next to him. "The stage is set up on the northern side of the building, the bar's along the opposite wall. A lit-up sign in blue is flashing the word 'Lite,' *l, i, t, e*—although why they spell it that way I could never figure out, even back when I was alive. There are three waitresses on duty and a female bartender with long red hair." He paused, looking hard at A.J. "But all this is moot, because there's no way I'm letting you go in there. We'll just have to prove I'm real another time."

"I'm okay," A.J. said. "But it doesn't matter. Your telling me all this wouldn't prove anything, even if I did go inside."

"It most certainly would!"

"Not for my mother. She'd point out that the door's been opened plenty of times since I've been out here. Maybe I saw all that from this perspective."

Jamie just looked at him. Then he disappeared again.

And again, A.J. was alone in the darkness. Still not drinking. Still just breathing. And still uncertain as to what he intended to do about Alison.

Maybe the pre-involvement speech he had to give her could be vague. *I'm not in a position to start something serious. You need to know that going in. . . .*

With the quietest of pops, Jamie was back, sitting exactly where he'd been.

"Okay," he said. "Here's something you couldn't possibly have seen. On the back of the door. There's a poster. It says, and I quote:

'Dreaming permits each and every one of us to be quietly and safely insane every night of our lives.' William Something, 1958. And there's no way in hell you could've seen that."

"Maybe there's a mirror on the wall opposite the door," A.J. said.

"Which means you read that," Jamie retorted, his skepticism heavy in his tone, "backwards, from all those yards away, across the street and the parking lot *and* the breadth of the honky-tonk itself, in the short amount of time that door's been open, with people coming and going, blocking your view?"

"The human brain's a pretty remarkable thing," A.J. told him.

"That it is," Jamie agreed. "And heads up, kid. Alison Carter at twelve o'clock."

Alison escaped the smoke and the noise of the roadhouse and stood for a moment in the relative quiet of the front parking lot, just filling her lungs with fresh air.

That had been a total waste of time.

She'd thought that Winter Baxter, the actress playing Melody Quinn, had wanted to talk about historical accuracy. They were, after all, filming the scene tomorrow morning where Kid Gallagher rode into town. Where the outlaw noticed the marshal's beautiful wife as she unknowingly went about her daily routine.

But instead of discussing the scene, Winter wanted to dance and kick back. She'd invited Alison to tag along because she knew that the older woman's presence would make Trace Marcus keep his distance.

Alison had ordered a ginger ale and tried to engage Winter in a conversation, but Winter was more interested in flirting with Kevin the sound engineer, who *was* pretty cute, but who was no A.J. Gallagher.

And yes, she *had* just thought that.

And double yes, she'd *also* tried her best this afternoon, standing in her kitchen, to touch A.J.'s tonsils with her tongue.

And somehow, despite the Hugh-induced return of her sanity, she'd spent most of the afternoon and evening thinking about kissing the man again.

And then, as if she'd conjured him up, he stepped out of the darkness and into the street, heading directly toward her.

Heading toward the bar, more likely.

Because saving naked women from rattlesnakes could give even the calmest, quietest man a hankering for a drink.

But he didn't seem surprised to see her. "Hey."

"Hey, yourself." Okay, that was stupid. Her grandmother used to say *Hey, yourself.* Great, she was turning into her grandmother at *the* most inopportune time. She didn't want to sound like a well-adjusted sixty-year-old. She wanted to be mysterious and sexy and youthful and desirable.

But the smile that A.J. gave her was as genuinely pleased as if she'd said, *Hi, come fuck me,* which made her wonder how he would've smiled if she *had* said, *Hi, come, et cetera.*

"You just taking a breather," he asked, "or . . . ?"

"What?" Alison asked, but then instantly understood that he was asking if she were going back inside. "No! No, I'm done. I'm not a big drinker and I've had enough secondhand smoke for this decade and the next, so . . ."

Great. All she had to do now was complain about the deafening volume of the music, and she might as well slap a sticker on her forehead saying *old* next to the one that already said *nerd*.

"Band's good, though," she added. "Country's not my thing, but the players are . . . proficient." And great, now she sounded like a professor. *Proficient.* God.

But he was nodding. "Country's not my thing, either."

"But you have a cowboy hat," she said, and as soon as the words left her lips, she realized how stupid she sounded. No—not that she sounded, but that she *was*.

But A.J. laughed, and the crow's feet around his sparkling eyes crinkled charmingly as he teased her. "Contrary to what most Yankees believe, I didn't have to pass a country music trivia quiz to get it. I just needed cash and a

185

desire to keep my head warm in the winter and cool in the summer."

"So what *do* you listen to?" And yes, her voice did sound a little breathless, a little girlish, but he didn't seem to notice or care.

"I'm a fan of the classics," he told her. "Jimi Hendrix, The Who, Eric Clapton, the Rolling Stones . . ."

"Ah," she said. "I'm . . . more of an *American Idol* viewer, myself."

"Eek," he said, laughing.

She laughed, too. "And just like that," she quipped, "it was over before it started."

He was still smiling, but something changed in his eyes. They got warmer. And his gaze slipped briefly down to her mouth. "Not a chance," he murmured. And he leaned in—she saw it coming, he took his time, giving her plenty of opportunity to back away, which she absolutely didn't—and he kissed her.

It was, quite possibly, the most gentle kiss she'd ever shared. While it was related to the inhalation attempt that had happened earlier, in her kitchen, it was far sweeter and much more tender and even almost reverent.

If kisses could carry messages, this kiss said, *I want to spend time with you, I want to get to know you,* as opposed to this afternoon's kiss, which had been all about the immediacy of them jumping each other's bones.

Not that there was anything wrong with that, either.

But Alison had been thinking about it, and thinking about it, and wondering about the best way to reconcile the conflicts between her personal and professional interests in this man. Safest thing would be to keep her distance, at least until she heard—and discounted—his version of the story. Which she was scheduled to do tomorrow night.

"I've been wanting to do that for . . . well, pretty much since I left your house," he told her, his hand warm against her chin as he smiled down into her eyes.

And Alison knew, with certainty, that she had no clue what to do where this man was concerned. But she also knew that she wasn't ready to say good night. Not yet. So she smiled back at him. "I know you were heading for the bar, but . . . Is there any chance I can talk you into walking me home?"

"Actually," A.J. said, "I *wasn't* going to the bar. I don't . . . I don't drink. I was just . . . kind of . . . out walking around. Honestly? I was hoping I'd run into you."

"Well," Alison said, with a smile, "looks like you did."

The woman probably didn't know it herself, but she was one giant green light.

187

Walk her home, my ass.

Sure, A.J. would walk her home, and then she'd say, *I'm going to make a cup of tea. Would you like some?*

And he'd say, *That sounds nice,* and he wouldn't be talking about the tea, which I happen to know he doesn't care for. At all. In fact, what Alison was *really* saying, beneath all the polite conversation, was, *Would you like to come inside and get both naked and horizontal in about thirty-five seconds after I shut and lock that door behind you?*

And don't get me wrong. I'm as open as the next man to the idea of consensual and mutual happy-fun between two sober, sane, and uncommitted grown-ups. And like I told Age, just a while ago, I'd originally been the conductor on board the get-A.J.-laid-now train. It had been years, after all, since he'd had that kind of companionship.

And I know what you're probably thinking. After Mel passed, I spent the last thirty-one years of my life alone, so I probably shouldn't offer an opinion on the subject. But that was different. I was already an old man, and getting older by the minute. I'd lived a good life.

But A.J. was still young.

And he was going to blow it, big time, with this woman, if he moved too fast, too soon.

The kid couldn't see the way he looked at her,

but I damn well could, and I was determined to do whatever I had to do, to keep him from making the mistake of his life.

They were talking about favorites as they quickly covered the ground between Mexicali and River Street. Books, more music, movies—they shared a love of a few in common, although I've yet to meet anyone who enjoys movies who thinks *Casablanca* isn't one of the all-time greats.

Any pair of maroons who wanted to knock knobs could use their mutual love for *Casablanca* as an excuse for impetuous sex with a near stranger. *But I thought we had so much in common. We both loved* Casablanca. . . .

Dogs or cats? They both preferred dogs.

Alison's grandmother, whom she'd lived with for a large part of her childhood—and there was a lot of personal information in that brief statement—had had a golden lab named Sparky.

A.J. confessed that he hadn't yet had the heart to replace his dog, Mac, whom he'd adopted from a shelter years ago. He'd brought Mac home on the one-year anniversary of his sobriety, although he didn't tell Alison that revealing little detail. He *did* say that Mac was already long in the tooth when A.J. got him, so it was no big surprise when the dog passed on, some two and a half years ago.

One of these days, A.J. told her, he'd get another dog, but it still felt too soon.

He changed the subject then to the lighter topic

of oceans versus lakes—and oceans won, hands down. Beach people unite.

Favorite restaurant. Alison's was some little French bistro in downtown Boston, at which point A.J. very strategically let drop the news that he was quite a good cook, which was a fact that, for some reason, always seemed to make a woman's heart beat harder.

By then they were approaching Alison's front steps, and A.J. slowed, because according to the rules of the game, he couldn't pretend that he already knew he was going in.

"Say good night and walk away," I said, but he didn't so much as glance at mc.

Until Alison starting digging in her handbag for her key, at which point he looked straight at me and shook his head, giving me a face that clearly said, *Get your ass out of here, ghost-man, because I am going in.*

"Nope," I said. "I'm not going anywhere. You want to get busy with this girl? Well, I'll be there, too, sitting right on the edge of the bed. If you want, I'll give you pointers."

Now before you get all squirrelly and horrified, you should know that I was purely bluffing. There was no way that I would actually do such a thing. Private moments, no matter how misguided, deserve privacy.

But I'd already learned that A.J. was unwilling to so much as *discuss* anything having to do with sex with me, and I was counting on his strong reaction to my words.

Sure enough, he started to retort, but realized how that would sound to Alison and turned it into a cough.

She'd found her key and had put it into the door, but now she turned back, concerned. "Are you all right?"

A.J. nodded, still coughing. He was damn good at faking it—it sounded like he'd choked on his own spit. Which maybe he had.

"Come on in," she said, "I'll get you some water."

And the look A.J. shot me then was triumphant, like *Look what you just helped me do.* He obediently followed her into her kitchen, shutting the door firmly in my face.

Which didn't stop me from following them.

"Or would you like a beer?" Alison asked, but caught herself, saying, "You don't drink," even as A.J. repeated it, "I don't drink."

"Sorry," she said.

"No, that's okay. A glass of water would be great," he told her, even though he'd stopped with the coughing. "Thanks."

She had one of those fancy filter pitcher things, and she took it out of that ugly green fridge, then reached up into the cabinet to get a pair of drinking glasses down. And all the while, A.J. let himself watch her.

"At least tell her about Craig," I said. But she brought it up first.

"You were in the army, right?" she said as she poured that water and turned to hand him a glass. "Maybe you can help. We're looking for someone with sharpshooting skills who might be able to help us re-create the shoot-out. You know, at the Red Rock Saloon."

The kid's open body language was unmistakable, and the way he let himself look at her? It sent a message, too. His admiration was right there—he wasn't trying to hide it or disguise it. He was telling her, with his eyes, that he found her beautiful.

And okay, yeah, I'm romanticizing it. I'm that kind of man. What he was really telling her was that he found her fuckable.

But she was a woman, so she probably thought the second meant the same as the first. Or maybe she was okay with it. Maybe she didn't want more than a brief boy-howdy with a good-looking near-stranger.

Maybe I was the only one here who wanted these two to give a damn about what they were about to do.

"It's been years since I've been in touch with anyone with that skill set," A.J. admitted as she refilled the pitcher from the tap and put it back into the fridge. "But I could make some calls."

"We're looking for some kind of laser setup,"

she told him, taking a long sip from her glass. "No paintballs in an historic building."

"Of course," he said, as if I hadn't told him that already.

"We're also looking to do this ASAP," she said. "The writers and Henry and I are in the middle of a battle to the death about what really happened."

"I can tell you what really happened," A.J. said. "But I'm thinking right now's probably not the best time."

She smiled at that. "Good call. It's definitely better to wait until the harsh light of day to try to crush my girlhood fantasies about Silas Quinn."

"Try?" A.J. said as he crossed the kitchen to set his now-empty glass in the sink.

She shrugged as she turned to face him, as she set her own glass on the counter.

A.J. took that for the invitation that it was, and he reached out and reeled her in. And then he kissed her.

I started to sing. *"Hello, young lovers whoever you are . . ."*

He ignored me, so when I finished the verse and chorus, I switched to a more rousing, upbeat number. *"Oh, the farmer and the cowman can be friends . . ."* I supplemented the song with some hand claps and even stood up and added boot stomps and something that might've passed for dancing. I made it good and loud, damn near bellowing at the top of my lungs. But it wasn't until I improvised my own version of a fiddle solo—"Diddle liddle liddle liddle, *liddle* liddle liddle! Dweep, dweep, reet, reet, diddle liddle liddle liddle liddle!"—that he lifted his head.

By then, I was starting the bass solo, "Bom, bom, bom, bom . . ." which required me to stand still and pretend to pluck the strings of some big old standup instrument, so I actually saw what happened.

The kid stopped kissing Alison and he opened his eyes and looked down at her uplifted face. Her eyes were closed and she looked as if his kisses had transported her to someplace wonderful. But then she opened her eyes and she smiled up at him, and I shut the hell up, because I knew, just from the look on A.J.'s own face as he met her gaze, that he finally understood exactly what I'd been trying to tell him.

Alison was the one.

And sure enough, "God damn it," he whispered.

She laughed, but she knew what he meant. "This is going to be a mistake, isn't it? An enormous one."

A.J. nodded. "I have to go," he said. "Because I really like you and . . . I think maybe it's mutual, and . . ."

"Very." She nodded, too, her eyes soft as she reached up to push his hair back from his face. He closed his eyes at her touch.

"I don't want to screw this up," he told her. "There's a lot you don't know about me."

"And vice versa," she pointed out, nodding her agreement.

"I think we should take some time," A.J. said. "And figure out, you know, what exactly this is, before we . . ." He laughed. "God, I want to . . ."

And then the fool didn't step away from her. Instead, he kissed her again. And again.

And again.

It was getting too damn hot in there as all of their careful resolve started to melt before my very eyes.

So I reached out and braced myself and, with a deep breath, put the palms of both my hands on A.J.'s shoulders.

Zzzzt.

Even though I was prepared for it this time, it was still startling as hell.

And of course, A.J. had no idea it was coming. "Holy shit!"

He stepped back from Alison, and she stepped back from him, and they both stood there, breathing hard and wide-eyed as they stared at each other.

"You're welcome," I said.

"What was *that?*" Alison asked. "Oh, my God, were we just . . . electrocuted?"

"Whoopsie," I said. "I didn't realize she would feel it, too."

"Um," A.J. said.

But she seemed okay with her theory. "This house was wired by a lunatic," she told A.J. "Right after I moved in, I called the landlord because I blew a fuse, and he had to go into the crawl space that's under part of the house and I peeked in and . . . I think we just got an electric shock from the refrigerator."

"This house has a crawl space?" A.J. asked. "Because I didn't check in there. If you want, I'll do that tomorrow. I'll look at the wiring, while I'm at it."

"Check the crawl space . . . ?" She was confused.

"For snakes," he said.

And she started to laugh. "I actually forgot about the snake. Oh, my God. Will you . . ." She made a face and said the rest, fast: "Help me search my house for snakes before you go? Please? I promise this is not just a ploy to get you into my bedroom."

He laughed. "I can't even begin to respond to that," he said, "so I'm just gonna go with the short answer—yes. Let's make sure there's not another snake in here."

And with that they went through the little house. Living room, Alison's tiny office, bathroom. Although it took them awhile, because they were holding on to each other's hand while they did. And they both seemed far more interested in looking at each other than looking for a snake.

At least A.J. knew enough not to kiss her again.

"Snakes head for heat," I told him, and he passed that information along to Alison. "Which is why they might crawl into a sleeping bag or a bed. Keep the AC at a warmer setting so it's not so cold in here tonight. Another trick would be to plug in a heating pad and leave it on the bedroom floor. 'Course, you should be sure your smoke alarms work, just in case it malfunctions and causes a fire. You're not any less dead if the cause is smoke inhalation instead of snakebite."

She had a heating pad in her bathroom cabinet, and A.J. helped her set it up.

While they were there, back in her bedroom— which absolutely was a dangerous place to be, considering the sparks these two made just from looking at each other—Alison yanked back the blanket and the sheet, as if afraid of what she'd find lurking there.

It was a whole lot of nothing.

Except there they now stood, staring at that big old empty bed—where they both clearly wanted to be.

A.J. made himself turn away first.

Then Alison flipped the covers back up. "I made sure there were snakebite kits in the first-aid station," she told A.J. as he led the way back to the kitchen, their fingers intertwined again. "I'm going to put my cell phone in the pocket of my pj's and . . . I'm going to be fine." She laughed then. "Huh. I wonder if . . . Were you touching the refrigerator before?"

"I honestly don't know," A.J. said. "I was a little focused on other things." He kissed her hand.

"Maybe it was where we were standing," Alison said breathlessly as he turned her palm over and kissed the inside of her wrist. "What if the wiring sends electric currents up through the floor—like those sidewalks in New York City, where those dogs were electrocuted? Did you ever hear about that?"

"No." A.J. stopped kissing her. "That's awful."

"Yeah, all these dogs had burned paws," Alison said. "Some even died. The current apparently went right through the concrete. But maybe that's what happened with the snake today. Maybe it kept getting zapped from the bad wiring, through the floor."

A.J. nodded, as if that were a real possibility. "I'll check it out tomorrow."

He leaned in and kissed her on the mouth, but only briefly this time.

"Are you sure," Alison started to say, but then stopped herself. "Sorry, I'm . . . shameless. Apparently."

"I want to stay," A.J. said softly, his forehead pressed against hers. "But I have to go. And you're not shameless. You're amazing. And I'll see you tomorrow."

With that, he let himself out the door.

Alison watched him through the screen, so I didn't say a word until we rounded the corner.

Then I said, "I'm proud of you, kid."

"Don't talk to me," he said, stopping short. "Don't follow me. I need a shower—a very cold one—and until I get it, which isn't going to be until tomorrow morning, I'm going to be pissed off. So just . . . don't. Okay?"

"She's falling in love with you," I told him.

And he looked at me as if I'd just suggested we play hockey using a fluffy baby bunny as the puck. "Is that supposed to *help?*" he asked, but added, "Don't answer that. Just . . . *don't.*"

So I didn't, and he stomped away.

July 8, 1898
Dear Diary,

A stranger is in town.

He stopped dead in the street, to watch me walk down the boardwalk. My injuries have faded. I have golden hair and a pretty face— I'd almost forgotten. Men are still drawn to me.

And this man didn't try to hide his admiration, even after one of the miners stepped close to warn him that I was the property of the monster. He didn't look away, and his dauntless, foolish courage makes me once again consider escape. Would this one help, this man with such blue eyes?

For a price, perhaps.

I think I am ready to pay, with the only thing I have left to offer.

Not my soul. My soul has long since faded to dust.

So. What have I become? No longer quite human, no longer completely alive, no longer caring of proprieties and conventions.

And yet the heat in a stranger's eyes sparks something I had thought was long dead.

Hope.

I know I am ready to pay the price. Still, I can't help but wonder if I would merely exchange one prison cell for yet another. One level of hell for a far worse one.

But perhaps another man, this other, pretty, blue-eyed man, would be easier to kill than the monster that I call husband.

Chapter Nine

Alison stood in the tent, behind the cameras, and watched as the production crew took yet another shot, from yet another angle, of the initial meeting of Kid Gallagher and Melody Quinn.

Jon White, the actor playing Gallagher, was on horseback, but his horse was skittish and kept moving sideways, out of the shot. Their horse wrangler had had a family emergency, and his assistant just wasn't getting the job done.

"Cut," Henry Logan yelled, clearly exasperated. "Set it up again."

The makeup head came running to freshen Winter's drooping blond hair as the actress playing Melody moved back to her mark just inside the swinging doors of the general store.

As Alison watched, A.J. approached Jon, who was still trying to gain control over the horse. A.J. took the horse's bridle and spoke to it, calming it almost immediately with his voice. Then he looked up at the actor, and the two men spoke. Alison couldn't hear the words, but she could see that A.J. was relaxing Jon as easily as he'd calmed the horse.

He'd done the same to her this morning.

There had been problems with Melody's dress that had kept Alison busy right up until the moment the AD called for quiet on the set. She'd then had a frantic few seconds to check the extras, one of whom was A.J., whom she hadn't seen since she'd kissed him good night.

"Hey," she'd said, and this time he'd responded with "Hey, yourself," which had made her laugh and say, "Great, now *you're* turning into my grandmother."

As the words came out of her mouth, she realized that she couldn't possibly take the time to explain. But it was okay, because he just smiled and said, "Later," and then backed away so the other extras could have their point-oh-nine nanoseconds with her.

When she'd finally stopped running, he was working—walking down the hot, dusty street with a saddle over his shoulder.

But now the camera angle was such that he wouldn't be in the shot. And maybe he'd use his precious moments of break to come over here, into the tent, to find her.

It was right then that A.J. turned and looked directly at Alison, as if someone—the horse, maybe—had told him that she was watching him.

He smiled, and her heart actually did a flip. What was she, suddenly in eighth grade again?

"Places!" the assistant director shouted.

And A.J. gave one final pat to the horse's neck, one last word to Jon, and then headed toward Alison. And her heart flipped over again. And again.

"Quiet!" someone else yelled as A.J. opened his mouth to greet her. Instead, he made a face, then turned to watch the actors.

"Speed!" shouted a third voice.

"And . . . Action!"

The day was so hot, A.J. was practically steaming. Silently, he took off his cowboy hat. His hair was matted and wet, and a steady stream of sweat ran down the side of his face. He wasn't standing all that close, but Alison could feel his body heat radiating right through his cotton shirt and faded brown pants. She could smell him, too—an interesting combination of his now-familiar and faintly spicy deodorant, the tanginess of his leather vest, a hint of woodsmoke, and the sweet scent of sunblock. He smelled very male— and very, very good.

He caught her looking at him and smiled.

Alison had to look away, pretending to be engrossed in the action on the set, but in truth, remembering the way A.J had kissed her last night.

I have to go, he'd said. *Because I really like you. And I don't want to screw this up. . . .*

Just the fact that he'd said those words had made her want to convince him to stay.

But the problem was, *she* was the one who was screwing this up. He'd traveled thousands of miles to tell her his story—a story that, if true, would not be made more convincing if word got out that she was sleeping with him.

And word would get out.

That was just the way the world worked.

And trying to convince that same skeptical world that her interest in this man's story had nothing to do with her attraction to him? That would be almost as hard to do as convincing the world that as a historian she would demand proper documentation and proof of everything A.J. told her, regardless of whether or not he was providing her with the best sex of her life.

And okay. Truth was, she couldn't even convince herself of that anymore.

And maybe it *was* just several days of considering the possibility that Silas Quinn *had* lied about everything, that was making her far more open to the idea that the legend was completely wrong. But maybe, instead, it was the promise of A.J.'s kisses that was making her interested in seeing things through his subjective lens.

Out in the street, the actor playing Kid Gallagher rode his horse—which was behaving very nicely now that A.J. had given it a talking to—toward the Red Rock Saloon, just as Winter, playing Melody, came out of the general store on cue. Gallagher slowed to a stop, to watch her. He lit a hand-rolled cigarette, squinting slightly as the smoke curled around his face.

Beside Alison, A.J. shifted slightly. He shook his head, just a little, as if he didn't like what he saw.

Out in the street, Melody caught sight of the Kid staring at her. She shrank back, as if in fear of the dangerous stranger.

"And . . . Cut!"

A.J. laughed. Alison looked at him, but he just shook his head as Henry called, "Nice job, everyone!" The director was happy—but not happy enough. "Let's do it again, same angle."

Melody moved back inside, and Kid Gallagher turned his horse around and went back to his mark. His assistant, Bonnie, snapped her fingers and several of her underlings went to bring the actor water, and to shield both him and the horse with giant beach umbrellas.

Alison turned to find A.J. watching her, still smiling.

"Go on," she said. "Say it. I know you want to. *This isn't how it happened.* We're guessing about a lot of this. That's what you have to do when you make a movie about historic events. There are holes that need filling in. We don't really know when or where Kid—Jamie—Gallagher first noticed Melody. Or whether he was even aware of her as anything more than a means to his revenge."

A.J.'s smile broadened. "He was aware of her. Very much so. This is actually pretty close to accurate. He rode into town and saw her, and he was toast. But the rest of it? The melodrama? You know, *Ooh, I'm so scared of you?*" He shook his head. "That didn't happen. And of course, the little details are wrong. Jamie wasn't on his horse when he first saw her. And the clothes she was wearing . . . But of course you wouldn't know that."

"And you *do* know what Melody Quinn was wearing on the day she met Kid Gallagher?" Alison couldn't keep the skepticism out of her voice.

"Like I said," A.J. told her. "Jamie noticed her. Big time. It was just after eleven in the morning on July 8, 1898. She was wearing a dark, I guess you'd call it navy, blue skirt and a long-sleeved white blouse that buttoned all the way up to her neck."

"Of course. To hide her bruises," Alison said, not knowing whether to laugh or cry.

"It was a hot day. Kind of like today. She wore a hat—a straw hat with a ribbon that matched the skirt."

Alison sighed. "A.J.," she started.

"Quiet on the set!" came the cry from the director's assistant.

Silently, she motioned for A.J. to follow her, and she led him out of the tent and far enough away from the filming to talk. They were filming MOS—without sound—so it was really just a matter of not disturbing the actors and crew.

"Speed!"

There was shade back behind the Red Rock Saloon, and she pulled him into it with her as the AD called, "And . . . *Action!*"

A.J. spoke first. "You have no idea how many times I've heard that story. Gramps said it was like being struck by lightning—his seeing her there. He used to tell me that his entire life was separated into before and after. And that day was the dividing line. His plan was to ride on. His horse had thrown a shoe and he'd stopped at the blacksmith's to get it replaced. He wasn't intending to stay in town for more than a few days. He was in a hurry—he was heading for San Francisco, where there was a high-stakes poker game he wanted in on. But then he saw Melody and . . . Everything else went out the window."

"A.J.," she said, and sighed again. Where to start? "You said you were ten when he died. You honestly expect me to believe that a ten-year-old boy sat around listening to a hundred-year-old man talking about what a woman was wearing when he first saw her seventy-five years earlier . . . ?"

"It wasn't my favorite story," A.J. admitted, "but I'd sit through it to get to the good stuff."

She nodded. Okay. She'd buy that. "So . . . he sees Melody," she said. "Lightning strikes. Then what?"

"Someone warned him off," A.J. said. "He was standing right in the middle of the street. He'd stopped, just dead in his tracks, as if, you know . . ."

"He'd been struck by lightning," she finished for him. "I got it."

"So someone sees him, notices who he's staring at, and tells him, Watch out, that's Mrs. Marshal Silas Quinn. You'd best take care, or you'll find your . . . male parts . . . in . . . some discomfort." He cleared his throat. "Yeah. But Jamie couldn't look away. She was that beautiful.

"He told me he didn't think Melody had noticed him at first, that she was like a sleepwalker, just drifting past," A.J. continued, his gentle western accent adding a touch of music to his softly spoken words. "Laudanum, he suspected, and his heart broke to think a woman so beautiful had fallen under the spell of that addiction. But then she turned and looked back at him and her eyes weren't empty—they were haunted."

How could he possibly remember all this? He had to be making it up.

"You know, it's hard—it would be hard—for him to watch this scene, because he *did* use to smoke," A.J. continued. "You got that right. He quit, pretty much right after they moved north to Alaska. When tobacco became a luxury. But he wished he'd quit sooner, because, well, she died of lung cancer. And he never really stopped blaming himself."

Melody Quinn had died of lung cancer. She wasn't abducted and murdered. She'd run away with and had a long, happy life with Jamie Gallagher. And A.J.—sweet, handsome, funny, kind, and courageous A.J.—was their direct descendent and unofficial proof of their enduring love.

Except two people didn't have to be in love to make a baby. Alison's own parents were proof of that.

"I'll need to see the original of your birth certificate," she told him abruptly. "And your father's birth certificate, and whatever records *his* father had—marriage certificate, military registration, death certificate, I don't know,

208

anything that might mention Jamie Gallagher's name, anything that required some account of paternity. Our best shot is records that belonged to your grandfather—Jamie and Melody's son. Alleged son. What was his name again?"

"Adam." A.J. thoughtfully rubbed his chin. "I told you, I'm not sure exactly what records are still available. There was a fire in Heaven in the late seventies, and the town building burned—"

"If you can't come up with records as simple as birth and death and marriage certificates," Alison said flatly, because a fire in town was just *too* convenient—it set off all her alarm bells—"then I'm going to have to assume you have a reason to hide them from me. A reason such as, the name listed on old Grandpa Adam's death certificate under 'father of deceased' is something other than Jamie Gallagher."

"But . . . Adam doesn't have a death certificate," A.J. said.

"He's *got* to have one—"

"No, he doesn't," A.J. said. "He's not dead."

He was smiling at her, but it was a gentle smile that shared the joke with her, rather than laughed at her surprise.

Alison had to smile, too. Then she sighed, and sat down on the cracked steps that led to a back door into the saloon. "Of course he isn't," she said, "because all the Gallagher men live to be a hundred."

"Or more," A.J. agreed as he sat down next to her.

And there they sat, shoulder to shoulder, outside the site of the most famous gunfight in the history of the American West.

"I'm sorry this is so difficult for you," he said.

She looked at him. At the deep blue of his eyes, the straight line of his nose, that mouth that was so quick to curve upward in amusement—a mouth that had kissed her so exquisitely just last night.

He leaned forward to kiss her again—no doubt she was sending out all kinds of pheromones and *kiss me* signals, including the fact that she'd just been staring at his mouth.

But she leaned back, away from him. "Please don't."

"Sorry, I thought, um . . ." He was a little embarrassed, a little confused, a little amused—this time with himself.

"No," Alison said. "You read me right. I want to kiss you. Very much."

Her words lit a fire in his eyes and he leaned in again. But she stopped him with a hand on his chest.

"I'm working," she said, "and . . . I have to be up front with you, A.J. If we keep up the kissing, or . . . even move things to the next level—the naked level? I'm going to need twice as much documentation, *twice* as much proof. The contents of your wallet won't cut it. I'm going to talk to your family, your friends. I'm going to wade through your life with hip boots on. And I'm going to make damn sure that you're who you say you are, and it's going to be weird, because people who kiss are supposed to trust each other, but I won't be able to do that. At all. Do you understand what I'm saying? I will not take your word for anything."

A.J. nodded. "I'm okay with weird," he said. "I've got some weirdness going on of my own, so . . ."

Alison had to laugh. "Doesn't anything ever faze you?"

"Just the big stuff," he said. "But the little stuff . . . ?" He shrugged.

"Having to find twice as much proof is *little stuff?*" she asked.

"I'm pretty certain that we'll find those diaries," he said. "You know, I've been playing phone tag with my sister, but she left me a message. They're real, she's read 'em, but it was a long time ago—right before she got married. She doesn't feel like she's any kind of authority on their exact content, because it's been so long since she read them, but she said she'd be happy to talk to you about the basics of what Melody wrote."

And didn't *that* sound suspicious. Alison looked at him, looked hard into his eyes. "If I find out that this is just some con, that you're playing me . . . ?"

"I'm not," he said.

"But if you are?" she countered. "If you're lying to me, about anything, I'm *gonna* find out. Because I will be thorough. And it *will* be ugly. And it'll be exponentially worse if we become . . . entangled."

He was looking down at the hat he was still holding in his hands, his long eyelashes thick and dark against his tanned cheeks. And when he looked back up at Alison, she was—not for the first time—startled by the vivid color of his eyes.

But he didn't respond. He didn't say anything. No promises, no *I'm not lying, not about anything. . . .*

"It's not too late to pack up your things and just clear out of town," she told him quietly. "You can disappear. Go back to Alaska or wherever, and we'll both just forget you ever came here."

Now *that* was a bald-faced lie. Even if he turned and walked away right now, Alison was going to remember the man who claimed to be A.J. Gallagher for a very long time to come.

"I'm not lying," he said quietly. "And I know that you think even if *I'm* not lying, that maybe someone lied to me. That my great-grandfather wasn't really Jamie. You want to work with that theory until my mother finds the diaries? That's fine with me."

Alison nodded. "Good. What do you know about your great-grandfather's life before he left Philadelphia? I'm curious about the older brother—Caldwell Gallagher."

A.J. was already shaking his head. "Jamie didn't talk much about his family back east. At least not to me."

"Caldwell's middle name was also James," Alison said.

A.J.'s reaction seemed genuine. Surprise—and amusement. "I didn't know that." He put two and two together. "You think Gramps might be Caldwell James. I'll ask him—I mean, my grandfather. Adam. I'll ask *him* about it. Next time I, um, talk to him. Adam. I'll see what I can find out."

Alison looked at him. He had these odd moments, where he stammered and stumbled all over himself in an attempt to clarify what he'd just said. For someone who claimed not to be fazed by the small stuff, he seemed rather fazed by something that was relatively small.

And then there were the times, like in her bathroom, with the snake, when he'd seemed to be giving orders to himself—*Do it now!*—or maybe to the snake. *You* are *real, aren't you?*

"I'd like to talk to him, too," Alison told A.J. now. "Your grandfather. And your mother. They both knew your great-grandfather for far longer than you did. But do keep me posted about the diaries." She stood up and A.J. rose, too. Always the gentleman. "I need to get back to work, but . . . Think about what I said, okay? About needing twice the proof, if we . . . ?"

Move it to the naked level. There was no need for her to say that again. She knew A.J. was thinking it.

But he cleared his throat, and said, "I know you can't completely trust me. Not right now, anyway. I understand that, but I just wanted you to know that I do. You know. Trust you. To find the truth. To be, um, open to a truth that might not be all that . . . comfortable for you. Bottom line, I trust you and I respect you. Very much."

And there she stood. Gazing up into the ridiculously handsome face of *the* most perfect man on the planet.

"Are you real?" she asked. "Or are you just a delicious little figment of my overactive imagination?"

He laughed, self-consciously. "I'm a little *too* real," he told her.

"I'm working," she said, more to herself than him, but he nodded and she knew he knew what she'd meant. That if she could have, she would've kissed him.

"Later," he promised her, just as he had earlier, and the smile he gave her made her feel as if she were going to melt.

"I don't know if that's a good idea," she said,

but it wasn't until Henry shouted, "Cut!" that she broke eye contact and turned, leading him back to the chaotic safety of the set.

Love is a strange, strange thing. There's no explaining it.

Look at me. I'd been happily single for years. Sure, I was young, only in my early twenties when I met Mel, but I'd hit the road and left home when I was fifteen.

When you're out on your own, you grow up fast, believe you me.

So there I was, the notorious gambler and gunslinger, Jamie Gallagher. I'd spent all those years stealing a night with one woman here and another woman there and never looking back when I left town the next morning.

Then one day, what the hell? I'm in some piss pot of a town called Jubilation in the Arizona Territory, and I look into this one girl's eyes, and my life takes a total hairpin turn.

Without rhyme or reason, I'm on my knees, struck dumb by Cupid's arrow.

Go figure.

Of course, I tried to deny it at first. Made excuses for why I was hanging around. My horse needed another day of rest. And then another. Then, there was money to be made at the poker tables in the Red Rock—miners with silver to spare, and relieving them of it was like taking candy from a baby. Except I didn't win all the time. And then I didn't win at all. And then I couldn't leave until I'd earned back enough to pay for the supplies I'd needed to get me across the desert.

And by then, I was in too deep. By then, I had to stay.

More than a hundred years after I'd first laid eyes on Mel, I stood out in the brilliant sunshine and watched as much of the fictional scene—vicious killer meets cherished wife—as I could stand. Curiously, it wasn't the fact that they portrayed Melody as being terrified of me that was hard to take, despite there having been a time when she was, indeed, horribly skittish around me, as she was around all men.

No, it was the reminder that, for quite a few years, I'd filled up her lungs with my secondhand smoke. It was those same lungs that failed her, decades later, and she'd slipped away from me.

Cause and effect? We'll never really know.

And don't worry, I'm not going to wallow. You don't have to skip ahead. In fact, you shouldn't, because after I bid A.J. farewell and left the moviemaking to wander around a bit on my own, I ran into my old friends Rob and Lombardi—whose first name was Charlotte.

This I knew, because she was wearing one of those name badge stickers that said *Hello, my name is* . . . as she helped set up the noon meal in the huge air-conditioned caterers' tent.

I almost didn't recognize her, because her hair—thick and red—was out of the brain-squeezingly tight chignon that she'd worn when I'd first noticed her out by the Circle K's pay phone. She'd also traded her dark suit for shorts and a T-shirt that fit her very nicely.

Rob was nearby wiping down tables, also dressed down for the occasion.

They were obviously undercover. Just a coupla thirty-year-old college kids working a minimum-wage summer position.

But people saw what they expected to see, and there were certainly all types working the equally wide variety of jobs connected to *Quinn*'s production.

"This is a giant waste of time," Charlotte murmured to Rob as she carried a tray of condiments to the table he'd just cleaned, and began setting them out.

"Yup," he said, clearly resigned to it.

"Hey, when you go back to the trailer," she said, "will you pick up my phone charger? My battery's flipping out. It's dying after about only an hour. I don't want to be caught without it."

"Sure thing, pumpkin," he said, and she gave him a disbelieving look.

"What?" he added under his breath. "We're supposed to be together."

She just walked away, shaking her head.

"You don't call a redhead pumpkin," I lectured as I sat up on the table across from him. "My son Jim's eldest granddaughter was a redhead, and she was on the stout side, with a round face, kind of like her father's. So all through grade school the other kids—the mean kids—called her *pumpkin head*. Of course, she had the last laugh when she grew up and turned into the prettiest girl in town and wouldn't give those fools who'd teased her the time of day."

Clueless Rob couldn't hear me. He just kept on grimly wiping down tables, and I realized that he was bone-weary exhausted. He probably hadn't slept well in days, and probably wouldn't in the near future, because he was sharing a trailer with his beautiful and smart partner who was also, if I remembered correctly, his foolish brother's ex-girlfriend.

"You're going to have to snap out of it," I advised him. "Because the men you're after are dangerous."

Of course, he did not respond.

Lunch wasn't due to start for another hour. I figured I'd return at that time, see what questions they asked the cast and crew as they dished out the food and replenished the salad bar. Because that's why they were here, working this particular job. As part of the catering team, they could talk to everyone. Provided everyone came into the tent to eat.

Which everyone didn't always do.

I was just about to drift away, see if I couldn't try to identify the mysterious Gene—who would be new in town and thus, hopefully, stand out—when Charlotte came back.

"I'm delivering his lunch tray," she quietly told her partner, who instantly woke up. "In twenty minutes."

"Come on, kids," I urged them. "Give us a name. Who's your suspect? Because I can watch him when you can't."

But Rob didn't tell me. He didn't say a word.

"He asked for me," she said. "I made sure he saw me at breakfast. Guess we'll see if the rumors are true."

"Rumors?" I said. "What rumors? You mean like your suspect is some VIP like Trace Marcus or Henry Logan himself, with a reputation for ruining the reputation of every pretty young girl on set?"

Although the movie's star and director weren't the only men in positions of power. There were probably dozens of others, less well known—and one of them, I believed, went by the nickname Loco.

My friend Rob didn't say a word. He just nodded an affirmative, the muscle jumping in the side of his jaw.

His beautiful partner nodded, too, and walked away, shoulders back, head high, like she was heading for her execution.

But then Rob straightened up and called after her, "Charlotte."

She turned back, her heart in her eyes. How he didn't see that, I'll never know.

Because all he did was shake his head. "Nothing. Never mind."

She nodded. "Don't bother getting my charger. I'm going to get it myself."

"Okay," he said.

And now she practically ran away, heading out of the tent.

"Rob," I said, "you big dope."

He muttered profanities to himself as he wiped down the next table.

I didn't want to follow Charlotte, because I figured she hadn't just gone to their trailer to make sure her cell phone worked. If I knew strong women—and I did know my share of strong, stoic women—she was also going there for the privacy, so that no one would see her if, despite her best efforts, she leaked a tear or two.

She deserved that privacy, so I headed to the kitchen. I'd meet her there. But twenty minutes was a long time, so I did a quick check-in with A.J., who was back to lugging a piece-of-crap saddle down the street, over and over and over again while the movie cameras rolled.

I walked beside him for a bit. He was the one who was sweating like a stuck pig, his shirt glued to his back, rivers running down the side of his face, but as soon as the director called "Cut," he muttered to me, "Are you all right?"

"Don't ever smoke," I told him.

He smiled as he used his arm to wipe the sweat from his brow. "You know, you said that to me every single night, when you tucked me in."

"I wanted to make sure it would stick," I said.

"It did," he told me, "although I wish you'd said *or drink*."

I wished I'd said that, too. But it was then that I saw him.

Gene.

Had to be.

He was standing back behind the cameras, with the same kind of dangerous edge as his friend, Tall-Man-with-Ponytail, aka Killer-of-Wayne.

He had a baseball cap on his head, and sunglasses covered his eyes. His shirt was long-sleeved, so I couldn't tell if he was tattooed the way Wayne had been. Which I suppose wasn't really any kind of a clue, since most of the cast and crew were permanently decorated in some way or another.

Used to be a tattoo was a way to tell that a man'd been to jail or served in the navy. Those days were long gone.

"Excuse me, son," I said to A.J. and headed over toward the man.

He was nervous. That was for sure. He kept tapping his foot, and shifting from side to side.

His shirt was definitely large enough to conceal a weapon beneath.

But before I reached him, Alison stepped in front of me. I had to stop short or I would've gone right through her. Which would have been a shock to both of us.

"Mr. Sylvester," she said, holding out her hand to greet him. "Welcome, sir. Nice to see you again. How are you?"

"I'll be damned," I said, adding, "not literally," because be careful what you wish for and all that.

This dangerous-looking man was Neil Sylvester, as in Silas Quinn's great-great-grandson—the man who still owned most of Jubilation, and was ponying up the cash to build more hotels and motels after *Quinn* put the town back on the map.

He was small and wiry and looked nothing like the marshal.

I was usually pretty good at reading a man, and this one obviously had secrets, but even I wasn't paranoid enough to think that one of Neil Sylvester's was that he moonlighted as a hired killer named Gene.

It was right about then that I realized my twenty minutes were nearly up. I had to meet Charlotte in the kitchen, or I'd lose my shot at locating the FBI's key suspect in the Headless Wayne murder case.

I couldn't risk zapping myself to the wrong

222

location, so I zoomed over to the caterer's tent doing my not-really-flying thing, and went straight down through the canvas and into the kitchen area. Where, sure enough, trays were being prepared for the folks who were too important or busy to eat in the tent with the proletariat.

But Charlotte was nowhere to be found.

And I realized that, as the trays were made ready, a whole pack of young women and men were standing by to deliver them. They left on their assignments, one at a time, moving quickly so that the meal was delivered hot.

Charlotte, no doubt, had already left.

So I shot myself back up and out of that tent, giving myself an aerial view of the rows of trailers that were back there, behind the motel. I could see a number of trays being carried, but I didn't see Charlotte's blaze of red hair.

I scanned the area again, and then a third time. But she wasn't outside.

Which was when I knew what I had to do.

She'd gone into someone's trailer with that tray, and I could find her by doing a quick pass through—literally through—the rows of 'em. Starting with the fancier ones that belonged to the bigwigs.

It was an unpleasant idea—invading the privacy of all those people, some of whom were surely picking their noses, or having an argument with their boyfriend or girlfriend, or having the opposite of an argument with . . . You know what I mean.

But I wanted to find her, and I figured her hair would be easy enough to spot, so I could breeze through quickly.

I braced myself and I went for it. It didn't feel like anything. It was just the same to me as moving through the air, but it looked a whole hell of a lot different, that was for sure.

I usually closed my eyes when I went through a wall or car ceiling, but this time I had 'em open because I was moving so fast, so I saw not just inside the trailers, but I also got an up close look at the wiring and the insulation and the spiders that lived in the insulation within the flimsy walls.

Now, I'm not a fan of spiders, particularly not the big hairy ones that thrive in hot climates, so I'll be honest and admit that I may have vocalized a bit as I made my journey down that first row of trailers.

I got an eyeful—mostly of people doing the little boring things that they do when they're on a break from work.

A dark-haired young woman read a book while her toenail polish dried.

A heavyset man sat on his commode, with his laptop, answering email while he took a dump.

A pair of girls were in the midst of trying on every piece of clothing in their little closet as they decided what to wear to lunch.

A woman was doing some kind of yoga-type stretches—naked. I had to slow down to double-check, but no, it wasn't Charlotte.

A young man was in his shower, doing what most young men do in the shower, pretty much everywhere in the world.

Some people napped, some facedown on their bunks, some lying back on their sofas, arms up and over their eyes.

And many, many, many people paced their trailers as they talked on their cell phones.

I had to dodge them, which was hard, because they were moving targets, and I did yet more shouting when I missed and we collided—which happened more often than not, because I was moving pretty damn fast.

I left behind a trail of *What was that*s and *Holy shit*s as I came out the far side, having not found Charlotte.

So I took a deep breath and searched the second row of trailers.

It was more of the same—*Holy shit, What the hell?*—until I caught a glimpse of red hair that made me hit my brakes and double back.

But it was only the production assistant. Alison's friend. What's his name. Hugh.

He was lying on his bunk on his back, staring sightlessly and expressionlessly up at the ceiling, and for one disturbing second, I thought maybe he was dead.

But then he blinked and he wiped his face between his eye and his ear, and I realized he was lying there, crying.

I knew the boy was gay. I'd lived a long time and had learned a thing or two about being human, and how it's nature or even God, if that's what you believe in, that makes that choice for us—whether or not we'll be attracted to a woman or another man.

But I'd also learned that a man's a man regardless of who he loves, and this one cried the same way most men cried—in silent, private pain. It was the way I'd cried, before loving Mel had made me feel safe and secure enough to be willing to share such intimate emotions with her.

"Sorry, son," I told Hugh, before diving back in, and getting a face full of spider.

Now I was the one screaming *Holy shit,* and I kept screaming because in the next trailer over, I saw more naked yoga—this time being done by the rotund actor who was playing Dick Eversfield, the owner of the general store. I got an eyeful, too, of someone cutting up what I guessed were lines of cocaine, in between a cell phone talker, a cell phone talker, and yet another cell phone talker.

I came out the other side, longing for the ability to take a shower.

There were still more rows of trailers, and as good as the idea of surrender seemed, it just wasn't in my nature to give up.

There was a life at stake—whoever the woman was who'd witnessed Wayne's murder—and all I could think was that, were it Melody or even A.J.'s Alison who was being targeted, I'd sure as hell want me to go above and beyond in order to protect them. Whoever this was, she was, at the very least, someone's daughter. I knew what that was like, having had a daughter of my own.

So I went for it. Row three.

The trailers were getting smaller and shabbier and older, and the spiders and webs within the walls were now a given.

Most of these were occupied by two or sometimes three people, and sometimes I hit all of 'em on my pass through. But there was no sign of Charlotte, and it suddenly occurred to me that whomever she was delivering that tray to could well have been staying over in the motel. And I was just on the verge of turning around and making *those* rooms my next sweep when I saw it.

Charlotte's unmistakable red hair.

I only caught a glimpse, but I did know this— she was not alone. She was also not doing naked yoga, but whatever she was doing, like naked yoga, there was very little of her clothing involved. And whoever she was doing it with was saying, loud and clear, "Oh, God, oh, baby . . ."

I peeked back in, and yes, that was, absolutely, Charlotte.

And yes, she was engaging in an intimate

moment with a dark-haired man whose face I couldn't see because his back was to me as he diligently worked to pin her to the wall.

I quickly popped back out, hating the fact that I was violating Charlotte's privacy this way, and more than a little shocked by the level to which she seemed to be enjoying herself.

It didn't make sense.

When I'd overheard her conversation with Rob, back in the catering tent, I'd believed that she'd been prepared to share intimacies with their suspect, in order to get closer to the man, but I'd also believed—completely—that she would hate every minute of it. And I would've sworn on my third-born son's hero's grave in Arlington National Cemetery that she was merely pretending to be tough as nails.

But what I'd just seen was an extremely enthusiastic woman who was not faking her enjoyment. On the contrary, she'd looked as if she were *exactly* where she wanted to be and . . .

Huh.

I closed my eyes so that I was just barely able to see through my eyelashes, and stepped back into that trailer and . . .

Bingo.

In the few seconds since I'd left, the pair had ricocheted off that wall and over to the little built-in bed, where Charlotte had assumed the position of power.

She was a good-looking woman, even just from the back like that, and I got no surprises this time as I moved just a smidge closer so I could look to see exactly who was locked there, between her lovely legs, before I popped away, giving them the privacy they deserved.

And yes, fellow romantics, you are correct. It was none other than our old friend Rob. Who, no doubt, had finally pulled his head out of his ass, mere moments after I left the catering tent.

Now, I don't know for sure what had happened between *Nothing. Never mind,* and *Oh, God, oh, baby* . . . except for the obvious—that he'd followed her back here.

Maybe they'd had a big, long conversation where they'd each confessed their undying love. Or maybe Rob opened the trailer door and went inside and found her crying and one thing led to another. Or maybe he went in there, and they both just looked at each other, and suddenly clothes were being removed.

It could happen.

Clearly, *some*thing had happened.

I walked back to find A.J., careful to avoid any additional collisions with any living creature, human or arachnid.

As glad as I was for my FBI friends, I was still aware that my above-and-beyond efforts to find Charlotte had yielded no positive results—at least as far as finding either Gene or the mysterious

Loco, with whom the tall and ponytailed Killer of Wayne had spoken on the phone.

No doubt about it, I made a lousy caped crusader.

Despite my X-ray-comparable vision and built-in cloak of invisibility, I was back to square one.

I hadn't felt this helpless and ineffective since the last time I was in Jubilation, when I was sorely afraid that, despite my best intentions, I wouldn't be able to rescue Melody from the hell that she found herself in.

Although, back then, I was ready and willing to die trying.

Chapter Ten

July 10, 1898
Dear Diary,

He's working with them. He's made some kind of deal with that gang of outlaws who have caused such damage to this town and its inhabitants.

Last night, I heard voices in the kitchen, and went to see who could be visiting so late. It was the Texan—the gang leader, the man with the missing tooth.

He's come to scratch on the back door before, but I've dared not let him in.

But my husband did.

They were arguing now about money.

The Texan had given my husband what looked to be a small bag of silver. But the monster wanted more. He grabbed the Texan's shirt and pushed him hard, so that the back of the man's head hit the wall. I know how that feels. I've been in his shoes.

The Texan clawed at his throat, but the monster was holding his shirt, twisting it, choking him with it. I know what that feels like, too. I have felt the same rush of panic and desperate need for air.

Later, the Texan came back with a bigger bag.

"From now on, that's my share," *my husband said, and that was when I understood.*

They have bought him, this gang of killers and thieves, and I am not surprised.

I am surprised, though, by the realization that hope has once again been awakened within me. Perhaps I don't need the help of a stranger after all. . . .

Craig Lutz got really quiet.

"Yeah," A.J. said into the cell phone his mother had forced on him, as he sat in the shade behind the Red Rock Saloon—on the same steps where he'd sat with Alison just that morning. The steps where he hadn't kissed her. But he'd wanted to. "That's kind of what I thought, too. Time to take

231

a long, quiet vacation with the nice men in the white coats."

"Fuck you," Lutz said. "I didn't say that. I'm just . . ." He stopped, exhaled hard. "A.J., man, I'm just a little thrown, that's all. I mean, *Hi, how are you, Lutz? I've ignored your calls and emails for all this time, but I'm back on the planet, and I'm ten years sober*—ten freaking years, like you couldn't've called me nine of 'em ago?"

"No," A.J. said, answering honestly. "I'm sorry, but I couldn't."

Lutz was silent again. But then he said, "Fair enough. Who am I to dictate the way you should or shouldn't've embraced your newfound sobriety? But still, fuck you twice. I could've helped you, dipshit. I haven't exactly made a secret of the fact that I'm in the program, too. Shit, forget about me helping you—you could've helped *me.* I'm still scrambling my way to five years—same way I was five years ago. Although, this time? I'm the master of the steps. I'm doing them all. No screwing around."

"That's . . . good," A.J. said.

Even after nearly twenty years, Lutz could still read him like a book. "Shit," he said. "Really? Ten years and you haven't gotten past . . . what? Step four?"

"There were . . . things," A.J. tried to explain, "that I was trying to ignore. Things I still try to ignore."

"So are you really sober, sir?" Lutz asked bluntly. And when he called an officer *sir* that way, with that particular tone, what he really meant was *asshole*. "Or are you just a super-dry drunk?"

"Hang on," A.J. told him, just as tartly. "Let me ask the ghost of my long-dead great-grandfather what *he* thinks."

Lutz's laughter was so familiar. A.J. had to close his eyes against the sensation of time falling away. Suddenly, he was twenty-four years old again. An old man by army standards. An experienced officer, leading nineteen- and twenty-year-old troops into battle.

But he wasn't experienced half enough for what he'd seen, what he'd done. Most of it with Lutz, two years his senior and a Special Ops NCO, by his side.

A.J. still didn't know exactly what Lutz had been doing over there, what his top secret assignment was. All he knew was that the two men had found and identified each other as people who actually got shit done. And they'd become friends.

Lutz came and went—sometimes with his Navy SEAL teammates, sometimes by himself—but he'd nearly always been there when A.J. had needed him.

Nearly always.

"Ignoring all the bad shit doesn't make it go

away," Lutz said now. "It festers until you start self-medicating again. Or seeing ghosts. Is he a scary ghost or a friendly one?"

"Friendly," A.J. told him.

"Well, that's good at least."

A.J. had to laugh. Trust Lutz to find the bright side. But then he instantly turned it back to serious.

"You planning to tell her about Hor al-Hammar?" Lutz asked. "You know, the potential girlfriend— what's her name. Alison?"

"No," A.J. said. "Nope."

"So what's the big about not introducing her to the friendly ghost?" Lutz pointed out. "It's not like you're lying. You're just withholding private information. If she asks you if you've seen this ghost, you can say yes. If she doesn't ask . . . No harm, no foul."

"It's such a major thing to withhold," A.J. said.

"And Hor al-Hammar isn't?"

Good point.

"Odds are," Lutz said, "Hor al-Hammar is haunting you far more than your great-grampa ever could. From what you just told me, he was just filling my spot until you got your ass in gear and called me. He got you back in the habit of actually having a conversation, maybe asking for a little advice. Hey, you know what would really convince *me* that he was real? If he went into the future, just a few days, and found out the winning California SuperLotto numbers."

"I don't think he can time travel," A.J. said.

"Have you asked him?" Lutz asked. "Because if we win a few hundred million dollars? Neither one of us will ever have a problem getting laid again. You can be batshit crazy with that kind of money, my friend. And you'll still have three-ways, every night."

"I don't want three-ways," A.J. said.

"And there's the proof that you're batshit crazy," Lutz said, adding, "For what it's worth, you don't sound any *more* batshit crazy than you ever did before. I mean, yeah, if you're hallucinating, that's kinda weird. But the brain is a complicated organ. We only use, like, ten percent. Maybe you've started using more and you really can see old Grampa. Tell me this: Does he, like, tell you to do shit?"

"He told me to call you."

"Well, all right. I like him already," Lutz said.

"He wants me to tell Alison about him," A.J. said, running his hand down his face as he remembered Jamie in Alison's kitchen, singing that song from *Oklahoma!* A traveling theater troupe had come to Heaven and performed the show one weekend when A.J. was nine. He and Gramps had gone to see it every single night. Of course, it worked both ways. Gramps had gone to *Star Wars* with A.J. seven times in the months before he'd died.

"On that," Lutz said, "he and I will have to

235

agree to disagree. Hey, I'm kind of afraid to ask this, because the answer might be *dead,* but how's the über-sexy Dr. Rose?"

"You know," A.J. said, "I *still* hate it when you call her that."

"So . . . not dead?"

"Very not dead," A.J. said. Lutz's own mother had died just before A.J. had met him and his father was on the man's permanent persona non grata list. "She thought I should call you, too."

"She wants me," Lutz said. "Even after all these years."

"Yeah, I don't think so, Lutz."

"Face the facts, bro," Lutz said cheerfully, the same way he had when they'd talked about A.J.'s mother in the past. "She was a child when she had you. That plus the dominatrix thing that she's got going on—that ice queen attitude. *I will chew you up and spit you out without even breaking stride.* I find her undeniably hot. You don't have to agree. She's your mother, that's creepy, I know. But unless you've undergone an intense personality change, I happen to know that you still don't even bother to look twice at a woman who can't—somehow, in some way—kick your ass." He paused. "You *do* still go for women, don't you?"

A.J. laughed. "Uh, yeah."

"Wait," Lutz said. "That came out wrong. I didn't mean for it to sound so much like I was saying, *I hope to Christ you're not a homo.*

236

Because that's not what I meant. Remember Reilly, from my team? Big guy—bigger than me? Had that motorcycle that he'd fixed up that he used to ride all over Kuwait?"

"I remember Reilly," A.J. said. "He never said much, but he was hard to miss."

"Yeah, well, he's in the program now, too," Lutz said. "Three years—he's doing great. Anyway, turns out he's gay. He's always been, you know. Gay. Now that he's out, he actually talks. And smiles. He's happy—happier. His partner died around five years ago, and he went into the tank, hit bottom, and bounced instead of splattered. He was with this guy for, like, sixteen years—even back in Iraq. I never knew—don't ask, don't tell, you know?"

"I'm not gay," A.J. said.

"I'm just saying," Lutz pointed out, "that it's okay if you are. But all right. Alison's not really Albert—not that it would matter. But she's really a woman, so your strategy—if you really feel like you have to tell her about old dead Grampa— should be to shag her, then tell her. You do it the other way around, you won't get to the *shag her* part. She'll be out the door. But if you shag her first, like for about a week before you break the news, she'll have already bonded with you. She becomes *we*. And your problem—the fact that you're seeing a ghost, if that's really what you're seeing—becomes her problem, too."

"I don't know," A.J. said.

"Whoops, shit, I gotta go," Lutz said. "Look, I'll call you later and let you know if I can organize the equipment and manpower we'd need to re-create your gunfight out there in What-the-Fuck, Arizona. I'm pretty sure I can—either way, though, I'd love to come out. You know, just to get Winter Baxter's autograph. If that's okay with you."

"It would be great, actually," A.J. said. "I'd like to see you."

"Hey, Gallagher, I'm really glad you called me," Lutz said.

"Yeah," A.J. agreed, and even though he still didn't know what he was going to do about Alison, he found that he meant it. "Me, too."

July 16, 1898
Dear Diary,

He caught me. However did I think I could do this without any help?

But it worked—to a point. The Texan came to the door in the early hours of the morning, and this time I opened it. Just enough to take the bag of silver he offered. "I'll give it to my husband," I lied. I hid it instead. And I watched the clock as I served the monster coffee and cakes, and he finally, finally left the house.

I packed a small bag—only the essentials—

and was quickly ready to go. But when I arrived at the livery, his deputies were there. Just leaning against the walls, passing the time.

I pretended to visit the horses. My plan was to ask the stable hands to saddle up both mine and the monster's, as if we were going for a ride or a picnic, despite the blistering morning heat.

But I couldn't do that with his men watching.

All day they were there, and as the shadows grew longer, I prayed for them to leave.

Darkness fell, and I should have surrendered. I should have quickly unpacked my bag, left the silver on the table for him to find. I should have accepted that my plan was folly. Even if I had a horse, I had no map, no knowledge of the countryside, no real hope.

Perhaps I wanted to die.

First he screamed at me as he rushed in the door. Then I was the one to scream and cry as he hit me, hard enough to break a rib and bloody my nose.

This was the end. I was so sure. This was when he would kill me.

I almost welcomed it.

But then the door opened with a crash, and miraculously, amazingly, the monster stopped. There was a man in our house. The gambler.

The stranger I'd noticed when he'd first ridden into town. I'd seen him several times since then, and he always watched me, always smiling. Some men are drawn to golden hair. I had figured this man to be one of them.

But he was not smiling now. Cold anger was in his eyes and his gun was drawn and aimed at the monster's head.

"I will not stand idly by and let this continue," the gambler said, his voice so icy a chill went down my own spine.

My husband's hand moved toward his gun, but the gambler cocked his weapon.

"Move again," the gambler told him, "and I will not hesitate to gun you down."

"You'll hang for it," the monster said.

The gambler smiled, tipping his hat to me, but the ice did not leave his eyes. "Gladly," he said. "But I don't think so, considering what I know about you and the Kellys."

The monster ordered me upstairs.

I turned to look back at the gambler and his eyes were still on me, softer now, warmer, full of concern.

I wonder if he knows that no one has ever dared stand up to my monster of a husband before this. I wonder if he knows that he is the first to care to risk his own life for mine.

For the first time in years, I am more than just afraid. I don't know what this is that I feel, but it makes me want to weep, and that frightens me even more than the fear of the pain I know is sure to come my way.

I will pay for this gambler's gallantry. Not today, perhaps. Not tomorrow. But I <u>will</u> pay.

The wind was already starting to kick up when A.J. walked with Alison back to her office trailer.

They were both carrying dinner trays, which a very cheerful man named Rob had recommended they cover with Saran wrap before venturing out of the catering tent.

A spray of dust and dirt now bounced off that plastic, and A.J. closed his eyes to a squint, wishing he had the sunglasses that he'd left on the dashboard of his truck.

He'd dressed carefully in a clean pair of jeans and a shirt that Bev had bought him because she said it matched his eyes. He didn't see it, but who was he to argue with an older sister who, more often than not, *did* know best?

Alison, too, had gone to some effort to look nice. She was not only wearing gracefully flowing pants with her usual sandals, but a colorful scoop-necked top that wasn't particularly daring, unless he could somehow engage her in a post-dinner game of Twister.

She'd taken some pains with her hair, too—

although the wind now blew it around her face. A face to which she'd applied more than her usual amount of makeup. Not that she needed it.

But A.J. liked the extra eyeliner because of the message it sent. *I want to look good for you. You're special.*

"They canceled tonight's shoot," Alison told him as she wrestled her key into the door's lock. "We're supposed to get some weather—although out here it could just be wind and dust. No rain."

Canceled? "Does that mean you have the whole evening free?" he asked as he held out his hand to take her tray. She handed it to him, along with a smile of thanks as she used both hands to pull the door open.

"I do," she said. "An actual evening off. Imagine that."

"Except here I am, making you work," he pointed out, now holding the door with his hip. "I got it. Go ahead."

"Thanks." She took her tray back from him. "To be honest, this doesn't feel like work," she said, and went up the stairs first, leaving him standing there, smiling like a damn fool.

The lights were already on inside, the AC chugging away.

The cooler air felt good as A.J. latched the door behind him and followed her.

She'd done as she'd promised and cleared off her desk, pulling up a chair on the far side for A.J.

It was radically different from the last time he'd been in here. All of the stacks of papers and piles of books were gone.

"Wow," A.J. said and she smiled again.

"I actually filed," she told him as she set her tray down.

"I'm honored."

"You should be."

"Hey, kids." Jamie was already there, sprawled out on the leather couch, feet up, jacket off, sleeves rolled up, and tie loosened.

So much for his mother's theory that calling and talking to Lutz would make Jamie vanish. And so much for A.J.'s hopes that he could spend a few hours with Alison and pretend he was just another guy, like any other guy whose great-grandfather *wasn't* the American West's notorious and most often slandered outlaw.

"And how was *your* day, dear?" Jamie asked. "Mine was a bitch. Lotta spiders. Hey, I know this isn't on the official agenda, but would you do me a favor and see what Alison's heard—if anything—about the dead guy that was found forty-five miles north of town?"

"Please," Alison said, "sit."

And A.J. realized he was standing there, holding that tray, probably looking both disappointed and dismayed. And a little relieved. Which was understandable. During his early childhood, going back as far as he could remember, Jamie

243

had been his rock, his lifeline, his primary caregiver. For most of that time, A.J.'s mother had either been emotionally unavailable or working her butt off to get her degree.

And as much as A.J. complained, as frustrating as it was, as much as he feared for his sanity . . . Truth was, he enjoyed Jamie's company.

And maybe that's why the ghost was still here. Maybe he'd stay until A.J. truly wanted him to go.

But as far as what he wanted right now? That wasn't hard to figure out. He definitely didn't want Jamie sitting in on this, his first real date with Alison.

He'd made up his mind—that he was going to tell her the truth, that he saw and heard and spoke to Jamie, before moving their relationship, as she'd put it, to the naked level. He had to. And if, as Lutz had warned, that meant they didn't move to that level? So be it.

But he didn't want to do any of it tonight. He'd just wanted to sit across a dinner table—or desk as the case was—and look into her eyes as they talked.

A.J. put his tray on Alison's desk and looked hard at Jamie before he said, "I can't tell you how much I've been looking forward to this. Just the two of us." Hint, hint. "A chance to talk privately, without interruption . . ."

"I've been looking forward to it, too," Alison told him with a smile. "Except the part where you break my heart by trash-talking my homeboy, Silas Quinn."

"Yeah, kid," Jamie said, "I don't think so. You definitely need a chaperone. Look at the way she's looking at you. If I leave you alone with her, you'll be toast."

"I'm glad we could do this tonight," Alison continued as she used a pair of scissors to cut the plastic from her tray. "Because tomorrow's going to be crazy. Hugh and I are actually going out location scouting. Henry wants us to find a relatively flat, completely desolate part of the desert, where he can set up a camera and do a three-sixty pan. It's supposed to be Quinn's point of view, during the scene where he's gone after Gallagher and Melody? He didn't bring enough food or water, and he realizes that trying to rescue his wife could kill him—but he pushes on anyway."

She smiled at A.J. as she leaned forward to cut the wrap from his tray, too, and he made note of the fact that her bra was black. And almost nonexistent. And her body, beneath it, was very nice. He had to look away, down at the chili and rice that he'd chosen for his dinner. It smelled great, but not as great as Alison.

"Even you have to admit that that was heroic," she said. "To cross that particularly treacherous part of the desert, at the hottest time of the year . . . ?"

"Thanks," A.J. said as she sat back down.

"Except he didn't do it," Jamie said from the couch as they started to eat. "The lying sack. He got that far, realized he wasn't going to catch us, knew that he didn't have enough water, so he turned back. I'm pretty sure it was then, too, that he realized he could rob the Jubilation Bank and Trust and blame it on me. He went back, killed Bert Perry, the night guard at the bank, took and hid the money, and didn't cross the desert until a day later. Not until he was completely outfitted for it."

"Where are you going to be scouting tomorrow?" A.J. asked Alison.

"Henry wants us to head north, because that's the direction Quinn actually took," she said between mouthfuls. She, too, had picked the chili. "Oh, my God, this is delicious."

It *was* good. The dull aqua tray gave it a middle school cafeteria feel, but the food was four star, and they *did* provide linen napkins and real silverware.

Jamie sat forward. "You better tell her about dead Wayne. Well, don't call him Wayne, but—"

"I heard there was some kind of trouble up to the north," A.J. interrupted him. "A police investigation, someone found a body . . . ?"

"You're right," she said. "I did hear something about that—some hiker wandered off the trail, but they still need to make sure it wasn't foul play."

"Is that really the story they're putting out there?" Jamie said. "Because there are at least two FBI agents working undercover in the catering tent."

"Seriously?" A.J. slipped and said, but thankfully it worked equally well in his conversation with Alison.

"I'm sure it's just standard procedure," Alison said.

Jamie nodded and said, "Rob and Charlotte. I saw them checking out the pay phone where you called in the murder."

Rob was an FBI agent? Happy Rob with the Saran wrap? Go figure.

"Or was your *seriously* about the fact that a hiker could just die out there?" Alison asked. "If you're caught without water in the desert, you really don't last long. People die all the time. Didn't you get one of those packets when you filled out your employment information forms? *Do's and Don'ts in the Desert* . . . ?"

"No," A.J. said, "but . . . I'm aware."

"That's right," she said. "The First Gulf War."

He nodded.

She ate in silence for a moment, just watching him. It was clearly an invitation to tell her something—anything—about his time overseas, but A.J. just kept eating, too.

In the distance, thunder rumbled ominously and the wind whistled past the trailer.

"Well, thanks for the reminder," Alison finally spoke. "About the investigation. All we need are police helicopters on the horizon in a scene that's supposed to be 1898. We'll definitely want to keep our distance."

"That's probably a good plan," A.J. said. He put down his fork. "Can I . . ." He stopped. "May I ask you something?"

She opened the bottle of water that had come with her dinner and took a sip. "Of course."

"What's next for you?" A.J. said. "After the movie's finished?"

She wiped her mouth with her napkin. "Wrap party?" she said, but then acknowledged that she was kidding. "No, I know what you mean. I'm on sabbatical until the January semester, so . . . I'm probably going to use that time to write most of my next book. Provided Penny Eversfield's letters ever arrive." She smiled. "Of course, I can do it without the letters, and I will, but I'm hoping for some really candid information that will make the four hundred and thirty history buffs who buy my books swoon with delight."

He had to smile at that. "After this movie comes out, you're going to sell more books than that."

"Maybe," she said. "Maybe not."

"What if you write Jamie's book?" A.J. asked. "Jamie's story?"

"Ooh," Jamie said from the sofa, "I like that idea."

Alison held A.J.'s gaze. "In order to write it, I'd have to believe it," she told him. "Completely."

"I remember," he assured her. "Plus, you'd need twice the proof. That's the model I'm . . . hoping to work with."

She smiled, and A.J.'s pulse skipped. "Me, too," she said. "That's the . . . Model. I'd prefer. With a reminder that if you're lying—"

"I'm not."

"But if you are," she said, her voice trailing off in a dot-dot-dot. She didn't need to put words to her threat.

Because he wasn't going to lie to her.

"Kid," Jamie said, apparently unable to read A.J.'s mind, which was interesting. "Think about this. If you just—"

"I have been thinking about it," A.J. told him, told Alison, too. "I'm not lying—I'm not going to lie." He glanced at Jamie. "Okay?"

"Really?" Jamie asked.

"Really," A.J. told Alison, too. "But I'm wondering . . . What happens in January? You go back to Boston College . . . ?"

"That's the current plan," Alison answered. "Yeah. How about you? After the movie . . . ?"

"Back home," he said. "At least that's my plan. Currently."

She nodded. Laughed. "I hear you," she said. "May I be blunt and quit with the coded messages and just say, I think we're both on the same page?

I'm not looking for something long term, and I'm *certainly* not looking for anything long distance. But at the same time, I'm always willing to acknowledge that there's a chance—a slim chance, because I suck at relationships—that it could turn into something bigger or . . . I don't know exactly, but I'm not looking to force anything, and I'm definitely not going to hold my breath." She paused. "*Are* we on the same page?"

"Mostly," A.J. said, and then, because he'd just told her that he wasn't going to lie, he added, "I have a terrible track record with relationships myself, but . . . I don't know what it is about you. I'm just, um . . . Smitten."

"Nice one, kid," Jamie said with approval.

A.J. shot him a quick look—*Go. Away.*—and the ghost made a zipping and locking motion across his mouth, tossing away the imaginary key. As if that were going to help.

But now Alison was looking at A.J. the same way she'd looked at him in the alley, when she'd told him that she couldn't kiss him because she was working. "I am, too," she whispered. "Smitten. What a good word for it. And . . . how lovely that it's mutual."

A.J. nodded, looking back down at the dinner he'd barely touched. "How often does that happen?" he asked.

"Never," Alison said. She'd stopped eating, too.

"Once in a lifetime," Jamie murmured. "That's

250

what I've been trying to tell you, kid. Sorry. Sorry. I'll . . . Shhh."

It was a moment—a very nice moment—despite Jamie's interruption. A.J. was getting damn good at ignoring the man—it wasn't hard to do when he lost himself in Alison's pretty eyes.

And there they sat, gazing at each other, thunder rumbling more persistently now, but still in the distance, until Alison looked away first. She stabbed at a few kidney beans, pretending to eat. "Did you get a chance to call your grandfather?" she asked. "You know, to ask about Caldwell?"

Across the room, Jamie sat up straight. "Did she just say . . . ?"

"Caldwell James Gallagher, known to his friends as Wells," A.J. repeated for Jamie's benefit, because the ghost hadn't been there when Alison had first brought up the subject of his older brother. And face it—the idea of Jamie sitting there silently was a ludicrous one. If he were there, he might as well contribute. "The theory being that Caldwell didn't die back in 1891, that he was Austin James's cohort in the robbery of the Jubilation bank. That he survived even though Jamie and Melody didn't, and he went to Alaska and started calling himself Jamie and settled down with a woman that he told me and the rest of the family was Melody Quinn, but really wasn't."

Alison was amused. "Nicely summarized."

"Wells was dead," Jamie said flatly. "He died—the same day I left Philadelphia."

A.J. glanced at him. *Go on.*

But the ghost shook his head. "I don't want to talk about it."

And wasn't that the ultimate irony.

"I haven't reached him yet," A.J. told Alison. "Adam. It's possible he knows, but . . . I'm betting he doesn't."

"He doesn't," Jamie said. He was disgusted. "I knew, Mel knew, but that was it. What the hell does *Wells* have to do with—"

"When you talk to him," Alison instructed, "ask him if your great-grandfather ever mentioned his reasons for leaving Pennsylvania. The thing I find curious is that Jamie's not the only Gallagher who wasn't buried in the family plot. It's understandable why he's not—he was a black sheep, he left home and broke the law, his family disowned him—the list is long. Plus he was killed—according to my information, okay? Let's not throw down about that right now. But according to my sources, he died in the middle of the desert in the summer, and was buried by Quinn right where he fell. But Caldwell . . ." She shook her head. "Records show he died in Philadelphia. But we just have that single piece of information—the date of his death. We don't know why he died—was he sick, was there an accident?—plus no one I've spoken to has any idea why he wasn't buried with the rest of his family."

Over on the sofa, Jamie was still grimly shaking his head. "Wells wasn't buried with the family," he said, "because he supposedly killed himself, and they wouldn't lay him to rest in consecrated ground. He blew out his brains, right in my father's study—at least that's how the old man's story goes. But it's not the truth. I saw what really happened. That gun was in my father's hand. He shot Wells, his own son, right in the face, point-blank."

Jesus.

A.J. pushed his chair back from the desk, put his napkin on the tray. "I'm sorry," he said to Alison. "May I, um, use your bathroom?"

She pointed down toward the narrow little door at the far end of the trailer. "You okay?"

"Yeah," he said. "I just, um . . . Excuse me." He shot Jamie a look as he went past the sofa.

The bathroom was tiny, like something you'd find in a train, with a sink that pulled down from the wall, directly over the toilet. A.J. closed the door behind him, turned on the fan overhead and it rattled and bumped as it fought the wind outside—but Jamie didn't appear.

"Come on, Gramps," A.J. said softly, aware of how thin these walls were.

And Jamie appeared. He stood petulantly in the tiny shower, arms crossed.

"Now you see why I didn't want to talk about it," he said, his mouth a tight line. "It didn't have anything to do with anything."

"You saw your father murder your brother," A.J. pointed out as quietly as he could manage. "It has everything to do with everything. To start, it made you leave home."

"I was gonna do that anyway. Just maybe not quite that soon." Jamie sighed. "I really shouldn't have told you, kid. You didn't need to know. It was an awful thing. For years, I blamed myself. I didn't stop him. I didn't even try."

"You were fifteen," A.J. reminded him.

Before this, he'd never quite understood why Jamie had left home. He'd always thought that his great-grandfather had been a spoiled rich boy, playing the outlaw, getting away—quite literally—with highway robbery. Somehow he'd survived the thieving phase of his career, and by the time he'd hit his late teens, he'd gained a reputation as a professional gambler, in possession of one hell of a quick draw and not a whole lot of scruples when it came to winning the game.

A.J. had always thought that Melody, by needing to be rescued, had somehow tamed Jamie. Forced him, out of necessity, to grow up. To man up. But now it was clear that there was so much more to the old family legend.

"I was the only witness to the murder," Jamie

told him now as the fan rattled overhead. "And I heard my father telling the servants to call the police as well as the parish priest. I heard him lie and say that Wells had killed himself."

As Jamie spoke, he changed, and A.J. realized that he was getting smaller, younger. Right before A.J.'s eyes, he became the fifteen-year-old boy that he'd once been, with shaggy dark hair, his face rounder, more like a child's, his frame slighter, skinnier.

"And I knew, in that instant, if I claimed that my father killed Wells, it would come down to his word against mine." Jamie shook his head. "And I would lose."

"Why would he kill his own son?" A.J. asked softly.

"I don't know," the boy said, confusion and disbelief in his brilliant blue eyes. "I didn't hear the beginning of the fight, but I did hear the raised voices, so I came downstairs to see what was happening. I stayed in the hall, because it didn't make sense. Wells didn't fight with my father—I did. He was the golden boy. He could only do right—*I* was the family screw-up. But then, that day . . . I couldn't hear what my father was saying. He'd stopped shouting, but Wells was crying. He was . . . just weeping, and he just kept saying *I'm sorry, I'm sorry.* . . . I don't for the life of me know what he did. But whatever it was, sorry wasn't good enough. Not for my father.

255

When he pulled that gun, I was so surprised. I couldn't believe it was more than a melodramatic threat. A stage prop to gesture with. I didn't believe it was loaded, but it was. He never loaded it, it was a showpiece, but this time he must've done it in advance. It was goddamn premeditated murder—he was intending to use it. And he pointed that thing at Wells and he said—and I remembered this to the day I died: *I gave you life, boy, and it's mine to take it away at will.* And he pulled that trigger. I saw him do it, but I never told anyone."

Just like that, he was back—the twenty-something man. "Except Mel," Jamie said, in his deeper, grown-up voice. "I told Mel, of course. Because the sins of the fathers are not revisited upon their children, I don't care what it says in Exodus—that's just plain wrong. A child is innocent and cannot be blamed for his father's crimes. And this I don't just believe—this I know. And I told her about my father, so that she would understand."

"I'm sorry you went through that," A.J. whispered.

"I wish Wells *had* gone west with me," Jamie told him. "Whatever he'd done, I would've forgiven him. He brought such light and life to everything he did. He was one of God's miracles, truly gentle and kind. But he died, Age. Alison's grasping at straws."

A.J. nodded. "If you don't want me to, I don't have to tell her about—"

"No," Jamie said. "It's all right. You can tell her whatever you want. You know, consecrated ground or not, I've run into Wells a few times. In the after. But I've never come face-to-face with my father. I'll let you do that math." He motioned toward the door with his head. "You better get back out there. But first . . ." He pointed to the handle of the john.

Right. "Thanks," A.J. said, and flushed, running the water a bit in the sink, too.

He unlocked the door and . . .

Alison was sitting behind her desk, wearing that nice shirt, with her pretty face made up just a little bit more than usual. And he should've said, *Hey, sorry about that. I just had to have a private conference with the ghost of my great-grandfather who, it turns out, witnessed a brutal murder as an impressionable child.* But instead, he said, "The cemetery where the Gallaghers are buried. It just occurred to me—that's probably consecrated ground."

"Whoa," she said, and the questioning look in her eyes—*Did you seriously just get up to take a leak in the middle of our dinner conversation, practically right after saying you were smitten with me . . . ?*—instantly was replaced by realization. "You're right. I never thought of that, but . . . Suicide. Of course. If Caldwell Gallagher had killed himself, he wouldn't have been allowed to be buried there." She reached down to open a drawer and pulled out a legal pad and pen, and made a note on it. "There also wouldn't have been any news about it—a suicide—in the papers. The Gallaghers were powerful enough to hush up something like that—and they would've wanted to. Imagine the talk."

"I actually just remembered," A.J. said as he sat down across from her. And it wasn't a lie, because he *did* just remember Jamie telling him this, even though it was only moments earlier, "Jamie talking about witnessing something terrible—something his father did—the day he left home for good."

"Something his *father* did," Alison asked. "Not his brother? Although, wow, here's a theory—when you bring suicide in as a possible reason for the lack of both Caldwell's grave and any newspaper articles about his death, it's also possible that a family as powerful as the Gallaghers covered up a murder by calling it a suicide. Can you imagine? If Jamie killed Caldwell and then ran?"

"No," A.J. said. "That's not—"

"Just hear me out," she interrupted him. "It's just a theory, but it's a good one. What if Jamie kills Caldwell and runs, only his father knows the family reputation will be in jeopardy if there's a huge manhunt, so he covers it up. Caldwell's

258

death is called a suicide, and Jamie's disowned by the family."

"Except that's not what happened," A.J. said.

"But you don't know what happened," Alison pointed out. "You just said that yourself."

And there it was.

The perfect invitation to tell her how he *hadn't* known what had happened a few minutes ago when he'd said just that, and yet how he *did* know now.

I see dead people. . . .

Lightning flashed outside, lighting the windows and brightening the room even more. A.J. braced himself for the thunder, but it was still relatively far away.

"I'll see what Adam knows," he said instead.

Alison nodded as she flipped a page on her pad. "Why don't we get a record of what you *do* know. You told me this morning that Gallagher first came to Jubilation in July."

"July 8, 1898," A.J. confirmed.

"Right around the same time that the Kelly Gang returned to town," she commented.

"That's not quite true." A.J. glanced over to Jamie, who was back on the couch. It was hard, now, to look at him without seeing that young boy who'd witnessed a horrible crime—and had left home rather than live in wealth and comfort with a father who'd literally gotten away with murder.

It was funny how, now that he knew what to

look for, he saw the echoes of that boy within the adult's face. And he wondered if Jamie, while looking back at A.J., saw traces of the little boy that *he'd* once been, as well as pieces of the twenty-four-year-old army lieutenant who'd seen enough death and destruction for a lifetime, and then some.

"Early July was definitely when the Kellys returned to Jubilation," Alison said. "It's not just Quinn's word on this one. There's a whole list of people who made a point of mentioning they'd seen Bo Kelly and his boys back at the Red Rock Saloon."

"The Kellys were definitely at the saloon," A.J. told her. "They were in town, but I wouldn't've called it *back*. They'd never left the area. They were still around, even after Quinn pretended to run them out of Jubilation some months earlier."

"Pretended." Alison smiled.

"My apologies," A.J. said, smiling back at her, "for commencing the crushing of your girlhood fantasies."

"You haven't crushed anything yet."

"I'm getting there," A.J. said. "How does the legend go? The Kellys had control of Jubilation, so Marshal Quinn was called in and he cleaned up the place in less than a week, running Bo and company out of town. Am I right?"

"In a nutshell," Alison confirmed. "Yeah. I'd add that Silas made a point to leave Melody behind, until he was satisfied that Jubilation was safe enough for women and children. You do know that Melody was pregnant when Silas left for Arizona, but she miscarried while he was away . . . ?"

"Nope." Jamie spoke up from across the room. "She just told him she was pregnant so he wouldn't hit her as hard."

"That, too, falls under the not-true category, but I want to focus on the Kelly Gang for now," A.J. said as Alison tapped the end of her pen on her pad. "Like I said, Quinn didn't run them out of town. He cut a deal with them."

She laughed. "With Bo Kelly, whom he killed at the Red Rock?"

"Things were going south between them," A.J. said, telling her the story that Jamie had told him, countless times. "At the beginning, though, Bo worked with Quinn, to make it look like the marshal was some kind of superman. He shows up, the Kellys run. High drama. On top of that, Quinn had what was essentially a *hands-off* list. People who'd paid for protection didn't get hit—not just in town, but in the surrounding mines as well. Everyone else was up for grabs. They either learned to pay up, or they were robbed and sometimes even killed. It was effective marketing. Although there were key streets in town—Main and River in particular—where everyone was safe. Which increased the property values for those addresses—conveniently for Quinn, who took a lot of his initial fees in land."

"There were definitely parts of town," Alison argued, "that took a little bit longer to get cleaned up. And yes, there was still crime in Jubilation. Silas couldn't control who came into town—the fact that Gallagher could just stroll in is a case in point."

"Quinn got a cut of the Kellys' take," A.J. told her, pushing his tray slightly to the side. He was long done with attempting to eat dinner. "He was working both sides of the game. And even though *he* couldn't control who strolled into town, the Kelly Gang usually did. They had a good deal going, and they didn't want someone else undercutting them. They happened to be fine with Jamie coming in, because they knew his reputation. They knew he'd be a better target to rob when he was on his way *out* of town, after he'd won a few dozen poker pots and liberated quite a few miners from their silver. They couldn't hit those select miners, right, because they were on Quinn's list, but they could hit Jamie Gallagher after he took their silver. It was a big win."

Alison sighed, because she saw the logic to it. But she wasn't done arguing. "Still, you're telling me that a band of outlaws spent *all* of their time in the hills outside of Jubilation, and never came into town for so much as a bath in the hotel?"

"They had all the comforts they needed," A.J. said. "Jamie told me he saw their camp, and it was just fine. Quinn gave them access to women and alcohol. And when they wanted a place to spend their silver, which they were raking in, hand over fist, they would ride into Tucson. Or down into Nogales, to Mexico. And of course, there were also the times when they showed up back in Jubilation—so Quinn could run 'em off again. Make sure the townfolk appreciated all his hard work."

"And none of those 'folk' in town cared that Silas Quinn—their U.S. marshal—was profiting from their misfortune?" she asked.

"He wasn't just profiting from theirs," A.J. said. "Quinn used to send the Kellys out to other towns, at which point he'd ride in and bring law and order. For a fee."

"That's what U.S. Marshals did back then," Alison said. "I know it sounds mercenary—"

"They didn't do what Quinn did," A.J. told her. "They didn't have a deal going with the outlaws who were causing the trouble."

"Why didn't anyone complain?" Alison asked. "No one in town said, *Hey, this is unusual. It seems as if Silas Quinn is always after Bo Kelly and his boys. . . .*"

"Bo had a lot of men," A.J. said. "And remember, Quinn did ride in and quiet things down. People didn't know, though, that he was responsible for stirring up trouble in the first place. And as for the good people of Jubilation—nobody knew about the money Quinn was getting from the Kellys. Nobody but Melody."

"And me," Jamie said.

"And Jamie," A.J. told Alison. "See, he'd had a recent losing streak at cards, and this one evening, things started to turn around and he began winning again. Only he was playing with Bo Kelly, who kept throwing his I.O.U. into the pot. Jamie wasn't about to let that much cash walk out of his sight, so without Bo knowing, he followed him back to his camp up in the mountains. And who does he see, hanging with the Kelly boys—with five of the territory's ten most wanted—just waiting for Bo to get back from town?"

"I'm supposed to say Silas Quinn, right?" Alison asked.

A strong gust of wind rocked the trailer, making the ice tinkle in the glass of lemonade he'd gotten with his dinner, and A.J. paused. "Is it really okay to be in this thing in a storm like this?"

"I think we're okay," she reassured him, "unless it's a tornado. Two-thirds of the cast and crew are housed in trailers. I'm sure they'll call us if we need to evacuate."

"Come on, kid," Jamie said. "She's actually taking notes."

"Where was I?" A.J. asked.

"Silas Quinn, hanging with the Kelly Gang,"

Alison said, as Jamie told him, "I'd just followed Bo Kelly back to camp, and saw Quinn there, waiting for him."

"Right," A.J. said. "So Jamie's sticking to the shadows. No one knows he's there, and he overhears Quinn and Bo start to argue. Quinn's angry about something, about some missing bag of silver. His week's payment is what Quinn called it."

Thunder rolled, ominous and no longer quite so distant, but Alison's full attention was on him, so he kept going.

"Bo told Quinn they were down a bit that week," A.J. told her. "A few of his boys had been shot in a scuffle up at one of the mines, and the take was slimmer than usual.

"But that's not what Quinn's upset about. Turns out he hasn't even seen this week's payoff. He's there to collect, only Bo tells him, no, he's already paid him off. He says he dropped the silver at Quinn's house early that same morning—right on schedule. He says he left it with Mrs. Quinn. With Melody. Before Quinn had even risen for his morning meal.

"Well," A.J. continued. "Quinn took off out of there like a bat out of hell, and Jamie followed. He'd only been in town for a few weeks, and he'd only gotten a few short glimpses of Melody in that entire time, but he'd seen enough to be wary of what the marshal might do to his wife when he caught up with her."

"I was scared to death for her," Jamie said. "Quinn was furious. I truly thought that he might kill her."

"When Jamie made it back to town, to Quinn's house on River Street, Quinn was already there, already inside, and already shouting," A.J. told Alison.

"I could hear his voice, but not the words," Jamie remembered. "He sounded goddamn crazy. And then I heard something break and, then, God, Mel . . ."

"There was a crash," A.J. said, "and Melody screamed, which is when Jamie kicked the door in and told Quinn that the violence had to stop."

"He kicked down Quinn's door and the marshal didn't kill him?" Alison didn't sound convinced.

"The marshal was otherwise engaged," Jamie said, and A.J. told her that.

"Jamie drew on him and the two men stood there, at an impasse," A.J. continued, "because Jamie knew as soon as he backed down, as soon as he walked away and that door closed behind him, Quinn would start in on Melody again, and maybe this time, he'd kill her.

"So he did the only thing he could, short of pulling her out of there—which he had no right to do, since, well, I assume you know that Melody was considered to be Quinn's lawful property."

"I'm aware of that, yes," Alison said. "At that time, women were . . . Yes."

266

"Killing Quinn right there and then was a possibility," Jamie interjected. "I considered it, but knew if I did I'd hang."

"He blackmailed the marshal," A.J. told Alison. "In an attempt to keep Melody safe. He made a deal of his own with Quinn. As long as he refrained from beating his wife, Jamie would keep his mouth shut about Quinn's little financial arrangement with the Kelly Gang. He took a cut of Quinn's share, while he was at it. He figured Quinn wouldn't understand—wouldn't trust him to stay silent if there wasn't an additional payoff of some kind."

Alison leaned forward. "I'm not sure I understand. Why would Jamie risk so much for someone he says he didn't know. Is it possible that part's been conveniently misremembered?"

A.J. glanced over at Jamie, who'd stretched out on the sofa, feet up, arms folded up behind his head. "*Why* is a good question."

"It's God's truth," Jamie said. "Mel and I hadn't exchanged as much as a hello before that night. And I was no hero, so why I should suddenly start acting like one, I can't explain. Sure, I wanted Melody in my bed, but . . . At first I tried to tell myself that I only wanted her for the thrill of the hunt. Seducing the marshal's wife would be a kick. He was a son of a bitch, and I tried to tell myself that if I had her, I'd be hurting him. Double the pleasure, you know, kid? But in truth? That wasn't it at all."

Alison was just watching A.J. Waiting for him to speak.

So he spoke. "I think," he said slowly, "that even then, even before Jamie really knew Melody, he saw something special in her. Something that he didn't want to live without."

"Did it work?" Alison asked. "You know. Jamie's blackmail. Did it keep Melody safe?"

"For a little while," A.J. told her. "Of course, it made Jamie a target. Quinn had to get rid of him. And that's what it was about, you know. The shoot-out at the Red Rock. The Kelly Gang wasn't after Quinn. They were *with* him. They were part of an ambush, set up to kill my great-grandfather. And the only reason he survived is because Melody came to the saloon to warn him."

Chapter Eleven

Alison sat in her office trailer with a man who believed that the shoot-out at the Red Rock Saloon—*the* most notorious and heroic gunfight in the history of the American West—was all about Silas Quinn's criminal need to silence a man who had seen and heard too much.

And Jamie Gallagher had survived not by dumb luck or blind chance, but because Melody—Mrs. Silas Quinn—had ventured outside the safety of her home, in the middle of the night, risking not just her reputation but her life, to warn him.

"Okay," Alison said.

A.J. Gallagher blinked at her. Frowned very slightly. "Okay?" he repeated.

She nodded. "Okay," she said again. "Let's have it. The rest of the story. I'm curious, though. Why did Jamie and Melody wait so long to leave Jubilation? The shoot-out was early in the morning on Tuesday, July twenty-sixth—unless you're disputing that, too."

"I'm not," A.J. said. "That's really when it happened."

"Oh, good," she said. "At least we got something right."

He smiled at her sarcasm, his crow's feet crinkling attractively around his eyes. "The battle took a hell of a lot less time than Quinn said it did, though."

"I don't think he said how long the gunfight went on," Alison pointed out.

"Implied," A.J. corrected himself. "He kind of implied it was long and drawn out. But it was over pretty fast."

"I took that as hyperbole," she said, sitting back in her chair as outside the wind picked up and pushed at the trailer, almost as if a thug or two were throwing a movie star against its flimsy side. Funny how, after that incident, Trace Marcus had been keeping mostly to himself. And showing up on time.

The lights flickered and she mentally located

her candles. Top drawer, right side. Matches were in there, too.

She tapped her pen on her pad again. "According to Quinn, it was another two and a half weeks after the shoot-out before Gallagher grabbed Melody and ran. Why not just go then, on the twenty-sixth? If she was in such a hurry to leave with him . . . ?"

A.J. was always so deliberate, as if taking a moment to think his answers through. He paused again now, before saying, "Because that was the very first time they spoke—in that back room at the Red Rock, the night before the gunfight. Melody didn't know him, didn't trust him. But he'd saved her life a week earlier, when he'd kicked in Quinn's door, and she was returning the favor."

"It *is* a romantic story," Alison started to say, but the door blew open with a startling crash as a solid swirl of dirt and dust blew inside.

Alison was on her feet along with A.J., but she was behind the desk. She didn't get more than a few feet around it before he was down the steps, grabbing the door and pulling it shut.

He coughed as he latched it, but then had to grab the frame to keep from losing his balance as another gust of wind rocked the trailer.

"Damn, it *does* look like hell out there," he said.

Alison went to the window and pulled back the curtains and . . . He was right. Dirt was chokingly

270

thick in the air and flashes of lightning gave the sky an eerie red-orange glow.

"I hope it starts to rain," Alison said, "or we won't be able to leave here. Can you imagine going out in that? It'd be like getting sandblasted."

Lightning flashed again, and she jerked away from the window, startled, as thunder cracked, almost right overhead. And the sky opened up—not with rain, but with what sounded like hail. Large, noisy pieces of hail, bouncing off the metal roof of her trailer.

Alison started to laugh at the din, which was when the lights flickered one last time, and went out.

Hail, even hail this size, went right through me without any problem.

So I went outside, because I had some experience with a certain type of a trailer, similar to this, known as an RV or recreation vehicle.

Now, it was true it had been some decades since my daughter, Rebecca, and her best friend, Irma, convinced me to set out with them on a road trip through the lower forty-eight. That was back in 1958, in fact. Their children were grown—they'd both had the challenging task of raising them on their own, since neither of their husbands had returned from World War Two.

They'd joined households in 1945 in order to

put those kids through college, and had been housemates ever since.

They traveled a lot—even going to the South Pacific, to the Philippines, to places called Guadalcanal and Leyte Gulf, where their young husbands had died.

But that one summer of '58, they dragged me from Portland to Chicago to Key West and over to the Grand Canyon—who knew such a thing of beauty was lurking a few hundred miles from Jubilation's dusty hills?

But my point here isn't to provide a travelogue of our journey, but instead to state that every time we stopped for the night in that little trailer we pulled along behind our Buick station wagon, if we thought we were going to get any kind of weather at all, we'd anchor that damn thing down so it didn't bounce around or blow over.

Now, I'm sure technology has changed, but as I walked around outside of Alison's trailer, I did not see any anchors whatsoever, tying that puppy in place.

Next trailer over? Guy wires and hooks. True, it was a different make, different model. But the one after that? Little support feet that came out from the side of the thing. The one after that? More wires and hooks.

The wind was howling now, and Alison's trailer was quite definitely listing to one side.

I went back inside, where Alison was shouting

over that racket on the roof, "Well, I *thought* I put some candles in this drawer. *Crap.* Where *are* they?"

I could see quite well in the dark—part of that being-dead thing—so I found A.J. and spoke in his ear. "This thing's gonna blow onto its side. You need to get yourself and the girl out of here."

"Alison, you have a jacket?" A.J. called.

"I don't," she called back. "Oh, maybe I put the candles in the bottom drawer."

"*Now,* Age," I told the kid as the trailer was buffeted again, and one of those food trays went off the desk and onto the floor with a crash.

"Oh, shit," Alison said.

"She doesn't have a jacket," he said through his teeth.

"What?" Alison called.

"How about a blanket?" A.J. asked. "Something to wrap around yourself?"

Even in the darkness, I could see her surprise. "No. There's nothing. . . . Paper. I have lots of paper and books. Are we going someplace?"

"We need to get out of here," A.J. told her, moving toward her. I could hear him rustling something, and then he said, "Here, put this on," and I realized he'd given her the shirt off his back.

"What?" she said. "Why?"

"Wind's pretty intense in a storm like this," he said. "There's stuff flying around that could cut you. You need to cover yourself up—put it over your head, kind of like Cornholio."

She laughed. "Oh, my God, when was the last time I had dinner with someone who brought up Cornholio? I think maybe I love you."

A blast of wind hit the trailer and I thought it was done. I thought we were going over, and it wasn't going to be pretty with those massive file cabinets and bookshelves shifting around. But the damn thing rocked back down, thank God.

Alison, meanwhile, got the hurry memo. She pulled on A.J.'s shirt. "Where are we going?" she asked. "Shouldn't we have a destination in mind?"

"My truck," A.J. said. "It's in the motel parking lot—halfway between us and the motel. Give me your hand. You ready?"

"Hail stopped," I reported, "but still no rain."

I was more than ready, but Alison hit the brakes. "Wait! Oh, my God. You're . . . You gave me your *shirt . . . ?*"

Lightning flashed and lit up the inside of the trailer, where Alison had her hand on A.J.'s bare arm. He was tying one of the linen napkins around the bottom half of his face, jamming his hat down on his head.

"I can't take your shirt, Gallagher," she said, but A.J.—good man—wasn't going to stand there and argue.

"Let's go," he said, and pulled her out into the maelstrom.

• • •

This was crazy.

As soon as Alison stepped outside, at the very first blast of sand and dirt, she was glad she had A.J.'s shirt. She held it tightly around her, over her head, leaving only a very small hole to peer out of.

Exactly like Cornholio. God, she was old.

And God, the flying dirt and dust stung, even through her clothes. What it felt like to A.J., she could only imagine.

"Lead the way," he shouted, but he must've been saying *I'll lead the way,* and the *I'll* had been lost in the buffeting wind, because he moved purposely away from the trailer.

The sand was so thick, it was like being in whiteout conditions, and Alison immediately lost her sense of direction, even of up and down. It was suffocating, blinding, almost like being buried alive. She stumbled, and A.J.'s arm went around her, holding her tightly, keeping her from falling.

He brought his mouth close to her ear. "Are you okay?"

"Yes." She was okay—if *okay* meant being barely able to breathe, and scared half to death. And ick, that would teach her to open her mouth in a dust storm. She was going to be spitting out sand for weeks.

"Halfway there," he told her.

How did he know that? And clearly he either liked the idea of sandblasting his teeth and gums, or he cared more about being able to talk to her, to reassure her.

Lightning flashed, and for the briefest of instants, Alison found herself looking up, directly into A.J.'s eyes. Her body was molded against his, and they were nose to nose—or rather linen napkin to shirt. She heard him half growl, half laugh in frustration, and she knew without a doubt that if their mouths hadn't been covered, he would have kissed her.

And the really stupid thing was that she would have kissed him back. Right there, in the middle of this craziness.

Her grandmother's expression—*Too stupid to come in out of the rain*—flashed through her mind, but it wasn't raining. Not even close.

A.J. pulled her forward, half carrying her. Visibility was nearly zero, yet he seemed to have some kind of sixth sense or radar that told him exactly where to go.

"Oh, shit," he said, his voice a rumble with her head against his chest. "Is anyone hurt?" Then, "Are you sure? Be *sure*."

Who are you talking to? Was he actually on the phone? Alison was just about to ask, when a tumbleweed slammed against her legs—at least she thought it was a tumbleweed. Whatever it was, it hit her with enough force to knock her over. But A.J. was there, holding on to her, somehow keeping their balance.

And then, thank God, his truck appeared, parked on the edge of the motel lot, just as he'd said. It was an older model, he couldn't beep the door open—he had to use a key. But he had it out and ready, and he pulled the door open, and pushed Alison inside.

He climbed in right behind her and slammed the door shut.

Inside the truck, the sound of the storm was muted. They both sat in silence, just catching their breath.

If he'd been on the phone, he was off it now.

Alison pulled A.J.'s shirt off her head, and dirt hissed as it fell from her hair and clothes and hit the vinyl seats and floor mat. She felt abraded and battered—and could only imagine how he was feeling. His entire upper body had been exposed.

But he didn't do more than glance at her before he put the key in the ignition and turned over the engine. He switched on the lights, and they did little to cut through the dust. But he put the truck in gear, moving slowly, maneuvering around so that . . .

"Oh, my God," Alison said.

He'd pointed his truck's headlights at her row of trailers, where her office was no longer standing. It had blown over, exactly as he'd predicted, and it lay on its side, partly crushed.

Alison reached for the door handle. "Someone might be under that!"

"No," A.J. said, reaching out to stop her. "There's not."

"You don't know that," she said. "You can't know that."

"But I do," he said. "There's not. Although, shit, there's at least one other trailer that isn't properly anchored. Two, maybe . . . Three. Fuck! Four? Excuse me. Sorry. I was, um, looking at them, earlier, yeah, and I noticed . . . *Damn it.*" He rummaged back behind the bench seat and pulled out what looked like a rain slicker, yellow with a hood, and started jamming his arms into it. "Can you drive?"

"Of course I can drive," Alison said as he zipped it up. He tossed his hat behind the seat and pulled the jacket's hood up, tightening it around his face. "That's kind of a weird thing to ask—"

"I've never seen you drive." He spoke over her, reached over her, too—to open his glove compartment and pull out a bandanna. "Give me a break. Some people don't drive. But okay, you drive. That's great. I need you to drive. We're going to evacuate the trailers that aren't anchored—along with the ones downwind of 'em. We'll get the people into the truck, and get them over to the motel." He handed the bandanna to her. "If you get out, put this on. But don't get out—I need you to drive. Slowly, because it's

278

hard to see. Second row of trailers, fifth one down. We're going to work our way west. When we clear out this one, I'll tell you where the next one is. Do you understand?"

Alison nodded.

"Good," he said, and he kissed her—hard—on the mouth before he yanked that linen napkin back up over his face, and vanished into the night.

It was starting to rain.

Everyone had been warned of the danger, and, where necessary, moved over to the motel. But A.J.'s evening activity wasn't over yet.

Alison was by the motel lobby, talking—with many large gestures—to her production assistant friend, Hugh, whose red hair was getting plastered to his head from the rain. Now that all of the people were safe, she was turning her attention to her next priority.

"Yeah, but I've still gotta figure out where all these people are going to sleep," Hugh was telling her.

"But some of those books are irreplaceable," Alison said. "Yes, I have digital copies of everything, but that's not the point. The historical value of the *books themselves*—"

"Is this what you're looking for?" A.J. interrupted her, holding out the tarp that Jamie had found and A.J.'d borrowed from whatever department was responsible for setting up extra tents.

"Bless you," Alison said.

"I've already checked it out," A.J. told her as they hurried over to her toppled trailer. "The seams are all holding and I was able to secure the door. That's the biggest potential leak point—it's not designed to keep water out from that angle."

Now that the trailer's center of gravity was lower to the ground, it wasn't going anywhere. Although it was also true that the wind seemed to be less strong. Or maybe it just felt less powerful now that it was sending water, instead of dust and dirt, into his face.

There were plenty of places to tie down the tarp, and with Jamie's help, they made swift work of it.

Not swift enough, though, to keep from getting soaked.

And not that it really mattered, since he was already drenched with perspiration. Nothing like wearing a hooded and rubber-lined raincoat in eighty-degree heat, although A.J. had pulled back the hood and unzipped the front as soon as the rain washed the dust from the air.

The water was cool, and he tried to pull the jacket away from his back as they walked to his truck—to let the rain soothe his roughed-up skin.

It was coming down in buckets. It was kind of funny actually—like walking through a car wash.

He unlocked the door to his truck, but Alison shook her head. "I'm a mess. I'm not getting in there."

"It's easy enough to clean," he said, trying to convince her, but she just kept shaking her head, no. So he locked the truck. Pocketed the keys. Gestured toward River Street. "I'll walk you home."

Jamie sighed as the rain passed right through him. He clearly foresaw disaster, but he knew there was no point in arguing. There was no way A.J. *wasn't* going to see Alison safely home.

"You're doing more than dropping me at the door," Alison informed him. "You're coming in so I can make sure you're okay."

"I'm fine," A.J. said.

"Give it up, kid," Jamie told him. "She knows there's a reason you haven't taken that jacket off. In fact, maybe you should do it now, so her first look at your back isn't in brighter light."

"It's not that big a deal." A.J. aimed his words at Alison, who was wearing her *I don't believe you* face. "It feels like I've got a sunburn. A mild one."

"I have some lotion," she told him, "that works well on sunburn. It's got aloe in it. You can take it with you, for after you shower."

"That's very thoughtful," A.J. said, "but not necessary."

"I still don't know how you knew that the trailer was going over," Alison mused.

"It's really simple, actually," Jamie said, as if answering for A.J. "I was warned by the wise and generous spirit of my—"

"It just didn't look that sturdy to me," A.J. said.

"And I really can't believe that you actually remembered seeing that there were other trailers that—"

"I can also name every U.S. President," A.J. cut her off, "and list batting averages for dozens of Major League baseball players, starting in the early 1900s. But the periodic table? Forget about it."

Alison laughed as she led him up onto her porch, as they both shook off the excess rain. But then she stopped. "Ah, crap. My handbag. It's back in the trailer." She could see he wasn't quite following, so she added, "My key. It's in my bag." She closed her eyes and groaned. "The landlord made a point to tell me not to get locked out— he's out of town."

"Did you leave any windows open?" A.J. asked, as Jamie gave him a nod and an, "I'll check."

But Alison shook her head. "It hasn't been open-window weather since I got here. Plus I double-checked them, you know, after the snake got in? Just in case."

"Maybe Hugh still has a key," A.J. suggested.

"Nope," Alison said, looking at the brand-new piece of glass that had been installed in her door just that morning. "He gave it back to me. It's in my purse. At the bottom of my trailer. Probably crushed beneath a four-hundred-pound filing cabinet." She smiled at A.J. "Which, to focus on the bright side, is not also crushing you or me. Which is a definite bonus." She took a deep breath. "The way I see it, we have two options. We break the window—again. Or . . . you could, maybe, invite me to stay, you know, with you tonight?"

"Uh-oh, kid," Jamie said, returned from his waltz around the perimeter of the house. "Back away. Fast. While you still can."

Alison tried not to cringe as her words came out sounding much more tentative than they had before she'd said them, back when they were still rolling around inside of her head, in brilliant-idea format. *Ooh, I have a good idea. We could go to your place.* Somehow it hadn't come out quite like that.

She'd meant to sound worldly and experienced, flirtatiously matter-of-fact—like it was no big thing to suggest she spend the night with A.J. in his motel room.

But her slightly stammered, extremely pathetic-sounding inviting-of-herself into his room and his bed had clearly surprised him. In fact, he looked as if he weren't sure what to do first: run away or run away really fast.

Instead, he laughed. Well, okay, it was more of a voiced exhale of surprise. And then he said, "Um . . ." Which was what he always said when he was trying to figure out what to say.

"Wow, I'm sorry," she interjected quickly. "I seem to be hurtling forward on the too-much-too-soon bus. I'm just, you know, even more smitten than ever, after seeing you go all alpha male on everyone's ass. You know, *Get out of the trailer now, sir,* and, um . . ."

Now she was doing it, too. *Um . . .*

But now his laughter sounded far more real as he said, "Me, too. I mean, *you* were . . . really great, too. You *were* . . . But I'm not . . . It's not . . ." He looked as embarrassed as she felt, and he started over. "There *is* a plan B. I looked at the door when I put the plywood up and the lock's pretty . . ." He took his sodden wallet from his back pocket, pulled out his credit card and, as Alison watched, he used it to jimmy the lock. The door popped open.

"Wow, that was easy," Alison said. "That's . . . a little scary. Hello, Mr. Burglar, come on in."

"Always use the night lock," he told her, tapping the chain. "Whenever you're inside."

"Yeah," she said. "Thanks." And wasn't *this* awkward. "I'm sorry that I said, you know, what I said. I'm usually not so desperately pushy. I must have storm madness."

A.J. laughed at that, which was good. She liked making him laugh.

"Well, maybe," he said. "Storm madness . . . Could be, but, I wasn't . . . Um. See, I'm not staying at the motel. That's what I was trying to tell you. If I were, I would've . . ." He cleared his throat. "I would've invited you. In out of the rain. But I'm kind of looking at overnighting it in my truck, so . . ."

"You're not at the . . . ?" She looked at him. In his *truck* . . . ? "Don't you even have a trailer?"

"No," he said. "They ran out. I'm, um . . ." He nodded, gesturing out toward the soggy night as if that meant something. And then it did mean something because he added, "I've been camping. Just outside of town."

"Camping." She looked at the deluge coming down on the other side of the tiny porch roof. But forget about the rain. This was just one night. He'd been camping, in this relentless, oven-hot heat . . . ?

A.J. smiled ruefully. "I can say with certainty that with the wind that we had, my tent's in the next county."

"At least," Alison said. "If not New Mexico. Not just your tent, but all your stuff. And if it didn't get blown away, it's soaked."

"It's all right. I've slept in my truck plenty of times before," A.J. said just as Alison said, "If you want, you could sleep on my couch."

"Not that I make a habit of it," A.J. added, just as Alison also added, "Unless I've made it too awkward and weird for you to be able to accept any invitation at all."

"It's not awkward and weird," he said. "It's . . .

285

incredibly tempting. I just . . . I don't want to mess this up."

She nodded, but she knew that *he* knew she didn't really understand.

And she just wasn't ready to say good night. It was true, she'd made jokes about being crushed by that file cabinet, but . . . They *could* have been crushed by that file cabinet. People died when heavy things fell on them.

And then there was the bit with the trailer that, from the force of the wind, went up on two wheels. As she'd watched from the truck, A.J. had gone inside *after* it did that dance routine.

And yeah, he'd briefly explained—before he went dashing off to save more lives—that some girl who was inside was too short to get a suitcase down from a closet shelf, and he realized that he wasn't going to get her to leave without it.

For several long, horrifying seconds, Alison had sat there in A.J.'s truck, certain that she was about to watch him get crushed.

Which had sucked—far more, even, than inviting herself to his nonexistent motel room and being shot down for a variety of reasons, the least of which was the fact that he didn't *have* a motel room.

And now he was just standing there, looking at her as if she wasn't completely bedraggled, with her wet hair slicked back from her face. As if she didn't look half-drowned and extremely worse for wear.

"Come here," he said, and he reached for her, as if he could read her mind, as if he knew that she needed at least a *little* bit of human contact, and yeah, who was she kidding? What she needed was a whole *lot* of A.J. Gallagher.

If that was really his name. But her inner snark was shouted down by the rest of her, who was beyond eager to let him pull her into his arms and hold her close, even as she clung to him.

How he managed to smell so good, despite everything he'd just been through, she couldn't figure out. So she just held on to him, with her head against his shoulder, her eyes closed.

He was touching her hair, gently stroking it, as if it weren't a mess of sodden string and knots.

Alison may have lifted her head first. She wasn't sure. But she knew she didn't lift her mouth to kiss him. At least she hoped she didn't. But then she didn't care about the stupid details behind *who* had done what first, because it was clear that they'd *both* moved. Both she and A.J. had moved, right at the same moment, to look into each other's eyes. And then they'd both moved again.

And now A.J. was kissing her the same way she was kissing him—fiercely, passionately, as if there were nothing in the world he'd rather be doing.

And the gentle, tender embrace instantly changed, too. She was now plastered against him, and he was trying to pull her closer as he all but staked a claim inside of her mouth.

Not that she was complaining. It was exhilarating to be kissed like that, with that much ferocious hunger.

Apparently, she wasn't the only one on the too-much-too-soon bus. Despite everything he'd said, he'd just jumped aboard, solidly planting himself beside her.

And maybe it wasn't too much, too soon, if they both wanted this as badly as they both seemed to want it.

Although it was certainly true that, when it came to relationships, her MO in the past involved boatloads of miscommunication, misunderstanding, and general all around poor judgment.

She kept kissing A.J. as she pulled him with her into the house, or maybe he pushed her inside with him. Either way, they moved into her kitchen, and she kicked the door shut behind them.

Which was when he pulled back. "Alison," he breathed.

She could see, in his eyes, an echo of everything she was feeling, everything she wanted. And he, too, wanted it all—right here, right now.

And, absolutely, she could feel the poor

judgment kicking in, because she knew—she *knew*—that at this moment in time, after the hellish night they'd both just had, she should be solicitous. She should offer him a chance to shower. She should check his back and shoulders—see just how much he was lying about that *feels like a mild sunburn* thing. At the very least, she should offer him something to drink along with a chance to think through and discuss the fact that two minutes ago he'd specifically said that he didn't want to mess this up.

She should at least suggest that maybe he wasn't messing up anything. Maybe this was the beginning of something wonderful. Something special. Something amazing.

But instead, she kissed him again.

Instead, she pushed his jacket from his shoulders.

Instead, she took her own shirt and pulled it over her head, unfastened her bra and let it, too, fall on her kitchen floor.

Alison was intending to jump him, right here, right in her kitchen.

And A.J. couldn't, for the life of him, think of anything he'd rather do than be jumped.

But he'd promised himself he'd be honest with her. He'd told himself he'd be the perfect gentleman tonight. He'd kiss her good night and he'd walk away.

And then tomorrow, after she got back from her scouting trip with Hugh, in the light of day, when A.J. wouldn't come off quite so much as a scary psycho lunatic freak, he'd tell her about Jamie. And he'd try to prove that Jamie was real—prove it both to himself and to her.

Jamie, who'd popped away, thank God, as soon as Alison had taken off her shirt.

The ghost was a lot of things, but disrespectful of others' privacy wasn't one of 'em. And it was clear that Alison was immediately embarrassed— afraid that, once again, she'd gone too far.

Of course, instead of telling her that she had, indeed, gone just a *bit* too far, a bit too quickly, A.J. grabbed her by the hands and pulled her in to kiss her. And, of course, as long as he was kissing her, he figured he might as well run his hands across that silky smooth skin that was right there—*right* there. Her breasts were cool and soft and the hard truth was, he didn't want her to put her shirt back on. In fact, he was pretty damn certain he wanted her to never wear a shirt ever again.

Only for him, though.

And then she was the one who pulled back, who stopped kissing him, and he realized he was in trouble, because Jamie was *gone*. Which meant there were no ridiculous versions of ancient show tunes to distract him from the gorgeous half-naked woman who'd already bared her breasts and was now in the process of peeling her soaking wet pants from an ass that was probably not perfect according to most of the world's measurements, but sure as hell could have been in his own personalized dictionary next to the word *exquisite.*

She hopped on one foot as she kicked off her pants and then there she was, wearing only a pair of silk panties and that smile that he loved.

And he knew what he had to do. He had to open his mouth and say, *Alison, wait . . .*

But she kissed him again, her mouth so soft and sweet against his, and he kissed her back, harder, deeper, longer, his hands somehow finding their way back to her breasts, which were undeniably the closest thing to perfect he'd ever seen. But he wanted to see her like this tomorrow. And the day after that, too, so he made himself stop kissing her long enough to say, "Alison, I was hoping we could . . ."

Talk. He'd meant to say talk, except she'd reached down into his jeans, the back of her hand cool against his stomach, and—Jesus!—she took hold of him, her fingers wrapped around him.

And now she was smiling up at him, her delicious lower lip caught between her teeth as she stroked him, and there was no way in hell he was going to say anything to make her stop doing *that.*

And when he unfastened his belt buckle and

291

yanked down his zipper—and yes, sue him, he did it himself, okay? Fumbling in his haste to give her more access—a shower of dust and dirt rained onto the kitchen floor. She laughed, but she didn't let go. She just kissed him again and murmured, "We could both use a shower, huh?"

"Yeah," he agreed, because a shower would both cool him off and slow him down. He could wrap her in a towel and hold her at arms' length and say, *Baby, we should wait . . .*

But he pulled one of her chairs out from the kitchen table, because he had to sit down to get his boots off. And he had to get his boots off, in order to get out of his jeans. And he had to get out of his jeans.

They were around his knees, and she didn't make it easier on him even though she let him go so he could sit. Because as soon as he sat, she straddled his lap. Her breasts were right there, and—Hoh, God—she was now pressing the slip of silk that was between her legs against his now-raging erection.

And yes, they needed a shower. And yes, he wanted his boots off. And yes, there were a whole list of important things he needed to say to this incredible woman, but nothing mattered more than getting inside of her, ASAP.

He grabbed for the back pocket of his jeans, where he kept his wallet, and he dumped its contents on the floor in his haste to find the condom that Jamie had made him put there, just a few days ago.

You never know, the ghost had said.

But somehow he *had* known. And maybe Lutz was right and Jamie *could* time travel. Maybe he could tell A.J. that everything was going to turn out okay, that he wasn't messing this up by being completely unable to refuse this moment's immediate gratification.

And God, maybe it wasn't too late to stop this, to slam on the brakes, only Alison saw what he was doing, saw that he had a condom, and was now helping him cover himself. In fact, she was doing all the work, which freed up his hands to touch her, to explore between her legs, where she was hot and wet and ready for him.

And she moved—off him for just a second—and when she was back, her panties were gone, and he didn't think. He just pulled her hips forward and she slipped down on top of him as he slid all the way—*all* the way—home.

He heard himself groaning her name because, sweet God, it felt so ridiculously good. It was new—new lover, new body, new sensations. There were so many unknowns, and yet one brilliantly clear absolute that erased any uncertainty.

This felt right. It *was* right.

He was where he was supposed to be.

There was no turning back. There was only here and now.

And Alison.

She was running the show, which was both wonderful and a little odd, because he didn't think he'd ever made love for the first time with the woman on top. And he knew damn well he'd never before had a first encounter like this, atop a kitchen chair. Which made him smile, because it was such a nice metaphor for their entire relationship. Where this woman was concerned, he couldn't wait for anything.

She was no doubt thinking the same thing, because as she moved on top of him, she breathed into his ear. "This is the best shower I've ever had."

"This is the best everything I've ever had, ever," he told her in return, which made her both laugh and kiss him.

And the sound of her laughter made him feel such lightness, of soul and heart and even body. It was joy—this feeling—and he wanted it to never stop.

But God, then he had to hold her down, hold himself tightly inside of her, or he was going to finish too soon, and he wanted . . .

He wanted to make her feel all that he was feeling.

But she didn't want to be held down like that, didn't want to not move and of course, he couldn't really keep her from moving altogether, he could only restrict her movement, make her make it smaller. But she also moved harder. And faster.

"Oh, God, A.J.," she breathed. "Oh, my God . . ."

And he was history. He came with a rush of pleasure so intense that colors pinwheeled and spun behind his closed eyelids. He released her, but she didn't change her rhythm, and he realized that she, too, was coming, around him, on top of him.

She was beautiful with her head thrown back, arms stretched out, hands pressed against his chest, nipples taut, stomach tight, legs spread to receive him.

But God, now what?

The reality of what he'd just done crashed down around him, and the lightness vanished as absolutely as Jamie did when he popped away. And he found himself actually considering Lutz's suggestion. If he wasn't going to tell Alison about Hor al-Hammar, why bother telling her anything about Jamie?

Of course maybe what his mother thought would happen by A.J. calling Lutz, had happened, instead, here tonight. Maybe Jamie was finally gone.

But somehow A.J. knew that wasn't the case. Somehow he felt Jamie, out there. Still, it was entirely possible that the ghost would stay away for a while, out of sheer disapproval. Although *he* was one to throw stones. The woman *he'd* been unable to resist had been married to someone else.

Alison shifted slightly on his lap as she came back to earth. She took a deep breath, exhaled hard, and opened her eyes to find him gazing up at her.

She was instantly embarrassed, scrunching up her face and bringing one arm up and across her breasts. "Oh, God," she said. "It's hard enough in a bed, when you can kind of burrow into the pillows. Who was the genius who had the brilliant idea to get it on for the first time on a kitchen chair?"

A.J. laughed. "I think we have to share responsibility for this. I was trying to get my boots off, but then . . . I stopped trying."

She glanced back over her shoulder at his jeans that were still down around his knees. "Classy," she said. "I'm classy all the way."

He pulled her down for a long, sweet kiss. "You're beautiful," he told her when he let her go. "And that was amazing. I've got somewhere close to a thousand things I want to make sure I get to say to you before I fall unconscious, which is going to happen pretty soon. You up for a shower and then . . . a talk?"

Alison laughed. "The new man actually wants to *talk?* What is wrong with this picture? Ah, wait a minute. You're too perfect, *that's* what it is." She kissed him again. "I would love to shower, then talk."

She had no clue, and he didn't have the heart to tell her, that their talk was going to send her reeling. Because as persuasive as Lutz had been, A.J. knew he had to tell her about Jamie. And he had to do it now.

While the excuse—*I couldn't stop myself from letting you jump me, you're just so hot*—was still an honest excuse, if he let himself have an entire night, which would be really easy to do—God give him strength—or even a week of nights, doing so would negate any potential positive power that came from his honest admission: *I was planning to tell you, I meant to tell you, I should have told you. . . .*

He had to do it now, but showers first.

Separate showers.

Except Alison was looking at him as if she had a vastly different agenda.

"Why don't you shower," he said, motioning to the sandbox's worth of dirt on the floor, "while I clean up in here?"

"Oh, my God, A.J. . . ." She leaped off him, which was startling. And weird.

He'd been alive for forty-two years. How could one short sexual encounter and several brief minutes of a post-sex, still-enjoined conversation make him believe—and he was totally convinced of the fact—that his penis belonged inside of this one particular woman? That *that* was its rightful place in the world, right there, although he had to smile at the idea of him walking around, for the entire rest of his life, with Alison's legs locked around his waist.

But then he stopped smiling, because when the hell did he start thinking things like *the entire rest of his life?*

He quickly pulled his shorts up, his jeans, too, ready to handle the mess on the floor, but then he realized that that wasn't what Alison was upset about.

She'd caught sight of his shoulders, which, if the way his back had felt against that chair was a clue, were no doubt looking a little angry. He glanced down. Yup.

"Mild sunburn," he said.

"Yeah, right," she said, "and even if I announce a hundred different times that I'm the pope, that doesn't mean I should pack my bags and move to Rome."

She was so indignant. And naked. A.J. couldn't not smile. And pull her back onto his lap for another kiss.

Chapter Twelve

I went back to Alaska, to talk to Rose.

Well, okay, to talk *at* Rose, since she couldn't see or hear me. But I thought it might help.

I also thought, since I'd been having such recent interference with my jumps, that I might end up not in Alaska, but sitting next to the tall man with the ponytail who'd shot and killed Wayne.

But no.

I wound up in Rose's private study, in her doctor's office. And I remembered that this was one of the many nights wherein she kept evening hours. Which was a plain-as-day example of her generosity and kindness to the community, since most folks worked days, and couldn't afford health insurance, let alone the missed time that they'd need for a daytime doctor's visit.

She was sitting behind her desk, typing something into a computer. And I realized, as I looked over her shoulder, that she was making notes into a patient's file.

She had a stethoscope looped casually around her neck, but other than that, she didn't particularly look like a doctor.

I cruised around, looking at all of her framed certifications and degrees. Her desk was big and made of oak. It took up most of the room. There was a big shelf behind it, filled with books of all shapes and sizes. Over by the window was a file cabinet, and in front of the desk were a couple of chairs—the kind you sit in when the doctor is about to tell you that your lover and best friend in the entire world has six months left to live.

I avoided the chairs and went around to Rose's side of the desk. It was remarkably uncluttered—or maybe not remarkably. Rose always had been efficient and neat. It made sense that she should continue to be that way.

There was only one picture sitting there—a picture of me and Adam and Bev and A.J., taken back when the kids were small. Age must've been about five, and he grinned toothlessly at the camera, his arms wrapped around my neck. I was barely recognizable with all my wrinkles, but I did, however, have all *my* teeth, and I, too, was grinning like the devil was inside of me. Adam, his hair only laced with gray, was holding little Bev, and the two of them looked like they were fit to burst from laughing.

It was a good picture, despite the fact that I looked like some old mummy dug up from ancient Egypt. I suppose I'd keep it on my desk, too, if I had one.

There were only a few other photographs in the room.

Bev's bridal portrait.

Bev and her husband, Charlie, holding their firstborn daughter, Kaeli, the three of them looking impossibly young; another picture with Kaeli's little sister, Morgan, in Bev's arms.

A.J. That one must've been after he'd opened up Adam's wood shop again, after he'd come out of rehab. He still looked pale and skinny. His face looked almost fragile, like if you pushed him too hard he might break.

I wondered why Rose chose to keep that picture

on her wall, when A.J. looks so much healthier and stronger these days. Surely she had a better picture now. But who could know? Maybe she didn't want to forget where he'd been.

The last picture in the room was on the bookshelf, apart from the others.

It was Ryan. It wasn't the stiff picture that the army had taken, with him in his military uniform. Rather, it was an old snapshot. He must've been about nineteen, maybe twenty, and he was laughing into the camera's lens, as love danced in his eyes.

It broke my heart seeing that picture there.

The boy had died when Rose was twenty-three. It hurt to think that she'd been alone for all those years since.

"You had men calling on you all the time," I said to her. "But when I was alive, you never even went out on a date with a single one of 'em. Why the hell not, Rose?"

She didn't answer. She couldn't hear me, of course.

"You're still a beautiful woman," I pointed out. "Do you really think that Ryan likes thinking you're down here all alone like this? It's not too late, girl. Get off your butt and find yourself a little companionship, damnit."

She just clacked away on that computer keyboard.

"Ah, hell," I said. If I was going to talk to Rose,

I'd have to do it through A.J. And that would go over real well. I could just hear myself saying, *Come on, kid, let's go have a sit-down with your mother about her lack of a sex life.*

Which reminded me of why I was here—because A.J. was making the mistake of his life down there in Jubilation by his brand-new *lack* of a lack of a sex life.

And okay, my emotions were mixed about the whole thing. On one level, I was overjoyed to see the kid so head over heels and out of control. That was one of the things that struck me the hardest about him, when I'd first returned. Everything he did was so careful, so cautious, so deliberate. Like, he was afraid that all it would take was one slip and he'd sail over the edge and past the point of no return.

But when he was with Alison?

The kid came alive with every fiber of his being. He listened with his lungs and his knees. He looked at her with his stomach. He sat with her, with an awareness that extended to his toenails.

"You should see him with her," I told Rose, who ignored me. "And you should see the way she looks at him, too. It's what you want your kids to find." I sighed. "I just don't know what advice to give him. Part of me's afraid he's not even trying, because he's already written himself off. You know? Like he doesn't believe he's worthy.

302

Damaged goods. Kind of the way I felt after I ran away—too much of a coward to bring Wells's killer to justice. It took me having something to believe in—having something worthwhile, to be willing to die for . . . That's what turned my ass around. But everyone's gotta take their own path, right? Still, I wonder . . ."

She didn't answer, but the intercom on her desk buzzed.

"Dr. Gallagher, Amy Stone finally arrived," a woman's voice said.

Dr. Gallagher. It still sent chills of pride down my spine.

Rose leaned forward and pushed the intercom button. "Bring her into the examining room, Ariana," she said. "I'll be right there."

She pushed her chair away from her desk, but instead of heading toward the door the way I expected her to, she walked toward the file cabinet. Directly toward me.

I tried to move out of her way, but I couldn't move fast enough. She passed through me, and stopped, startled. She'd just gotten one hell of a buzz.

I quickly moved to the other side of the room.

She looked around her, frowning slightly.

"Yeah," I said. "That's right. It's me. Jamie. I'm in here with you, Rose."

But even concentrating the way she was, she still couldn't hear me or see me.

She shook her head, as if she'd figured she must've imagined that patch of electrically charged air that she'd just walked through. She got what she needed from the file cabinet and went out the door.

I sighed, and zapped myself back to A.J.

"Too soon!" A.J. shouted, his voice echoing off the bathroom tile and the walls of the shower stall.

Alison had to laugh. "I'm kind of not in control here," she told him.

He had her pinned against the tile wall, the shower running and steaming up the entire room, creating a thick fog that swirled around them.

"I'm not either," he breathed. He didn't stop moving as he lifted his head to look into her eyes. He'd set a rhythm that was both slow and steady—and not quite complete. He was withholding, just a little bit, and try as she might to change that, even by tightening her legs around his waist, her efforts were fruitless.

"You're killing me," she told him, and he smiled.

He'd carried her all the way from the kitchen, and although he was a big man, she was no lightweight at five-foot-eleven. But he made it seem effortless, one big hand beneath her butt as he used the other to turn on the shower.

She'd reached for her medicine cabinet, where

304

she had a small supply of condoms—a gift from Hugh, who'd told her that even though he wasn't allowed to be a Boy Scout, he'd embraced their motto: *Be prepared.*

So she'd grabbed a handful and carried them with her into the shower stall.

Only then did A.J. set her down.

He'd washed her, which was lovely, even as she returned the favor, careful of his shoulders and back—which really weren't as badly scraped as she'd feared. She marveled at how nicely he was put together, loving the way he responded so visibly to her touch, but then finding and tracing a scar that he had both on his abdomen, and on his back. It looked like something had gone clear through him, but when she'd murmured, "That must've hurt," he didn't stop kissing her long enough to say more than "Hor al-Hammar."

She'd wanted to know more. Was Hor al-Hammar a place or a person's name or a type of weapon? She honestly didn't know.

But he just kissed her and kissed her, his hands urgent against her body, lighting her on fire all over again.

He'd used one of her condoms to cover himself and . . .

Here they were.

Making love for the second time in an hour.

"Please," she gasped. "More, *please* . . ." And just like that he pushed himself all the way inside of her, giving her exactly what she wanted. Just because she'd asked.

And God, it felt so good and yes, maybe it *was* too soon, but it felt right to her and she felt herself go and she heard herself shouting, both his name and *yes,* like women did in clichéd romantic comedies. But maybe there was a reason shouting *yes* was a cliché—because she had never before in her life felt such a positive affirmative, and maybe the feeling was universal, at least when it came to off-the-chart orgasms and the amazing, wonderful, sexy men who delivered them.

Yes, this was great.

Yes, she was coming.

Yes, she couldn't believe how in tune she was with this man, who was coming now, too, with his own strangled shouts of her name—Alison, Alison, *Alison*—as if she were a goddess he was worshiping, or the answer to his lifelong prayers.

But then it was over, and they were both breathing hard.

Alison kept her eyes closed, wanting to hang on to that feeling, that *yes,* just a little bit longer. But the tile was hard and cold against her back, and as strong as A.J. was, his muscles had to be well past the straining point.

So she sighed and shifted slightly.

But he didn't release her. He just broke the silence. "Is it weird," he said, his voice just slightly louder than the rush of the water, his forehead against the tile above her left shoulder, "that I'm filled with this . . . longing. To stay just like this, and maybe even take a nap, right here?"

Alison laughed. "Yes, that's a little weird," she told him. "Come on, let me down. I'll get us some towels."

He did just that, and she stepped under the spray for one final rinse, pushing open the shower door as he took a turn under the water.

She opened the linen closet carefully—her new procedure was to check every cabinet, every closet, every room for snakes before going or reaching in—and pulled out a clean towel for him. Hers was already on the rack.

She turned to hand it to him as he shut off the water and stepped out of the shower. "Is Hor al-Hammar a city?" she asked.

He hesitated just slightly before answering. "It was an area—a region. A part of Iraq that was . . . It was also a marsh. There was a village—a really small one—at the edge that was called . . . Well, the name was long and difficult to pronounce so the army just called it Hor al-Hammar."

"I don't know much about the First Gulf War," she admitted.

"Most people don't."

"Yeah, but I'm an historian."

"It doesn't matter," A.J. said as he finished drying himself. "You still wouldn't have heard of Hor al-Hammar. The village, anyway. It was tiny.

It was . . . People lived there and . . . A lot of good people died there."

"Then I'm sure that I should have heard of it."

"No," he said. "They were civilians. Iraqis. They didn't count."

"That's awful," Alison said.

"Yes, it is." He met her eyes only briefly as he wrapped the towel around his waist. "I'm going to go sweep up the kitchen floor."

He left the bathroom, but then turned back. "Look, I just want you to know that . . . This is going to sound nuts, but . . . That's the most that I've talked about it, since it happened. I mean, you know, aside from the times that they . . . *made* me talk about it, and even then, it wasn't really me talking. It was me, telling them what they wanted to hear and . . . I do trust you. Very much. I just . . . Don't like to talk about it."

She had her own towel wrapped around her and she held it on with both hands as she looked back into the familiar blue of his eyes. "I'm just glad that you weren't one of the people who died there."

"For a long time," he said, "I almost was. I still sometimes wonder . . ."

"You're alive," she told him past her heart, which was lodged firmly in her throat. She made herself smile. "I know, because . . . Well, let's just say you definitely have a pulse and a very healthy circulatory system. Good blood flow."

A.J. laughed. And then stepped back into the bathroom and kissed her.

July 26, 1898
Dear Diary,

He is going to hurt me badly. Not tonight, because he is still recovering from a gunshot wound.

No, not tonight, but soon.

I am locked here in this tiny room beneath the stairs. I've tried to get out, but there are no windows, and the door is sealed with an iron bolt.

I don't regret what I did. I saved a man's life—the gambler who came to our door, who risked his own life for mine.

When I heard of the plot to kill him, I knew I had no choice.

The monster was still in the parlor with the Texan, planning the ambush, and I slipped out the back door into the unearthly darkness before dawn, wearing only my nightdress, with my feet bare.

I ran to the saloon, where the Texan had said the gambler was still playing poker, but went in the back door. The tiny kitchen was empty, save for one serving girl, whom I didn't recognize. She didn't seem surprised to see me in my nightgown, I suppose because she was wearing even less than I.

I asked her to give a message to my gambler, requesting that he come to the kitchen to speak with me. I gave her the locket around my neck for the favor, and off she dutifully went.

It seemed forever before the kitchen doors opened, but they finally did open, and he was standing there.

It was only then that I realized the immodesty of my nightgown and my state of disarray. I could see in the gambler's eyes that he was not immune to my charms.

He moved toward me—he knew my name. "Are you all right?"

He was bigger, stronger than I'd thought, and my instincts were to shy away from him. But I lifted my chin and held my ground.

"You're the one in danger," I said, and told him about the monster's plan to kill him.

The gambler checked his gun and his supply of ammunition as I talked.

"What are you going to do?" I asked.

"Well," he said. "They want me to leave the saloon, so . . . 'Pears to me that first thing I need to do is, not leave the saloon."

"But the barkeep will be told to shut the game down," I said.

"There are . . . other games to be played in an establishment like this," he told me, and I knew he was talking about the women who worked on their backs.

I used to scorn them, but unlike me, they get paid for their pain.

He seemed embarrassed. "Not that I'd . . . actually . . . It would just be to have someplace to go," he explained, "until I have time to think things through."

I started to protest—he should leave now, leave town for good—but he reached out and put a finger on my lips, then pushed my hair back from my face. I couldn't believe a man could be so gentle. I still wonder if I imagined his caress, imagined the softness in his uncommonly pretty eyes.

"I'll be fine," my gambler said quietly. "Thank you, but . . . Go home. Run quickly, before he misses you."

I stopped at the door, looking back at him. "Don't die," I said, wondering at the fact that I should even care. It is an odd sensation, this caring.

He smiled at me, a sparkling smile that I shall hold tightly to in my mind even as the monster hurts me.

He smiled and it was like the sunrise, but then I slipped out the door, back into the darkness of the night.

This time, after it was over, A.J. had fallen asleep.

He woke up now, still sprawled half on top of

Alison, entangled together in the sheets of her bed, his face against a sweet-smelling pillow that he was—nice—drooling onto.

He lifted his head and wiped his mouth and chin, and found her awake and watching him.

"Sorry," he said.

"For what?" she asked. She was so beautiful, lying there, her hair disheveled and her eyes half-closed, her smile wide and warm.

As he shifted off her, she turned on her side to face him, head propped up on one hand, elbow out. She didn't try to cover herself, even though it hadn't been that long, hours-wise, since she'd been embarrassed by her nakedness, out in her kitchen.

Of course, that third time he'd made love to her, here in her bed, he'd spent a lot of time looking and touching and tasting.

And nearly no time talking.

So much for his plan.

He could've stopped what he was doing. And okay, certainly not that first time they'd gone at it. And not the second time, either. The urgency had been off the charts in both cases.

But number three?

The massage oil and the cunnilingus and the hours—literally hours, plural—of foreplay, before he'd slid inside of her and rocked himself to heaven . . .

That was on him. That was him knowing he'd

screwed this up and willfully screwing it up even further.

"You hungry?" she asked now. "I don't have a whole lot of food here in the house. A couple cans of soup, some frozen waffles . . ."

"Oh," he said, "no. Thanks, but . . ." He wasn't hungry. In fact, his stomach was tight, because it was long past time to get the conversation started. Unless . . .

"I've already kept you up way too late," he added. "If you have to be up early for that location-scouting thing—"

She shook her head. "I haven't spoken to Hugh yet, but he's going to have to go without me. My priority has to be getting my books and files out of my trailer. As soon as it's light, I'm going to start organizing that."

"I can help," A.J. said. "We can use my truck."

"That would be great, thanks." She leaned over and kissed him, her mouth soft and cool against his lips. "You scare me a little sometimes. You just seem too good to be true."

A.J. laughed as he shook his head. "I'm not, um . . . I'm . . . Um . . ." It was the perfect segue, but he couldn't do it. He couldn't find the right words. Probably because there were no right words. *Oh, by the way? I'm probably crazy.*

She kissed him again and sat up, swinging her long legs out of bed. "I know the idea of a postmidnight waffle didn't thrill you, but I'm starving. You don't have to move if you don't want to. I can bring it back in here."

She'd found a bathrobe that had been tossed over the back of a chair, and she pulled it on as A.J., too, sat up.

"No," he said. "Actually, something to drink would be nice." His towel was on the floor where he'd dropped it, and he picked it up now and secured it back around his waist.

This was good. This would get them into the kitchen, where they could sit at the table, and he could tell her . . . what he had to tell her.

He followed her down the hall as she said, "You know, I've been thinking about what you said. You know, before the sky fell in? About Melody warning Jamie, and I just can't make it work. But that's part of the problem. I've never been able to make sense of the reported logistics of the shoot-out at the Red Rock. Silas Quinn left something out. Maybe if Melody were having an affair with Jamie, and Quinn was trying to protect her—"

"That's not what happened," A.J. said. And damn it, their wet clothes were still on the kitchen floor, along with all that dirt he'd never managed to sweep up.

"I'm just thinking aloud here." Alison just stepped over most of it, scooping up her own clothes and tossing them into a laundry basket that was in the corner of the room. She went to the fridge and got out both a pitcher of lemonade and what looked like iced tea. "Help yourself. There's OJ, too."

She opened the freezer and frowned inside of it, rummaging around as he got out the same dustpan and broom that he'd used to sweep up the broken glass. Was that really just yesterday?

"You know, even if we embrace your story"— she turned to point at him with a box of waffles— "and I'm not saying that's what I'm doing. I'm just theorizing. But you said yourself that you were just a child when your great-grandfather told you what he told you. You might've gotten the kid-friendly version. You know, Great-grampa helped Great-gramma escape from her mean first husband, instead of a more sordid truth. Great-grampa was fooling around with Great-gramma even though she was a married lady, and she fell in love and left her first husband to be with him. You don't have to do that—it can wait until the morning."

"I don't mind," A.J. said as he kept sweeping.

"Then I'm not going to stop you. Who am I to say no to a man doing housework?" She closed the freezer door as she said, "Maybe Quinn hit Melody—and mind you, I am *not* condoning it—but just *maybe* the domestic violence happened because he found out that she was stepping out on him. She was so pretty and so young—much younger than he was. Plus, he was away so often . . ."

"He kept her under lock and key," A.J. said. "Not so much in Jubilation, because the town was isolated, there was really nowhere for her to go. But in Kansas City and in Denver, he locked her in her room. Kept her under guard when he was gone."

"Which could support my theory. That he had a compelling reason to keep her locked up—to him, I mean, obviously not compelling to modern standards," Alison pointed out as she put two waffles in the toaster and pushed the button down. She got a plate from the cabinet. "I'm going to assume you'll shout if you change your mind about having something to eat."

"I'm good," he said. "But yeah, thanks." As he dumped the dust from the pan into the trash it hissed against the plastic liner. "May I just point out that even if your theory is true, it means we've caught Quinn in a lie. According to everything he wrote, his marriage to Melody was all sweetness and light. And if he lied about *that* . . ."

"I'm not sure that's really lying," Alison argued as she watched him pick up his boots and set them down by the door. "It's like when someone asks, *How are you?* and you answer, *Fine,* even though you've got a migraine starting and your car just broke down for the third time in a week."

"Hmm." A.J. wasn't sure he agreed as he set his still-damp jeans and his yellow slicker next to his boots, and swept up the rest of the dust and grit from the worn linoleum floor.

Alison continued. "And Quinn's omission of . . . whatever he omitted in his report of the gunfight at the saloon . . . ?" Her waffles had popped, and she moved them quickly from the toaster to her plate and added what looked like real maple syrup from a tiny maple-leaf-shaped bottle. "If Melody *was* there, and he was trying to protect her, or . . . Okay. Maybe he was trying to protect himself. If word got out that she was there, people might've figured out that she was getting it on with the gambler on the side. And maybe you're right. Maybe Jamie and Melody didn't die, but Quinn said they did, because in his world a dead wife was better than one who'd run off with an outlaw."

It should have been the perfect lead in. She was talking about lies of omission. And still the words stuck in A.J.'s throat.

"Lemonade or iced tea?" she asked, as she got two glasses down from the cabinet. "Or a mix of both?"

"A mix sounds good, thanks," he said, and clearly it wasn't his throat that was the problem. He got those words out easily enough.

He also had no problem saying, "The story Jamie told me is that he didn't even speak to Melody for the first time, until early in the morning—before dawn—on the day of the shoot-out. And I believe him. I just . . . I do."

Alison carried her plate and both glasses over to the table and sat down. Leaving him the chair that he'd sat upon earlier.

God, what was wrong with him? He wanted her again. Just watching her walk across the room in that pale-colored bathrobe, knowing that she had nothing on underneath it . . . It looked as if it were made of slippery fabric, soft to the touch, and he wanted it off her.

And the bitch of it was, he knew that if he sat down in that chair, and let his towel drop, let her see for herself where his thoughts had gone . . .

He could put off this conversation until the morning. Or day after tomorrow. Or next week, next month, next year . . .

Yeah, that wouldn't work.

She wanted to go to Alaska. She wanted to talk to his mother and Bev. Adam. All zillion of his cousins. And one of them would let slip his secret.

And that would really suck—her finding it out from someone else.

"So let's have it," Alison said, and then laughed at what was, no doubt, his startled expression. She explained, "Jamie's version of what happened on July 26, 1898."

Ah.

"What did you think I was talking about?" she asked, laughing. "Sex? What are you, part Energizer Bunny?"

A.J. felt his cheeks heat as he adjusted his towel

318

around his waist. Great, now he was blushing, too. So he went for honesty.

"I don't really know what's up," he said. "I mean, besides what's obviously . . . up. Again. I mean, you're sitting there, eating waffles, and it's turning me on. Which, I guess is kind of weird, but that's what it's been like, pretty much since I met you. I just . . . I can't get enough."

She'd stopped eating, and she set her fork down on her plate. She didn't seem to know what to say, so he kept going.

"I just . . . I really love listening to you talk and . . . following the way your brain works? It's just . . . You're so smart and . . . *funny* and . . . I love making you laugh and I . . . I'm really falling for you, Alison. And maybe there's a part of me that thinks that maybe if I, I don't know, just keep making you feel good, you'll . . . fall for me, too. Which . . . is as stupid as it sounds, isn't it?"

A.J. turned away from her, because—talk about awkward. Even though he hadn't said *I love you,* it was a mere few steps removed. And similar to *I love you,* any declaration like the one he'd made—*I'm falling for you*—had a perceived appropriate response. *I'm falling for you, too.* But he didn't want her to say it if she didn't mean it.

And considering what he was warming up to, he was pretty certain he didn't want her to say it, period. In fact, an *Oh, gee, Age, that's so sweet, but . . . I'm just not that into you, babe* would be

319

far better, considering that the dead last thing he wanted to do here was hurt her.

And *that* was something he should've focused on with far more intensity several hours ago when he was pulling off his jeans in order to get the best lap dance of his entire life.

She was silent, and he didn't want to look at her, so he carefully picked up his jeans and went out the kitchen door, intending to shake them out over the porch railing—and nearly went right through Jamie, who was sitting on the top rail.

"Jesus!" A.J. said.

"Nope, it's just me," Jamie said. "Sorry about before. FYI, I didn't see anything."

"It's not another snake, is it?" Alison called from back in the kitchen.

"No," A.J. told her. "It's not. It's okay. I was just . . . startled."

"I should have realized," Jamie said. "You're a Gallagher, and Gallaghers are—"

"Yeah, stop right there, thanks so much," A.J. whispered from between clenched teeth as he shook his jeans over the other rail.

Alison appeared at the door. "You're seriously going to say . . . what you said, and walk away?"

"No," A.J. said, giving his jeans one more shake. "I'm not going anywhere. You, um, wanted to hear Jamie's version of the story, right?"

He went back into the house, holding the door open behind him, so that Jamie knew he was welcome inside. "It's not just Jamie's version," he told Alison, who definitely had more to say. But now he was terrified to hear it, so he just kept telling the story. "It's Melody's, too. Jamie told me she woke up to the sound of voices in the parlor. Bo Kelly was back, and he and Quinn were arguing again. It was about money, as usual. Bo thought he was paying Quinn too much, Quinn thought it *wasn't* enough and on and on it went. But then Jamie's name came up. And they started arguing about how and when to kill him."

"Kid," Jamie said, but A.J. shook him off.

He just kept talking. "Kelly wanted to wait until Jamie was flush. He was in the middle of a losing streak, which meant there'd be nothing in his pockets to steal after he was dead.

"But Quinn wanted it to happen immediately. He was afraid of what Jamie knew, afraid of what he'd say and who he'd talk to. For Quinn it was worth two weeks of his share of the Kellys' take—to have Kelly and his boys handle the problem that very morning. And Bo Kelly finally agreed."

"She doesn't want to hear this right now, kid," Jamie murmured.

But A.J. plunged on. "The plan was for the Kelly boys to ambush Jamie on his way home from the saloon," he said. "Apparently my gramps had spent the entire night in a poker game—a game that showed no sign of ending.

The Kellys would hide in the alleys between the Red Rock and Jamie's hotel, while Quinn provided insurance by putting himself with a rifle in the Red Rock itself, at a second-floor window. Even if the Kellys all missed, Quinn wouldn't. Not with that weapon, and with a target as broad as Jamie's back."

"No." Alison shook her head. "Silas Quinn never shot a man in the back. That was something he was very clear about. He never killed a man who wasn't looking him in the eye. Everyone who knew him said the same."

"Well, that might be true," A.J. said, "because even though he was in position at that window, he never had the opportunity to shoot Jamie in the back. Because Melody heard about the plans for the ambush, and went to the Red Rock to warn Jamie. She told him that at a prearranged time, the barkeep would come into the main part of the saloon, shut the game down, and send everyone home. If she hadn't warned him, if Jamie *had* headed for his hotel, he'd have been dead a matter of seconds later."

But Jamie was right. She wasn't really listening, she was just shaking her head and waiting for him to stop talking.

So he stopped. And braced himself.

"A.J.," she said. "I need to be honest with you. You scare the crap out of me because . . . Well, I keep waiting for the other shoe to drop. If this is,

I don't know, some kind of elaborate con . . . ? But I just don't know what you get, if it is a con, because I don't have that much money. And you know, maybe you're a player and you get to score, which you did, and maybe it's somehow worth more if you get me to fall in love with you . . . ?"

"I'm not conning you," A.J. said, "and I'm not playing you. I'm just . . ." He took a deep breath. "Will you sit down? I kind of need you to sit down."

Chapter Thirteen

Alison sat at the kitchen table in her quirky little rented house in Jubilation, Arizona, as a man who claimed to be the great-grandson of the infamous outlaw, Jamie "Kid" Gallagher, sat down across from her.

A man she'd spent most of the evening having sex with.

Great sex.

Fabulous sex.

Creative, inventive, extraordinary, laughter-filled, passionate sex.

In the single overhead light, in the chair he was now in—the very chair upon which they'd first made love, not all that many hours ago—the way he was sitting put his face into shadows. And because of that, he looked older, harder, more weather-beaten and world-weary.

And just a little bit dangerous.

He looked up at her, meeting her eyes as he cleared his throat. "There's something I need to tell you."

Not the words one wanted to hear from a new lover. But it could be anything. It didn't have to be disastrous. Maybe he was allergic to peanut butter and he needed her never to eat it again. Maybe he had some kind of weird obsession with cleanliness that meant he would have to sweep her kitchen floor and clean her bathroom every morning.

Alison nodded, because he seemed to be waiting for her to say something. So she said, "I'm listening."

But he still hesitated, looking down at the table as he fidgeted with her napkin tray.

And every second that he delayed, she knew whatever he *needed* to tell her was going to be a disaster.

He'd lied about not being married. He was gay— no, probably not. She had very good gaydar. And then there were all those hours of sex. He could be bi—*that* was possible, but so what? Maybe it wasn't about sex. Maybe he was terminally ill. Or HIV-positive—there was a scary thought, except they'd been careful about using protection. Still, if it were true, she was going to kick his ass for not telling her first. That was just wrong not to talk about first with a new sexual partner.

But it seemed so unlike him—unlike the him, at least, that he was pretending to be.

Maybe he wasn't married, but he was engaged. Or he had a girlfriend.

Maybe he was an undercover cop, a superhero in disguise, a vampire with a soul, a priest on vacation from the Vatican . . .

"There's someone else in this room with us," A.J. told her.

"I'm sorry . . . ?" she said. His words didn't make sense. His mention of *someone else* meant she was right about him having a girlfriend or fiancée, the rat bastard, but the rest of what he'd said didn't line up.

"We're not alone."

They weren't . . . ? She pulled her feet up. "You said there wasn't another snake."

A.J. shook his head. "No snakes. Just . . . Jamie."

"Jamie," Alison repeated, and it was weird, because she knew they were alone in there—the room just wasn't that big—and yet, she suddenly had the urge to turn and look behind her.

"You can't see him, but he's here. He's . . . over there. Right now."

And then she did look around—at a kitchen that was definitely empty, save for the two of them. "Jamie?" she asked. "As in . . . *Jamie?*"

"Gallagher," A.J. said. "My great-grandfather. His, well, ghost, actually." He looked over her shoulder. "Spirit. He prefers spirit."

Alison laughed. "Very funny," she said.

But A.J. didn't laugh, too. "I'm not kidding, Alison."

Or . . .

Maybe . . .

He was crazy.

That was one possibility that Alison hadn't considered.

Dear God.

He was dead serious. She could see from his eyes that he wasn't teasing. He *wasn't* kidding. He truly believed that there was someone—some *invisible* one—in the room with them.

She didn't know what to say. The other shoe hadn't just dropped—it had kicked her solidly in the face. Of all the potential problems and issues she'd imagined . . .

"I know it sounds nuts," A.J. told her, looking like he wanted to reach across the table for her hand, so she dropped hers into her lap. "I didn't believe it myself at first, and me, I *can* see him. But I'm the only one, and—"

. . . mental illness wasn't one of them. Alison stood up.

"Shit," A.J. said, his hand against his forehead as he briefly closed his eyes. "Please. Wait. I know how it sounds. I know what you're thinking, because, believe me, I've thought it, too. I've had a CAT scan, it's not a tumor, it's not physiological. So yeah. Either I'm, I don't know, maybe schizophrenic or delusional in some other way, or . . . Maybe he's real. And Alison, God help me, after tonight? I think he's real. He was the one who found the trailers that needed to be evacuated. Please, will you sit down and hear me out? Please."

He looked up at her, and now, from this angle, with the light shining more fully on his face, he looked younger and almost angelic. His blue eyes held disappointment and regret, as if he knew that whatever he said, she wouldn't—couldn't possibly—believe him.

His hair fell forward into his eyes and he impatiently raked it back with one hand.

Alison's stomach churned, and the smell of the waffle and syrup she hadn't finished seemed suddenly cloyingly, overpoweringly sweet. So she took her plate to the sink, ran water over it to rinse it into the garbage disposal.

She turned off the water, and just stood there, looking down at the chipped and worn white ceramic, as all of the little weirdnesses that she'd noticed about A.J. Gallagher suddenly made sense.

He talked to himself—or rather, to his hallucinations. She'd caught him often enough, but she'd brushed it off. He was quirky. A man that attractive, that funny and smart, couldn't possibly be mentally ill.

Except he was.

"He first appeared to me," A.J. said quietly from his seat at the table, "about two and a half weeks ago. He's been following me around ever since. He's the reason I came here. To Jubilation. He asked me to help him clear his name."

"There're no such things as ghosts," Alison said.

"That's what I used to think."

She turned toward him, and God, he looked as gorgeous as he had in her shower, in her bed, with the light glinting off of his nicely sculpted body and too-handsome face. "You can see him?" she asked, her voice breaking slightly despite her efforts to not cry. "Right now?"

"I'm so sorry," A.J. said, his voice thick with his regret. "I know I should have told you. And I meant to tell you before things went too far. I tried, but I didn't try hard enough, because I just . . . I was selfish. I've never met anyone like you, and I couldn't say no."

She wiped her eyes, nodding. "You *should* have told me. You're right, that was wrong. It was . . . deceitful and . . . very wrong, but . . . One thing at a time, all right? Just tell me. You see him. He's here, right now?"

"Well, he was," A.J. said, "but he stepped outside, because . . . Jamie," he called, then looked over by the door. "He's back," he told Alison.

"By the door." Where there was no one and nothing.

A.J. nodded. "Yeah."

"Why can't I see him?" she asked. "If he's really there, tell him to let me see him, too."

"He can hear you," A.J. told her. "I don't have to repeat . . . and . . ." He paused, as if he were listening to someone speak, then nodded and said, "It's one of the rules. For returning. I guess there're rules. If he'd chosen to return to a specific place, like his house, everyone who went in could conceivably see him, but he wouldn't have speech. And he never particularly liked charades, so . . ." He cleared his throat. "He'd also be restricted in terms of his movement. By choosing to appear only to me, I can not only hear him, too, but he can go anywhere I can go. But no one else can see him. It's a trade-off—*what?*"

And God, that was freaky—watching him give his full attention to the emptiness beside the door, nodding slightly and then saying, "That's right, that's right. . . ."

He turned back to Alison, and he must've seen the expression of dismay on her face, because he apologized again. "I'm sorry. That must be bizarre. It must look . . . But the snake. Remember the snake? That was Jamie. And the odd electric shock that was kind of cold and hot at the same time . . . ? That was Jamie, too. For some reason—he doesn't know why—but when he comes into contact with living things, he gets that reaction."

"The *snake* was Jamie . . . ?" she asked. Oh, God . . .

"No," A.J. said, laughing. "Jesus, no. Jamie *zapped* the snake. That was why it didn't bite me. Jamie was there and he touched it, and it flipped out like that. You saw it. That wasn't me, Alison. Was it you?"

She shook her head. She *had* seen the snake act strangely, but . . .

"It was also Jamie," A.J. told her, so intently, so convinced, "who knew you were trapped in your bathroom. You were supposed to meet me, remember? But you didn't show up, and I got worried and . . . He found you and he thought maybe you'd fallen and hit your head. You were lying on the floor in the shower. He didn't see the snake and I didn't either at first, but then when he did see it, he touched it. He didn't know it was going to react that way, but I was glad that it did. And he touched it again and again and . . . That electric shock we felt, here in your kitchen? That was him, too."

Alison just shook her head. This was just too much.

"He's going to touch you," A.J. told her. "Jamie is. He's right next to you and he's going to put his hands on your shoulders and—"

"Oh, my God!" It was the same peculiar electric current that had gone through Alison that first time she'd kissed A.J. It wasn't exactly unpleasant, except it was, because it was *weird*. "Don't do that!" she told A.J., suddenly—for the first time—frightened. "I don't know how you did that, but you *stop!*"

"Back off!" A.J. stood up and he was so tall, so big that she quickly backed away, bumping into the wall between the kitchen and the hall.

He immediately sat back down. "I'm sorry, I'm sorry, I wasn't talking to you, I was talking to Jamie—"

Her voice shook. "I think you better go."

"Please," he said, his hands carefully out on the table in front of him, as if that would help her to see he wasn't a danger to her. "Jamie won't do that again. I promise. I can see how . . . that was too much. Too soon."

Except how did she know he *wasn't* a danger, to her or to himself? She didn't.

"Yeah," A.J. was saying, but not to her. "Yes. That's . . ." He turned to her. "In the living room there's a bookshelf. There's not a lot of books on it, but there's a Bible."

Alison was already shaking her head. "I'm not going to read the Bible with you, A.J. I want you to go."

"I don't want you to . . ." He exhaled hard, but then started over. "Alison, please. I can prove that he's really here," he implored her. "And if you want to know the truth, it'll help me prove it to myself, as well. No more shocks—he won't touch you and . . . I won't touch you again either, okay?"

He sounded so lucid. So present and coherent. But she just didn't know enough about this kind of mental illness. For all she knew, this was normal. He'd be articulate and reasoned—until he wasn't.

God, the last thing she wanted to do was get the crazy man angry. What she had to do was call for help, but of course, her cell phone was with her keys—at the bottom of her handbag, in her crushed tin can of a trailer.

But as if he knew what she was thinking, he added, quietly, "If you still don't believe me after we do this, then . . . I'll go."

So Alison nodded.

"I'll stay right here," A.J. told her. "While you get, you know, the Bible."

She backed away, turning on the lights in the living room, listening for him to make any noise—to push back the chair—although what she would do if he did, she had no clue.

And there in the bookcase that she'd all but ignored because it held mostly knick-knacks and tchotchkes from tourist destinations such as the Grand Canyon, Mount Rushmore, and Wall, South Dakota, was a cheap, faux-leather-bound Bible.

She took it from the shelf—it was covered with dust—and brought it back into the hall, where she could see A.J. still sitting at the kitchen table.

Looking so normal.

"I know you said you've been to a doctor," she said, unable to keep from asking, "but have you seen a psychiatrist?"

"No," he said. "My, um, mother's been pushing for that."

"Your mother, the *doctor,* knows that . . ."

"I see Jamie," he finished for her. "Yeah. She's not convinced he's real either, even though he helped her find an old oil tank that was buried in her backyard—which used to be Jamie and Melody's backyard."

A.J.'s mother lived in the same house that Jamie and Melody had shared. Supposedly shared. Alison shook her head, not allowing herself to be distracted. "What does your mother think about . . . ?" she asked. "You know . . ."

"What does she think is wrong with me?" A.J. asked, and she nodded. "She thinks it's PTSD-related."

"Is it possible," Alison said carefully, "that she's right?"

He smiled. "Over the past few weeks, I've learned that just about anything is possible, so . . . Yeah." He looked away from her, again as if he were listening to someone speak. "That could do it," he said, then turned back to Alison. "There are no mirrors behind you, right?" he asked.

"Mirrors?" she said, turning to look. She was in

the hall that led to the bathroom and the bedroom. "No. Why?" She looked back at A.J.

"Open the book," A.J. said, "and put your finger to the first verse you see."

Alison looked at him. He was sitting on the other side of the kitchen, at least ten feet away from her. There was no way he could read the tiny print of the Bible from where he was. Still, when she opened it, as more dust fell from its cover and onionskin-thin pages, she kept it carefully angled away from him. She moved closer to the hall light, because the print was so small, *she* was going to have trouble reading it from where *she* was.

Her finger fell on what looked like some kind of poem.

And across the room, A.J. said aloud, *"Asleep on my bed, night after night, I dreamed of the one I love—"*

Alison slammed the book shut and spun around. There was no one behind her, no mirrors, nothing. She spun back and stared at A.J. How had he done that?

"That was the Bible?" he asked, pushing his hair out of his face. "What the heck *was* that?"

"I don't know," Alison said. It had to be some kind of trick. The book was rigged somehow, made to fall to exactly that page. He'd planted it there. Made it appear to be dusty. And maybe he could tell from about where her finger was, at which verse she was looking.

"It was Song of Songs," A.J. said. "At least that's what Jamie says. I'm gathering from your reaction that I got it right?"

Alison nodded.

And A.J. laughed. "Son of a bitch," he said. "I just might not be crazy. Go on. Try it again."

She backed up even more, so that she was all the way at the end of the hall, against the plain wooden door of a closet. She couldn't see A.J. from here, and he couldn't see her. Still, when she opened the book she held it very close to her chest. She put her finger down.

"Proverbs 12, verse 19. *A lie has a short life, but truth lives on forever,*" A.J. recited the words that were printed just above her finger, raising his voice so she could hear him clearly from the kitchen.

She snapped the book shut and went back toward him. "How are you doing this? How does it work?"

"I'm right again?" he asked. "Alison, don't you get it? This is *great*. Jamie's *real*."

"Is there something—some kind of sensor hidden in this Bible?" she asked. "Or . . . a camera, in the hall light fixture . . . ?"

"No hidden cameras," A.J. told her. He was grinning—*grinning*. Like this was the best night of his life. "No tricks. Just a ghost. Jamie stands beside you and reads aloud the words that you point to. Of course, you can't hear him, but *I* can and—"

"No," Alison said, tossing the book onto the table, flooded with anger and grief and terrible, crushing disappointment. "You take that with you and you get the hell out of here. You think this is *funny?*"

"No," he said, his smile wiped from his face. "I'm sorry, I'm . . ."

"I'm sorry, too," she said. "But you said that you'd go, if I did what you wanted and . . . I did. So now *go.*" There was a landline here in the kitchen, inches from where she was standing, but she didn't have the phone numbers for security—or even for Hugh. Those were all programmed into her cell. She wiped her eyes with hands that were shaking and her voice shook again, too, as she went for the bluff, picking up the kitchen phone. "Don't make me call security."

He looked crushed—like she was the one who'd broken his heart, instead of the other way around.

"Go," she said again. "*Now,* A.J."

"I'm sorry," he whispered again, and he picked up his boots and his jeans and his jacket, and went out the door, closing it gently behind him.

It was only then, after Alison had put on the night lock and she was as secure as she could possibly be, that she let herself cry.

"You know, you're not the first ghost I've ever seen," A.J. said to me, as we sat in his truck, just waiting for the sun to come up.

I'd followed him out of Alison's after that total fiasco. He'd stopped on the porch and pulled on his jeans and boots in silence, after warning me, "Don't say a goddamn word." I figured it was wise to keep my thoughts to myself as he neatly folded that towel and left it carefully hanging over her front railing.

He didn't tell me to go away, so I stayed nearby as he stomped over to his truck and climbed inside. I resisted the urge to tell him that sitting around in wet jeans was not the best way to remain chafe-free. Instead, I just sat beside him as he put his head back and closed his eyes and pretended to sleep.

But then, about an hour after we got into the truck, he surprised me by saying that. That I wasn't the first ghost he'd seen.

"Is that right?" I said, since he'd started the conversation.

"Yeah," he said. "I was in San Francisco. A little over ten years ago. I was drunk off my ass. Completely shitfaced."

"You're not drunk now, son," I said. "I'm real and you know it. I just wish Alison—"

"Yeah," he said tightly. "I wish Alison, too. But I don't blame her, I would've done the same thing. Get the lunatic out of the house, as quickly as possible. I've been sitting here, waiting for security to show up and escort me off the set."

I wanted to tell him that she'd come 'round, but

I wasn't sure that she would. I'd scared her, badly, with that jolt. That was piss-poor judgment on my part. "I'm sorry, kid."

"I was living in Golden Gate Park," A.J. said. "Sleeping in the daytime, walking the city at night. I learned a lot of tricks in the army, ways to stay hidden, because sleeping in the park wasn't legal. But the more I drank, the less I cared about keeping to a schedule or staying out of sight. I just didn't give a damn."

This was hard to hear. I knew about it, but this was the first time A.J. had spoken to me about any of this. I tried not to squirm though, because I didn't want him to stop talking.

"One day I passed out, not too far from the Japanese Tea Garden, and I woke up to find myself getting hit in the ribs by a boy with a length of pipe. He was with four other boys, and I knew right away that this was some kind of gang initiation—that they were going to kill me."

A.J. turned to look at me. "I was dead," he told me, his voice matter of fact. "I knew I was dead, and in that split-second before that kid tried to bash in my head, I felt regret. I didn't want to die. You know, I hadn't been alive, not really, for close to a decade, but when it came to the end of the line? I honestly didn't want to go.

"So I fought back," A.J. continued. "I didn't exactly win, but they didn't kill me. My rib was broken and I looked like I'd been hit by a car, but

I was alive. I managed to crawl to a sidewalk, where I knew someone would find me. And then someone *did* find me. Which is where it got a little weird."

"You saw a ghost," I surmised.

"Sort of," he said. "I saw Tom Fallingstar. He's the shaman—"

"I remember Tom," I interrupted. He was the spiritual leader of the local Inuits up in and around Heaven. His son Charlie had married A.J.'s sister, Bev. "But . . . he's still alive."

"Yup," A.J. said. "Still, I was lying there, waiting for someone to find me, wishing I had a bottle of tequila to numb the pain in my side, and wishing that I had the strength to never touch another bottle of tequila again, and guess who appears out of the fog?"

"Tom Fallingstar," I said.

"Yup," A.J. said again. "Old Tom sat down next to me and just chatted for a while. It was nice to see him—it had been years since I'd been home. He told me that my mother and Bev were worried about me—that nobody knew where I was. And then he gave me a hundred-dollar bill. He said it was bus fare. He told me that now that I'd decided to stop drinking, I should come back to Alaska. And I said, *Wait, I didn't decide anything,* and he said, *Yeah, I'm pretty certain you just did.* He told me there was a good rehab clinic in Fairbanks—a place called Renata Hospital—and that they had a special program for vets. The VA wouldn't pay for it because of the way I'd been discharged, but Tom said he'd lend me whatever I needed to cover the cost. He knew I was good for it. He said, *See you in a few days,* and then he disappeared."

"He tracked you down," I told him. I'd always liked that Tom Fallingstar, and now I liked him even more.

But A.J. was shaking his head. "He never left Alaska. His uncle was ill. Tom was with him, almost around the clock, for months before he died."

"Maybe," I suggested, "you *were* so drunk you were hallucinating."

"Then where'd I get the bus fare? A hundred-dollar bill—it was in my pocket."

"Maybe one of those boys felt bad about trying to kill you."

A.J. shot me a look, and yeah, I know. It was a ridiculous idea. But at the same time, even if Tom had tapped into some kind of superhuman ability to spirit-surf away from his body, how would he have managed to bring along that money?

Unless, of course, he was spectacularly superhuman.

"And how come there was a bed already waiting for me at Renata when I called?" A.J. asked.

"Well, what did Tom say when you asked him about it?"

"He just smiled," A.J. said, "and told me that he'd dreamed I was coming home."

"The world is full of mysteries and miracles," I told him, as there, right in front of our eyes a daily miracle occurred. The sky turned all shades of yellows and golds and pinks and blues and purples as the sun poked its head over the distant horizon, and a new day dawned.

A.J. was staring out at it, but I wasn't sure he was seeing it. His gaze had gone inward, and I knew he was trying his damnedest not to cry as he'd thought about the past night and all he'd gained and then lost.

"We'll figure out a way to get Alison to listen to you," I told him gruffly, feeling a little choked up myself.

"How exactly are we going to do that?" he asked.

"That," I told the kid, "is another one of life's mysteries. *How* doesn't really matter. What matters is our resolve to get the job done."

A.J. nodded, but I could tell that he wasn't quite convinced.

So I zapped him. "You want this girl?" I asked.

"I don't know," he said.

"You don't know?" I loaded my voice with disbelief.

"Yes," he said, some of his misery transferring to anger and irritation. "I *don't* know, is that all right with you? I'm in love with her, okay? Enough to want to protect her from the crazy-ass bullshit that is me."

"So, what?" I said, trying to sound as if his confession hadn't made me want to get out of the truck and dance. He was in love with her. I knew it. I *knew* it. That was half the battle won. "You're just going to make that decision for her? Treat her like a child and not let her make up her own mind about whether her definition of *crazy-ass bullshit* is the same as yours? Everyone has a different threshold, kid. A different line."

"And I'm on the other side of hers," A.J. pointed out. "We proved you were real, but she kicked me out. If she won't let me near her . . ." He shook his head.

"Right now," I pointed out. "It's only right now that she won't let you near her. Tomorrow's another day. And there's another day after that. We'll do whatever it takes," I reassured him. "It's that simple. I've faced adversity, too, kid. I know a thing or two about keeping on when the chips are down. Literally. And you know how you start? You don't quit."

And with those words of wisdom, the dawn burst into a morning that was astonishing in its brilliance.

Because last night's soaking rain had made the desert bloom.

"But how do you know," A.J. whispered, "when it's finally time to surrender? When the best thing you can do for the woman you love is . . . to let her go?"

"I've been there, too, A.J.," I reminded him as I remembered the sharply antiseptic smell of the hospital, the grave faces of the doctors, Mel's thin hand in mine. "I've been there, too."

Chapter Fourteen

Sandra Busard was going in Alison's place, to scout locations with Hugh—and he was not at all happy about that.

"She hates me," he said, as he followed Alison to the catering tent which, amazingly, had survived the storm.

"No, she doesn't," she said, getting in line to get a tray, even though the thought of breakfast made her stomach hurt. But this morning, *everything* made her stomach hurt. Breathing hurt. "*You* hate *her*."

"Because she hates me."

"Because you *think* she hates you. That's not the same thing."

"Couldn't you just wait to clean out your trailer," he started.

"Couldn't *you* just act like a grown-up for once and tell the woman you don't want her to go with you? You know, other people are dealing with things that are a little more devastatingly awful than a four-hour car ride with someone you're embarrassed to spend time with because she overheard you being a prick and saying she had the creative instincts of a trained rat in a maze."

And whoops, she'd slammed her tray down on the metal runners in front of the breakfast buffet much harder than she'd intended. From all around the tent, people were looking in their direction. And Hugh's mouth had dropped open.

But this was a movie set. Dramatic outbursts were not that unusual, and the attention never lasted for long.

"Sorry," she said grimly as she took a plate and helped herself to a small pile of scrambled eggs. Maybe some protein would make her feel better, even though she felt as if she'd never be hungry again.

"So . . . what's going on?" Hugh asked as he followed her, taking a small mountain of eggs himself, with a bacon side.

Alison just shook her head.

"Devastatingly awful?" he repeated. "Did things go south with Cowboy McDreamy?"

She took a mug and held it under the coffee spigot and filled it. "South doesn't begin to describe it."

"Uh-oh," Hugh said. "Did you—"

"Yes," she told him. "Yes. Whatever you're asking, the answer's probably yes, even before I've heard the question. I did. With him." She leaned close and lowered her voice. "You know what happened with Kent?"

"Oh, crap," Hugh said. "The cowboy already *dumped* you?"

"No," Alison said, "but I'd rather he'd done that than what he *did* do."

"He's married? The bastard—"

"He's crazy," she interrupted him.

Hugh stopped and laughed. "Honey, who's *not?*" he asked.

"No," she said. "Hughie, I'm talking scary schizophrenic. Off his meds mentally ill."

"Oh, crap," Hugh said again, leading the way to a table in an empty part of the tent. "Are you all right? Did he get, what? Violent?"

"No," she said. "But he sat there and told me—completely seriously—that he's being followed around by the ghost of his dead great-grandfather. He sees him and talks to him and . . . It was . . . Devastatingly awful." To her horror, her eyes filled with tears.

Hugh took her hand. "Oh, babe," he said, his voice filled with sympathy. "That bites. I know you really liked this guy."

"What's worse, is he set up this whole elaborate scheme to make me believe that this ghost is real. I haven't found them yet, but I think he might've broken into my house and planted minicams. At the very least, he broke in and left a Bible on the bookshelf, that somehow opens to predetermined pages. I don't know how he did it, but the point is, he went to a lot of trouble—a lot—to convince me that this ghost is real. Which it's not—how could it be?

"The doubly stupid thing is," she told her friend, "that I didn't sleep at all last night. I spent the night online, researching schizophrenia and other illnesses that can cause hallucinations. I keep thinking, maybe with the right medication . . . And then I think, God, no, I don't want that in my life. I grew up with a mother who was . . . She was crazy and she was a drunk, and when she drank, she got crazier, and I've done Al-Anon and I've gone through all the therapy for adult children of alcoholics, and I know, I *know* that her alcoholism was a disease that she couldn't control, that it was a mental illness, and I've forgiven her, I have, but I don't want that in my life. Except then I think about how great he is . . . How great he *could* be . . . And goddamnit, I'm sitting here, and I'm looking around, because there's this big, sick, enabling, doomed part of me that desperately wants to see him again. Because maybe I can help him, right? Maybe I can save him. Kind of the way my grandmother went to her grave believing that she could somehow save my mother, when she couldn't."

"Wow," Hugh said after sitting for a moment in silence. "Overload. I am never, ever whining to you about Kent again."

"Kent's a jerk," Alison said. "And you don't

346

whine about him. You just grieve. Loudly. And I think that's what I need to do."

Hugh nodded. "I'm so sorry."

"Please tell me that I can't save him," she whispered.

"You know you can't save him," Hugh said. "You don't need me to tell you that. But if you're only looking for a short-term thing, and the sex was so great that you're looking for him despite the fact that he has conversations with invisible dead people and breaks in to put Bibles on people's bookshelves . . . ? Where's the harm in having a fling?"

Alison pulled her hand away. "That's no help. I really liked this guy. I really thought . . ." She pushed her tray away. Stood up. "Where was the harm in your having had a one-night stand with Kent?"

"But I hooked up with Kent," Hugh said, standing, too, "dreaming of a Cape Cod summer wedding. Last I heard from you, A.J. Gallagher—"

"Don't say his name!" Alison hissed, looking around. All she needed was for him to find her talking about him. But he wasn't in the tent.

"He who shall be nameless," Hugh substituted, "was, last time we spoke, a con man or a naive yokel who'd been lied to by his family, that you happened to think was particularly hot. What happened? Were you seriously going all traditionally girly on me? After just one night?"

Alison picked up her tray and took it over to the garbage. "I might've been," she said. "I might've started . . . falling for him. I'm a complete moron."

"Okay," Hugh said. "I get it. If you're falling for him, or you've already fallen—"

"Don't say that, either," she whispered.

"You can't do the casual thing," he told her, "if you're not feeling casual. I shouldn't have suggested it."

Alison scraped her untouched eggs into the trash, feeling guilty on top of everything for serving herself food that she knew from the start she wasn't going to eat. "I don't know what to do," she said.

"Yeah, you do," Hugh told her. His plate was clean. Somehow he'd managed to eat all his breakfast. "You'll do what I do. You'll hide when you see him coming and you'll grieve. And eventually? Honey, you'll move on."

A.J. was waiting by Alison's trailer, leaning against his truck, when he saw her approach from the direction of the catering tent.

She faltered when she saw him, but then squared her shoulders and kept coming, head held high.

"I don't need your help," she said as she got within speaking range.

"Are you okay?" he asked.

"I'm great," she said, but she was obviously

lying. She looked exhausted. As if, like him, she hadn't slept since they'd parted.

He'd worked some crazy magic in order to get in a shower and a shave, and to rustle up clean clothes so he didn't look like crazy sleeps-in-his-truck man. He'd even talked the technicians in the hair and makeup tent into giving him a haircut. Nothing too radical, just a trim.

He'd looked in that mirror and seen his familiar weather-beaten face looking back at him. His healthy, solid, filled-out, grown man's face.

He'd seen himself looking thin and ill, during all those months at war when he'd had near-continuous diarrhea from the crap water that the troops had been given. He'd looked even worse in the hospital after Hor al-Hammar, after he'd nearly been killed. And then during and right after rehab, he'd had the street-worn, hard-edged, big-boned skinniness of a man who'd spent months drinking every dollar he could beg, steal, or borrow.

He'd seen himself, too, in the mirrors in the bathrooms at the shelters, in the grip of the worst of his wild-eyed addiction.

So, yeah, he knew what crazy looked like, and it wasn't looking back at him.

Not today, anyway.

But Alison wouldn't even look at him, gazing past him at the ruins of her trailer, obviously intending to breeze right by.

"Alison," he said, stepping forward, which

made her stop short. And, God, now she looked as if she were ready to run, should he try to reach for her. So he backed away immediately, apologizing. "I'm sorry, I'm—"

"No, you know what?" she said. "I *do* have a question for you. About the story you told me last night. One of the stories you told me, anyway. It's been bothering me. You said Quinn was the only person inside the Red Rock Saloon—that the Kellys were all waiting outside, to ambush your . . . Gallagher. The Kid. But the gun battle happened inside. I've seen the bullet marks in the walls. So don't you dare try to tell me it went down in the street."

Okay, this was good. She was talking to him, even though hostility was radiating off of her in waves, and was thick in her voice.

A.J. nodded. "No, you're right," he said, "it took place inside the saloon. The barkeep broke up the poker game at the designated time, you know, after Quinn and the Kellys were in position. But Jamie didn't leave the table. Instead he told the barkeep to go on out and give a shout and invite Bo Kelly inside so Jamie could buy him a drink."

"That's not really what happened." Jamie got out of the truck. He'd been sitting inside, slightly removed, but close enough to offer support. "That's an old family embellishment—the bit about me offering to buy Bo a drink?"

"I'm sorry," A.J. told Alison, "I was wrong."

He paraphrased Jamie's words as the ghost told him, "It makes for a good story, but truth is, I lost big that night and barely had enough to get into the next night's game. In fact, I was in the middle of a losing streak that lasted for another two weeks, which is one of the reasons it took so long for me and Mel to leave town. We couldn't go without proper provisions. And I also had to, uh, win back my horse. Which was embarrassing, so I kind of didn't mention it before this. But that morning? I did invite Bo Kelly in to talk, figuring the drinks would be on the house, since no barkeep in his right mind would stick around for *that* meet-and-greet. The rest, kid, is as you know it."

"Jamie sent a message out via one of the girls who worked upstairs," A.J. told Alison. "He told Bo that he wasn't the kind of man who held a grudge, and that whatever deal that gang had going with Quinn, *he* could make them a better offer.

"See, Jamie knew that Bo Kelly was unhappy with how things were shaking down between himself and Quinn, and sure enough, Bo and two of his men came into the saloon—staying close to the edges of the building, so that the marshal didn't see them come inside from his second-floor window.

"Jamie went behind the bar, which not only gave him protection from the balcony above, but also access to the liquor. Which he started serving the Kellys, rather liberally. He told Bo that he was gunning for the wrong man. That Quinn was the one squeezing them for a too-substantial cut of their hard-earned pay each week. Jamie told them if they got rid of Quinn, he'd see to it that Bo Kelly got elected sheriff. He and his boys could run the town—earn the money Quinn was making, without any bloodshed or peril."

"The people of Jubilation would *not* have elected Bo Kelly sheriff," Alison countered.

"Yeah, but Bo didn't know that," A.J. said. "And Jamie was pretty good at making people believe the impossible." He still was.

Although look at him. He was standing here, talking to Alison. He wouldn't have believed *that* was possible just a few short minutes ago.

It was true, her body language was angry and tight. Impenetrable. But they were talking. That was good, right?

"Bo called the rest of his boys in," A.J. continued, "and they all stood there arguing and drinking, which of course got loud. Quinn came out of his room and realized his plan was deteriorating before his eyes. So he stood on the balcony, looking down into the saloon, and he ordered Bo to kill Jamie.

"Bo refused. In fact, he drew on Quinn, but missed. Quinn shot Bo and *didn't* miss—"

"Lucky shot," Jamie murmured.

"And just like that, Bo Kelly was dead," A.J. told Alison. "All hell broke loose, with half the Kellys aiming for Quinn, and the other half shooting at Jamie. It wasn't long before it was just Quinn and Jamie left. But before Jamie could rid Melody of her marital problems for good, Quinn's deputies arrived, having heard the gunshots. Jamie slipped out the back door, and Quinn—wounded in the leg—was an instant hero and credited with single-handedly wiping out the Kelly Gang."

"So Jamie was behind the bar," Alison said. "And Quinn was on the balcony. That actually explains . . ." She shook her head. "Thank you. You never finished the story, and . . . I was curious. That's all." She turned to walk away.

"Wait," he said. "I know you don't need my help, but—"

"Don't need it, don't want it," she said. "Don't want to see you, don't want to talk to you."

"You're kind of talking to me right now," A.J. pointed out.

"No," she said. "I'm done talking to you. I want you to stay away from me—*far* away. Do you understand? Because if you don't, I *will* get security involved, and they'll help you to understand."

Beside him, Jamie whistled through his teeth. "She's still furious. Which is good, kid. You want there to be passion."

"I just thought you might, at least, want to borrow my truck." A.J. held out the keys, offering them to her, dangling the ring on the end of his finger so she could take them without touching him. "It'll make it easier to move your books."

"No, thank you," she said, crossing her arms.

"It's also going to be hot in the trailer," he tried, because at least she wasn't walking away. "But I'm used to that kind of heat. I'd be happy to go in there—"

"No," she said, no *thank you* this time.

"See, I thought maybe we could, you know, get someone to work in the middle, between me and you. Like a chain. They could take the boxes from me and pass them to you so you could put them in the truck. . . ."

She just stood there, shaking her head, looking anywhere but at him.

"That way, you don't have to see me or talk to me," he pointed out as he attempted a smile.

"Look, A.J.," Alison said, "I can't help you." She looked up at him, finally meeting his gaze, but only for a fraction of a second. "Go back to Alaska. Listen to your mother and go see a doctor."

He cleared his throat. "I appreciate your—"

She cut him off. "I need you to leave me alone."

"Kid," Jamie murmured. "I know I've been advocating that old *never surrender* approach, but I think it's time to give her some space."

But A.J. couldn't do it. He couldn't just turn and drive away. "Alison," he said again, his heart in his throat. "Come on. You're telling me that you're not even remotely curious? You don't want to see if I can't do it again—the reading thing—with a different book. You get to pick it, or, God, okay, you can get a pad and a pen and write something, and I'll be twenty yards away. We can do it outside, wherever you choose. I'll be blindfolded and I'll still be able to tell you what you just wrote, because Jamie will read it to me."

"No," she said, backing away. "I don't want to. I won't. I'm going to go get boxes. If you're here when I get back? I *am* calling security. So don't be here. Go home, A.J. Just go. *Home*."

And with that, she turned and rapidly walked away.

"Kid," Jamie said again, his voice gentle. "You haven't slept, and she clearly hasn't either. Why don't you back on down and get some rest? Tomorrow's another day."

A.J. nodded. "Yeah," he said, and he got into his truck and drove away.

I'm always astonished at people's fascination with the gunfight at the Red Rock Saloon.

I mean, here was Alison, in the middle of all of this emotional pain, unable to keep from asking A.J. about it.

Of course, maybe she really just wanted an

355

excuse to stand there with him, even just for a few minutes, and she couldn't figure out any other way to do it.

But the thing is, she saw talking about the shoot-out as a legitimate excuse.

It was that infamous and legendary.

It's become the classic tale of good versus evil in the history of the American West. It's the age-old fable of the loner versus the pack, one lawman standing up to the gang of ferocious criminals and coming out the victor.

Except that the lawman wasn't alone, and most of those criminals were well on their way to becoming soused. I was serving those drinks fast and furious, folks. They weren't good marksmen to start with, and add a little alcohol . . . It's a recipe for success if, like me, you're on the other side.

But I also want you to take into consideration that the so-called good guys, Silas Quinn and myself—and I'm sure I'm risking eternal damnation for lumping myself into the same category as that bastard Quinn—were 1) up on the second-floor balcony, which offered a great deal of cover to hide behind, or 2) behind a bar that was built to withstand a hail of bullets.

Meanwhile, the Kelly Gang, a bit sodden and, if not quite staggering around then at least pretty damn close, were smack-dab in the middle of the saloon.

Like ducks in a shooting gallery, my friends.

I'd also like to point out, for the official record, that I saw Jed Kelly shoot and kill his first cousin, Johnny Johnson, before he turned and hightailed it out of there with his kid brother Nathaniel who, records show, no one even knew was at the saloon that day.

So when the smoke first cleared, there were two men dead—Bo Kelly, killed by a lucky shot from Quinn's gun, and Johnson. I'd shot three of the other Kelly boys—Zeke and Abe Kelly, and Frank Porter. I was careful only to wing 'em. I find killing a stupid man distasteful. But those three fools weren't even smart enough to crawl to cover. And they died for it, because Silas Quinn apparently had no qualms about shooting a wounded man. He gutshot them all, the bastard, probably because a man's belly is the easiest place to hit.

According to the legend, and to those dime store novels, Quinn and the Kellys were shooting it up inside the Red Rock Saloon for most of the day.

In truth, the entire gunplay took maybe two minutes, maybe a little less.

And I spent at least one and a half of those minutes trying to kill Quinn.

I would've felt no distaste in sighting that sombitch's head and squeezing the trigger. I have no problem killing a mean man.

But just as Quinn found it difficult to draw a bead on me, I found him likewise elusive.

In fact, I spent most of my ammunition, but only managed to hit Quinn in the leg.

Then, right when I was getting ready to rush that staircase for a second time, and find and finish him up on the second floor, his deputies arrived.

But still, I didn't quit trying.

"Quinn's had it out with the Kellys," I told them. "He's upstairs—the marshal is—and one of the gang is up there, too, gone after him. He's wounded and dangerous, so shoot to kill, boys, shoot to kill."

See, I was hoping they'd do the dirty work for me and shoot Quinn, thinking he was a Kelly.

But no luck.

They didn't shoot Quinn. Instead, they brought him downstairs and called in the doctor to look at his leg.

While I went out the back door.

Melody Quinn had saved my life that night, but unfortunately, try as I might, I hadn't been able to return the favor.

Chapter Fifteen

It was just before midnight when Alison got the call from Henry Logan himself, and the day went from bad to worse.

"I'm sorry to bother you this late, Carter, but I know you're friends with Darcy, you know, Hugh? Little red-haired Hugh."

"Yes, sir," she said.

"Is he with you?"

She turned on the light on her bedside table. "I haven't seen him since he left this morning. I turned in early—"

"Do me a favor," the director said, "and see if he's maybe camping on your couch. I know he's done that before."

"Yeah, but never when I didn't invite him," Alison pointed out. Still, she got out of bed and slipped on her robe and went into her living room. It was empty. She looked through the other rooms. She was definitely alone.

Unless, of course, A.J.'s ghost was with her.

"He's not here," Alison reported. "What's going on?"

"Apparently he never came back from his location-scouting run," Henry told her. "And he's not answering his phone."

"No," Alison said. "He must've. Come back. I saw Sandra at dinner. She went with him."

"No, she didn't," Henry said. "He went out alone. Look, I know you were originally going with him. Did you talk about where he was heading? Because we're going to call the state police and organize search teams. If we wait until morning . . . Once the sun comes up . . . If he's injured, he's already been out there too long."

"Northeast," Alison said as she flashed both hot and cold. *Injured?* She went back into her bedroom and started pulling on her clothes. "That's where he said he was going. I made a point to remind him that there's still a police investigation ongoing over to the northwest, even though that's the way Quinn would have actually gone. Where are you, Henry? I'll be right there."

August 6, 1898
Dear Diary,

The town has thrown me a welcoming "ball." It was hardly grand, barely fashionable, with women in ill-fitting, cast-down gowns with mud-stained hems and ghastly musicians playing barely recognizable tunes.

Half of the town—the people who have been the kindest to me—had not been invited.

But this ball is the reason he has kept my face clear of bruises and cuts so I can hardly complain. Still, the ruling class of Jubilation, those Lords and Ladies lifted from their place in the mud by the silver they've found in the surrounding hills, murmured at how ladylike I was. What small steps I took. They don't know that I took those small steps in an attempt to keep my latest broken rib from paining.

Or maybe they do know. Maybe everyone knows. Yet they do nothing. Save one man.

He was there tonight, my gambler. He came, even without an invitation. He just leaned against the wall, watching me, for what seemed to be an eternity. When my husband finally went down to the street to have one of his cigars with the other men, the gambler approached and asked me for a dance. For the first time all night, the music seemed to be in tune.

I accepted, even knowing that my husband would of course find out, knowing I would be beaten for it.

He held me politely, this gambler with the quicksilver smile. He held me at the distance propriety demanded. Still, he managed to touch me, if only with his eyes.

"Are you well?" he asked.

I replied that I was, thank you.

Then he surprised me by asking, "Would you tell me if you weren't?"

This time I answered him honestly. "No."

He was quiet for quite some time, and then he asked if my husband had hurt me again.

With the outlaws gone, there was nothing with which to blackmail the monster, to keep him from harming me. And likewise, my gambler believed himself to be safe, because he no longer posed a threat. And yet the monster still marked him, watched him, waited for him to make a mistake. Just one was all it would take and my gambler would be brutally gunned down.

I told him this, told him that he'd done enough, that he should leave this godforsaken place.

But he said he would not, that he liked this little town. But his eyes and his smile told me that what he liked, in fact, was me.

But I know that he saw my despair because he fell silent again. And when we were some distance away from the other dancers, he asked me, in a low voice, did I want him to kill my husband? And I knew if I said yes, he would do it right then, right there.

I was shocked—not at the thought of killing, but at the fact that if this gambler tried such a thing, he would surely hang. When I told him this, he agreed, but said he was willing to take his chances.

For me.

I told him no and thanked him for his concern, pressing his hand as the dance ended.

He bid me good evening and told me he would see me soon.

Tonight I have begun to plan in earnest. Because in this gambler, I have finally found the man who can help set me free.

A.J.'s camp was right where he'd said it was.

He'd either found his tent or gotten a new one. It was pitched near his truck, near the cold remains of a fire that had been carefully doused.

"A.J.," Alison called, suddenly feeling really stupid that she'd come out here alone.

This was crazy. She was as crazy as he was, and it wasn't going to help at all in their search for Hugh.

But what if . . . ?

"A.J.," she called even louder, and she heard movement from the tent. "Wake up. There's an emergency."

He scrambled out, wearing only a pair of briefs, his feet jammed into his boots, his hair standing straight up. "Alison. What's the matter? Are you all right?"

In the glow from her flashlight, he looked . . . a lot like she'd looked in shorts and boots. Except she'd only looked ridiculous. He also managed to look ridiculously sexy.

"I'm fine," she said, "but Hugh went out scouting locations and he hasn't come back. We've sent out search parties, but no one's found anything, and . . . I thought . . ."

She'd thought that—maybe—if there was the slightest chance that Jamie really was real, that he could find Hugh the way he'd found Alison when she was trapped in the bathroom with that snake.

And God, yes, it was crazy, but the sun would be up in less than an hour. And the state police were starting to make noises that sounded an awful lot as if they were preparing the production crew for the very real possibility that they weren't going to find Hugh alive.

But A.J. didn't make her say it. He didn't gloat. He didn't rub her face in the fact that, yes, she'd come to him for help. He just closed his eyes and put his head back and said, "Jamie, where are you?"

And God, that was weird, but weirder still was this hope she had that Jamie truly existed. And she couldn't help it, she started to cry.

"Hey," A.J. said, moving toward her, but then stopping, as if self-conscious about getting too close. "We're going to find him, okay?" He closed his eyes, again. "Come on, Jamie, I need you—*now*."

"The theory's that he's had some kind of car accident. Jeep. He was driving a Jeep," Alison said in her stupid wobbling voice, wiping her eyes with the back of her hand as she willed herself to stop. "A Jeep without a LoJack signal, without GPS."

A compass. Each of the production company

Jeeps was outfitted with a compass and a first-aid kit and plenty of water and Gatorade. Which was great and would keep Hugh alive—provided whatever accident he'd been in wasn't so severe that he couldn't reach that water or Gatorade.

"We've tried calling him, tried to track his phone, but we've had no luck with that, either," she said. "Should I . . . not interrupt you?"

"No," he said. "It's okay. He's here."

Jamie was here.

Oh, good . . . ?

A.J. quickly explained the situation to the empty air, then paused, as if listening intently, before turning back to Alison. "He wants to make sure he's . . . Hugh's the redhead, right?" he asked. "With . . . the broken heart?"

Alison looked at him. "How do you know about that?"

"I don't," A.J. said. "But Jamie apparently does."

"Yes," Alison said. "Hugh Darcy. He's in his mid-twenties, red hair, definitely a broken heart. He's also gay. Is that going to be a problem for . . . Jamie?"

"No," A.J. said, absolutely. "Jamie says don't worry, he'll find him. With a little luck, he'll be able to focus on Hugh and just zap himself to wherever he is." He pointed to his tent. "I'm going to get . . . pants on. Pants will . . . be good. On. I'll be ready to go when Jamie gets back. Which should be pretty quick."

Ready to go.

Of course.

After Jamie—the invisible ghost—found Hugh, the only person he'd be able to tell about it was A.J. Who would then have to go out in his truck and find Hugh himself.

"I'm coming with you," Alison called. "Is that okay?"

A.J. emerged from his tent, still fastening his belt, a T-shirt over his arm. "Of course. Are you sure?" But he didn't wait for her to answer. He turned and, God, it just didn't get any less weird. He was looking and listening to Jamie again, who was, apparently, already back.

Provided that he was real and not just a figment of A.J.'s psychotic imagination.

"Jamie found Hugh," A.J. told her, and she wanted to believe him so badly, her knees went a little weak.

Please God, don't let him just be crazy.

But A.J. returned his full attention to the empty space beside him. "He's where . . . ? Yeah, that's really not good." He turned back to Alison, his face serious. "He went south, not north. His Jeep's in a ditch, like he went off the road, but then he left it, which he shouldn't have done, and he went south again. Walking. He must've gotten completely turned around. But Jamie says now he's just lying there, at the side of a dirt road that leads down to Mexico. He's alive, but he's really weak. Jamie tried, but can't get him to move, hardly at all. It looks like he's been pretty sick. Possibly injured."

"Should we call for a chopper?" Alison asked. "There's one standing by in Tucson, but it'll take awhile to get here."

A.J. shook his head. "He's not that far," he told her. "Twenty minutes, tops. But he's in the total opposite direction from where the search teams have been looking."

Alison nodded and held out her hand for the keys. "I'll drive," she said.

It would've been crowded with the three of them in the front seat of his truck, had Jamie not elected to ride on the cab roof.

When he wanted to talk, he stuck his face down through the plastic of the ceiling, right where the overhead light was, which was quite the bizarre effect.

Still it was better than the ghost sitting next to Alison and involuntarily jolting her again.

"Left here," Jamie instructed, and A.J. passed the information on to Alison, who was driving like a NASCAR champion, fast and sure, her hands tight on the steering wheel.

"Thank you for asking me to help," A.J. said, and she glanced at him.

"If he's not here," she said, "I'm kicking you out and you're walking back."

"He's here."

She drew in a deep breath and exhaled, hard. "How do I know you didn't kidnap him and stage this whole thing?"

"And yet you're in my truck with me," he pointed out. "Probably because you don't really think I'd do that."

"But apparently," she said, "I'm known for being wrong. According to you, I've written a whole book that's wrong."

"You wrote a book about a legend," A.J. pointed out. "As for what happened to Hugh? After we find him, he'll be able to tell us."

"Unless you gave him the date rape drug," Alison countered. "That would've made him forget what happened."

"Damn," Jamie said from the ceiling. "She's got an answer for everything, doesn't she?"

"We'll make sure he gets a blood test," A.J. said. "To see if he was given roofies. And after we get Hugh to the doctor? We can go someplace where there can't possibly be a camera or a sensor or whatever you can imagine, and I'll put a freaking bag over my head, if that's what it'll take—"

"While I write something on a pad," Alison finished for him, "that Jamie then reads and you repeat."

"Yeah," A.J. said. "We can do it as many times as you want, however you want. You make the rules. We'll do it till you're satisfied—and okay, *that* came out sounding . . . That's not what I meant. I meant—"

"I know what you meant," she said.

They drove for a few more minutes in silence, as he berated himself for being an idiot.

This was, no doubt about it, a precious second chance that he'd been given, and he was not going to blow it.

But then she said, "I'll do that, if we find Hugh. I'll sit down with you. And Jamie. But you have to promise that, if we *don't* find him . . ."

"We're going to find him," A.J. said.

"But if we don't?" she said. "After you walk back to town? We're going to sit down, you and me, in a very public place, and we're going to call your mother and we're going to make arrangements to get you the help that you need. Does that sound like a fair deal?"

"Alison," he started.

She cut him off. "Yes or no," she said. "Is that a deal? Either way, we're going to talk, and you're going to answer my questions. *All* my questions. I agree to this deal, do you?"

"Yes," he said.

"Good. How much farther?"

A.J. glanced up at Jamie, who lifted his head and soared high above them, to get a bird's-eye view.

"Half a mile, then a left onto the dirt road," he

reported, and A.J. relayed. "Then another two and a half miles, maybe a little less, and he's off to the right side. I'll go and be with him, and flag you down."

He popped away.

"Are we alone?" Alison asked.

A.J. nodded. "Yeah."

"Is he . . . always with you?" she asked. "I mean, was he . . . Did he . . ."

"No," A.J. told her. "When we were . . . together, he wasn't there."

Alison glanced at him, shaking her head as she focused on the road, slowing to make the turn onto what seemed little better than an off-road trail. "I was going to say, *Good, because that would be weird,* but really, what about this *isn't* weird?"

"I should have told you," A.J. said, "before we got too . . . hot and heavy. But . . . you just . . . swept me off my feet."

"I'm sorry," she said, "but that's bullshit. You swept *me* off *my* feet. I didn't carry you into the shower. And then into my bedroom, where I'm positive my feet didn't touch the ground once."

"Okay," he said, "so maybe my choice of expression was wrong, but I just . . . You're irresistible."

"Yeah, well," she said, "you were, too."

Were. Past tense. Ouch.

"I should have told you," A.J. said again. "Bottom line? I was wrong, and I apologize."

"And I don't accept your apology, thank you very much," she shot back. "I think you purposely deceived me. I think you knew damn well how I was going to react to your little news flash, so you lied."

"By omission," A.J. pointed out. "Funny how it was okay when Silas Quinn did it." He could see, up ahead, Jamie in the middle of the road, waving his arms. "Slow down—there he is."

And there he was.

Hugh Darcy. A slight figure collapsed at the side of the road.

Alison was out of the truck almost before she'd braked to a stop and put it in park. But A.J. was closer and he beat her to the man.

Hugh was lying in a puddle of his own vomit, and even though he'd tried to cover his head with a spare shirt, he was still badly sunburned—as if he'd been lying out here since early in the afternoon.

It was a miracle that he wasn't dead from that, let alone any potential internal bleeding from the accident.

"Please, help me get him in the truck," Alison said, tears running down her face—a mix of fear and relief.

A.J. picked up the smaller man easily as Alison dug for her cell phone, already trying to call ahead for an ambulance. It wasn't until they hit the main road that her cell worked, but she finally reached the police and coordinated with them so that they'd meet on the road back into town.

A road that A.J. didn't walk.

In fact, he drove.

Chapter Sixteen

I was real.

What a relief.

Seriously though, Alison was still in Whoo-whoo-land about the whole thing, and her body language screamed *Don't touch me.* She carefully kept her distance from A.J. as they got red-haired, broken-hearted Hugh transferred into the hands of the paramedics, who immediately gave him fluid intravenously.

His blood pressure was surprisingly stable, which was an indication that his injuries weren't internal, thank God. Until they discovered otherwise, though, they were going on the theory that he'd thrown up because he'd hit his head, which wasn't so good. Head injuries could be tricky.

As the ambulance sped off, leaving Alison staring after it like a worried mother who'd just put her kindergartner on the school bus, I knew A.J. wanted to put his arms around her. But he didn't dare.

"He's going to be okay," he said instead, and Alison looked at him in surprise, almost as if she'd forgotten he was there. The pair of them were going on severely limited sleep. "And Jamie can pop in and check on him, so we don't have to wait for a phone call for news about how he's doing."

"Is Jamie here?" she asked. "Right now?"

A.J. glanced at me, almost as if he were checking to see if I were at my desk and taking calls. So I nodded and spread my hands in a silent *Here I am,* and he said, "He's here."

"Where?" Alison asked.

"Leaning against the hood of the truck."

Not that I needed the truck to be able to lean. I could lean anywhere, or even sit on thin air if I wanted to. Still, I figured it would be less disconcerting to A.J. if I used bits of his physical world whenever possible.

Alison turned to face me. "Which side of the truck?"

"This side."

It was then that she surprised the hell out of me by moving toward me, her hand outstretched, as if she were going to try to touch me.

"She's gonna get zapped," I warned A.J., who told her just that.

She pulled her hand back. "Is it . . ." She started over. "Will he get zapped, too? Because I won't do it if he doesn't want me to."

"Well, it's an odd sensation," I told her through A.J., "but I'd be happy to shake your hand, dear."

It was the strangest handshake of my afterlife. And maybe because we both knew it was coming, it didn't buzz quite so badly.

"Oh, my God," she breathed, her pretty eyes looking right through me.

Up close like this, I could again see why A.J. found her so appealing. She wasn't particularly young, yet she radiated youthfulness. It was her attitude that gave her that freshness and life. I wished I had a sense of smell, because I would've bet my entire stake that she smelled really good, too. Not from heavy artificial perfume, but, again, fresh and clean. Like a gorgeous spring day.

And okay, yeah, too Hallmark, I know. But A.J. was my kid, perhaps in some ways even more than any of my actual children, because Melody had done most of the hands-on raising of them. Of course, I'd been there, but I was just their father, and in those days that meant something very different than it does today. But for a while there, at the very end of my life, I was A.J.'s mommy, which sounds odd, I know. But it's true.

The bond between us is a strong one.

And I wanted him to find someone worthy. Someone who'd bring light and laughter into his life.

"Please," Alison said. "Do you mind if we . . . ?"

She opened up the truck cab and reached in behind the seat, where she'd stashed her giant bag. It was half purse, half briefcase, and she pulled a script from it. It was, I saw, the latest version of that blockbuster-to-be, *Quinn*.

Dawn was lighting the sky with streaks of purple and blue, but it still wasn't bright enough yet for her to read. So she stepped in front of the truck's headlights and motioned for A.J. to move off a bit, down the road.

He kept going until his white shirt was just a blur, even to me. Which meant Alison probably couldn't even see him. "That's far enough," she called, and she opened her script. "Tell him to start at the top of the page."

"He can hear you fine, you don't have to shout," A.J. called back.

"All right, spirit of Jamie," Alison muttered. "If you're real, start reading."

So I did.

"*Interior, Red Rock Saloon, back room,*" A.J. recited, his voice distant but clear. "*Kid Gallagher has Melody trapped against a wall. She is clearly frightened. He kisses her roughly, she struggles. This is a total load of horse*—Sorry. I think that last must've been an editorial comment. Jamie says nothing like that ever happened. Not even close."

Alison looked at the headlights, frowning slightly.

"Tell her she can move away from the truck," I called to A.J. "My night vision's good. Although if I have to read anything more from this ridiculous script, I just might go blind."

A.J. paraphrased—the kid was nothing if not polite. And Alison dug through her bag for a pen. She uncapped it with her teeth as she backed away from the truck's headlights.

She started to write, right on the white space of the script's page.

One of the reasons this is so difficult for me, she wrote, *is because I needed a hero—a lot— when I was a little girl. And I used to pretend that I was Melody and if I could just hang on a little longer, that Silas Quinn would come and save me.*

I read the words, and A.J. repeated them—his voice quiet in the stillness.

Alison sat down, right there in the road. A.J. dashed back, but he stopped before he got too close, afraid that he might scare her. I knew what *that* was like.

She looked up at him in the dimness. "I could really use some breakfast," she said. "Let's head back to town."

August 9, 1898
Dear Diary,
I never knew a man's hands could be so gentle, or his lips so sweet. I never dreamed of such pleasures.
I knew of the word "passion," but had little real idea what it meant.
Not before this past night.

• • •

Hugh was going to be okay.

But he was so severely dehydrated that the ER doctors at the hospital in Tucson were adamant in their opinion that he'd been found just in the nick of time.

He hadn't been hurt when his Jeep went off the road, as they'd originally feared. There was no sign of bruising or any injury to his head or internal organs.

But apparently he'd ingested something that had made him violently ill, the theory being that something he'd had in the Jeep—either food or drink—had gone bad. The ensuing illness had made him unable even to find his phone, which was in the pocket of his jeans with its voicemail box filled with messages from all the crew members who'd been frantically searching for him.

They were pumping him with fluids and an anti-nausea drug, and he'd actually roused once, which was a good sign. But he wasn't able yet to talk and to turn their theories into facts.

As A.J. followed Alison into the catering tent where breakfast was being served, they received a round of applause for finding the young production assistant.

"We just thought we'd go out there and drive around," Alison told the man named Rob, who was refilling a vat-sized tub of scrambled eggs, and who was also—according to Jamie—an FBI agent. "We headed away from where the teams were searching. It was on a whim."

He looked at them both somewhat skeptically so A.J. added, "We got lucky."

Alison was silent then, as she served herself some eggs and bacon and poured them both mugs of dark, rich coffee.

"Thanks," A.J. said, taking one from her.

She was standing there, just holding her tray of food, looking out at all the empty tables.

"As soon as we sit down," she said, "we're going to be mobbed. And I hate doing this— having to lie to everyone about how we found Hugh. That was just really unpleasant."

"Yeah," he agreed. "I know."

"You're good at it, though," she pointed out.

"No," A.J. said, "actually I'm not."

"Better than me."

"Look," he said, "we can go back to your place if you want, and I won't take that as anything more than a . . . desire to be able to talk privately. Jamie'll come with us, and I'll leave when you ask me to."

Of course, A.J.'d also stay if she asked him to, but he figured that was probably understood.

Alison nodded. "All right."

And he followed her out of the tent.

It wasn't far to River Street, wasn't long before she balanced her tray on the railing and unlocked her door.

And A.J. was back in Alison's kitchen.

"Can I be honest with you?" she asked as she set her tray down at her table, as she took the same chair she'd sat in when he'd first told her about Jamie.

"Of course." That left him the sex chair, although to be honest, despite learning the truth that Jamie's ghost was real and A.J. wasn't crazy, the vibe he was picking up from Alison was completely unlike the one he'd gotten the night she'd taken off her shirt.

"I'm still struggling to believe that it's true," she admitted. "I'm just too much of a scientist. I keep trying to figure out ways you could've done all that—including the jolt."

"It does take some getting used to," A.J. agreed, taking a sip of his coffee as Jamie sat up on the counter, across the room.

"And I can't apologize to you," Alison said. "Not yet. Because if this is a scam, if you're somehow tricking me, if you nearly got Hugh killed to make me believe in this crazy, *crazy* scenario . . ."

"You don't have to apologize," he told her.

"It'll be worse if I've apologized on top of being fooled," she explained.

"It's okay," A.J. reassured her. "My own mother thinks I'm suffering from . . ." He shook his head. "If there's anything I can do to help you believe that I'm being truthful with you . . ."

Alison nodded. "I'm thinking about it," she said. "I'll let you know." She looked around. "Is Jamie here?"

Jamie waved at her, but of course she couldn't see him.

"He's over by the sink," A.J. said.

"Tell her I want her to get out that sorry-ass script and show you that scene that she had me start to read," Jamie said. "We need a little levity here."

"He wants you to show me the script for *Quinn*," A.J. told her. "That scene with, you know, *Kid Gallagher has Melody trapped against a wall . . .*"

Alison pulled the script out of her bag, which was on the floor next to her chair. She plopped it onto the table. "It's marked with the orange Post-it note," she told him as she dug into her eggs. "Knock yourself out."

A.J. pulled the script closer to him and opened it and . . .

"Read it aloud," Jamie ordered, sliding down from the counter, to come stand behind him. "It's ridiculous. I know, I'll be Mel, you be 'Kid' Gallagher. You read the stage directions, too, because I'm going to have to work hard to get into character here. Let me practice a few times." He pitched his voice high. "No! *Nooooo!*"

A.J. couldn't help but laugh as he read aloud, "Interior, Red Rock Saloon, back room. Kid

Gallagher has Melody trapped against a wall. She is clearly frightened. He kisses her roughly and she struggles to get free. Melody: *Stay away from me.*" Jamie read the lines along with him, in that silly high-pitched voice. *"My husband ordered you out of town!"*

"Gallagher, laughing:" A.J. added an appropriately sinister sounding *Mwah-ha-ha*. *"I'm going. And guess what? I'm taking you with me."* He looked up at Alison. "Hmm."

"It's a dramatization," she said defensively, biting a piece of bacon. "It's supposed to be dramatic. Exciting. Maybe a little over the top."

"A little," A.J. agreed.

"Keep going," Jamie prompted.

"Melody struggles even more and he pushes her harder against the wall, nearly throttling her," A.J. read. "Melody: *No . . .* Gallagher:" He deepened his voice. *"Yes. And you know what else?* Still holding her tightly with one hand, he caresses her throat, his fingers moving lightly across the bare skin exposed by the torn top of her blouse. She still struggles."

"Noooo," Jamie said, even though that wasn't his line.

"Gallagher, continued: *You're not going to tell him a thing. It's going to be our secret. Because if you tell him? I'll kill him.*" He stretched out the vowel and the *Ls* in *kill,* pronouncing it *keel.*

"Okay," Alison said, laughing and rolling her

eyes, "maybe it's a *lot* over the top. But the writers were basing this on the legend. They tried to imagine what might have transpired between Melody and Jamie before he kidnapped her. They were also going on the assumption, because it was believed to be a fact, that he *did* kidnap her. As opposed to your story that she went with him of her own free will. Of which, by the way, I've still seen absolutely no proof."

"I'm working on that," A.J. said.

"Keep reading," Jamie said.

So A.J. kept reading. "Melody freezes. She very nearly stops breathing because she believes him. Gallagher, continued: *You know that I can, and I will. I'll kill him, and I'll take you with me anyway.* Melody:" He looked up at Alison. "All together now: *No . . .*"

She shook her head, but she was laughing.

"Gallagher: *Be ready for me,*" A.J. read. *"Tomorrow night. If you want Quinn to stay alive."*

Jamie snorted. "Total, stinking horse manure. Plus, it's badly written. A two-bit melodrama. *Nooo!* Pah."

"It's what our audience wants to see," Alison said. "They want bad guys who are really bad."

"Like, say, a six-and-a-half-foot-tall man who regularly beat his wife?" A.J. asked.

"Touché," she said. "So okay. Tell me. How did it really happen? Jamie approached Melody and

382

said, *Excuse me, I can't help but notice you need to be rescued from your brute of a husband?*"

"Nope," A.J. said. "She approached Jamie. August 7, 1898. It was the evening after that party the town threw for Melody. Quinn was drinking a lot. He was really pounding it down after the shoot-out at the Red Rock, because he was at something of a loss without Bo and the Kelly Gang. Plus he'd seen Jamie shoot, and he knew he couldn't beat him at a quickdraw, so he was afraid to confront him. I think he was hoping Jamie would just win at cards and move on—he'd've been happy to see him go. But in the meantime, his injured leg was hurting and he was drinking to medicate that, as well.

"That night, he'd already put away a few bottles of gin and was snoring in their front parlor, so Melody used the opportunity to sneak out of the house. She put a cloak over her hair and went in through the back of the hotel, praying that no one would recognize her. She went to Jamie's room— she bribed another serving girl to tell her which room was his—and she knocked on the door."

"That was a shock," Jamie said. "She was the last person on earth I expected to find when I opened my door at midnight. I actually had my gun drawn, because I thought it might be Quinn, come to kill me for dancing with his wife the night before."

"He wasn't even dressed, but Melody pushed

her way into his room," A.J. told Alison. "She couldn't risk being seen standing in the hall."

"She didn't even notice that I wasn't wearing my pants." Jamie sighed. "Here I'd been fantasizing about her for a full month, and she doesn't even give my well-turned ankles a second glance."

"Jamie quickly got dressed," A.J. said, "and Melody came directly to the point of her visit. She'd come to make a business deal. She was looking for help getting out of town. Far out of town. She wanted to go to San Francisco. But there was a catch. She had no money to pay him, and no money to buy the food and supplies they'd need to make that long, dangerous trip to California. So instead, she offered to trade the only thing she had of any potential value." He cleared his throat. "Her body."

"Oh, God," Alison said. "I am *so* glad I don't live back then."

"She took off her cloak and started unfastening her dress," Jamie said. "I'm standing there thinking, *Am I dreaming?* And then her words sink in. She's got nothing on her face, no emotion, nothing. She's not in my room because she wants to be. She's there because she has no choice."

A.J. repeated Jamie's words to Alison.

"So I stopped her," Jamie said. "I couldn't believe I was doing it, but I actually stopped her. I buttoned her dress back up and I told her she didn't have to do this. I told her I'd take her to San Francisco anyway. I told her we'd leave tonight if we could, but . . . there was one little problem. Cash. As in *no* cash.

"I was in the red, both for my hotel bill and with a couple of gents I'd been playing cards with over the past few weeks," Jamie continued, through A.J. "All I needed was one good game, one big win. I told Mel to pack a small bag, nothing too much, just a few things she might want to take with her, and be ready to go at any time. And then . . ."

"He kissed her," A.J. said, because he'd heard this story often enough before. "He couldn't resist. He kissed her, and he knew he was right to turn down her offer. Because she didn't move. She didn't kiss him back. It was as if she were completely numb."

"I buttoned my shirt and put on my jacket," Jamie said, with A.J. repeating the words for Alison to hear. "I was going to walk her back home, make sure no one saw her coming out of my room. I wrapped her cloak around her and was about to open the door when she suddenly asked why was I doing this? Why would I help her? And why didn't I take what she had offered?

"I answered her honestly. I didn't want sex. Oh, I wanted her, all right, but not as part of a business deal. I told her I knew it was crazy, but . . . I was in love with her."

Jamie fell silent again, still as bemused by that revelation as he'd been that day, more than a hundred years ago.

"My great-grandmother didn't say a word," A.J. told Alison quietly. "She just looked at him as if he was speaking a language she didn't understand. So Jamie saw her safely home, then went back to his room to pray for some divine intervention in the form of several winning hands in the next evening's poker game. It took Jamie several more days, but he finally won enough to pay off his debts and ride out of town. So there you have it. All the events that transpired between Jamie and Melody before they left Jubilation."

Jamie cleared his throat. "Well . . ." he said. "Not exactly all of 'em."

"With Jamie's reputation, it's hard to believe he turned her down," Alison said skeptically.

"There's more?" A.J. asked Jamie.

Jamie sat back up on the kitchen counter, which put his face into shadows. "Tell Alison that I *did* turn Mel down—but only that first time. The next night, well . . . she sort of came back."

"Really?" A.J. said.

"I never told you this part of the story before. You were too young."

"You sure you want this on the record?" A.J. asked him.

Alison tapped the table in front of him. "Hey," she said. "Let him tell it. Come on, Jamie. I'm listening." She turned back to A.J. "No editing, okay?"

"The next night, Melody came to my room again," Jamie said, A.J. repeating his words for Alison. "And this time she was nervous, almost shy. She told me that she couldn't stop thinking about what I'd said the night before, about me being in love with her. That got her thinking about love, and about Quinn and how he'd never really loved her—he'd just wanted to possess her. Own her. And she started thinking about all that she'd missed. She told me that when I touched her, when I'd kissed her, she felt cherished and . . . safe. For the first time since she could remember, she felt safe." He paused, clearing his throat. "She asked me to kiss her again, so of course, I did. And this time she kissed me back. It was so, *so* sweet and . . ." He paused, letting A.J. catch up before he said, "Long story short? This time? When she took off her dress, I most certainly did not turn her down."

And there they sat, in silence.

Until Alison cleared her throat. "So they left Jubilation," she said. "When?"

"Saturday morning, August 13, 1898. Three solid hours before dawn," Jamie answered and A.J. relayed.

"And they outran Silas Quinn," she said. "Even though Jamie couldn't possibly have gone full speed with a woman riding sidesaddle."

"She didn't ride sidesaddle," Jamie told her. "She rode astride, wearing a pair of my pants. The myth that she was an inexperienced rider? That was just another of Quinn's lies. Her inexperience was with the desert, with camping, with hiding from Quinn. That's where she needed my help."

"The legend says that they left in haste," Alison said. "Jamie left behind that famous pair of boots."

"We took very little with us, in the way of clothing," he countered. "Nearly all of our luggage held water and food. That's why I left those boots behind. We weren't in a hurry—in fact, we waited an extra day for Quinn to get a good old drunk on. He was hungover as hell that morning when he awoke. Some hero, huh? And can I just say? Mel didn't mind leaving her dresses behind, not one bit. Even after we got to San Francisco, she preferred wearing those old pants of mine. But she was starting to make waves, and we were looking to stay low profile, so . . ."

"Huh," Alison said after A.J. passed on that information. "There were rumors about Kid Gallagher bestowing affection upon another man in San Francisco. But that was before he went to Jubilation and—" She stopped herself. "Except everyone always assumed it happened *before* Jubilation, because Quinn said Gallagher died shortly after he arrived in town."

"It was after," Jamie said. "And it was Mel. Wearing pants. Although whoever looked at her and thought she was a man probably needed a new pair of eyeglasses."

"Well, that's certainly interesting," Alison said. She paused. "What does Jamie know about Melody's diaries?"

"He knows she wrote them," A.J. answered. "But he didn't know if she'd destroyed them or . . . what. He doesn't know where they are."

"Could he find them?" Alison asked. "The way he found Hugh?"

Good question. A.J. looked at Jamie, who shrugged. "I can certainly try," the ghost said. "And I will—after we finish here."

"I think we're finished here," Alison said. "I've got a production meeting in a half hour, so . . ."

A.J. started piling her dishes onto his own, so he could stack the two trays and carry them both at once. "I'll take these back," he said.

She stood up. "Thank you."

"If you don't mind, I have a quick question for you." He glanced at her. "That thing you wrote, that Jamie and I read aloud. About wanting Quinn to rescue you . . . ?"

She sighed as she slowly sat back down. "Pathetic, huh?" she said. "When I was around twelve, though, I stopped waiting to get rescued. I started pretending that I was Quinn. Because even though he was big and strong, bad things still happened to him. And all he could do was his best, you know? Even when he didn't win, at least he tried. At least he fought back. And at least he had his code and his honor." She rolled her eyes. "Or so I thought."

"There are a lot of legends," A.J. pointed out. "A lot of stories that were made up to provide inspiration. And you were right. Bad stuff can happen, regardless of who you are. If Quinn's self-legend helped you when you were a kid, then that's a good thing. Then his lies did good. Although I honestly believe that the real story— what really happened—would have helped you more. Because same as you, Melody didn't wait to be rescued. True, she needed help, but she found that help in Jamie, and together they rescued her from Silas Quinn."

Alison nodded, and they sat for a moment in silence.

She cleared her throat as she looked up to find him watching her. "It was nothing really awful," she told him. "That happened to me. I know you're probably curious. Your restraint is amazing, because if I were you, I'd have to ask. It was just . . . my mother was . . . hard to live with. A lot of drama."

"Drama," he repeated.

Alison shook her head. "Mostly noise. The worst thing that happened to me, physically, was when she was so drunk that she didn't stop when she pulled the car into the garage and she went through the wall into the playroom and part of the wall fell on me. I had to go in for X-rays—it was just a concussion. But it sucked because my grandmother asked me to lie and say that *she* was driving so my mother wouldn't get arrested."

"Your mother was an alcoholic," A.J. said. It wasn't a question, but she nodded. Yes. And his heart sank.

He didn't look over at Jamie, but he heard the ghost sigh and mutter, "Shit."

"I'm an alcoholic," A.J. said. "I figure I should go for full disclosure here."

"You . . . ?" she said. And yes, God, the expression on her face was one of total incredulity. She actually managed to laugh, but tears also sprang into her eyes. Tears that she grimly fought back.

"Oh, perfect," she said. "I mean, yes, I knew you didn't drink, but I thought . . ."

"I'm ten years sober," he told her.

"Which means absolutely nothing," she scoffed, but then corrected herself. "I'm sorry. It does mean quite a lot, of course. Congratulations. I actually do know how hard it must've been—must still be. But I also know—first hand—that it just doesn't mean as much as most people think. My mother was eight years sober, until she wasn't anymore. I was seven, and that was it. Every now and then she did a month, month and a half, but

. . . Three months once. Three months, seventeen days. And then she went right back down the toilet. On my tenth birthday."

"Jesus," A.J. said. "And you were a kid—you couldn't walk away."

"Nope."

And there they sat in silence until he cleared his throat. "You're not a kid anymore. You could, um, walk away from me."

"I already have," she said, and then winced. "I'm sorry, that came out sounding harsh. But I see no point in . . . pretending otherwise. Really, A.J. If things hadn't already gone past the point of no return for us, that news would've just done it."

"She's lying," Jamie said from across the room.

Maybe, but A.J. didn't think so.

"I'm sorry that you feel that way," he said quietly. "But it's probably for the best. Because you're right. I can't give guarantees. I'm sober today. Right now. I don't think too much about tomorrow, because that doesn't serve me. So I don't try to plan and say, here's where I'll be in a month or a year. All I can tell you is that I'm not drinking now. And I'm not drinking now. Or now. And I'm doing okay, so when we get to the *now* that's hanging out there, a year in the future, it's highly likely that I won't be drinking then either. But there *are* no guarantees. And Jamie's not the only ghost haunting me."

Hor al-Hammar. She didn't say it, but A.J. knew she was thinking it.

He picked up their trays.

This time she was the one who stopped him. "Before you go," she said. "Could you ask . . . Jamie. To check on Hugh."

Jamie didn't wait for him to say it, he just popped out. And then popped back in. "He's continuing to improve," he reported, "but he's still not conscious."

"Thank you," Alison said, after A.J. relayed that information.

A.J. nodded and went out the door.

August 16, 1898
Dear Diary,
I am free. My gambler and I have been riding hard for three days, and there is no sign of pursuit. J. paid off two others to ride due north, hoping that the monster would follow them instead. So far, it seems to have worked.

But even if he catches me and kills me tomorrow, I will have had these three days.

And these three nights.

I am shameless, but I wait most eagerly for the night.

A.J. went back to the tent to lie down, although the heat of the day had to have made it unbearable in there.

He made me promise I'd wake him if I located Mel's old diaries, and he stripped down to his shorts, turned on that battery-powered fan that he'd bought at the Circle K, and lay back in his bunk with one arm up and over his eyes.

I used to lie just like that after Mel got diagnosed. I didn't want her to see my tears or know how truly frightened I was by my helplessness.

"Don't quit," I told him.

"Too late," he said.

"Now, A.J.," I started, but he cut me off.

"Just find the fucking diaries," he said, "so we can get the fuck out of here. I want to go home."

I knew when the *fuck* and the *fucking* started flying that there was no real point in conversing with the kid. Still, I had to say, "You won't feel any better there."

He pulled his arm off his eyes and looked at me. "Thanks for the encouragement."

"Encouragement," I said, "would be me saying *Don't quit. Don't give up.* Everything Alison said, everything she's feeling right now? That's knee-jerk. She's a smart girl. She'll come 'round. She knows that you two fit."

"But she'll always wonder," A.J. said. "She'll always worry."

"She'll just have to take it one day at a time, too," I pointed out. "Come on, kid. She needs to be told that you don't have to start drinking again for her to lose you. You could get hit by a bus. Or get cancer."

"That's different."

"No, it's not," I said.

He was silent.

"Just think about it. Your mom lost your dad because there were no guarantees—just like you said to Alison. There's never a guarantee. And on the flip side of the coin is Bev and Charlie. Maybe after we find those diaries, we could get Bev to bring 'em down here. Introduce her to Alison."

A.J. still didn't say anything.

"I'm going to see if I can't locate them," I told him. "Mel's diaries. You gonna be okay?"

"Yeah," he finally said.

"Don't quit," I told him. "Love you, kid."

"I love you, too, Gramps," he said, which warmed my heart as I closed my eyes and focused on Mel's diaries—somewhere in Heaven, Alaska—and popped away.

Not Alaska.

That was the first thing I recognized as I staggered a bit, trying to get my bearings.

Wherever I was, it was *definitely* not Alaska. The sun was scorchingly high in a sky that was so pale blue it was almost white. The little rolling hills, the cactus and scrub . . . I was in the desert.

And then I heard a sound from behind me— someone grunting as they lifted something heavy, and I turned to see a man taking some kind of contraption out from under the front passenger seat of Hugh Darcy's Jeep.

That was definitely Hugh's Jeep, nose pointed down in that ditch at the side of that same road where we'd found him, just a few hours earlier.

Whoever this man was, he had his own truck—a big one, like A.J.'s.—and he put the contraption that he'd taken from the Jeep into a container in the back of it.

I tried to get a look at the thing before he locked it up, to figure out what it was. And maybe you would've known what it was right away, but because I'm technologically challenged, having died in 1977, I was at a disadvantage. Yes, sure, I've kept up with quite a bit, and of course I did an additional burst of contemporary studies while I was waiting to return, but this device was beyond my knowledge or experience.

All I could see was some kind of electronics brand name, TechWhiz, and a number, 7842.

7842, I repeated to myself as I turned my attention to the man himself.

Medium height—a little bit shorter than me. Brown hair, worn commando short. Mirrored sunglasses on a relatively nondescript face.

I leaned in closer, looking for a distinguishing mark. A scar or a tattoo or . . .

I got nothing.

7842.

The man had a face. It wasn't particularly handsome, but it wasn't anything to run screaming from, either.

His most distinguishing features were eyebrows that were bushier than most, and a small bald spot, about the size of a half dollar, right at the top of his head. Fool wasn't wearing a hat, and in this hot sun he was going to get a burn.

As I watched, he humped several containers of Gatorade out of the back of the Jeep and into his truck. He replaced them with other bottles of the juice or whatever it was in the same unnatural colors—bright blue and neon green—that he took from the front seat of his cab.

He opened one of them, and poured about half of it out on some poor unsuspecting cactus, before putting it on the Jeep's front seat.

Which was when I realized that he was wearing gloves.

In this heat.

7842. TechWhiz. Whatever that device was, it got me thinking about the way that Alison's cell phone didn't work after we'd found Hugh—not until we were some distance away from where we'd found him. And how we'd found him not that far from his Jeep.

I started thinking about the fact that no one had been able to reach Hugh the entire time he'd been missing—that their calls just went to voicemail. And I thought about the fact that he hadn't used his cell phone—which had been in his jeans pocket—to call for help.

And I started thinking that maybe Hugh hadn't accidentally consumed something that had gone bad, but rather that he'd taken a sip—or more—of Gatorade that had been poisoned in some way.

It wouldn't have had to have been poisoned with something that could kill. Just something that would make a person upchuck. In this heat, sunstroke could kill a man *without* the added dehydration that came from puking one's guts out. But add a little, oh, say, antifreeze to a bottle of disgusting sports drink . . . ?

As I stood there watching, I started thinking that maybe I'd misheard the tall and ponytailed Killer-of-Wayne. Because here, now, was this stranger messing around with nearly-dead Hugh's Jeep. It wasn't a robbery. There were plenty of things in the back of that Jeep to steal. No, what I was seeing was manipulation of a crime scene. I'd watched enough episodes of *The Streets of San Francisco* to recognize that when I saw it.

Except . . . Hugh wasn't a woman.

I tried to recall the conversations I'd overheard. And I could not remember Mr. Tall Ponytail ever saying anything about "the woman." It was all *if we have to kill her* and then *kill her. . . .* Maybe he was one of those intolerant types who thought it was funny to call a gay man *she* and *her*.

Except, wait a minute. I'd overheard Alison

saying that Hugh was originally supposed to make this trip with *her,* and then, when her plans changed, with some other woman named Sandra Something.

So maybe the real target was Alison or Sandra, and Hugh was merely collateral damage, which was a very disturbing thought, on a variety of levels.

As I was standing there, pondering all that, this man with his half-dollar bald spot and caterpillar eyebrows got into his truck and pulled away. I hurried after him, quickly slipping into the front seat beside him.

He'd pulled off the gloves and was driving with one hand on the wheel, his other hand dialing a cell phone, which he put up to his nondescript ear.

Whoever answered obviously knew who was calling, because there was no identification made. No, *Hi, Loco, this is Gene.* No doubt about it, I now officially hated caller ID.

He spoke, my nameless new friend with that bald spot, in a husky voice with plenty of southern drawl. "Swing and a miss," he told whoever was on the other end of that call. And then he said, "Uh-huh." And, "Nope," with a heavy pop on that *P.* "I'm not ready for that quite yet. Gimme one more go. In fact, I've already got a backup in place," he said, then paused again. And another "Uh-huh." And then a final "Yes, suh," before he hung up his phone.

By then, my new friend—let's call him Gene, just on a whim—he'd reached the end of that little dirt road, and he turned, heading north.

Toward Jubilation.

I settled in for the ride, ready, this time, to stick with Gene like white on rice, until I got me some answers and made damn sure that no one else got hurt—be it brokenhearted Hugh, A.J.'s Alison, or Sandra, whom I'd never met, but who was surely somebody's beloved wife, daughter, and/or mother.

"I'm sorry, sir," Alison said, hurrying after Henry Logan. "I must've misunderstood you."

The director stopped in the middle of the street, radiating impatience. "What's not to understand? Just a few days ago you were talking about taking some research trip to Alaska after the shoot is done. Today, I'm telling you that filming is on hold for the next four days—at least. So take my plane and go. I've already called Julio and given him the flight plan. Talk to Debbie in the production office, she'll have all the information. Pack your things and hit the road."

"Trace Marcus is . . . *where,* exactly?" she asked.

"He's in the hospital," he said. "Back in L.A. Appendicitis. Or so he claims."

Alison shook her head. "That's how Quinn died."

"Yeah," Henry said. "Coincidence much? Marcus is such an asshole, I'm actually going to call my lawyer, have her request a note from the surgeon."

Alison laughed, surprised. "If you think Trace is lying about having major surgery . . . Why did you cast him?"

"I didn't. He came with the project," Henry told her, heading for the catering tent at his usual brisk pace. She had to trot beside him to keep up. "He was part of the deal that got us permission to film here in Jubilation. Neil Sylvester was involved in some way—I don't know how. Maybe he's a fan. I just thought . . . Making this movie right here, where it all happened . . . ? It was too good to pass up."

"That's why I'm here, too," Alison said.

"No," Henry said. "You're here because Hughie gave me a copy of your book and I read it and I said, *She's my consultant, do whatever it takes to get her on my set.*" He lowered his voice. "You sold yourself cheap there, Carter. I would have paid twice as much."

"May I have a raise?" she asked.

"Nope," he said, "but you can use my private jet to fly to Alaska and find out if this Gallagher guy is for real. Hughie told me all about it a few days ago—that he says Jamie helped Melody escape from Quinn, who used to beat the hell out of her. I love it—plus it's the perfect sequel. And you *know* they're going to want a sequel, even though,

401

hello? Historical biopic? A sequel isn't possible. Except now it is. We'll turn the legend upside down in *Quinn Part Two: The Legend Revisited*. When you get back, you can write up a treatment—and *then* I'll give you a raise. A big one. Do you know how much money we can save the production company if we move from one film right into the other with the same cast and crew? Even Marcus—the asshole. I'll have to bring someone else on board to contain him. His assistant's just not getting it done. But regardless of that bullshit, the writers need to start working on the script immediately."

"*Hugh* told you about . . . ?" Alison asked, bemused. "Do you regularly listen to your bottom tier production assistants?"

"Only when they're my nephew," he said, stopping outside the tent.

"Hugh Darcy's your *nephew*," she repeated.

"Thank you, by the way, for saving his life." Henry kissed her on the forehead. "Now, go to Alaska and make us both rich."

He turned and went inside, raising his voice. "I need a breakfast to go. I'm heading out to the hospital to see Hugh."

"Um, sir," Alison called after him. "The timing's a little inconvenient."

"I don't care," he said, without stopping or even looking back. "Go to Alaska. But be back in four days, Carter. Tick tock, people."

Chapter Seventeen

"I don't mind driving," A.J. said.

"And I don't mind either," Alison told him from behind the wheel of the Jeep, her eyes hidden behind a large pair of sunglasses.

"I'd actually prefer taking my truck," he said.

"Sorry," Alison said, coolly. "We're doing Debbie a favor and returning this thing to the rental car company at the airport. Two birds with one stone. So just get in if you're getting in, and let's go."

A.J. put his duffel in the back, on the floor, and climbed in, pushing the seat back as far as it went and then reclining it a bit so his legs would fit.

Alison was already driving as he fastened his seat belt, bouncing over the potholes in the motel parking lot, where he'd left his truck.

"This was not my idea," she said—again. She'd told him that earlier, too, when she'd come out to his campground and told him Henry Logan was sending her to Alaska. To Heaven, to be precise.

Instead of taking her research trip at the end of the movie shoot, she was going now. Because they all had several days of downtime while Trace Marcus was in the hospital, and as the production team scrambled to reschedule the next week's scenes.

Unfortunately the next few days had been set to

be all Trace, all the time, and the actor playing Jamie was in New York doing a guest spot on a TV show. The earliest he could return was next Tuesday.

"I understand," A.J. said. "By the way, Jamie had no luck tracking down Melody's diaries. He popped in, a few hours ago, to let me know that."

Jamie had also been adamant about A.J. staying close to Alison. He didn't go into detail—he was in a hurry to get back to whatever he'd been doing. But A.J. had promised to keep an eye on her.

Which was definitely much easier to do when they were in both a car and then a plane together.

"I left a message for my mother," he continued telling Alison, "to see if maybe it would help if she described them to Jamie. The diaries. He's not really sure what they look like."

"You don't have to talk," she said, as she took the turnoff that led to the road down the mountain. "Sorry. That came out sounding extra-hostile, didn't it? What I *meant* was we both know that this is incredibly awkward. It's going to be a really long trip, and when it's finally over, when we arrive in Alaska, it's going to be even *more* awkward, because, great, I'm going to have to meet your mother and your sister and all forty bazillion of your cousins, and I'm a little freaked out by that, if you want to know the truth."

"Don't be," he said.

"What am I supposed to say to your mother? *Hi, how are you? Yeah, I had a small lapse in judgment last week, and had sex with your son.*"

"That might be, um, too much information."

"You think she's not going to know?" Alison asked, glancing up from the road and over at him. "Mothers know these things. And you know *how* she's going to know? By looking at you. It's all over you, it drips from you. It oozes. You might as well be wearing a shirt with an arrow pointing at me saying *I had sex with Stupid.*"

He had to laugh. "You're not stupid," he said.

"Oh, yeah?" she said. "I had sex with you way too soon. I didn't even know you—I *still* don't know you. You're, like, the King of Withholding Information and I completely didn't see that. It's as if, when I get into that gotta-have-sex place, my brain shuts down or I see only what I want to see. Like that old saying. *Love is blind.* Not that what we did had anything to do with love," she added hastily.

"For the sake of full disclosure," he said, because her description of him as the King of Withholding Info hit a little too close to home. He could talk until he was blue in the face—as long as the subject was Jamie. Or his sister and nieces. Or anything else for that matter, anything that wasn't intensely personal to him or his life. "That's not entirely true. I'm in love with you."

They were driving up the mountain, heading for

405

the pass that would take them down into the desert valley, and Alison pulled over onto the shoulder and hit the brakes hard. The Jeep stopped in a skid of dust and gravel as she turned to look at him in outraged disbelief.

"Don't you dare," she said.

"Don't what?" he asked. "Tell you the truth? I tried *not* telling you the truth, and look where that got me."

"Yeah, into my bed, you jerk," she said. "God *damn* you, A.J. You're not allowed to *love* me. What's wrong with you?"

"Allowed?" A.J. said with a short laugh. "I'm not *allowed?* I don't think you get to decide that."

"I don't *want* you to love me, or to think that you love me or whatever this is that you think you're feeling," she said, as she hit the gas and pulled back onto the road, again with a spray of gravel and a squeal of the tires. She was gripping the steering wheel so tightly that her knuckles were turning white. "Is that better? And for the record, even though I brought up sex? Which I really shouldn't have done even though your mother *is* going to know, so I'll just have to deal with her disapproval when it comes, but I *am not* sleeping with you again. Because face it, that's what this is really about. You don't love me. You just said that because you don't want to be bored on the trip north. Seven hours on Henry's private

406

jet—you probably figure we can spend the entire time doing the nasty."

"I didn't even know we were taking a private jet," A.J. protested. "And for the record, I don't think there was anything even remotely nasty—"

"Oh, stop playing the innocent yokel," she said. "You know damn well what I mean. And let me say it again: I am not sleeping with you."

She was protesting just a little too much, but A.J. kept that comment to himself. Because she had, after all, brought up the subject of sex. Why would she talk about it if she weren't thinking about it?

Truth was, it was hard *not* to think about, sitting close to her in the car like this.

"I meant what I said this morning," she told him. "Your alcoholism is a deal breaker. I know that makes me a bad person—so be it. It's a huge issue for me. I'm happy to be friends. I can be a very good friend. I will not enable you and I can be ruthless with the truth, which is exactly what an alcoholic needs in a friend."

"Recovering alcoholic," A.J. interrupted her.

"It's moronic to call it that," she said, "because you'll never be . . ." Her voice wobbled and broke. "Recovered." She made a noise that was part laughter, part despair. "Ah, God, A.J., I like you so much, I really do, but I just can't do this, and damnit, I'm watching myself teetering on the edge of that slippery slope, because *I'm* the one who can't stop thinking about the fact that we're going to be all alone on that airplane, with that big private bedroom—I've flown on Henry's jet before. And God, the sex we had was so good, and the way you made me laugh was even better, and I see myself backing into this . . . this . . . *thing*. Just this weekend. Just this week. Just until the shoot ends . . . And suddenly I'm doomed. I don't want to hurt you, but I *will* walk away from you. I will. Sooner or later. Probably sooner, because I can't live like that again. And whatever happens? I will not—*will not*—let myself fall in love with you."

And there they sat, in a silence that was really quite noisy, considering the sound of the big tires on the road, and the Jeep's hardworking engine as they continued to climb up the mountain.

Jamie wasn't in the Jeep, offering encouragement, but A.J. could hear him, anyway. *She's scared, kid. Don't let up. Don't quit. . . .*

And he finally broke the silence. "It's a disease," he reminded her. "I was genetically predisposed. I got it from my mother's side of the family. She's fine, but her father was . . . Anyway, you probably are, too—predisposed—so it's a good thing that you choose not to drink. Still, who knows? You could go, too. You come with no guarantees, either. And how about cancer, Alison? That's something Jamie reminded me about this morning. Does cancer run in *your* family? Can you write me a guarantee that you won't get sick and die?"

She shook her head. "That's not the same thing."

"That's what I said, too, but . . . When you think about it, it's *exactly* the same thing," he said. "Would you seriously throw me away because cancer runs in my family? That's pretty stupid, so I guess I *should* be wearing a shirt that says, *I'm in love with Stupid.*"

"Stop saying that," she whispered. She was driving much too fast as she took them over the crest of the mountain and down the other side, as if she were trying to get away from him.

"Why?" he asked, holding on to the grab bar. "You only want *some* of the truth? I made a mistake. I make them from time to time, on account of my being human and yes, occasionally stupid. I should have told you about Jamie right from the start, and I'm sorry that I didn't. I should have told you about everything. I'm an alcoholic Gulf War vet, thank you very much. I lost a kidney in Hor al-Hammar, and my liver was damaged, too. Which makes all those years of hard drinking even more self-destructive, but I'm doing okay—I'm doing quite well actually, health-wise. Thank God. Mentally, I'm also feeling pretty good, especially since you helped me prove that Jamie's not something my brain fabricated. That's a *huge* relief. But I have to be honest. It's been awhile since I've attended an AA meeting, and my friend Lutz—he's a former Navy SEAL—he was verbally bitch-slapping me when he found out I never finished the twelve steps. He's in the program, too. Along with a lotta guys I served with over—"

"So what am I supposed to do?" Alison interrupted him. "Just say *Oh well?* And instead throw away everything I learned from my mother, growing up?"

"You really think *she* was a good teacher?" A.J. asked.

"You *know* what I mean."

"You're not a child anymore," A.J. said. "And I'm not your mother."

"I don't want you to love me."

"Then stop being so fucking amazing."

She laughed at that, but then shook her head. "But I'm not," she said.

"Being with you makes me happy," he admitted, "in a way that I haven't been in a really long time."

"I refuse to be responsible for your happiness," she said quietly.

"*I'm* responsible for my happiness," A.J. told her. "I don't want to hurt you either, and it kills me to see how hard this is for you. But I'm not going to just slink away quietly into the night. Not this time."

"Oh, shit," she said.

"I'm sorry, I'm *not*," he said. "It's too important—"

"No," she said. "A.J.—oh, shit—I have no brakes."

"What?"

A.J. looked down at the floor beneath Alison's feet, and sure enough she had the brake pedal pushed all the way down. She stomped it again and again, but he could see that there was no resistance.

The Jeep was going too fast and began to pick up even more speed. The road ahead of them was steep but relatively straight—for now. But signs were posted warning of an impending curve—a big one. Thirty miles per hour, another sign said, with a picture of a truck on two wheels, tipping over.

"Use the emergency brake," A.J. said, even as Alison was already frantically searching for it.

"I don't know where it is!"

"Left-hand side," A.J. said. "Look low, under the dash."

"Got it!" Alison said.

"Don't pull it too fast," A.J. warned.

"Slow and steady," she said, "I know—oh, *shit!*"

It had come off in her hand—a little plastic handle that was now completely useless. She handed it to A.J. as if he could somehow fix it from where he sat.

"Downshift," A.J. said.

The car had an automatic transmission, but it could still be downshifted. Alison grabbed the shift and went from overdrive to drive to third, and the engine whined horribly.

But the Jeep didn't slow.

She shifted lower. Second.

Nothing. Just more noise.

"Jamie, where are you?" A.J. said.

"He's not here?" Alison asked, her eyes glued to the road in front of them. It was clearly getting harder for her to control the Jeep. The speedometer read sixty-five. Seventy. And that big-ass curve was coming.

"No, he's not," A.J. said as he reached over and helped her hold the wheel. "Come *on,* Jamie. I need some help here. Switch with me, Alison. Quickly, while the road's still relatively straight."

She didn't argue. She just scrambled out from beneath him as he lifted himself over her and into the driver's seat.

"Climb into the back," he told her as he struggled to keep the Jeep on the right side of the double lines. "And strap yourself in. Other side of the car from me and be ready to throw your weight, hard, to the right. Jamie, for the love of God, where *are* you?"

"What?" *Now* she argued.

"Get into the back," he ordered again as—thank God—Jamie popped in.

412

"What the hell?" Jamie said from the backseat. "Kid, you know, you're going just a *little* fast."

"Brakes are out," A.J. told him tersely. "I need to know what the road looks like ahead—if there's any traffic. Or a runaway truck ramp. I could use one of those. Find me one, will you?"

But he'd been on this road coming into Jubilation, and he hadn't seen one then.

Jamie instantly disappeared.

"Get. In the back," A.J. said again to Alison. "Right-hand side. You'll have a better chance of surviving an impact back there."

"Oh, my God," she said, finally scrambling over the seat. "What about *you?* A.J., I don't want you to die."

"Good to know," he said as he approached the big curve. He'd been on similar mountain roads plenty of times before. The speed limit was thirty, but the curve could be handled by an experienced driver at forty-five. Fifty, and the tires would squeal. Fifty-five and you'd skid. Sixty-five you could maybe do if you turned the wheel hard to the right, and went way over the double yellow line and into the left lane, into the oncoming traffic.

Please God, let there be no oncoming traffic.

And please let him have missed seeing a runaway truck ramp. Cut into the side of the mountain, it was an enormous pile of gravel that would grab at the tires and slow them down.

413

There should be one here—why wasn't there one? If he survived this, he was going to write someone a letter.

"There's a driver's side airbag," he told Alison now. "Plus, Jamie's here, he's going to help us."

As if on cue, Jamie popped back in, into the front seat this time. "No ramp, but no other cars," he said, and A.J. repeated his words for Alison to hear. "Nothing coming in either direction, for miles. But kid, there's a curve coming up that's gonna be a bitch."

"I know," A.J. said. But first there were a series of smaller curves—slight bends in the road, at least comparatively.

"After you make it around that curve," Jamie shouted over the whine of the engine, "there's a kind of a cutaway about a quarter mile farther down the mountain, right-hand side. It's not a ramp, but it looks like some kind of big parking lot, like it was flattened and cleared for trucks to access, I don't know, maybe a barite mine. You'll have to bust through a fence—nothing more than a run-down chain link, gate's not even locked— then you'll have about a hundred, maybe a hundred fifty yards to play with. At the edge of the clearing, to the left, there's a cluster of orange barrels. They might soften your impact—at least more than the mountain will." Jamie's face was lined with worry. "I wish I could help you in some way, A.J."

"Just keep watching for traffic," A.J. said, focusing on the road. One more slight curve to the left, and then the big one to the right. "Get ready to lean right," he shouted to Alison.

If he turned the wheel too hard, they'd flip. If he didn't turn hard enough, they'd go through the guardrail and off the side of the mountain.

And then, there it was. In front of him.

A long, tight, hairpin curve that made the rest of the road—and any oncoming traffic—disappear from sight.

"I'm ready. You'll tell me when, right?" He felt Alison as she reached forward to touch his shoulder and then the back of his neck, her cool fingers briefly in his hair.

"I will."

Her life—both of their lives—were in his hands.

Never had he been more glad that they were steady.

He turned the wheel, trying to stay in the right lane for as long as he could.

The tires squealed, then screamed, drowning out the roar of the engine.

"Now!" he shouted, and he, too, threw as much of his weight as he could over to the right side of the Jeep, and they didn't go onto their side.

The guardrail came toward them, much too quickly, and A.J. turned the wheel hard, harder, still leaning. The Jeep skidded, sideways now, into the oncoming lane, scraping along the guardrail, metal on metal, with an unholy screech.

Alison was screaming—he was, too.

And the friction from the guardrail was slowing them down. But not enough.

Because then they were free of the curve, the Jeep rocketing out of the guided track of the guardrail like a pinball. As they headed downhill, they once again began to pick up speed.

A.J. glanced into the rear-view mirror to make sure Alison was okay. She was holding on for dear life, but she smiled at him, a fierce smile of victory. They'd made it past the deadly curve.

The first one on this road, anyway.

A.J. saw the cutaway before Jamie pointed to it.

It was big, but nowhere near as big as it needed to be to stop a heavy vehicle with no brakes. But it was at least as wide as it was long.

And it was flat, and he saw those orange barrels that Jamie had told him about.

"Hang on," A.J. shouted to Alison. "We're going off road."

The Jeep bounced crazily as the tires left the pavement and hit the uneven dirt at the side of the road. A.J. had about four short seconds to decide whether to aim for the gate or the fence itself, and because the gate looked like it might pop right open, he went for the fence instead, hoping it would help slow them down.

But they smashed into the thing with all four

wheels off the ground, and it didn't offer much resistance—it just went down.

They landed on top of it with a bone-jarring crunch, bounced, bounced again.

And mud—or what was left of what must've been huge puddles of thick mud after that drenching rain and which had since turned into something softer than the usual hard, dusty ground—pulled at the tires and the Jeep skidded and slowed.

Sixty-five, sixty, fifty-five . . .

A.J. dragged the steering wheel left, trying to point the Jeep toward those barrels, and then he realized this was a lot like driving in the snow and ice of Heaven, and he pulled the wheel harder, to make a donut the way Jamie had taught him when he was ten, out in the field behind their house in celebration of his first Christmas after turning double digits.

Alison was screaming again, and they hit the orange barrels with the very back of the Jeep, which did little to slow them, since they were empty. They went flying like bowling pins, but the impact somehow triggered the airbag, a blinding cloud of white directly in A.J.'s face, making it impossible for him to see.

He swore as he tried to push it out of his way as they continued to spin back out into the middle of the pull off, like a Tilt-a-Whirl ride gone horribly wrong. Around and around and around.

Until finally, they were going slowly enough for A.J. to put the Jeep into park and it lurched to a stop. The engine sputtered and stalled.

"Alison?" He pushed the airbag out of his way to turn toward the back.

She was sitting there, still gripping the grab bar over the window, her eyes bright and her face flushed as she worked to catch her breath.

"You all right?" he asked.

She nodded, let go of the bar, unfastened her seat belt. "Are you?"

"Yeah." His hair was in his eyes and he pushed it back with a hand that was shaking. So much for steady. But, to be fair, it was adrenaline. The shaking was all after the fact.

Next to him, in the front seat, Jamie exhaled long and hard. He may have said something, but A.J. didn't hear it, because Alison sat forward and grabbed him around the neck and kissed him.

It was not a *Thank you for saving my life* kiss, either.

It was a *Do me right now* kiss.

He knew, because she'd kissed him like that before.

Her hands were in his hair, on the back of his neck, tugging at his shoulders, pulling him toward her.

And A.J. couldn't think of a single thing he'd rather do to celebrate the fact that they were both still alive, so, as she kissed him the entire time, he scrambled awkwardly over the seat back, only vaguely aware as he did so that Jamie had popped away.

Alison just kept kissing him as he landed on top of her in the backseat. She welcomed the weight of his body by wrapping herself around him, intertwining their legs, as if she wanted every possible inch of them to touch, to be connected. And God, he wanted that, too.

Which was why, when she started removing clothing—both his and hers—he didn't protest, even though he knew—he *knew*—that this was going to land right at the very top of his current list of mistakes. Things he should—or shouldn't—have done.

Sex with a woman who'd already claimed to have walked away from him, who'd just spent a lot of time insisting that she wasn't going to have sex with him ever again. It couldn't possibly end well, and yet he didn't give a damn. He just wanted inside of her.

She wanted that, too, and as she scrambled out of her jeans, she stopped kissing him long enough to say, "Condom."

He answered, "Yes."

He'd replaced the one in his wallet and he used that replacement now to cover himself, sitting up for a moment on the bench seat as she finished her wrestling match with her jeans. He'd barely gotten it on when she straddled him. No *May I?*

No discussion. Just bam. Hot, hardcore, full penetration sex—from zero to sixty in the beat of a heart.

A.J. heard himself cry out, heard Alison, too, but then she kissed him again, possessively, ferociously, even as she rode him hard and deep, setting a rhythm that made his heart race. This was a woman who knew what she wanted, who didn't hesitate, didn't sit back and wait, and God, her self-confidence totally turned him on.

She was on the verge of coming—he expected as much, expected her to come fast. And here she thought they didn't know each other.

He wished there was time for him to hang on, so he could make her come again, more slowly her second time, because God, he'd loved doing that, that night when they'd finally hit her bed. But right now they were in a car, and it was broad daylight, and if someone passing by saw the broken fence, the scattered barrels, and the airbag sagging now in the front seat, they might stop to see if they could help.

And A.J. didn't need any help, thanks. He knew exactly what to do to rock this woman's world. He tightened his stomach muscles and pushed up his hips so that she could take him as deeply as possible. It felt beyond good on his end, and the noise she made, her moan of pleasure as she came undone, made him come, too.

He almost told her he loved her, but he knew

she didn't want to hear that, so he clenched his teeth over the words.

But as he sat there, in the back of that Jeep, with his arms tightly around her, her head down on his shoulder as she, too, caught her breath, he knew he had to say something.

But she spoke first, her breath warm against his ear. "What am I going to do?" she said. "I can't seem to stay away from you."

A.J. ran his hand down and up her back, wishing he had some kind of magical answer. "Sometimes it's things that are the hardest that are . . . most worth having."

She lifted her head to look at him, pushing her hair back out of her face. It was getting hot back there with the air conditioner off, and they'd both recently done some sweating.

"And sometimes things that are hard? They just suck. Getting hit in the face with a two-by-four," she said. "Over and over again? *That's* hard. It also sucks."

"Good point," he said, unable not to smile at her.

But she looked down at him, into his eyes, her face so serious as she shook her head. "I'm not going to fall in love with you, A.J.," she said. "I can't."

A.J. nodded, because she seemed to want a response. "Okay."

"Really?"

"No," he admitted, "but what am I going to do? I can't make you love me. Is it okay with you if I hope that you'll change your mind?"

She laughed. "What if I say no, it's not okay?"

"Tough shit?" He phrased it as a question, adding plenty of tentativeness to his voice, but he knew as she looked into his eyes, that she could see that he meant it.

She laughed again, but this time she pulled off of him, and once again, he immediately missed her closeness and heat—despite the fact that the temperature in the Jeep was becoming unbearable. He opened the door for some air and a chance to stretch his legs as he cleaned himself up.

Alison, meanwhile, was searching for her panties, then turning the legs of her jeans right side out. She opened the door on her side of the car, too.

"I can do this," she said as she dressed, and he got the sense that she was talking to convince herself as much as him. "I know you don't think so, but I can. I can spend these next few days or weeks or even months with you, and walk away when it's over, without blinking. Because I'm *not* going to let myself fall in love with you. It's no longer an option. It's completely off the table. So if that's going to be a problem for you . . ."

"I'm going to have to think about it," he said. "Okay. I thought about it, and it's not going to be a problem for me as long as you keep jumping me like that. The only thing better than hope is hope with a lot of great sex."

Alison laughed. "I'm serious, A.J."

"I am, too," he said, opening up his phone. "That was seriously great sex. I'm looking forward to more of it as I work to convince you that I'm worth the risk. You got cell coverage here? Because I'm showing no bars."

Chapter Eighteen

Alison's cell phone had bars.

Which, for me, was a great relief.

I was already looking under the Jeep's front seats for another of those little TechWhiz boxes that I was now more convinced than ever were some kind of cell phone signal jammers.

They'd had that type of thing on *Star Trek*— *They're jamming the signal from our ship, Captain!* And they'd been able to do similar things with radio signals and even radar back during WWII. Since I'd had a son who flew bomber raids over Africa and then Europe, I knew a great deal about the importance and mechanics of jamming the enemy's radar.

But that wasn't happening here, since Alison's cell phone worked. As she called the production office for help, I pulled A.J. aside and shared with him what little I'd learned since running into the man I suspected was Gene, as he'd removed the evidence of his nearly-foul-play from Hugh's Jeep.

I told A.J. about the TechWhiz 7842, and the mysterious swapped-out Gatorade.

I told him about Sandra Busard, who was supposed to go with Hugh, but only after Alison had canceled on him.

And I told him about the holes in the ground that I'd found, which seemed to suggest that Alison's nearly demolished office trailer had, at one time, been anchored with guy wires. There was also what I thought of as a suspiciously placed dent in the side of the trailer. But A.J. interrupted me before I could reveal my theory about that.

"You think someone intentionally removed those anchors before the storm," A.J. said, his skepticism ringing in his voice. "That seems a bit of a stretch. There was no way for anyone to know how strong those winds were going to get. That's kind of like me saying I think I'd like to trip Beverly, so I'll sit in my living room on the sofa with my leg stretched out. She's bound to show up sooner or later and take a fall."

"They want it to look like an accident," I told him a touch peevishly, because he was right. As far as accidents went, it was pretty dumb and relied far too much on luck. But they could've been playing into their hand. Seen that the storm was coming, and gone for it when it appeared to be the doozy that it was. "Plus I'm pretty sure the plan was to put a little shoulder into it, too, when the wind blew. There's a dent, right where someone could've heaved and helped the thing tip."

"There are, like, four hundred dents all over that trailer," A.J. argued, shaking his head. "And what about the other trailers that didn't have anchors? Gramps, you're letting your imagination run wild. And why would they tip it, anyway, after we got out?"

"Because they didn't see you leave." I didn't have an answer for *What about the other trailers,* so I said, "Okay, all right, let's leave the trailer alone and focus on what just happened here. As in, you nearly died. Have you looked under the Jeep? I suspect you're going to find that brake line was tampered with. I think my tall killer with the ponytail, and his buddies Gene and Loco, are trying to kill Alison, and I don't think they care who gets caught in the crossfire."

A.J. just kept shaking his head. "You honestly think Alison witnessed a murder and didn't *tell* anyone?" he asked, looking me dead in the eye.

I stared straight back at him. "She knows something. She's seen something. She's somehow involved."

"In a murder?" he asked, lowering his voice and glancing over toward the other side of the Jeep, where Alison was still on her phone. "Seriously, Gramps, if you think Alison would help anyone cover up the fact that they hit the bumper of someone else's car in a parking lot, let alone a *murder* . . ."

"Just check that brake line," I told him. "I'll be beyond thrilled to be wrong. I'd do it myself, but you're going to have to see it anyway. . . ."

A.J. glanced at Alison again, and I knew what he was thinking. Here she'd just gotten used to—barely—the fact that A.J. was being followed around by a spirit from beyond.

And she was struggling—hard—with the news that A.J. was forever destined to fight his alcoholism. That that battle was never going to end.

She wasn't going to welcome the paranoid-seeming warning that someone was trying to kill her. And A.J. was right. She'd think—again—that he was certifiable.

But I strongly believed that she had to be told. Told and talked into going to the police. Or the FBI. She and A.J. could go back to Jubilation and knock on the door of Rob and Charlotte's trailer, and ask for immunity in exchange for the information for which Gene and company were trying to kill her. Whatever that information was.

Surely Alison would know.

The tall man with that ponytail had said that he'd exploded Wayne's head all over the back windshield of his car. If Alison had seen that, then she was certainly still having nightmares. Although A.J. had a point. Why she hadn't gone to the police right away was . . .

Huh.

And I realized, as A.J. pulled himself back out from under the Jeep and dusted off his jeans, that maybe Alison *hadn't* seen Wayne's murder. But Wayne, with all of his tattoos, may well have been an easily identifiable man. As was his tall, ponytailed killer, with that easy-to-distinguish scar near his eye.

What if Alison had seen them together, just prior to Wayne's death?

I wasn't any kind of lawyer, but that made me scratch my head, because it seemed to me that simply seeing two men together before one man died, didn't provide evidence—beyond a reasonable doubt—that the second man was guilty of murder.

So maybe there was more to it than that. Which seemed to make sense, because despite Wayne's being as charming and lovely as he no doubt must've been before death had stolen him, it also seemed odd that the FBI had been called in to solve a simple homicide.

Which made me twice the fan of the knock-on-Rob-and-Charlotte's-door idea.

"Brake line's severed," A.J. reported. "But it was badly frayed. It was definitely an accident."

427

I shook my head. "There are ways to fray a line. Remember, they wanted to make it look like it wasn't deliberate."

A.J. sighed heavily. "Look, Gramps, I just—"

"This is a rental car," I pointed out. "You think they don't check these things regularly?"

"Apparently not regularly enough," A.J. said, and I knew, just from looking at him, that I wasn't going to convince him, even though I went on and told him everything that I'd just been thinking.

This accident was just that to him—an accident. Plus he saw it as a good thing, a happy occasion—because it had thrown him back into Alison's willing arms. The boy was besotted, that much was clear.

He was also in that place—I'd been there myself—where, after a long stretch of no sexual congress, he'd gotten some, and now desperately craved more. He wasn't about to listen to reason when all he wanted to think about was planning the logistics behind the next time he could get this girl alone.

I wanted to suggest to him that right now—and over the next few days—might be the perfect time to keep his belt fastened and his pants zipped. He'd achieve more by refusing to be Alison's cheap and meaningless plaything, but I knew that A.J. wouldn't be able to hear that news flash right now either. So I kept that to myself.

"Let's talk to the rental car company," I said.

"Find out the date when the brake line was last checked. See if it was starting to fray and I'd bet you it wasn't. In the meantime, I'll keep an eye on the man I think is Gene, while you get Alison safely to Alaska and stick close to her. Like that's going to be a hardship."

He smiled a little sheepishly. "Sorry about before. In the Jeep. I kind of kicked you in the head."

"I don't have a head to kick," I told him. "Besides, I saw your intention and got the hell out of Dodge. Lookit, do me a favor? Will you at least let me ask her about Wayne and Gene and the tall man I saw burning that car?"

He sighed. "She's not an idiot."

"I'm aware of that, kid."

"Let's do it later," he said, "please?" and he went toward Alison, who'd just closed her phone.

"Paula's coming with another car," Alison reported. "She's going to drive us to the airport. She's already on the road—she'll be here in about ten minutes. It's going to be close, but we're still going to make our departure time."

And then she stopped talking because A.J. kissed her.

A.J. definitely wasn't bored on the plane.

And Alison wasn't either.

She didn't even try to pretend that, after they'd boarded the aircraft—luxurious and plush, with that king-sized bed lurking there in a private, spacious room—they weren't going to end up napping.

Together.

After not napping together.

They sat in the comfortable captain's chairs in the main cabin during takeoff. And A.J. must've seen her anxiety. She'd never been a happy flier and somehow he knew and reached over and took her hand, lacing their fingers together.

It was so thoughtful and sweet, it nearly made her cry.

Of course it seemed as if almost everything, over the past few days, nearly made her cry.

And she was still badly shaken by that plunge down the hill.

Not to mention how quickly and thoroughly she'd thrown away her resolve to, as she'd stated quite succinctly moments earlier, never have sex with this man again.

So, okay. A little near-death experience had made her realize that life was too short to not take advantage of the kind of connection that she and A.J. had made.

As long as they both understood that their time together was temporary.

It had to be.

They reached cruising altitude and the seat belt sign went off, and Alison stood up. And this time, she held out her hand for him.

He didn't argue, didn't say a word. He just followed her into the bedroom, where she locked the door behind them, and pulled him in close for a kiss.

He tasted like A.J.—sweet and funny with familiar coffee overtones, because he drank so much of the stuff. It was odd how quickly that had happened—that familiarity. It wasn't long ago that kissing him had been new and strange and wonderful. And now it was just wonderful.

He got her naked—with her enthusiastic help, of course—and then he made her come, hard and fast, just blowing the top of her head off, leaving her gasping and weak and yet, somehow, longing for more.

And then he delivered more, for longer than she would have believed possible. Slowly, sweetly, tenderly, and this time when she came it was in glorious slow motion. This time he came with her, sighing her name as if, for him, she were the beginning and the end.

And again she nearly cried, because she wanted this, but she didn't want *this*. She wanted someone a lot like him, but different. She didn't want this man, *this* A.J.—not with the luggage with which he came burdened. It was luggage he'd never lose and the thought of handcuffing herself to it, too, was too much.

Somehow he knew that as well, and he whispered, "I'm sorry."

And then he fell asleep, as did Alison.

For a little while.

She awoke to find him moaning, still fast asleep, and she shook him to try to wake him, afraid he was caught in the claws of some horrible dream—something he'd done or seen or lived through. He'd lost a kidney, he'd told her. In Hor al-Hammar. And she knew that wasn't all that he'd lost there.

But when he opened his eyes—they were so blue—he smiled at her. "Hey," he said. "Don't tell me we're there already."

"No," Alison said. "I think you were having a nightmare."

He looked surprised and then he laughed. "No," he said. "That was . . . Not a nightmare. I've had my share of nightmares and . . . But you were there in this one and, um . . ."

"Um?" she said, smiling back at him. "Really? Then I'm sorry I woke you."

He pulled her down for a kiss. "Dream versus reality? I'll take the real thing. Although you *were* wearing this incredible lingerie. I was sitting on this chair—like the ones in your kitchen. And I was tied up—to the chair. And you came in, in these black panties, with these really high heels and I knew you were going to, you know, jump me. Which I love, very much, when you do it, not just in my dreams."

She had to laugh. "Shades of dominatrix," she

said. "Was I wearing leather and maybe carrying a whip?"

A.J. laughed, too. "No, it was that stretchy kind of lace, like you were wearing today. I don't know why, but I've always really, *really* liked that."

"So . . . do you also really, *really* like being tied up?" Alison asked.

"Actually," he said, "I don't. I don't find it even remotely appealing. I'm not sure why I dreamed it. Although, in my dream, it wasn't a bad thing."

"Your hands are tied," she said. "Maybe it was symbolic. Was it just your hands?"

"God," he said, "I can't remember that. All I know is that I wasn't trying to get away."

"Do you always remember your dreams so vividly?"

A.J. looked at her, as if deciding how to answer. He was a smart man, and he'd no doubt figured out exactly the direction she was heading. But then he nodded and said, "Yeah. Usually."

"Do you have nightmares a lot?"

"Not so much anymore."

"Really?"

"Yeah," he said. "It's been awhile since I've done the whole wake-up-screaming thing. You'd know it if I was having a nightmare, by the way. None of this *are you or aren't you* ambiguity. You'd know."

Alison propped her head up on one hand, elbow out, so that she was looking down at him as she played with the hair on his chest. "Do you have those nasty recurring ones, with the same dream every time? Or . . . ?"

"They usually start out differently," he told her. "And end up the same."

And of course, her next question was, *Will you tell me about it?* She could see him bracing himself for it, see him start to consider his options—what to say, what to do.

"If I asked you to tell me about your nightmare," she said instead, "would that be a bad thing? Would, you know, talking about it make you more likely to have it again?"

He was both surprised and amused. "You do know you just gave me an out."

Alison shook her head. "No, I gave you a chance to answer—honestly—what I believe is a very serious question."

"My honest answer," he said, "is that I don't know. Because I've . . . kind of, um, never talked about it."

"Kind of?"

"Never," he clarified with an apologetic smile. "I do that a lot, don't I? Equivocate."

"Yes, you do. Don't change the subject."

"I wasn't trying to." He reached up and pushed her hair back behind her ear with the gentlest of caresses.

"You've never talked to your friend Lutz?" Alison asked.

"No," A.J. said. "I was always trying to push that part of my life away. It was over and I was moving on. Revisiting what happened didn't seem like a good plan. So I didn't talk to Lutz about anything. I didn't talk to Lutz at all."

"Wow," Alison said. "Maybe I should be wearing the *I'm with Stupid* shirt."

A.J. laughed. "But I'm doing okay."

"Wouldn't you rather be doing better than just okay?"

"When I'm with you, I am," he told her. And he meant it, which scared the crap out of her.

So she said, "Tell me about your nightmare," because she wanted him to back away, to admit that he was unwilling to open up and tell her. Of course, that would be more brutally awful fuel to add to the fire upon which all of her doubts blazed. More reasons to help convince herself that there was no way in hell this relationship could ever be anything real and lasting.

And she could see from his eyes that he knew why she was pushing him to tell her, and it made him sad—but not sad enough to douse his relentless hope.

"It's one of those dreams," he told her quietly, "where I know exactly what's going to happen. I see it coming, but I can't stop it. It just bulldozes over me. I think that's one of the reasons why I stopped having the nightmares. I finally realized that even if I'd seen it coming, back when it really happened, even if I hadn't been so naive and trusting, it wouldn't have mattered. I still wouldn't have been able to stop it. It was not a situation that I could control, even though I tried. I did the best I could, and nearly died."

He took a deep breath and let it out in a rush.

"At the time, it was hard not to blame myself. We went in knowing that the enemy was . . . cruel. They allegedly answered to the Republican Guard, but they were led by a powerful local warlord who was even more brutal. And although he had plenty of ammunition, he preferred to crush any opposition in a far more up-close and personal way, starting with his opponents' children. And if you didn't have children, his men would kill your nieces and nephews or even the neighbors' kids. They didn't give a damn. They also liked to draw it out. The killing. And make it public. Witnessing it kept everyone else in line."

He was telling her what had actually happened, not what he'd dreamed. He was telling her about Hor al-Hammar.

"And yet, when we went into the village, into what we called Hor al-Hammar, there were still people willing to help us. I told them—because this was what *I* had been told—that after we'd liberated Kuwait, we were going to push, hard, into Iraq. So they helped us set up a base. They helped us make it secure. But then, just like that, it was over, and we were being ordered back over the border. I was so goddamned young and naive. I remember running to find my commanding officer, because I knew it had to be a mistake. And when I couldn't find him, I went further up the chain of command. And when I realized we really were leaving, I told the major that we had to get those people out of there—we had to take them with us—all the civilians who'd helped us. But he said there was no time. And even if there was, there was nowhere to put them—they'd be refugees. Imagine the uproar if we showed up back in the States with a few thousand stray towel-heads. He actually called them that. Besides, he said, they wouldn't want to go.

"I told him he was wrong, and then I told him to go fuck himself, which kind of ended my career— there's that *kind of,* again. It ended my career, but that's okay, by then it was already over. I was ready to get out. He got pissed and he called for the MPs, but everything was in chaos so I just walked away. And then I ran. And then I stole a Jeep, which went onto my list of transgressions. I made it out to the village, but the fighting had already started. Our people—our allies, the so-called *towel-heads* who'd already helped save countless American lives—they were armed and they were holding off the attack, but they weren't going to be able to hold it forever. And they knew by then that we'd abandoned them.

"And one of them—Nouri—in his heartbreak

and rage, he shot me. And then he shot his family and himself, and it was . . ."

"Oh, God," Alison said.

"It was happening all around me," A.J. whispered. "These people, they all knew what was coming, and they chose a quick and painless death for their children."

"So the massacre," Alison whispered, "was . . . self-inflicted."

"No," A.J. said with certainty. "*We* inflicted it."

"How did you survive?" she asked.

"This girl," A.J. said. "Zaynab. She was maybe seventeen. She wanted to be a doctor and I was . . ." He cleared his throat. "Smitten." But then he added, "Not like with you. This was entirely from afar, because she was so young, but we were friends. She and her brother got me back into the Jeep and they drove me out of town. Not out of kindness or affection. I'm sure they hated me by then as much as Nouri did. But they told me that if the warlord's men found me there, even if they just found my body, they would raze the entire village—they'd even kill the people who didn't actively help the Americans. Which those bastards ended up doing anyway.

"I'm not sure where we were when Lutz and his men found us. I'd lost a lot of blood by then and things were pretty surreal. I know I wanted to stay and fight. I remember trying to kick Lutz in the balls. I think I wanted to die there, but Lutz got me onto a chopper, and I didn't. But Zaynab and her brother did. Die. Not right away. Lutz told me later that they escaped into the marsh where they formed a resistance. They did pretty well for a while. Until they were gassed—and the entire marsh was drained."

"Oh, God," Alison said again.

"But in my nightmare, it's always Nouri," A.J. told her. "Weeping as he puts his gun to the head of his ten-year-old son as his three-year-old screams. His wife picks her up and sings to her as she uses her own weapon to kill the girl, then turns her gun on herself, so her husband doesn't have to do it. One final act of love as their world comes to a violent and bloody end—as I lie there, helpless, unable to do anything but watch."

"I'm so sorry," Alison said.

"At the time it seemed so black and white to me," A.J. told her. "I was so sure that we should've invaded. We could've kicked Saddam's ass. But we've all since seen what an invasion looks like when there's no strategy in place for winning the peace. And it wasn't in place back then, either. Goddamned idiots, all of 'em. That could've been the easy part and they screwed it up, royally. They're so busy with the big picture—with the money that their corporate overlords can earn—that they don't see that it's all about the little things. About the people. It's about Zaynab wanting to go to school to become

439

a doctor, not in some big city, but in her village. It's about Nouri risking everything because he wants a better life for his children. It's about Nouri's wife, who loved him and her children so deeply, and thousands of people, individuals, just like them, who *would have* been our friends if we'd greeted them with food and water and shelter and medical aid—and an organized way for them to get it. And then jobs and homes and education . . . Instead, we treat them—these proud, courageous people—as if they're insignificant. Just a bunch of numbers, statistics. Vermin living in the rubble above a land rich with oil. Plus, their babies are brown, so they don't count as much, back here in the *homeland,* when *they* die."

He'd gotten louder as he'd said that last bit, and now the cabin seemed to ring with silence.

"Sorry," A.J. apologized. "I didn't mean to . . . I'm still a little angry and . . ."

"A little," she said.

"Did I scare you?" he asked, his eyes worried.

"No," she said, absolutely.

He kissed her then. It was a sweet kiss, but then he kissed her again, and his intention became very clear. He was done talking. At least for a while.

But Alison stopped him from kissing her again. "Thank you," she said, "for telling me."

"Thank *you,*" he said, "for not running away, screaming. At least not yet."

He softened his words with a smile, but they both knew that he was kidding on the square.

As he kissed her again—longer, deeper—and her pulse kicked up a notch, Alison couldn't help but wonder exactly what this was that she was doing here.

And then she stopped wondering about anything at all as he took her to heaven.

August 18, 1898
Dear Diary,

We were forced to stop early today. One horse has gone lame. J. was tense and angry. I made dinner, usual camp rations, but he did not eat.

I confess, I was frightened. His face looked so dark, so unforgiving. I also confess, that I had been waiting for this moment all these past days, waiting for the monster within him to reveal itself to me.

The horse's lameness is not my fault, but fault is not necessary for punishment.

He asked me if there were any biscuits left, and there weren't and in my fear and worry, I dropped my plate. He saw that I was shaking, and came swiftly toward me. I reacted instinctively, dropping to the ground and curling up, protecting my head from the blows to come.

But no blows came.

He picked me up and held me in his arms, and I swear to the stars above, he wept.

Never, he told me, <u>never</u> would he strike me. If there was only one thing in life I could count on, it was that—because he truly loved me.

I would try to remember, I told him. I didn't mean to mistrust him.

He'd earn my trust, he said, through time, if nothing else.

I have never seen a man cry before. It touches my heart that my gambler should have tears so like mine.

But one thing he said rings in my mind, louder and stronger than all of his vows and words of love. It was a promise that he made me give to him.

"If ever I hit you," he told me with those tears in his beautiful eyes, "you <u>will</u> leave me. You'll walk away. Or hell, you'll pick up a gun and order me out of our house, if we ever have a house. Promise me right now that you won't take that abuse from me or from any other man, God forbid something happen to me."

"I promise," I whispered, and he kissed me so gently.

In the morning, while the plane was refueling on the ground in Seattle, A.J. had called Bev from the comfort of that big bed.

Alison was in the bathroom, on her own cell

phone, hoping to get some information from Paula the intern. Something about the packet of letters from Penelope Eversfield to her sister Horry, that were being sent from Denver. Had Neil Sylvester received them yet?

A.J. could hear her asking about tracking numbers and dates as he let his sister know that his flight was going to land over at the old Air Force field, just outside of Heaven, shortly after noon.

She was more than happy to come and pick him up. And to lend him their old truck—the one that Charlie was trying to sell—to use while he was back in town.

Bev's legendary curiosity had reached new levels though, when, in response to her offer to reserve a room at the local B&B, A.J. had informed her that Alison would be staying with him for the few days she'd be in town.

Which was exactly the kind of information that Bev had been fishing for.

"So Mom's right," she said triumphantly. "I thought she was just doing her usual crazy-mother thing. I'm impressed. You're actually making time with the famous Hollywood writer. Go, A.J."

"She's not a Hollywood writer," A.J. told her. "She's a history professor, from Boston."

"Now I'm even more impressed. What's she like?"

And that was where A.J. made his fatal mistake.

He not only told his incredibly secrecy-challenged sister that Alison was brilliant and funny and beautiful, but he also admitted that he'd told her about Hor al-Hammar.

Which Bev—after she'd finished crying—correctly interpreted to mean that he'd fallen hard for Alison.

And *that* was why, as the jet came in for their landing, A.J. looked out the window and saw not just Bev's truck parked near the hangar, but his mother's SUV, as well as around ten other vehicles.

"Oh, damn," he told Alison, as she held tightly to his hand for the descent. "We've got a welcoming committee."

She looked out the window, but saw only the mountains. "Oh, my God, A.J., it's *so* beautiful."

And it was—with the lush green trees and the sparkling blue of the intercoastal waterway. Heaven was in the part of Alaska that was an arctic rainforest, which meant that the days were often overcast and gray. But today the sky was blue, without a cloud in sight—as if someone had ordered the perfect sunny, early-summer day.

A.J. was beyond happy to be home. But he wasn't all that thrilled about the fact that they were going to have to face the twenty-questions brigade immediately upon stepping off the plane.

And then Alison, who was leaning across him, her hand on his thigh, saw all the cars. And the

444

crowd of people standing around them, or sitting on their hoods. "Whoa," she said as the jet's tires grabbed the runway, as her hand tightened on his leg. "Are those *all* relatives?"

"Not all of them," A.J. reported. "My mother's there. And my grandfather—Adam. I see a bunch of cousins, too. My sister and her husband . . . And a lot of other miscellaneous people from town."

"They must've missed you," she said. "It's sweet."

"Nah," A.J. said. "It's pure curiosity, combined with it being lunchtime. Word must've gotten out that you were coming home with me. Everyone wants to check you out."

"Am I that much of a novelty?" she asked, bemused.

"Actually," A.J. said as the plane finally turned and taxied toward the hangar, "it's more about me. I tend to keep to myself."

"Ah," she said. "No hordes of wild women lined up at your door, I take it."

A.J. smiled at that. "Not exactly. I dated a second-grade teacher down in Juneau for a while, a few years back, but it wasn't serious. She never came up here, I always took the ferry down there. I'm not sure anyone even knew I was, um, seeing her."

"Would you rather that no one knows about me?" Alison asked. "We could keep a low profile.

If you want, I could stay at that bed and breakfast. That way people wouldn't have to know—"

"That horse has already left the barn," he told her. "Sorry about that. Bev kind of pried it out of me and . . . I'm just going to apologize in advance, for anything bizarre that my mother or anyone else in my family might say to you."

Alison laughed. "What could they possibly say?"

"Welcome to Heaven. So. Alison. When are you and A.J. getting married?"

"No one's going to say that."

The plane stopped and Alison unfastened her seat belt.

"Care to put some money on it?" A.J. asked.

"Dinner," she said. "Loser buys tonight." She paused. "You do have restaurants in Heaven, right?"

He looked at her. "What's a rest-ee-rant?"

"Very funny."

"Italian, Thai, Vegan, Middle Eastern, seafood, or seafood," he told her. "I recommend Fishy's, the second seafood place."

"Fishy's," she said.

"Yeah, big-city woman. Mock it now. You're going to be apologizing later. And picking up the check." Not that he was actually going to let her do that. Still, it was nice to see her smile. To pretend that he really was bringing her home to meet his family.

He stood up. Kissed her. Kissed her again, longer this time, because he wasn't going to be able to kiss her that way after they got off the plane. At least not in the immediate future.

She sighed and melted against him. "Hmm. Maybe we should ask the pilot to run us over to Boston so I could pick up my raincoat. You said it rains here all the time. It's only a seven-hour trip, each way. . . ."

He laughed as he kissed her again. "You know, *my* bed's pretty nice, too."

"I've just really enjoyed the fantasy element of all this," Alison admitted.

"Yeah," A.J. said. "Me, too."

And there was the flight attendant, whom they'd seen very little of, knocking on the cabin door.

A.J. went to open it, but Alison stopped him with a hand on his arm. "Is Jamie . . . ?"

"No," he said. "I haven't seen him in a while. He's, um, working on some big mystery back in Jubilation." He cleared his throat. "I'll tell you more about it after we run the gauntlet of misplaced curiosity, okay?"

She laughed as he opened the door. "You're so mean to your family."

"The stairs are in place, sir," the flight attendant said. "Ma'am."

"Thank you."

"Oh, my God," Alison said as she stepped out of the plane and took her first deep breath of that

447

impossibly clean, fresh, cool air. But then she took A.J.'s arm and said, "You do realize that nothing's changed between us, right?"

It was funny she could say that when, for him, so much had changed. He'd told her the truth about Hor al-Hammar, about Nouri and his family—just several of the dozens of people he'd thought of as friends whom he'd helped to kill as absolutely as if he'd pulled the trigger himself.

And Alison had listened without judging him. And without trying to minimize or make insignificant his feelings of responsibility.

"But I won't embarrass you by being too honest," she added, slipping her hand down into his, so that they were obviously holding hands— for his mother and Bev and the entire rest of the town to see. "No pronouncements that I'm in this purely for the sex and that I see you merely as the steaming hot man-stud that you are, servicing me immediately upon my command."

A.J. laughed. "You know, my cousin Bill is deaf. He reads lips."

"Oh, no, really?" she said, covering her mouth as she laughed.

"I'm kidding," he said. "I mean, he does read lips, but he's not here. Besides, aren't you also here for the diaries?"

"Yes, I am," Alison said, but they'd hit the tarmac and his mother was leading the crowd who'd come to meet them.

"Everyone, this is Alison," A.J. said. "Alison, this is . . . everyone."

Alison recognized A.J.'s mother immediately.

Dr. Rose Gallagher was tall and elegant looking, with regal, almost harsh features and brilliant green eyes. Her gray hair was pulled back into a single braid that hung down her back. She wore a plaid flannel shirt and well-worn jeans, but her casual attire didn't detract from her queenly appearance. She gazed back at Alison, one eyebrow raised.

A.J.'s sister Bev was beside her—had to be. She looked like a younger version of their mother. But her eyes were a softer shade of hazel, her face slightly more round and her mouth curved up into a welcoming smile. Her long hair was brown and wavy—Jamie Gallagher's hair, Alison realized.

And there was Adam. The old man was A.J.'s grandfather, there was no doubt about that. They were nearly identical in height and build, and despite Adam's age he still stood straight and tall. His hair was white but thick and full, and his face was leathery and lined. The eyes that sparkled at her from under bushy gray eyebrows were that of a much younger man—in fact, they were very much like A.J.'s eyes. And like Jamie Gallagher's. Who was allegedly Adam's father. As Melody Quinn was allegedly his mother.

For a moment, Alison couldn't quite breathe.

Adam didn't hesitate. He swooped in and enveloped his grandson in a hug.

A.J.'s mother, however, hung back. "I'm not *everyone*," she said. "I'm Rose Gallagher. Dr. Rose Gallagher."

"It's so nice to meet you," Alison said, shaking the older woman's hand. This was not a woman one greeted for the very first time with an embrace.

In fact, if Alison were casting a movie about A.J.'s life, she'd build a time machine and go back to 1968 to hire Katharine Hepburn to play his mother. Rose Gallagher had the same no-nonsense attitude, the same almost aloof air of authority that Hepburn had brought to many of her later movies like *The Lion in Winter*.

"You're looking tired," Rose said to A.J. as Adam released him. "Are you well?" Her tone was cool, businesslike, but Alison knew that the older woman was hiding a great deal of anxiety and worry. She cared about her son, and quite deeply, despite her lack of obvious outward affection.

"I'm fine," A.J. said. "I'm . . . *really* fine."

"Welcome to Heaven," Adam said to Alison, distracting her so that she never did see if Rose smiled at her son. Rose finally did hug him, though—thank goodness. If she hadn't, Alison would've been tempted to smack her.

But Adam was now holding out a hand for

Alison to shake, and his grip was firm and strong. "I'm Adam, and I'm real pleased to meet you, dear. Anyone who's responsible for Age answering *fine* to that question instead of *I'm getting by* or *I'm surviving* deserves a ticker tape parade."

Age? It was a shortening of A.J., Alison realized. A nickname for a nickname. She liked Adam and his twinkling blue eyes instantly.

"I'm Bev." A.J.'s sister also shook her hand. "And this is my husband, Charlie, and my father-in-law, Tom."

Everyone else in the crowd started calling out their names and waving, which was a little overwhelming. A.J. put his hand on her shoulder, but it was Tom—Tom Fallingstar, the old shaman—who reassured her.

"You'll get a chance to meet them all back in town," he told her quietly. "They don't want to be rude. Just smile and wave."

A.J. had told her about Tom on the plane—a kind of crazy story about how, just as he'd hit bottom with his drinking, Tom had seemed to appear. He'd given A.J. the money he'd needed to get back home.

The way A.J. had spoken of him, Tom was at least a million years old. And he did look both simultaneously ancient and ageless. He could have been anywhere from forty to seventy, with hair that was still mostly dark. He wore it long,

451

much as Rose wore her hair—back in a single braid. His face was all sharp angles and well-defined planes, as if he'd been carved from stone. But his eyes weren't cold. They were brown and warm and welcoming.

"Thanks," she whispered back to him.

"I can't tell you how happy I am to meet you," Bev said. "We've all read your book. We're *very* impressed."

"Well, thank you."

Bev may have been impressed, but if Rose Gallagher was, too, she certainly wasn't letting on. Alison felt the woman's cool gaze on her, studying her. So she faced her head-on.

"I'm eager to get a look at those diaries," Alison said. "They'll go a long way toward verifying A.J.'s claim."

"Claim?" Rose repeated, eyebrows elevating to new heights, the chill in her voice dropping to sub-zero. "Don't you believe what A.J.'s told you?"

She felt A.J.'s hand tighten on her shoulder. But before he could run interference between her and his dragon of a mother, who apparently didn't have a problem with confrontations in front of an audience, Alison stepped up to the task.

Public speaking didn't frighten her. And Rose Gallagher didn't frighten her, either. Regardless of the fact that she clearly knew that Alison and her son had gotten it on. And on. And on.

452

Alison smiled. "I'd *like* to believe A.J., Dr. Gallagher," she said, the perfect balance of sweetness and light, refusing to be intimidated or even remotely defensive. "I'm sure you know that. His story is very convincing. His nonverbal communications are convincing, too."

The crowd laughed and Rose Gallagher glanced at her son, who was now nonchalantly examining the toes of his boots and hiding his face from view beneath the brim of his cowboy hat.

From most people's view. Alison was standing close enough to achieve eye contact, and the look he gave her was a mix of amusement and disbelief.

"But I'm an historian," Alison continued. "I can't let my personal interest in A.J. sway my good judgment. The fact is, he's given me no written proof—so far—that anything he's told me is true. To counter that, to date, it's been documented in writing that Silas Quinn killed Jamie Gallagher in Arizona in 1898. I'm here to find documented proof that Jamie Gallagher in fact lived quite a bit longer."

Dr. Gallagher stared back at Alison, the expression in her eyes unreadable.

"It's my job, ma'am," Alison said quietly but firmly, "to question your family's claim. I'm sure you can respect my need to do my job as well and as thoroughly as I possibly can."

Tom Fallingstar chuckled softly.

"En garde, Mom," Bev said, with a broad smile.

Rose Gallagher blinked and glanced at her daughter. "Yes," she said. "Indeed."

She smiled then, and to Alison's surprise there was now genuine warmth and amusement in the older woman's eyes.

"You'll do," Rose said to Alison. "Quite nicely, in fact. I hope we'll have time to chat while you're here in town. But in the meantime, you'll want to get to work, I imagine. You're staying at A.J.'s, I assume?"

"Uh, yes," Alison said, slightly off-balance at the older woman's sudden total acceptance.

"Good," Rose Gallagher said, briskly leading the way back to the cars and trucks parked at the edge of the field.

A.J. grabbed Alison's hand and pulled her along.

"I've got to get back to work," Charlie Fallingstar, Bev's husband, said. He kissed his wife and waved to Alison as the rest of the crowd dispersed, too. "Nice meeting you, Alison. I'm sure I'll see you later. Come on, Adam, I'll give you a lift."

"For the record, I want more grandchildren," Rose said before Alison could even properly say good-bye to Charlie. "I make no bones about that. Of course I'd prefer it if you were married first. I'm old-fashioned that way—where children are concerned." She glanced at Alison. "You haven't, by any chance, agreed to marry my son . . . ?"

"Fishy's," A.J. murmured into Alison's ear. "Seven o'clock. I'm having the salmon."

"We've really only just started seeing each other," Alison said, trying not to laugh. "It's a little soon to think beyond the end of the year."

"What happens at the end of the year?" Rose asked, stopping in front of a bright yellow SUV with MD plates.

"My sabbatical ends and I'm back in Boston," she said. "Teaching."

"Hmm," Rose said. "American history, right?"

"Yes, ma'am."

"I didn't think I'd like you, but I do," she told Alison, just point-blank. Pow. "Your book was . . ." She paused, searching for the right word.

"Wrong?" Alison supplied, and Rose laughed.

"Not many people would be willing to admit that," she said. "Even as a remote possibility. Yet . . . here you are. Interested in the truth."

"I'm a history professor," Alison told A.J.'s mother, "because I'm fascinated by the lessons we, the human race, can learn from the past. But one of the things we need to keep in the forefront of any discussion about that past is that history has been and always will be recorded by the winners. We rarely get an unbiased picture of any event. I mean, even on a fairly innocuous level. Think about who recorded the history of this country from the time of Columbus until, well, about the mid-twentieth century. Men—and

455

predominantly white men. We view much of our past through that white male filter. Which is one of the reasons why I'm extremely interested in reading the story of Melody's life with both Silas Quinn and Jamie Gallagher—in her very own words. I suspect Jubilation, Arizona, and even Heaven, Alaska, too, will look a little different through her lens."

"I don't just like her," Rose pronounced to A.J. "I love her. Marry her immediately."

She didn't wait for an answer, she just turned and beeped open the door of her car.

"And I'll have the Death by Chocolate for dessert," A.J. murmured in Alison's ear. "Although, I'm gonna order it to go."

"I like you, too, Dr. Gallagher," Alison told Rose, this time trying not to think about sharing a dessert called Death by Chocolate with A.J.— back in the privacy of his home. "But like I said. Too soon."

The last of the cars and trucks were gone, leaving A.J. and Alison alone with his mother and Bev and Tom the shaman. Who appeared to be considered part of the family.

Rose turned back to look at her. "You know about it all?" she asked, again point-blank. "The Gulf War, the injuries, the hospital, the drinking, rehab . . . Everything?"

"Well gee, Ma, if she didn't, she'd sure as hell know now, wouldn't she?" A.J. said dryly.

Alison glanced at A.J. His mother may have exasperated and frustrated and sometimes even embarrassed him, but he didn't really let that bother him. It amused him instead, his fondness for her clearly evident in his wry smile.

Alison looked back at Rose. "I know about everything."

"Including Jamie?" Rose asked.

"She knows, Mom," A.J. said.

But for the first time, Alison couldn't quite hold the older woman's steely gaze. She faltered, but for only a moment. Still it was enough.

"Hmm," Rose said. "Another nonbeliever in the spirit world. Well, I guess it's all right. I don't buy it, but I love A.J., too."

"I'm still sorting through what I've seen and . . . felt," Alison tried to explain.

A.J. squeezed her hand, his fingers warm, his presence solid. "It's okay," he said. "It's not a problem. We'll see you later, Mom. Tomorrow. We'll stop by."

He nodded to Tom and leaned forward and kissed his mother on the cheek before opening the door to his sister's truck and helping Alison inside.

It's not a problem.

Tom Fallingstar moved to stand next to Rose and her bright-colored car, a silent pillar of support.

As A.J. climbed into the truck, as Bev started

the engine and pulled away, Alison could feel Rose Gallagher's brilliant green eyes, now tinged with sadness, still watching her.

I love A.J., too. . . .

Chapter Nineteen

I was getting really tired of Gene.

If he even *was* Gene.

He'd headed back to Tucson, where he'd gotten a room in a cheap motel and sat around watching crap TV and smoking some kind of foul-looking drug that made me glad I didn't have to breathe the air in there.

Twice a day a skinny whore with tremendously bad teeth would come in and do some of the drug with him and then pull up her skirt and give him a go as she leaned over the table and unenthusiastically watched whatever was flickering across the TV screen.

The first time I closed my eyes and stayed, but that made me want to rub myself all over with sandpaper, and then give myself a good bleaching. I'd always thought lovemaking was a beautiful thing—it certainly was whenever I had done it—but this was rutting, pure and simple, and about as beautiful as watching Gene take a dump.

It took him about five glorious minutes from start to finish, and really, the only reason I stuck around, staring at the sink in the bathroom, was in hope that she'd call him by name. Or that he'd say something. *Yeah, I'm waiting for a call from Wayne's tall friend, you know, the one with the ponytail . . . ,* and then he'd fill in the blank by calling Wayne's killer by name.

Because it was clear that old Maybe-Gene was waiting on a phone call. His cell was out and in a position of importance on the bedside table—within easy reach at all times.

But Gene and his hooker friend didn't bother talking. She'd knock, he'd let her in, and they'd start smoking. And then Gene would unzip.

By day two I learned to pop quickly away when she knocked, and this time, I went to check in on A.J., who'd just gotten back from dinner out with Alison.

She looked like a million bucks in a simple black dress and nice shoes, her hair shiny around her shoulders. She had her arms around A.J.'s neck and she was smiling up at him as they stood in his kitchen.

"You *really* should have let me pay," she was saying. "You won the bet."

I know he saw me pop in, at least out of the corner of his eye, but he purposely ignored me. In fact, he turned his back on me and kissed her soundly.

It was more than clear where *that* was going, so I said—somewhat crossly, "Sooner or later, kid. I need to talk to Alison about old dead Wayne."

"Later," he lifted his head to tell me, then kissed her again.

We'd had a bit of a chat last time Skinny had knocked on Gene's door—back when A.J. was on that fancy airplane, while Alison was in the shower.

A.J. seemed convinced that, even if Alison somehow was a target of some thugs back in Jubilation, she was safe here in Alaska.

And I had to agree. What I'd seen of Gene made it clear that he wasn't any kind of International Man of Mystery. He was strictly local talent, and I use that word *talent* with a great deal of irony and sarcasm. And as for the tall man with the ponytail, well, *he* was the genius who'd hired Gene. I didn't expect much from him, either.

Across the kitchen, that kiss wasn't ending anytime soon, so I sighed and popped away, back to Jubilation to check on my good friends Rob and Charlotte, the FBI agents.

I'd been monitoring them to see if I couldn't figure out who they were surveilling, but they were as bad as A.J. and Alison when it came to needing their privacy.

In fact, as I jumped in, I had my eyes almost completely shut, but then opened them when I realized Rob was dressed and sitting at their trailer's little built-in table. Charlotte was nowhere in sight, and Rob had a pensive expression on his face as he looked at a little blue velvet jeweler's box that was open to reveal a ring. I only got a glimpse, but I'm pretty sure the stone was a diamond.

But he snapped the box shut when the door opened, and he quickly made it disappear into the pocket of his jeans.

"God, I need a shower," Charlotte said as she started to take off her clothes, which, of course, was my cue to leave.

Rob's response was to assist her by taking off his own clothes, and I knew from the way Charlotte smiled at him that they were going to be useless in my quest for information, for an hour or so at least.

So I popped away, back up to Alaska, into downtown Heaven.

You know, supposedly, while I was down here on earth as a spirit, I'd feel nothing—no hunger, no thirst, no pain of any kind, no desire. I don't really have any form—I only appear as human for A.J.'s sake, to make it easier for him to deal with me.

But just because I couldn't feel hunger or thirst or desire didn't mean that I didn't want a big helping of chicken with mashed potatoes, or a tall glass of iced tea.

Or my beautiful wife in my arms.

I wished Mel were with me, holding my hand while we walked the streets of this town that we'd made from scratch, this town that we both still loved.

In some ways, Heaven's changed a lot in the past thirty-odd years. There're new houses, new stores. Some of the older buildings have undergone renovations. And the town is crawling with children and new babies.

But in some ways, Heaven hasn't changed a bit.

Dave Sanders still sweeps the sidewalk in front of his hardware store every morning, saying howdy to everyone who passes by. Merle still runs up a tab for you at the grocery, regardless of whether or not you can afford to pay on time.

Folks still smile at one another when they pass in the street, often stopping to chat, never too busy to greet an old friend.

And those mountains still loom nearby, sharp and beautiful and covered with snow, even in the summer months. I've always figured that those mountains are proof that there is a God. Something that beautiful couldn't've been an accident.

I headed toward Rose's doctor's office and stuck my head in, but the lights were off and the place was empty.

I'd been thinking a great deal about the way she'd reacted to bumping into me. She'd definitely felt my presence, the same as Alison had. I'd been pondering the idea of trying to communicate with Rose somehow, by standing in her way and letting her walk through me a few times or something.

Or something.

It was clearly another case of my hoping for divine inspiration to strike at the moment I needed it.

I jumped over to Rose's house and walked up the porch steps and through the wall, right into the middle of her living room. Of course, it used to be my living room. Mine and Mel's. So it didn't feel too much like trespassing.

"Honey, I'm home," I called out, but of course Rose couldn't hear me.

I could hear her, though. She was in the kitchen, rattling around some pots and pans and cooking up some of that vegetarian mishmash that she'd taken to eating lately.

Rose is capable of cooking the best damn pot roast in a five-hundred-mile radius, yet recently—well, sometime in the past thirty years, anyway—she became a vegetarian. Now, instead of pot roast that would melt in your mouth, she eats little sticks and twigs and curry this and tofu that.

"What's cookin', good-lookin'?" I greeted her as I went into the kitchen.

She was steaming some veggies and cooking some exotic blend of rice. There was nary a roast in sight.

I sat down at the kitchen table. "Lookit here, Rose," I said, even though she couldn't hear me.

"I've been thinking, and what I've been thinking is that it isn't right that you've been eating dinner alone for all these years."

That was when I noticed. There were two place settings at that table.

The back door opened without even a knock and Tom Fallingstar walked in.

Rose looked up from chopping broccoli and smiled. "Hi," she said.

"Hi," he said, taking off his jacket and hanging it on one of the hooks that lined the wall by the door. I'd hung my own jacket there more times than I could count. "Sorry I'm late."

"That's okay," she said.

"I was supposed to cook tonight," he said. He crossed toward her, and pushed a strand of her hair back from her face.

It was such a small thing, just the gentlest touch, but that, and the way they smiled into each other's eyes spoke volumes.

Good thing I didn't really have to breathe, because I'm not sure I could have right then. But for the two of them, this was just another day.

Tom crossed to the refrigerator and opened it. "I'll make a salad," he said. He knew exactly where all the fixings were as he moved around that kitchen. It was as if he'd made a salad there every night for the past thirty years.

If I'd been able to, I would've wept tears of joy. Rose wasn't alone the way I'd thought.

They worked together in companionable silence for a good two or three minutes as I studied Tom's face. He'd been a few years older than Ryan, but still, I couldn't remember him ever going to the town high school. Then I remembered that even back then, he was traveling and studying to become a shaman. Even back then, when he was just a teenager, it was recognized that there was something special about him.

His wife had died back when young Charlie, his son, was very small. Tom had been one of the many men lingering at Rose's door after Ryan, too, had passed.

I guess he'd simply lingered longer than the others—knowing a damn good thing when he saw it, and recognizing that Rosie was worth waiting for.

"A.J. looks good," Tom said, breaking the silence.

Rose nodded. "I like Alison," she said.

"I do, too," he said.

"But Heaven's very different from Boston."

"True," Tom said.

"I just don't want her to hurt him." Rose paused. "It scares me."

"I know," he said. "But from where I stand, I see only possibility. I see two very strong young people—"

"You see him as strong?" Rose asked, putting down her knife to look over at him.

He kept cutting a red cabbage as he answered. "Very. For ten years A.J.'s done something difficult, something that you and I can't even imagine. And he makes it look easy."

"No, he doesn't," she said.

Tom looked up. "Yes," he said, "he does. You need to let yourself really look at him. As he is today. Maybe it's time to put a new picture up in your office. He's not that fragile boy anymore, Rose."

Rose didn't respond. She just went back to cutting the broccoli and they worked again in silence for a while.

But then she said, "A funny thing happened a few days ago."

"Hmm," Tom said, cutting a yellow pepper now.

"I was in my office," Rose said, "and I felt the oddest sensation. You know when you swim and you hit a cold spot?"

"Uh-huh."

"Well, this was kind of like that, only it was a cold spot in the air," Rose said. "Plus there was this odd jangle with it—not quite an electric shock, but close." She put the broccoli into the steamer with the other vegetables and closed the lid before she turned toward Tom. "What do you suppose it was?"

He looked up at her and smiled. "Jamie," he said.

She smiled back at him. "Don't tease."

"I'm not," Tom said, matter-of-factly. "He's here, right now."

She glanced around the room, looking right through me. "Can you see him?" she asked Tom, her voice lowered, as if maybe I wouldn't be able to hear her that way.

He scraped the skinny slices of cabbage and pepper into the bowl with the lettuce, then put down the cutting board and knife. "Not exactly," he said.

"Then how do you know he's here?" she asked.

He smiled. "I feel him, his presence. He's here."

Medical science stared into the smiling eyes of mystical wisdom. Then medical science smiled, too. But it was a tremulous smile.

"Is Jamie angry with me?" Rose asked, searching Tom's eyes. "You know . . . because . . . you're here?"

"Oh, no, Rose," I said. "I'm happy for you. You don't know how happy. . . . And I know Ryan would be happy for you, too. It's long past time, dear."

Tom shook his head, and kissed her gently on the lips. "Jamie's not angry," he said. "He's glad." His smile grew broader. "In fact, if I listen very carefully, I can hear him. He's very frustrated, almost as much as I am, that we've been talking about getting married for almost three years now, and you won't agree that it's the right thing to do.

Right now, he's telling me that he wants—no, demands—that you come to a decision in my favor, and marry me."

Rose laughed as she wiped away the tears in her eyes. "You can't hear him, you big fake," she said. "Jamie did not say all that."

"Oh yes," I said. "I certainly did."

"Besides, when Jamie was frustrated with me, he'd tease and call me a ninny," Rose added.

"Jamie wants you to be happy, Rosie," Tom said, pulling her even closer and kissing the top of her head. "Come on. I promise not to hog the blankets and to keep the cap on the toothpaste. We've been friends for half a century, lovers for nearly ten years. The entire town knows that I'm your backdoor man. It's time you start letting me come in the front."

"I don't use the front door," Rose said.

Tom smiled. "That's beside the point." His smile faded and his eyes grew serious. "I know you'll always love Ryan. The same way I'll always love Marie. That won't ever change. But we're here and they're not."

"Jamie never remarried after Melody died," Rose said stubbornly.

Tom shook his head. "He wasn't lucky enough to meet someone else he could fall in love with," he said. "But we *were* lucky, you and I. I love you, and I know you love me. Come on, Rose, we're good together, and you know it."

Rose glanced around the room, searching for something. Me, I guess.

"Marry him, Rose," I all but shouted. "Don't be a ninny!"

"Marry me, Rose," he said. "Jamie says it's okay." He smiled. "He says, *Don't be a ninny*."

She looked back into Tom's eyes and started to laugh and cry both at the same time. "Oh, all right," she said.

Tom laughed, too. He tried to wipe the tears from her eyes, but soon gave up and just kissed her and held her tight.

And then, I swear to God, Tom Fallingstar looked straight at me and winked.

A.J.'s home was lovely.

When they'd first pulled up outside, earlier that afternoon, the cabin had seemed small and rustic. But as A.J. had brought Alison inside, she'd seen that it had been added on to repeatedly through the years, with several bedrooms and a den and a beautiful kitchen that had a wall of windows looking out over the harbor.

It wasn't large by any means, but it was warm and welcoming, and filled with richly polished wood and graceful furniture that had either come from A.J.'s shop, or had once belonged to Jamie and Melody, which was thrilling.

Assuming A.J.'s story was true.

July, 1901. The date was carved into the wood

mantel of the fireplace in A.J.'s living room—
right beneath the equally elegantly carved
proclamation *J loves M.*

Jamie loves Melody.

"They lived here for years," A.J. said as he saw
what Alison was tracing with her finger. He knelt
to stoke the fire that was crackling in the
fireplace. He'd lit it after they'd come home and
shared . . . dessert.

And no, she would never be able to order Death
by Chocolate again without smiling. Broadly.

Post-dessert, they'd showered—out of
necessity—and she'd slipped into A.J.'s bathrobe,
which was big and warm and fuzzy, like wearing
a blanket on a chilly night.

And it *was* chilly. The evening air was a touch
too cold, which was flat-out bizarre after all those
weeks in Arizona. So A.J. had pulled on a pair of
pajama pants, and lit a fire.

"They started out with only this one room," he
was telling her now. "Think about it. That was an
enormous change—for both of them."

She *was* thinking about it. Jamie and Melody
could have gone to Europe. To Asia. To Australia.
They could have gone anywhere in the world with
that money from the bank robbery. Unless A.J.
was right, and Jamie Gallagher hadn't really
robbed the Jubilation Bank and Trust.

Unless Quinn had shot and killed the night
guard, Bert Perry, and then lied about having

received an inheritance from an elderly relative.

An elderly relative whom he'd never named, whom Alison had never been able to trace. Which was not unusual, but God, in retrospect, it seemed obvious that Quinn had lied about everything.

"This was a man who loved crowds and people and parties and expensive hotels," A.J. was telling her, talking about Jamie, of course. "He loved glitter and gambling. But he moved to a part of the territory that wasn't even on the map at that time. He worked his butt off to build a new life up here, panning for gold when he could have earned ten times as much playing poker in San Francisco—which was the center of the universe back then, on par with New York City."

"Why didn't they stay there?" Alison asked.

"They did for a while—for a few years," he told her.

He tugged her down so that she sat beside him on his sofa, which was made from impossibly soft leather. She sank into it, leaning back against him, his arm around her shoulders, as she watched the dancing flames. Jamie and Melody had probably sat in this very spot countless times. Not on this particular sofa, of course, since it was one that A.J. had made. But they'd surely sat on something comfortable, pulled up close to the fire.

"But then Quinn found them."

"What?" She turned to look at A.J., and he took

471

the opportunity to kiss her, which, over the past few days had nearly always led to more kisses and, yes, the idea of making love on this couch, in front of a fire, was a tempting one, but she wanted to hear this. So she pulled back. "Quinn found them? In San Francisco?"

"Yeah," A.J. said, smiling at her. His hair had dried going every which way, making him look like an adorable blend of little boy and full-grown man. He was very good-looking, and in firelight he was even more attractive. Especially when he looked at her that way—as if he couldn't get enough of her. "It's kind of an ugly story. Nutshell version, Quinn hired Pinkerton agents to locate them. Jamie and Melody were careful, but these guys were good. It was the summer of 1900. August. Quinn hired someone to engage Jamie in a high-stakes poker game, and while it was going, he broke into their hotel room, and nearly beat Melody to death."

"Oh, God," Alison said.

"It was bad," A.J. said. "Jamie always hated telling this story, and it wasn't until I was older that I figured it out—that Quinn had raped Melody. Jamie blamed himself for leaving her alone, or for not being more careful, or God knows what. He also knew that he was lucky that Quinn didn't just kill her. And the only reason Quinn didn't do *that* was because he knew he didn't stand a chance against Jamie any other

472

way. This way, Jamie would walk in, and Quinn would be sitting there, with his gun aimed at Melody. Jamie would immediately surrender his weapons, at which point Quinn would be able to kill him. It was a two-fer for Quinn, because he wanted to make Melody watch as Jamie died.

"So he tied her up. And then he sat back and had a cigar while he waited for Jamie to return."

Alison sat there, her head against A.J.'s shoulder, gazing into the fire and trying to imagine the horror that Melody had felt. Beaten, raped, tied up, and knowing that her lover was probably going to be murdered because she couldn't do anything to stop his killer . . .

"It was the cigar that tipped Jamie off," A.J. told her. "He smelled it out in the hallway, before he put his key in the lock and, God, he must've just gone cold. He crept outside, climbed up to the balcony, and came in through the window, guns blazing. He shot Quinn in the chest, untied Melody, and got her the hell out of there." He paused. "You know, he never went into detail when he told this story. He never told me what it was like climbing up the outside of that building, even though their room was on the fourth floor. He'd pulled some kind of amazing superhero stunt, but he never wanted to talk about it."

"Because he got there too late," Alison pointed out. "He saved Melody's life, yeah. But . . . God, what a nightmare."

"Yeah," A.J. said. "Especially when they found out that Quinn survived his gunshot wound. Melody was certain he'd come after them again. It got to the point where she couldn't sleep or eat, her anxiety was so intense. So Jamie brought her up here. Built this cabin on this spot, because at the time, the glacier made this part of the mountain impenetrable. Now there's a road behind here that goes all the way down the hill and back again toward town, but at the time there was only one trail in and out. Plus they had the view of the harbor from their porch, so they could keep track of any ships coming in. Jamie kept the place stocked with food and ammunition. This cabin was a fortress."

"Why not just kill Quinn?" Alison asked. "Turn the table on him—hunt *him* down?"

"Jamie would have had to leave Melody alone to do it," A.J. said. "No way was he going to bring her back to Jubilation. And maybe the original plan was to bring her up here, put some guards in place, and head back south. But once they were here? She just loved it so much. She felt safe. Plus, by then, there was a baby on the way."

"I've got to find those diaries," she said. "You know, Henry Logan wants to make a sequel: *Quinn Part Two*. Or maybe he should call it *Gallagher*."

"Seriously?"

"Same cast, Jamie's version of the story. He was really lit up by the idea."

"Add an exclamation point," A.J. suggested, "and we can make it a musical."

Alison laughed. "I like it. Dancing cowboys. Singing silver miners. The Kelly Gang pirouetting wildly around the Red Rock Saloon."

"Right now," he said, with a laugh, "they're rolling over in their graves. So what's the plan for tomorrow? Because Bev called while we were at dinner—she left a message on my machine. She wants to have breakfast with you, if you're up for it. I figured you would be, since she's actually read the diaries."

"That sounds good." Alison reached for her bag, which was leaning up against the end table, and dug for her calendar. "I'm also hoping to interview Adam. And your mother. And . . . what is it you always say? For the sake of full disclosure, one of the things I want to talk to her about is . . . you."

A.J. wasn't all that surprised.

"Hmm," he said. "Are you thinking about forming an alliance and voting me off the island?"

Alison was wearing his bathrobe, with absolutely nothing on underneath it, and as she shifted to put her calendar down on the coffee table, the top gapped, giving him not just a flash, but an extremely nice display of her right breast.

He'd never been much of a look-but-don't-touch type, and when it came to Alison's breasts it was hard to touch without tasting, which resulted in his unfastening her entire robe and pulling her down on the sofa, and touching and tasting just about every part of her he could reach with his hands and his mouth.

They were both too tall to fit on the couch at the same time, so he moved onto the floor, kneeling there as he kissed her.

He felt more than heard her laugh, and he looked up across the fire-lit smoothness of her skin—her stomach, her breasts, and the graceful lines of her collarbone and throat—and into her smiling eyes.

"Hello," she said. "We *were* talking. I've noted that's your MO. You don't want to have a certain conversation, so suddenly—what a surprise—we're having sex."

"I didn't want to not talk. I just thought we were done," he said and lowered his head again.

"So . . . you don't want to know specifically what I want to ask your mother about?" she asked breathlessly, adding, "Oh, God, whatever you just did, do it again. . . ."

Now it was his turn to laugh. "I thought you wanted to talk."

"I do," she said. "But oh, my God. Whatever that was, remember that for later, okay?"

"I can do this and listen at the same time," he told her, then proved his point.

"No, you can't," she gasped. "Because I can't . . . do this . . . and *talk* . . . and make . . . any sense. . . ."

"You're doing okay," he said. At least he meant to say that, but it may not have come out clearly.

"A.J.," she breathed, her hands in his hair. "Oh, God . . . Oh, yes . . . Oh, *yes* . . ."

It was beautiful, the way she came undone and he wanted to watch her, but he wanted to taste her, too, and his need to taste won. Later, he'd do the same thing with just his hands and let himself look.

He loved that there would be a later almost as much as he loved the way she responded to him— always and instantly. As if her body felt absolutely no hesitation—that at least part of her believed they were meant to be together.

As if she were thinking along the same lines, her sigh of contentment contained exasperation. "Is that your plan?" she said. "Have sex for four days straight? Get me completely addicted so I'll just never leave?"

"I don't really have a plan," he admitted as he pulled himself back onto the couch, sitting with her legs across his lap. They were long and smooth, and again he couldn't look without touching. So he touched.

She made no attempt to cover herself back up as she lay there, just gazing at him. "Jamie's family—back in Philadelphia—was devoutly Catholic," she said.

It seemed like an abrupt change of subject, but A.J. went with it. "Yeah," he said. "I read that in your book."

"You didn't know?" she asked. "Before?"

"No," he said. "Jamie didn't go to church."

"Never?" she asked.

"Not when I knew him," A.J. said. "Although, he *did* go to weddings and funerals. The occasional Christmas pageant. But that was it."

"Huh," she said. "I guess I just expected . . . I don't know. Maybe that someone who's become a spirit—his word, right?"

A.J. nodded.

"I guess I assumed that in life he'd been . . . spiritual."

"You don't have to attend church for that," A.J. said. "He was . . . a deep thinker. A reader. He was always reading something. But he also kept his Bible on the table next to his bed. I know he read it, because sometimes when I went into his room, it was open. It had one of those ribbon markers, you know? A red one. I always liked to touch it, it was so smooth and shiny. He gave it to me—the Bible—for my eleventh birthday. Well, he was intending to give it to me. He'd written in it and bought some paper and a bow, but he hadn't wrapped it yet. I found it in his dresser drawer after he died."

"Really?" She sat up. "Do you still have it?"

"Of course."

Alison pulled her legs off him, so he could stand up and cross to the built-in bookshelves— the same shelves upon which Jamie and Melody had kept their few precious books when they'd first moved north. It was probably where Melody had stored her diaries.

"How about you?" Alison asked, as she closed her robe and tied the belt securely around her waist.

What a shame.

A.J. knew exactly where Jamie's Bible was, and he pulled it free. "How about me what?" he asked as he brought it to her.

"Do you consider yourself religious?" she asked, tilting her head to look up at him.

He had to smile. "What, do you think my seeing Jamie is the result of my having some super-fanatical religious paroxysm or something?"

"I'm just trying to figure it all out," Alison said.

"I believe in a higher power," he told her as he sat down next to her, "but I wouldn't go so far as to give it a gender and a name. Sure, I've read the Bible. And I've read a lot of books by people who offer explanations for what they think it all means. I don't agree with any of them—not a hundred percent. And I *really* don't agree with the people who get in my face and tell me that *their* interpretation is the only one of value, with this implication that they have some kind of direct line to their God. The really ridiculous thing is that they're too stupid to realize that by doing that, they're breaking one of their own commandments: *Thou shalt not take the Lord's name in vain.*"

She was flipping through the book, and he could tell that she was a little disappointed. It was a cheaply made edition, with a cardboard cover. It was clearly not the expensive leather-bound Bible Jamie had surely been given upon his first communion, back in Philly in the late 1800s.

In fact, she checked the printing date as, curious, A.J. looked over her shoulder.

1944.

"That makes sense," A.J. said. "Because Melody gave it to him. Probably after she found out that she was dying." He reached over to flip the pages to the front, where Melody had inscribed a note to Jamie, and years later, Jamie had written to A.J.

Melody's handwriting was careful and neat.

My darling Jamie, My body is worn, but my spirit still sings. And my love for you will never die. Words are cold comfort, I know, but I hope and pray you will find some warmth within. Always yours, Melody.

Beneath it, Jamie had written in his spidery hand, *To Austin James Gallagher the Second, on the eleventh momentous anniversary of his* *birth. A man needs to know right from wrong, but should <u>never</u> follow blindly. Also, a life well-lived with kindness and respect for others is the ultimate hosanna and will be recognized as such by whoever up there is in charge. (I suspect it might be Mel by now . . .) Live, laugh, sing, dance, but most of all, <u>LOVE</u> with all your heart. Eternally yours, Austin James Gallagher the First, aka Gramps.*

Alison was silent as she read both inscriptions. And then she must have read them both again, and yet again, because she didn't speak and didn't look up.

"I always thought he knew he was going to die," A.J. said quietly, "because he wrote that inscription months before my birthday. I mean, yeah, he always planned ahead, but . . . He told me he didn't know. I asked him—recently, you know—and he said he was as surprised as we were when he passed. But I still think he somehow knew it was coming. Subconsciously, maybe."

She turned to look at him, and her eyes were filled with tears. "You must have loved him so much. And his affection for you is apparent in every word that he wrote."

A.J. knew where she was going. Jamie was obviously so important to him. It made sense that he should imagine him back again.

"How did I do it, Alison?" he asked her, trying

not to let his frustration tinge his voice. "Reading those words that you wrote? I couldn't even see you clearly from where I was standing."

"I don't know," she said. "It's just so . . . I don't know. Maybe you *could* see me. Maybe you have really amazing vision, and you could tell what I was writing from the way my pen moved—"

"But I also read from the script."

"Maybe you got a copy. Maybe you memorized it."

"If you seriously think I'd do something like that—"

"I don't," she said. "I'm just looking for explanations."

"How about the simplest one?" he countered. "That Jamie really did come back, for whatever reason, and that I really can see and hear him."

"A.J.," she started.

"Let's do it again," he said, cutting her off. "I'll get Jamie back here. We can go into two different rooms, close the door. But okay. Maybe you think I've got my entire house wired with minicams or sensors. So we'll go somewhere else. You get to decide where. We'll just get in the truck and go. You can drive. Don't tell me where we're going, because that way there's no chance I'll call my dozens of minions and get that new location wired up. And when we get out of the truck, I'll strip naked and put a bag on my head. And I'll *still* be able to tell you what you're

482

reading, because I don't need minicams and I don't need to memorize the entire contents of the Library of Congress because *Jamie* will be reading it to me, whatever it is. Of course, maybe you'll decide that you're in the throes of a religious paroxysm, too. So we better bring a dozen witnesses and make sure they're all atheists or at least agnostics."

Okay. So much for keeping his frustration from showing. Alison was silent, just clutching Jamie's Bible.

"If Jamie's not real," A.J. pointed out, trying to sound measured and calm, but failing because his voice actually shook, "then I'm crazy. You really like that possibility better? You like thinking that I set this all up? That I, what? Ran Hugh off the road myself, so I could wait for you to come ask me to help find him? What if you didn't come when you did, Alison? What if he died?"

"I *don't* like that possibility any better," she said. "It's all bad, all right?"

"So what are you doing, then?" he asked. "Here with me?"

She looked down at the Bible in her lap, and shook her head. "I have absolutely no clue," she admitted softly. "I just . . ." She met his eyes. "I really like you, even though . . . I know that I shouldn't."

He spelled it out. "Even though I'm a potentially crazy alcoholic."

"Recovering alcoholic," she said.

"Yeah, but we both know what that means," A.J. said tightly. "There are no guarantees."

"I don't know what I'm doing," Alison said, louder this time. "It scares me to death, A.J. How much I . . . care about you."

And there they sat, in silence.

Until Alison spoke again. "This is what we were looking for, you know." She held up the Bible. "There's a sample of Jamie's handwriting in the church records back in Philadelphia. About a month before he left, he was a witness at his cousin's wedding. Not officially, because he was underage, but he signed the marriage documents anyway. So we have a sample of his handwriting. If it's okay with you, I'll send this out to have it analyzed and compared. They might be able to date it, too, from, I don't know, maybe the ink. If Melody really did write her inscription back in 1944—"

"She did," A.J. said.

"Well, then, we'll try to prove that," Alison said. "Maybe I'll . . . take it, this Bible, myself, to Philadelphia. In the morning. I mean, as long as I have access to Henry's jet. Of course, I'll call him first . . ."

"In the morning," A.J. said. He looked at her. "Damn it. I didn't mean to chase you away."

"Didn't you?" she asked as she stood up.

He stood, too. "Alison . . ."

"No, see, you're right," she said. "All I'm doing here is playing a game of make-believe. That's not fair to you."

"Hope plus a lot of sex," he reminded her. He forced a smile. "I'm doing okay."

But she didn't smile. "But I'm not," she said. "I love it here, A.J. I love the mountains and the ocean and the fresh air. I love this town, I love the people I've met, I love that everyone in that lovely, lovely restaurant with the stupid name knew you, and I *really* love the way that they all so obviously adore you. I love your house, and I love the carving on your mantel, and I love sitting in front of the fire in this beautiful room, and I love the idea that Jamie and Melody created all this, that they helped create *you,* and God damn it, I think I love you, even though I said I wouldn't, that I couldn't, but it doesn't work that way, does it? And now I really, *really* don't know what I'm going to do."

She may not have known, but A.J. did.

Two steps brought him close enough to pull her into his arms and kiss her.

And Alison kissed him back, through the salt of her tears, as if her world were coming to an end.

So he swept her up into his arms and carried her into his bedroom.

Because hope wasn't the only thing that went down a little better with a lot of sex. Sex could also temper fear. It could strengthen resolve. And when it wasn't just sex but also a beautiful and tender physical expression of deep emotions, it could even turn *I think* into *I do love you.*

October 29, 1900
Dear Diary,
    It's been nearly six months since I've taken up a pen, but this morning I feel the urge to write again.
    Perhaps it will cure me of my despair.
    But probably not.
    I am with child.
    Such joyful news—if only the child were my gambler's. But it is not so.
    The monster found us, more than two months ago. I still cannot think of it without my tears falling on this paper and smudging the ink. I cry so often, so easily these days.
    The monster violated me. How could such a gentle, loving act be done so violently, so offensively? To think, before J., I knew no other way. Perhaps I should be grateful for the reminder, but I am only angry. Bitterly so.
    Because the monster put his seed in me. He tied me up after, so that I could not clean myself or do the things I'd done in the past to prevent pregnancy. I know it is his child that I carry.
    And I cannot bear to tell J.
    It took me two weeks to tell him what the

monster had done to me, just how he had hurt me. But my gambler knew. He must've known from my bruises and pain. He held me at night, just held me, and waited for me to find the right words to tell him.

When I did, he swore to me such a thing would never happen again, even if it meant never letting me out of his sight. And then he made love to me, the way it should be done. With love, not violence. And I did feel safe.

He had shot the monster in the chest. There was so much blood, we were sure he was dead. And I was glad. Lord, I was so glad.

But today we heard the terrible news. We were wrong. He survived. The monster has recovered from his wounds, and is returning to the Arizona Territory.

If he found us in San Francisco, a city with so many people, he will find us again.

Where can we go that is truly safe? Where can we go, that the monster will not follow?

I laugh as I write these words, feeling the edge of hysteria start to overcome me.

Because we can never escape the monster.

Part of him is growing inside of me.

Chapter Twenty

Gene's phone finally rang.

I'd almost jumped away a few minutes earlier, because it was finally morning up in Alaska, and I was determined that today was the day that A.J. would talk to Alison and ask her about dead Wayne, and what she did or didn't see on the day that he'd been murdered.

I also wanted to be there when Rose and Tom announced their plans to get hitched. They'd probably get the whole family together for a cookout, and I didn't want to miss it.

Gene was snoring atop of his hooker friend when his cell phone erupted in an electronic version of "When the Saints Go Marching In," which was kind of a strange ringtone for a man who wasn't going anywhere even remotely good after he parted ways with his earthly remains.

He lurched awake and scrambled off the bed, pulling a huge-caliber handgun from a holster that must've been at the small of his back, fumbling it not once but twice.

I could've killed him six times over, but back in my day, we wore our weapons where everyone could see 'em, and where we could reach 'em easily. So he was at a disadvantage. That plus the brains-to-mush effect of whatever drug he'd been sucking down was another strike against him.

Luckily for the whore, he didn't kill her, although I'm not sure she would've reacted even if he had. As it was, she just blinked at the barrel of the gun he'd shoved in her face, and—amazing, she had a voice—she spoke for the first time. "It's your phone, Gene, you asshole."

Victory!

I was already over there, looking at the lit-up little screen. Hoping for an ID, but happy enough to settle for a number, which is what I got, starting with the main Los Angeles area code. The three-numbered exchange was easy enough to memorize—it was the twins' single-digit birthday, followed by that of my eldest son, Jim. That left me the final four numbers, which were nine zero four four.

Nine zero four four. Ninety forty-four.

Not that I had the fingers to dial this number or the voice to ask *Hello, who the heck are you?* But A.J. could. Calling from a pay phone, while disguising his voice. Or maybe we could use the Internet and access some kind of reverse phone directory—kind of the way Baretta and Columbo always used to do when they were trying to solve a case. Except back then, they had to call a friend at the phone company.

Nine zero forty-four.

"Yo," Gene said as he answered his phone. I had to move quickly, straight up in the air, to keep him from bumping into me. He was so stoned, he probably wouldn't have noticed, but we'd both been waiting for this call for so long, I didn't want to risk his dropping the phone in shock at our contact. "What's the word?"

My word was nine oh four four, and bingo, I got it. Ninety plus four plus four equals ninety-eight, which was the year I met Mel. Los Angeles, and the twins and Jim, and ninety-eight. So what if I couldn't carry a pen in order to write things down? My mind was a steel trap.

And I'd correctly IDed the man with the bald spot and bushy eyebrows as Gene.

I was having a good day.

"Uh-huh," Gene was saying. "Uh-huh." He laughed. "No shit? That's like a gift, right? Because this bitch is fucking hard to kill, man." He laughed again. "No, no, I'm just hanging." A pause. "A few more days? No problem. In case she comes back. You're paying, right?" More laughter. "That's my fee, Brian. Have a nice trip. And call me if you need me."

Brian.

Another small victory. But where was Brian going?

I stayed close as Gene hung up his cell and put it back on the little table next to the bed. He got up, scratching his belly, and went into the bathroom to relieve himself noisily.

His girlfriend-slash-personal-hooker rolled off the bed, sat at the table, and picked up that pipe and the cheap red lighter that was nearby.

And when Gene came out of the bathroom, zipping up his pants, he said, "Get the fuck away from there!"

Which pretty much canceled out the possibility of her saying, *Hey, hon, was that your tall killer friend Brian on the phone? The one with the scar near his eye and the ponytail? How's he doing? Who's he hiring you to kill this time? And where exactly is he going on that trip he mentioned?*

Instead she pouted and said, "Why? You got plenty."

"Yeah, because I earned it," he said. "Get the fuck out of here."

She grabbed her shoes and flounced out the door, slamming it behind her.

"I'm getting the fuck out of here, too, Gene," I said. "It's been disgusting and horrific and thank God it's finally time for me to go."

And I popped off to Alaska to tell A.J. what I'd learned, and found him—happily for me—awake and dressed and having breakfast in his kitchen with Alison, Bev, and Rose.

"I knew back in fifth grade," A.J.'s sister Bev told Alison, "that I was going to marry Charlie Fallingstar and that I was going to have babies and paint." She laughed. "It took Charlie a little bit longer to come to that same realization."

"Considering you were ten and he was thirteen," Rose said dryly from across A.J.'s

491

kitchen table, "that's not too hard to understand."

"But I was determined," Bev said. "I finally managed to catch his eye—"

"It was the summer she turned sixteen," Rose told Alison.

"We got married two months after my sixteenth birthday," Bev said.

Alison looked from Bev to Rose. "Oh, dear."

"It's not what you're thinking," Bev said. "I wasn't pregnant. We hadn't even . . ." She shook her head.

"She had my blessing," Rose said serenely. "I knew Charlie well, and I liked him very much."

"It was a unique situation," Bev explained. "For years, I spent almost every afternoon hanging out at his uncle's art supply store, painting and listening to music and talking to Charlie, who lived with his aunt and uncle when his father was out of town. The year I turned sixteen, he gave me the most beautiful earrings for my birthday. He'd picked them up in Juneau, and . . . I loved them and I threw myself at him to hug him and . . . Suddenly he was kissing me." She smiled. "It scared the heck out of him, because the next day, he enlisted in the Air Force."

"A month after that, he was back home," Rose said. "A routine physical revealed that he had leukemia."

"Oh, my God." Cancer. Alison looked across the kitchen to find A.J. leaning against the counter, just watching her as he took a sip of coffee from his mug.

And suddenly she knew why he'd been so gung-ho to have Bev come over to talk. Although her bringing their mother along had been a slightly awkward surprise.

Especially since Alison had just—moments before Bev's truck had pulled into the driveway—told A.J. that last night hadn't changed her mind. In fact, it had made her more determined than ever to leave.

"A.J.," she'd told him, "I know you think you've won something because I said . . . what I said. But just because I love you, that doesn't mean I can or even should stay. I just don't know how I can take that chance. I'm scared to death and . . . I have to walk away now, while I still can. I *need* to."

Of course that was when the doorbell rang, which Alison, coward that she was, had been grateful for.

"They gave Charlie a matter of months, even with his chemotherapy treatments up in Anchorage," Bev said now. "So he came and asked me—and then my mother—if he could marry me. He wanted to spend the time he had left—the rest of his life—with me."

"How could I refuse?" Rose asked. "Beverly had loved this boy for years."

"You didn't really have a choice," Bev said

cheerfully. "I was going to Anchorage with him, regardless of what you said."

"Oh, I had a choice," Rose said imperiously.

"She didn't have a choice," Bev whispered to Alison.

Rose ignored her daughter. "Charlie defied the odds. His prognosis wasn't good, yet he went into remission about six months after they were married," she told Alison. "It was something of a medical miracle."

"Personally," Bev said with a smile, "I believe it was a miracle of another kind. That was in 1980. Thirty years of cheating death. Even after all this time, when I wake up in the morning and see Charlie beside me, I still thank God for the gift of another day with him."

And now Alison didn't dare look at A.J., because she really *was* a coward, and he knew it, too.

She was leaving. As soon as Henry's private jet returned from refueling in Juneau. Which would happen that afternoon. She was just waiting for her phone to ring with the exact departure time.

"Jamie always used to say things happen for a reason," A.J. said quietly. "I used to think that was just a crock. But with Bev and Charlie, you've got to wonder. One of the theories is that he responded so well to his chemo because it was started as early as possible. If he'd delayed, if he hadn't enlisted and had that blood test . . ."

"Which he wouldn't have done if I'd been turning seventeen instead of sixteen," Bev pointed out. "You can get into this whole world of *what if*s that'll drive you crazy. You know, I almost didn't go into the art store on my birthday. I was supposed to go to the movies, but my three best friends all got the flu. At the time I was so upset. My birthday was ruined. And then Charlie gave me that wonderful present and then— God—*kissed* me. And I was flying, but he was so upset and even angry—at me, and I didn't understand, and then he was *gone,* and I cried for weeks. But that was nothing compared to the pain that was barreling toward me—when he came back and sat in our living room and told me that he was dying. . . ." Her voice broke, and she shook her head. "I'm sorry, I still . . ."

"No." Alison reached across the table and took her hand. "Don't apologize. I can't even imagine how awful it must've been."

"Awful and wonderful," Bev told her. "Because there was joy, too. He *loved* me, this amazing, beautiful boy that I'd loved forever. I knew my mother and A.J. and Adam and everyone in the family—even Charlie himself—were terrified for me. If he died, I mean, God, at the time, they thought it was going to be *when* he died, not *if*. But if he did? My mother had lived through that and it really must've scared her to death because she knew what was in store for me, but she said yes, because she also knew that love like that is worth the risk.

"As for me, I learned what really mattered. I learned to live in the moment. Tomorrow was coming—I knew that well enough. But Charlie and I, we made sure we spent every moment right there, living for today." Bev smiled. "It gets a little harder when you have kids, but . . . And speaking of miracles, both of our daughters were conceived in vitro. Charlie knew the chemo would sterilize him, so he did the sperm bank thing. We've been endlessly lucky. Amazingly blessed."

Alison looked up to find A.J. watching her again. *Live for today* was a variation on the theme of *one day at a time.*

She wanted to cry, because she wasn't as brave as Bev—and she knew she'd never be.

A.J., bless him, gently changed the subject, telling his mother and sister that Alison had been excited about finding the Bible that Melody had given to Jamie, and Jamie had then given to A.J.

"I'm still eager to read Melody's diary," Alison told them, "but things like this Bible are what I'm looking for. And we really do need to come up with a lot more than just one signed book to convince the skeptics. I have to be honest. The fact that there are no town records prior to 1978 is going to be suspect."

"The fire in the town hall is well documented," Rose pointed out.

"But awfully convenient," Alison pointed out. "Considering Jamie died in '77."

"Someone must have some records—originals of birth certificates," Bev said. "I have a lot of cousins. We can ask everyone to check their attics. And we haven't even tried contacting Great-aunt Rebecca. She and Irma usually visit starting in April, but Irma just had a knee replaced, so they're in Florida until early July."

"Really?" A.J. said, and Alison looked up, only to find he was talking not to them, but to Jamie. He was looking at an empty space near the refrigerator and nodding. "Of course. That would . . ." He turned to look from Bev to Rose to Alison. "Sorry, that must seem so strange."

"Jamie's here?" Bev asked. "Hi, Gramps."

"He says hi," A.J. said, and Alison could feel Rose watching her, no doubt picking up on her discomfort. "He says we should check into military records. But he's got a question I can't answer. He has a phone number and he wants to find out who it belongs to—you know, get a name, and maybe even an address."

"Google it," Bev said. "That's where I'd start. Tell him I'll help him with it. Whose number is it?"

"He says *Thank you, dear, but it's too long a story to go into right now,* because . . . He also says . . . Mom has some . . . really good news to share . . . ?"

Rose sat back in her chair. "Really," she said. She waved her hand in a grand gesture. "Then, by all means, let him tell you what it is."

A.J. returned his attention to the thin air beside him, and laughed, adding, "Wow," as he held his hand to his forehead, as if he'd just heard brain-breaking news. He turned to his sister. "Do you know about this?"

"I don't think so," Bev said. "No fair, Gramps. Why can't you haunt me?"

"He says Mom's getting married," A.J. told his sister.

"What?" Bev was astonished. "Okay, Age, now I'm on her side. That's crazy. Who on earth—"

"Tom," A.J. said. "Jamie says she and Tom have been more than friends for—holy crap—nearly ten years now."

Bev's mouth was open as she turned to her mother, who was looking at A.J. with suspicion.

"*Jamie* told you that," Rose asked. "Not Tom?"

"Oh, my God," Bev said. "You and Charlie's *father* . . . ? And you didn't tell me?"

Alison stood up. "Maybe I should . . ." She pointed toward the living room and the front door.

"Ten *years?*" Bev said, turning her indignation upon A.J., who held up his hands.

"Don't be mad at me," he said. "I'm just finding out about this now, too."

Alison tried to make herself invisible, figuring she'd go out on the porch to give them privacy as

Rose admitted, "I didn't know how to tell you. It started after A.J. finally came home from rehab, and . . . I didn't know what either of you would say."

As Alison slipped out of the house, gently closing the screen door behind her, she glanced back to see Bev hug her mother as she started to cry. "How could you think I'd say anything other than Tom's wonderful? Mommy, he's the kindest, most perfect man I've ever met—besides Charlie. I love him—do you love him?"

"I do," Rose admitted, and Alison stepped even farther out onto the porch, because the ice queen was actually starting to cry, too. "But he's not your father."

"I barely knew my father," Bev said. "Jamie was my father. And Adam and Tom, too. Although, oh, my God, does this mean Charlie's going to be my stepbrother?"

They both started to laugh as A.J. stepped out onto the porch, meeting Alison's eyes and smiling. "I figured I'd let them . . ." He shrugged. "I think it's great."

"Your mother needs to hear those words from you," Alison told him. "You make sure you tell her. She needs your approval."

"Yes, ma'am," he said. But then his smile faded. "Jamie's idea was a good one—military records. I don't know why I didn't think of that before. His three younger sons served in the Second World

War, and Jim and Skyler both served in the First. George—Rebecca's twin—was killed when his plane was shot down. It happened a week after Melody passed."

"Oh, my God," Alison said.

"Jamie just told me that there was extra paperwork that needed to be filed, because George listed both of his parents as beneficiaries, you know, to receive his death benefits? He also remembered that the telegram he received—about George's death—was addressed to Melody, too. I'll put the word out, see if someone in the family has the original or even a copy. I have this memory of one of the younger cousins writing a report about Uncle George for school a few years ago. Maybe Joey. He majored in history and . . . You'd like him—you should meet him. If you . . . stay."

Alison nodded, unable to hold his gaze. "I can't stay, A.J. I know you think I'm a coward and . . . I am. I'm sorry—I really am—that I can't be the person you want me to be."

He opened his mouth to respond, but whatever he said, it was drowned out by a loud boom. Sharp, like an explosion, it echoed across the mountains as Alison felt a sudden burst of pain in her upper arm.

Before she could look to see—had she been stung by an enormous Alaskan-sized bee?—A.J. tackled her, knocking the wind from her lungs as he pushed her hard to the porch floor, covering her with his body.

There was another explosion and something whistled past her head and slammed into the side of the cabin.

A.J. moved fast then, faster than she'd ever seen him move before, picking her up and hauling her back inside, slamming and locking the door shut behind them. "Get down!" he shouted. "Get away from the windows! Jamie! I need your eyes outside!"

Another explosion boomed and the front window shattered, and A.J. covered Alison again, shielding her from fragments of glass that sprayed into the room.

God, she was dizzy, and her arm really hurt, and she had no idea *what* was going on.

"Oh, Jesus," A.J. said, his voice hoarse as he pulled back to look down at her. "Bev, call nine-one-one! Mom! I need you!" It was odd, but his T-shirt—the same shade of blue as his eyes—was now sprayed and streaked with red. "Alison, God, were you hit anywhere else?"

Hit? She looked down at her arm and—holy shit. She was bleeding. The red on A.J.'s shirt was blood. *Her* blood.

There was another explosion and a solid *thunk* hit the sturdy front wall of the cabin. And suddenly it all became clear.

Someone was shooting at them. Someone was shooting at them, and she'd just been shot.

501

Alison had been shot by someone who was continuing to fire at the front of the cabin.

She'd been hit only once, though, thank God for small favors. A.J.'d run his hands across her, down her legs, making certain of that.

"Jamie!" A.J. called. "What the hell is going on . . . ?"

"Phone's out," Bev reported from the kitchen. "Line's dead."

"Use your cell!" A.J. ordered.

His mother was there, then, kneeling beside him, cool and calm. "She's going to be okay," she told him, then told Alison the same thing. "You're going to be fine. Nothing's broken. We just need to stop the bleeding."

"Here." A.J. yanked off his shirt, handing it to his mother, even as he called to his sister, "Bev, towels! Clean ones are in the middle drawer."

He had to get to his rifles—kept for protection against bears and wolves—but they were on the other side of the living room, securely locked in their case.

"My cell phone's not working either," Bev reported as she crawled across the living room floor, delivering a pile of folded kitchen towels to her mother.

The other front window broke with a crash and again A.J. tried to shield them from the glass.

"Get her into the kitchen," he sharply ordered

his mother and Bev, as if they were grunts in his platoon. How quickly it all came back—the ability to think clearly and decisively under fire.

He moved then—fast—across the room, skidding on the broken glass as he dove into the corner where he kept his weapons. His keys were in his pocket and he dug for them even as Alison called out for him: "A.J., don't leave me!"

"I won't," he said as he unlocked the case and grabbed both of his rifles and two boxes of ammo. "I'm right here. Bev!"

He sent one of the weapons skittering across the hardwood floor and into his sister's capable hands. Jamie had spent plenty of target-practice time with her, too.

"Is the back door locked?" she asked.

"Don't know," A.J. said, and Bev nodded.

"I'll check."

"Be careful," Alison called.

It wasn't hunting season, but for some of the residents of Alaska, the words *in season* meant nothing. However they were also less likely to fire away blindly in populated areas. And they'd damn well know where A.J.'s cabin was, and stay far away.

Unless, of course, excessive amounts of alcohol were in play, turning them into brain-dead idiots.

Tourists, on the other hand, could be brain-dead idiots completely on their own.

It was entirely possible that someone had set up

target practice out on the road, thinking they were in the middle of nowhere—not realizing his cabin was just around the bend.

A.J. was just about to dash back into the kitchen, to see if maybe his cell phone—charging on the counter—would work to call for help, when Jamie popped back in.

He didn't look happy. "Kid," he said. "You're in serious trouble. There're at least two of 'em. I haven't seen the second—he's somewhere hunkered down out in front, to keep you locked down and away from your trucks. The first man's mobile and he's carrying an arsenal. He's working his way around to the back."

"Doors and windows are all locked!" Bev reported as she returned to the kitchen, almost as if she'd heard Jamie's dire report.

But Jamie shook his head. "He's got an assault weapon," he told A.J., "that'll get him through any door or window that his black heart desires."

An assault weapon. "Are you sure?" A.J. asked. "Because I've only heard single shots."

As Jamie quickly described the gun, they were both sure.

"I know you don't want to hear this," Jamie continued, his eyes and face somber, "but I've seen this man before. He's got long hair and a scar and his name is Brian, and he murdered that man named Wayne down in Arizona, and your Alison is somehow involved, because he's here, now, to silence her permanently. And he'll kill you and Rose and Bev without blinking, in order to do it."

Alison's cell phone didn't work.

A.J.'s and his mother's didn't either.

Alison was sitting up, leaning back against the kitchen island with A.J.'s mother still applying pressure to her gunshot wound.

God, the entire world had gone completely crazy, and the only thing that Alison knew for sure was that A.J. would protect them from whoever was out there.

Or die trying.

A thought that scared her to death.

"Are they hunters who are lost?" Rose asked. "Can't we wave a white flag or shout to tell them to move away?"

"That's what we were doing when A.J. shot back at them," Bev told her mother. "When he fired over their heads, it was a very definite *Hello, we're in here*. Which they have since ignored."

A.J. had tried returning fire from the broken front window, which under normal circumstances would make a gunman duck for cover and momentarily stop shooting. But whoever was out there, he was either fearless or stupid, because he just kept firing at the front of the cabin, almost indiscriminately.

And if that wasn't crazy enough, there were the constant reports that A.J. received from Jamie.

There were two gunmen—one in the front and one in the back. There was also an SUV parked about a mile down the road, in the pull-off by a hiking trail. Jamie got the plate number, which Bev dutifully wrote down.

Like Bev, Alison was glad that the ghost, or spirit or whatever Jamie was, was there. But A.J.'s mother clearly didn't feel the same. She kept trying to call out on her cell phone, even after A.J. told them that Jamie believed the gunmen had something called a TechWhiz 7842—a cell phone signal jammer—which was keeping them from calling for help.

"How does a man who died in 1977 know about that kind of technology?" Rose asked, but A.J. didn't answer her.

Instead he turned to Alison. "Jamie thinks you're their target—that they're trying to kill you."

Dear God. Alison felt her entire world slip sideways. "What?" she asked. "Why?"

"Do you know a man named Brian?" he asked, as if his question were an important one. "Or Wayne?"

She shook her head. "No. You're the only people I know here in Alaska, A.J., I swear."

"They aren't from Alaska," he told her. "They're from Arizona. Wayne's dead. Brian apparently killed him a week ago."

Dear God . . .

"Jamie thinks you witnessed it," A.J. said. "Wayne's murder."

Again, Alison shook her head. "I didn't," she breathed.

"Brian shot him," A.J. told her. "In the back of a car."

She laughed—she couldn't help it. "I really think I would've remembered that."

"If Wayne is dead, then how could he be shooting at us?" Rose asked.

"He's not, Mom," A.J. said impatiently. "But Jamie says Brian is." He looked at Alison searchingly. "A tall man, long hair pulled back into a ponytail, scar on his face . . . ?"

She shook her head. With the exception of the scar, that described half of the men on the movie set. But a scar . . . Why did that ring a bell? Still, it was a distant one, and try as she might, she came up blank. "I honestly don't know any Brians."

"Maybe you don't know his name," A.J. said, but then his attention went to Jamie as he stared intently, grimly up at nothing. He nodded. Spoke to Jamie. "Go check it out. But be quick." Jamie must've vanished, because A.J. turned back to Bev and Alison. "Jamie says Brian's approaching the back more cautiously now that he knows we're armed. The other man hasn't moved from his position out front. Jamie's going to try to find him from his next muzzle flash."

"When the gunman fires," Bev explained to Alison, "there'll be a brief flash from the barrel of his weapon. That'll help Jamie find where he's hiding."

"I need you to watch from the front," A.J. told his sister, as his mother checked Alison's arm. "Stay down, use a mirror. Break the one in the bathroom if you have to."

"I've got a makeup mirror in my toilet kit," Alison said. "It's on the sink in the master bathroom."

Rose glanced up at that and Alison gave her a *Yes, I'm sleeping with your son* look in return.

Bev was already rummaging in one of A.J.'s kitchen drawers, pulling out a giant spatula—the kind you'd use during a cookout to keep your fingers far from the heat. "Rubber bands, Age?" she asked.

"Junk drawer," he told her. "Bev, I'm serious. Do not put your head up over that sill, but start firing over your shoulder, out the window, if you see any movement at all. Just to signal to me that the man's on the move, and maybe keep him from going too far. Okay?"

"Got it." She crawled for the bathroom.

"What can I do?" Alison asked. "How can I help?"

A.J. smiled, a short, fierce smile that, combined with the deadly intention on his face and the hardness and ice in his eyes, made him look like the soldier he once had been.

And still was, apparently.

"I need you to stop bleeding," he said, as he kissed her, quick but sweet. "Keep your head down—and make sure my mother does, too."

"What are you planning, A.J.?" Rose asked sharply.

"I'm going out the side window," he told her, told Alison, his smile replaced by grimness that would have scared her a little, if she didn't know him quite so well. "With Jamie's help, I can circle around behind the gunman in the back, and eliminate the threat."

"You mean, kill the man," Rose clarified.

A.J. nodded. "Yeah, Mom," he said. "If I have to."

"A.J.," she started.

"Jamie says he's got an assault weapon," he told his mother. "A submachine gun. From his description, it sounds like an MP5, which is nicknamed a 'room broom.' If he gets inside and uses it, just a few sweeps of this kitchen? We're all dead in less than five seconds. I'm not going to let that happen."

"And if Jamie's wrong?" Rose asked. "And this man's not even armed?"

"Jamie's not wrong," A.J. said with conviction.

His mother was not convinced. "And what if Jamie's not real?" she asked.

Boom. Thunk. In the silence there was another gunshot, another bullet hitting the front of the house—providing Jamie with that muzzle flash that he'd needed.

"Jamie's real, Dr. Gallagher," Alison spoke up. "I know it's hard to fathom. But . . . I think right now, especially now, I want to believe he's real. I've . . . felt him. And . . . I do believe A.J. I trust him about this, very much."

A.J. kissed her again, breathing, "Thank you," as he pulled back to look into her eyes. "I love you," he told her. "And I believe you, too."

His mother was watching, but Alison didn't care. "I love you, too," she said, because, oh, God, she did. "Be careful," she added, for about the thousandth time.

He nodded and picked up his rifle—about to go outside and face off with a man who had a machine gun that was called a *room broom.*

"No one else is getting hurt," he said absolutely, as Bev crawled back from the bathroom, her makeshift spatula mirror rubber-banded together and held in front of her along with her rifle—a soccer mom gone totally Rambo.

A.J. waited until Bev was in place, then headed for the hall that led to the back of the house. "Jamie, I need you," he called, as Alison watched him go.

This was not the time for tears, but she could feel them welling up. She fought them, refusing to succumb. Instead she turned to A.J.'s mother, who was sitting beside her.

"So," Alison said. "My mother was an alcoholic. I'm going to need a lot of counseling and support to make this work, because I'm terrified of A.J.'s disease. Will you help me with that?"

And now it was Rose, A.J.'s dragon of a mother, who had tears in her eyes. "Of course," she said, as she reached over and took Alison's hand.

But then A.J. came back, crawling down the hall toward them, saying, "Change of plans."

I'd been trying, ever since I'd seen that automatic weapon that A.J. called a room broom, to convince the kid to slow down and come up with a plan B.

It had been years since A.J.'d fired a weapon of any kind, let alone taken a life, while it was clear that Gene's buddy Brian had had a lot of recent practice in both skill sets.

Also, I was personally very familiar with the damage that six bullets, rapidly fired from a Colt 45, could cause. The thought of twelve bullets per *second*—all aimed at my kid—made me feel ill.

So no. I did not want A.J. anywhere near Brian. It was far too risky.

True, the plan was for A.J. to climb up onto the roof, and for me to find Brian and stand directly in front of him. That way A.J. could find me in his gun sight. His bullets would pass through me and damage Brian. Hopefully permanently.

But it still made me nervous—a single-shot rifle against a machine gun.

But now we had a real plan B, because the weapon being fired at the front of the cabin was the same style submachine gun. I took a good look at it after I tracked that muzzle flash. Apparently it could be—and was—set to fire a single shot. It wouldn't take much—the adjustment of a button—for A.J. to turn it into a hamburger-maker of his own, and even out the odds.

A few dozen rounds fired in Brian's direction would—I hoped—make the killer turn tail and run for his SUV. At which point, we could load the women into one of the trucks and race down to town. To the sheriff's office and the hospital, not necessarily in that order.

And if we were really lucky, the local law enforcement would send out an all-points bulletin with Brian's description and license plate number. And he would be caught so we could find out, as A.J. was fond of saying while under stress, "What the fuck?"

There was, however, one small catch. A.J. had to convince three very skeptical women that his running toward the "gunman" in the front wouldn't be suicide.

"According to Jamie, this guy Brian's set up some kind of robot device," he was telling his mother, his sister, and his lover—the three most important women in his life. Bev was still using her mirror to watch out the front, and I kept popping in and out as I kept an eye on Brian, who was hunkered down and no doubt wishing he'd brought Gene along for backup.

Or maybe not, on second thought.

He was probably wishing he'd never gone and killed Wayne, though. What a barge-load of trouble *that* had brought him.

"So there's not actually anyone out front?" Bev clarified. "Just a gun that fires on its own?"

"Jamie says it's a submachine gun—a 9mm—set up on some kind of swivel mechanism, kind of like a house fan, you know? So that the bullets don't hit the same place each time," A.J. said. "The weapon's probably programmed to fire randomly—I'm not sure how it works, but I haven't noticed a pattern. There seems to be anywhere from fifteen to ninety seconds between shots."

Rose shook her head. "I don't like this."

"Jamie'll watch the thing and shout when it's clear for me to leave the house," A.J. said as he made sure his rifle was locked and loaded. "I'm going out the front door."

"What?" His mother was aghast.

"It's the fastest route from here to that weapon. It's important I get hold of it quickly. As soon as I do, I'm going to start firing it. It's going to sound like a ripping noise, so don't get scared

513

when you hear it. Be ready to run for the truck on my command—but only on my command. Is that clear?"

They all nodded, and he held out his rifle to Alison, because he knew how much his mother hated guns.

"You ever fire one of these?" he asked.

"No," Alison said stoutly, taking it from him, despite her injured arm. "But I'm willing to learn."

But Rose took it from her. "Be careful," she told her son.

A.J. turned and looked at me. "Let's do this," he said.

This time it was Rose who stopped us. "Jamie," she said, speaking directly to me. "You keep my son safe."

"I will," I promised her, and I went up, right through the roof of that cabin I'd built with my own two hands, so I could verify that Brian was right where I'd left him.

He was, indeed, so I sailed over to that robot gun and watched as it jerked off a shot, then swiveled all the way to its right.

"Go now," I shouted to A.J. "Head to *your* right and circle around behind this thing!"

And he came charging out of that cabin, moving faster than I'd ever seen him run as I lifted myself up above the brush so that he knew exactly where he was heading.

The expression on his face, and his single-minded determination and speed reminded me, well, of me. I'm pretty certain that was what I'd looked like that godawful night I'd smelled Silas Quinn's cigar in the hallway outside of the room I was sharing with his ex-wife.

And yeah, I'm sure there're some of you who'd quibble over the fact that Melody and ol' Silas had never technically ended their marriage. But I'd always told Mel that I was pretty sure a black eye and broken rib were a legal form of divorce in God's eyes. In a similar way, I always believed that God married Mel and me the very first time we kissed. Back in 1944, when we finally said our vows in front of a preacher, beneath the most beautiful display of Northern Lights I'd ever seen, we were just cementing that lifetime commitment we'd both made in Jubilation, in 1898.

But I digress.

Here was A.J. running for that room broom, looking like he'd tear apart anything or anyone that got in his way.

And I knew just what he was thinking.

That son of a bitch Brian had shot Alison. A few inches to the left, and she would've been dead, not merely injured.

And even though the plan was to frighten Brian away so they could escape into town, A.J. *really* wanted to send the rat bastard straight to hell, where he belonged.

"Easy, kid," I told him, as he grabbed for the weapon.

It didn't come off the frame, so he just heaved and ripped the whole damn contraption out from where it was anchored in the dirt.

He'd used a weapon like that before. I could tell, because he didn't even look down, he just slammed at the setting, pushing it into automatic mode and hauling on that trigger as he ran out from the cover of the brush, screaming like a crazy man, unable in his anger even to form words.

Much in the same way that I'd gone through that hotel room window, all those years ago, guns blazing, because I knew—I *knew*—that that monster had beaten and raped the woman whom I loved more than life itself.

At the time, I was also damn near out of my mind with fear that he'd already killed her.

But today, unlike Silas, who'd been caught unaware and went down like a tranked elephant on *National Geographic*, tall, ponytailed Brian hauled ass and ran for his life toward his waiting SUV.

"Kid, kid, kid, kid," I said, keeping pace with A.J., "let him go, let him go! He's out of range of that thing now, and you know it. Come on, son, you've got to get your family in your truck. Alison needs to get to the hospital, and she needs to go now. She's lost a lot of blood."

It was that last, I think, that stopped him. He planted his feet as he kept firing that weapon, stopping only to shout toward the house, "Bev! Mom! Get Alison into the truck—let's move, let's *go!*"

"Good boy," I said as Rose and Bev helped Alison out of the house, the screen door slapping shut behind them.

A.J. looked at me as we hustled back to Charlie's old truck. His eyes were still a little crazy—adrenaline could do that to a man. "She doesn't know a Brian," he told me, talking about Alison, "or a Wayne."

I nodded. "I know," I said as he got behind the wheel, checking to make sure Bev, Rose, and Alison were safely inside. "At least not by those names. I was thinking though. Maybe the sheriff's office has one of those artists who can draw us a picture of the suspect. She might recognize him that way—Brian, I mean, because I never saw Wayne's face. Although I *have* seen a little too much of their cohort, Gene."

He nodded, and I jumped in the back as A.J. jammed the truck into gear, and roared off down the road, away from Brian's SUV, and into town and safety.

Chapter Twenty-one

November 11, 1900
Dear Diary,

I could put off telling J. no longer.

We've been traveling steadily north, staying no one place longer than a week or two, using made-up names.

I am so very tired, and often ill.

We are about to embark on a journey to someplace called the Territory of Alaska. It is dreadful cold there, but there is said to be quite a bit of gold.

I was afraid of going into the wilderness without proper supplies for the birthing of a baby. When I told my gambler we'd need such things, he was silent.

"When?" he asked.

"May," I told him.

He has a head for numbers, and it didn't take him long to realize why I hadn't told him sooner. Or maybe it was my sudden tears that led him to the correct conclusion.

He put his arms around me and held me close. "It might be mine," he told me, and then he gently scolded me for not sharing this burden with him sooner.

He teased me about growing round and fat, telling me he looked forward to loving a woman he could really hold in his arms. He teased until my tears stopped, until I laughed, too.

And then he kissed me and said, "Now we'll make this baby mine," and he made love to me.

After, he seemed so content, as if the thought that I was carrying another man's child didn't trouble him any longer. I wondered if perhaps he knew nothing of the science of biology. I wondered if he truly thought that now the babe would be his.

When I tried to explain that he was mistaken, he laughed. He was not ignorant. He knew of such matters, he told me. But he also told me that since he couldn't change that which had been done, it seemed silly to worry or suffer over it.

There would be a child, he said. Maybe, just maybe it would be his. If not, life would go on. And we would make a baby of our own in a year or two.

I must be silly—I know I am. But I can't stop worrying or suffering.

How can I possibly love a child conceived out of violence and hatred?

A.J. was in the hospital lobby, talking to the deputies, waiting for the sheriff to arrive, as Rose supervised the cleaning, stitching, and bandaging of Alison's wounded arm.

Bev peeked in through the curtain. "Everyone decent?"

"Is the sheriff here?" Alison asked in response, making sure her hospital gown covered her completely.

"Not yet," Bev told her, coming in as Rose went out. "But Joey's here. Another cousin. The family history buff. He found the diaries."

Alison sat up. "What?"

"Is it okay if he comes in?"

"Of course," Alison said, even as her arm started to throb. She forced herself to sit back as a tall, rawboned young man came through the opening in the curtain. He smiled and held a file folder out to her.

"Joe Gallagher, Alison Carter," Bev introduced them.

"A.J. thought you'd want to see this right away," he said in a gentle twang much like his cousin's. "It's not the diaries—Sarah went up to Sitka to pick them up."

"Joey's sister is a pilot," Bev told Alison.

"She should be back in about an hour," the young man said. "Still, there's quite a bit of information about Jamie's son George—Aunt Rebecca's twin brother—in here."

Alison reached for the file and he smiled at her obvious excitement—an easygoing, charming smile. There was something about him that was oddly familiar.

"Did we meet at the airfield?" Alison asked.

"No, ma'am," he said. "But my great-grandfather was Jim, Jamie's eldest son."

Joe was young, in his early twenties, and the way he dressed and stood and spoke set her gaydar pinging. His hair was sandy brown, his eyes an odd mix of brown and green. But it wasn't his eyes or his hair that was familiar, but rather something about the shape of his face, his cheekbones or jaw or forehead or maybe all of them combined. . . .

He was smiling at her patiently, as if waiting for her to figure out a puzzle.

A.J.'s grandfather Adam was Melody and Jamie's youngest son, and the only one of the four boys still alive. Rebecca was the next youngest. Her twin, George, had died in the skies over Europe, a mere week after Melody had succumbed to cancer, back in 1944. And God, the thought of the pain Jamie'd gone through, losing his wife and son within a week, still made Alison feel a little sick.

His second-oldest son, Skyler, had been a career navy man who'd come close to dying in that same war—at Iwo Jima. According to A.J., Sky had been born in January of 1903. And Jim, the eldest, had been born in . . .

May of '01.

May, April, March, February . . .

Exactly nine months after August, when Quinn

521

had tracked Melody and Jamie to San Francisco. Nine months after he'd beaten and raped Melody.

Dear God. *That* was why Joe Gallagher looked so familiar.

He looked quite a bit like the tintypes Alison had seen of Silas Quinn.

"I never met Jamie," Joe said, smiling at the recognition in Alison's eyes. "He died before I was born. But we still talk about him like he's just down the street at the grocery store." He looked wistful. "I kinda wish he'd picked me to haunt. I've been writing about him since I was fourteen. There're so many great stories . . . A lot of funny ones. He was . . . something else. My father remembers playing cards with him, and the old man would play hard and even cheat. Against a twelve-year-old. But Dad said you knew that going in—it was part of the game, that was what Jamie used to say. But he didn't cheat when it came down to the important things. He was a good man, Dr. Carter. The best. His love for his family—for *all* of his children—was legendary. And probably even more so on my side of the family."

Alison blinked back the tears that rushed to her eyes. God, the trials Jamie and Melody had overcome had been mountainous. Not only had Quinn raped Melody in San Francisco, but she'd borne a child as a result of that violence.

And instead of making a bad situation worse, instead of allowing the hurt and suffering to continue, Jamie had begun the healing with unconditional love.

Jamie Gallagher was indeed a very good man.

"It's a pleasure to meet you, Joe," Alison said. "I'm looking forward to reading those diaries."

"And I'm looking forward to reading your next book, ma'am," he said. "Let me know if you need a research assistant." He slipped out through the curtain before she could respond.

She *was* going to need an assistant. And an office with nearby mountains to gaze at, like the ones she could see from the windows of A.J.'s cabin . . .

The now broken windows . . .

Alison leafed through the file Joe had given her. It included a copy of the report about George Gallagher that he must've written for a college history class, along with about fifty pages of a document with the title *Jamie's Stories*. He'd stuck Post-it notes on both of them, saying *FYI only. Don't feel obliged to read this.*

She flipped past—she'd definitely read it all later—and found the original of the telegram that had been sent, notifying Jamie and Melody of their son George's death.

Beneath it was George's death certificate— again, an original. Father of deceased was listed as Austin James Gallagher. Mother, Melody

Patience Thompson, which were, absolutely, Melody Quinn's middle and maiden names.

"This is good," Alison said, looking up to see A.J. coming behind the curtain. "This is really good."

He didn't look happy, but he forced a smile. "Are you all right?" he asked, turning to his mother, who'd come in just behind him, to verify Alison's affirmative nod.

"She's going to be fine," Rose said. "The bullet didn't break up—there was a clean exit wound. She'll be on antibiotics for about a week as a precaution. All in all, it should heal nicely, with hardly a scar."

A.J. nodded as he stood there, at the end of her hospital bed, just looking down at her. "May we have a little privacy?" he asked.

"Of course," his mother said, and vanished, pulling Bev with her, and the curtain tightly closed behind them.

Alison put down the file that Joe had given her. "A.J., what's wrong?" she asked, because something was—very wrong.

He sat down in the chair his mother had pulled up beside the bed. "I'm just going to say it, okay?" he said. "Because it's awful and—"

"Who's dead?" she asked, filled suddenly with dread.

But A.J. shook his head. "No," he said. "No one's dead. Well, no one except for this man named Wayne that Jamie says this Brian guy killed. Jamie saw him—Brian—burning a car, with Wayne's body in it. It wasn't a hiker who died out in the desert, Alison. It was some man named Wayne. I called the police after Jamie saw the fire. Anonymously. I let them know about the body, too." He shook his head. "But that's not what, um . . ."

Alison just waited.

And he cleared his throat, and said, "The sheriff thinks it was me. Who shot you."

"But it wasn't," she said. "It couldn't have been. You were standing right next to me."

"He thinks I set up that robot." A.J.'s eyes were filled not just with frustration but with anxiety, as if he were afraid that she, like the sheriff, would think him capable of such a thing. "He doesn't believe that anyone else was there. At all."

She sat up. "But Jamie saw that SUV. Bev wrote down the license plate number—"

"It was a car owned by some winter people that I know. Not very well, but, I do know them. The Robinsons."

"Winter people," Alison repeated.

And he smiled wanly. "Believe it or not, there are people who only come up here in the winter, for the skiing. If this Brian really did use the Robinsons' SUV, he also returned it to their garage. Because it was there when the Sheriff's Department went to check."

"So he put it back," Alison said. "Can't they check its tires to see if it was used recently . . . ?"

He sighed. "Heaven doesn't exactly have a CSI unit. That kind of thing is expensive."

"How hard could it be to check?" Alison asked. "Mud or fresh earth versus dried dirt? If it was parked off the road, near a trail—"

A.J. interrupted her. "There's more."

This wasn't going to be good. Alison braced herself.

"The 9mm," he said. "The submachine gun. The sheriff has papers that say it was purchased at a gun show, four weeks ago. By me."

"My signature was forged," A.J. told Alison. "It's obvious. To me, anyway. But the sheriff doesn't see it that way."

I'd sat in on that conversation with Sheriff Bill Fenster.

The man was a fool, and unfortunately, among Heaven's townfolk, he was one of the few who rode on the A.J.-is-crazy bus. In fact, he sat in the front seat. He didn't believe that I was real. Plus he didn't like A.J. much, on account of an incident with a girl back in high school. Cindy Harris. She liked A.J. and Bill liked Cindy, and even though A.J. didn't take Cindy up on her loud and drunken offer, made at a party after a basketball game, to let him take her virginity, Bill, who'd overheard it, never quite managed to forgive A.J. for being the object of her desire.

Bill was only too happy to pay attention to the evidence that pointed to A.J.'s insanity and/or guilt.

A.J. had requested that Bill's deputies find the bullet that had injured Alison—to see whether or not it had been fired from that robot gun or from a different weapon, as we both believed. It wouldn't have taken much time or effort to figure out which one of the many bullets that had pounded into the cabin's front had the girl's blood on it.

But Bill had already judged A.J. and found him guilty. Besides, he was sending his team of deputies out to talk to the man who'd allegedly sold A.J. that assault weapon at that gun show. If the man agreed that the document was forged—a document that had rather randomly shown up in the sheriff's office just that morning—then and only then would they start digging bullets out of the cabin.

It was at that point in their interview that Bill made a crass joke about how maybe it had been the ghost of Silas Quinn who'd shot Alison. And A.J., who still had her blood on his jeans, wasn't ready to joke about that at all, so he told Bill to shut the fuck up.

Things got even more tense when Bill dropped another bomb and let us know that the deputies who'd gone out to A.J.'s cabin used some kind of electronic surveillance detecting equipment to locate a cell phone jammer. And yes, indeed, it was a TechWhiz 7842, and it had been wiped clean of all fingerprints.

I stood off to the side in that little curtained ER room, while A.J. told Alison everything.

And like A.J., I held my breath, praying that after she absorbed it all, she'd look him in the eye and say, *I still believe you.*

But she was silent, and I knew that A.J. didn't blame her for her doubt. It was a lot to take in. A lot to wonder about.

But then she said, "What about the picture?"

And A.J. didn't know what she meant at first.

I did, though, so I told him, "The police artist's rendering of the killer. The tall man named Brian."

A.J. had told her about my suggestion on the ride to the hospital, but he now shook his head. "No way is Fenster going to spend any of his budget on that. He thinks I'm crazy."

"So let's pay for it ourselves," Alison said, leaning forward to take his hand. "Or do it ourselves. Isn't Bev an artist?"

A.J. glanced over at me, hope in his eyes. "She paints," he told her. "She's not . . . But Charlie . . . He used to draw."

"But you know who's even better?" I reminded him. Or maybe it wasn't a reminder. Maybe he just didn't know. "His father. Tom. When he was a boy, he drew a picture of Melody—just from my description through the years."

Although, to be honest now, after that wink Tom had given me, I wasn't sure he hadn't actually seen her, maybe as a spirit or an angel come to watch over me.

Still, it was certainly worth a try.

Alison was moved out of the ER and into a private room. Bev's husband, Charlie, had brought her suitcase from A.J.'s, because the clothes she'd been wearing had been ruined.

He'd brought her toilet kit, too, so that she could wash up.

Rose had stayed with her at first, making sure she was steady enough on her feet as she changed. But then she'd left to give Alison some privacy—especially when Hugh called from Arizona.

"How are *you?*" Alison asked.

"Finally out of the hospital," he said. "It's you I'm worried about. Al, seriously, you've got to get out of there. Henry's shitting dancing monkeys—he's terrified the nutjob's going to kill you. And I have to be honest—for once I actually agree."

"A.J.'s not a nutjob," Alison said.

"Babe," Hugh said. "The state police are crawling all over his truck, because, well, it matches my description of the truck that ran me off the road."

"You were run off the road by a *truck?*" Alison asked, her heart in her throat. "Did you see the other driver?"

"No," he admitted. "And really, my description was big and dark colored, which, yeah, could be every other truck in the state. I really don't remember that much. Still . . . Lookit, you're not going to like this, but the production office got an anonymous phone call last night. It was on the voicemail this morning. A tip. Warning us about A.J. Gallagher. Telling us to be careful, because, well, he's . . . literally crazy."

"He's not," Alison said. "I know I said what I said, but—"

"And you are *so* sleeping with him again," Hugh said. "And it's against everything I believe in to trash-talk a friend's lover, but, honey, this is something you really need to know. We verified it, Alison." He took a deep breath. "A.J. Gallagher spent quite a few months in a psychiatric hospital."

"It was rehab," she said. "Your uncle Henry himself has gone in—"

"This was for way longer than your average twenty-eight-day program," Hugh said.

"A.J. needed more than twenty-eight days," she countered. "He'd seen some horrible things in the war."

Hugh sighed heavily.

"When people are ill, they go to the hospital,"

she told him. She tried, but she couldn't keep her voice from shaking.

"And sometimes," her friend told her quietly, "they're released before they're better. Honey, the state police found a cell phone signal jammer in the back of Gallagher's truck. I remember being run off the road and being pissed that my phone didn't work. I thought it was temporary—the lack of reception. It happens, particularly out in the middle of nowhere. So I sat there, in the Jeep, with the AC still running, waiting for phone service to come back on line. But it didn't. And it still didn't. And then I ate my lunch and I got incredibly sick. And there I am, heaving by the side of the road, and my phone *still* doesn't work. Kind of the way it stopped working when the police got that jammer up and running, to try it out. They had me test it."

"A.J.'s being framed," Alison said, but even as the words came out of her mouth, they felt odd and bizarre. People didn't get framed for crimes they didn't commit. Not outside of the movies or old episodes of *Charlie's Angels*.

"You need to get away from there," Hugh said. "Henry insists. He's sent the plane and he wants you on it. Today."

"Hugh—"

"Alison, think about it. Everything that's happened? It was supposed to be you with me, scouting locations. But even before that, there was that snake in your house—and you told me yourself A.J. opened your door with a freaking credit card. He certainly could have put that snake there."

"Why?" Alison said. "Why would he do that?"

"So he could save you," Hugh said. "Same with the missing anchors on your trailer. Again, who comes to your rescue? A.J. Gallagher."

"That's ridiculous," Alison said. "Mine wasn't the only trailer—"

"So he took *all* the anchors," Hugh spoke over her, "so he could be an even bigger hero. Paula told me about the accident you had with the rental car. The brake line was frayed. Yeah, right, how often does *that* happen? But who's there, so that you can fling your arms—and legs—around him after he saves the day?"

Alison was silent.

"Tell me that you're not sleeping with him," Hugh said, "and I'll revise my theory."

She was getting mad. Not just at Hugh, but at herself and at A.J. "So A.J. shot me this morning so I'd have sex with him," she said flatly. "That doesn't make sense, after I already spent the night with him. . . ."

But she broke off, because maybe it *did* make sense in a crazy way. She was going to leave. She'd told A.J. so.

Still, she shook her head, unwilling to accept Hugh's so-called theory. "Hughie, I know this sounds crazy, but Jamie—the ghost—he's real," Alison said. "I've felt him. He saved our lives today."

"Just get on the plane," Hugh said. "Please. You need a little distance from this man. Maybe you're right. Maybe there's really a ghost. But maybe there's not. Maybe you just *want* there to be a ghost. Just *get* on the plane, and we'll figure it out. I'll help you, I promise." His voice broke. "Alison, please, I'm really scared for you."

May 12, 1901
Dear Diary,
   A boy. The child is a boy.
   I wept when I saw him—he is so clearly not my gambler's. Yet I cherish this little babe so, it pains me inside. How could I love something that is part monster?
   And however could I ask J. to love him, too?
   But J. knew. Somehow, without my telling him, he knew what I feared.
   He cradled that baby in his arms, he kissed that tiny forehead, and he gave the child a name. His name. He looked right at me, and said, "He's my son now. Yours and mine and no one else's. We'll raise him right, with plenty of love, and he'll grow to be a man we'll both be proud of."
   I love them so, father and son, with all my heart and soul.

• • •

The diaries arrived while A.J., Bev, and Rose were still attempting to track down Tom Fallingstar—to see if the shaman could draw a picture of Brian, described by Jamie, with A.J. as information conduit.

There were two of them—the diaries. They were in plastic ziplock baggies that were tucked into an ancient-looking leather mailbag.

Joe Gallagher dropped them off in Alison's room, moments after she had signed her release papers and received her prescription for antibiotics from the nurse.

She didn't get a chance to open the baggies before two men—the co-pilot and the flight attendant from Henry Logan's private jet—came into her room, gathered up her suitcase and her belongings, and hustled her out of the back door of the hospital.

Alison found herself flipping back and forth between *this was crazy* and *Hugh and Henry had a point.*

If she *were* in danger from A.J.—and God, she just couldn't believe that she was—then leaving Alaska would ensure her safety.

Unless, of course, Jamie was real and A.J. wasn't crazy—and someone named Brian who wore his long hair back in a ponytail, who had killed another man named Wayne, and who had a cohort named Gene, really *was* gunning for her.

Which was ridiculous. She'd witnessed nothing—no murders in the backseat of any kind of car. Not ever, in her entire life.

She dug her cell phone out of her purse, but the co-pilot, a rotund little man named Julio Garcia, who was sitting in the back beside her while the flight attendant drove, gently took it from her, taking care not to jostle her injured arm.

"You can call Mr. Gallagher from the phones on board after we're in the air," Julio told her. He and Henry had gone to middle school together, in suburban New Jersey. He'd told her that the first time she'd flown on the director's private jet.

It was clear that Julio would do anything for his friend and boss.

"So I'm being kidnapped," Alison said.

"Absolutely not," Julio said. He signaled to the flight attendant, who pulled to the side of the road. "But be aware if you get out? You'll be sued for breach of contract. Henry needs you back on set, and the plane is scheduled to leave in a matter of minutes. If you're not on it . . . Well, that would be a shame. Your lawyers' fees will probably be around two hundred thousand dollars, even if you win, which you won't."

"Henry's not going to sue me," she said. But at the same time, she didn't get out of the car.

"Don't count on it." He nodded for the driver to resume. "Henry feels responsible for sending you to Alaska. If you get killed while you're here, your estate will sue him—no doubt about that."

"I don't have an estate," she informed him. "I don't have a family. I don't even have a cat."

"Then your publisher will sue Henry. Someone will. This is a litigious world we live in, Dr. Carter, and Henry wants you safe. Not merely because he's fond of you, but for financial reasons, too. He'll sue you, to prove that you broke your contract by staying in Alaska against his wishes. So if you *do* die . . ."

"I'm in love with this man," Alison said, "that everyone thinks is a lunatic. But he's not. I know it. And you're making me leave without even—"

"If Henry's wrong about him," the co-pilot told her, "he'll fly you back. And he'll explain to your friend that you were given no choice. You had to leave."

"A.J. won't understand," Alison said, but when they pulled up to the plane and she got out of the car, she didn't try to run away.

She just climbed the stairs, hoping that A.J. would follow her here, so that she could, at least, say good-bye. But she paused for just a moment before going into the cabin, looking out at the empty parking lot. And the pain in her arm was nothing compared to the ache in her heart.

A.J. heard Alison board the plane.

Jamie had told him that the private jet had landed in the airstrip north of town. The ghost had overheard, too, Alison's phone conversation with her friend Hugh.

And A.J. knew that there was no way he was going to be able to purchase a plane ticket down to Tucson or even Phoenix. Because the way things were going, it was really just a matter of time before Bill Fenster brought him in for questioning.

Not the semi-friendly questioning like this morning, but the kind where A.J. was fingerprinted and locked in a holding cell.

The kind where charges were going to be filed against him, where a judge would find him a flight risk and agree that he should be held without bail.

At which point, he'd be locked up and impotent while Brian and Gene were both still out there, on the loose and dangerous and—according to Jamie—gunning for the woman he loved.

So A.J. had made a decision—and he'd come here to the airfield and stowed away on Logan's private jet, sneaking on board with a food delivery.

He'd set his cell phone on vibrate, willing Alison to call him. But then he turned that off, too, when Jamie reported that her phone had been confiscated by the co-pilot.

"She really doesn't have a choice, kid," Jamie said as A.J. hid in the shadows of the plane's storage cabin. He knew it was pressurized, because there were dog crates built in, and a large, goofy-looking poodle/lab mix was curled up in one of them.

The dog had lifted his or her head when A.J. had first come on board, but there was no barking, which was good.

But he knew that the dog belonged to one of the pilots or the flight attendant—who would probably be down to check on it during the long flight.

Which meant he'd have to stay hidden.

All the way to Arizona.

Which was no big deal, if it meant keeping Alison safe.

He looked at the clock on his cell phone, wishing that Tom hadn't been tied up and unable to do that drawing. Tom was going to have to draw the picture of Brian via the phone, with Jamie jumping back and forth, which had to be taxing for the ghost.

A.J. wished he had his hat, too. He felt undressed and incomplete without it, but he knew without a doubt that if he let anything happen to Alison, his lack of hat wouldn't matter.

The plane began to taxi, and he knew it was time. He pushed send and sent the simple text message—*now*—to his mother's phone.

I went into the jet's cabin to sit with Alison, and to see what she saw out the airplane's little windows.

"Oh," she said as she spotted Rose's brightly colored car race into the airfield parking lot.

She pushed the button that connected her to the pilot's cabin and said, "Please, can we wait? Just a minute? I really want to—"

"No can do," the pilot's voice came back, cutting her off. "We've been cleared for take off. Make sure your seat belt is fastened, ma'am."

Alison started to cry, with big noisy sobs that she never would've allowed herself to make if she knew I was listening. "I'm so sorry," she said, as she leaned over to look out the window, where Rose and Tom had climbed out of that car, following A.J., whose cowboy hat seemed almost white in the bright afternoon sunshine. They both held on to him when he looked as if he wanted to run after the plane, and Alison craned her neck to watch him through her tears for as long as she possibly could.

What she and the pilots and the attendant didn't see, of course, was that A.J. wasn't A.J. beneath that hat, but instead was his cousin Joe—a good man and the spitting image of his great-grandfather, my beloved eldest son Jim.

I went straight down, through the cabin floor, and into the luggage holding area and told A.J. about Alison's tears, hoping it would make him feel better.

But I think it only made him feel worse.

Chapter Twenty-two

Alison cried until she was too tired to cry anymore.

And then she blew her nose and picked up the plane's phone, and dialed A.J.'s cell.

She was beeped right to his voicemail.

"Hey," she said, leaving a message. "It's me. I'm a coward, and I'm on a plane heading for Jubilation, and I am so sorry that I didn't kick and scream and insist that they wait until I talked to you. I wanted to just . . . let you know that even though it looks like I've run away, I'm still on your side. I know you're kind of new at using your cell phone, but maybe Bev or Rose can help you send that picture of Brian to my cell as soon as you've got it. I won't be able to see it until I land, because I can't use my cell on the plane, but as soon as I'm on the ground, I'll check for it." She paused. "I guess that's all. I know you're probably worried about me, but I'm going to go to the police as soon as we get to Arizona, and tell them about Brian and Wayne and Jamie's suspicions. It'll help if I have that picture, so . . . If you want to call me back, I'll be here. If not, I . . . don't blame you. I . . . hope to talk to you soon."

She hung up, because she'd started to cry again, which was ridiculous, because she just wasn't a weeper. But now she couldn't seem to stop.

She forced her tears away through sheer will as

she found the bag that held Melody's diaries and opened the first volume.

The first entry was dated from 1895.

Careful of the antique binding—the book's cover was a faded red velvet, and the pages were edged in a still-shiny gold—Alison began to read.

April 24, 1895
Dearest, lovely new Diary!

In a few short days, I shall become the wife of a legendary American hero. Aunt E. bought me this beautiful book, assuring me that as the wife of such an important man, it is my responsibility to keep a written chronicle of our lives. I agree. Someday when my future husband becomes President of this great country, schoolchildren will read my words and marvel at the excitement of our lives.

I have just turned eighteen. I am almost an old maid, or so Aunt E. keeps telling me. I could have had any man in town, but I wanted this one, so I waited, and sure enough, he is mine!

I am gloating, I know, but surely every new bride is allowed to gloat a little on the eve of her wedding.

My future husband is so big and strong. A United States Marshal.

I shall never have to worry about my safety again.

Alison turned the page. At eighteen years old, Melody's sweet innocence came through in her neatly penned words.

She was a child—and she was about to face a real-life nightmare that wouldn't end for three long years.

The next few entries were similar to the first, full of girlish gushings and dreams. Silas, Melody discovered with some shock, had never learned to read. She imagined herself teaching him, in the evenings, before the fire. She imagined his gratitude and admiration and heartfelt devotion.

He drank too much, she admitted, as men who lived a hard life were prone to do. She would help him limit the intake of his alcohol, and keep him entertained with her vast library of books. Once he could read, they would read them together.

Theirs would be a lovely life, exciting by day and quiet and peaceful by night.

Her entry for Melody and Silas's wedding day, however, was a bit less confident.

April 28, 1895
Dear Diary,
I am married, and now know the secrets only married women know. I know, too, why these things are kept confidential. If young girls knew, they'd every one enter a convent.

I am bleeding, and continue to bleed while my husband snores.

Is it too late, I wonder, to change my mind?

April 29, 1895
Dear Diary,

Aunt E. noticed my unhappiness and has reassured me that my conjugal duties will pain me less as time goes by.

I can only hope.

May 2, 1895
Dear Diary,

My bruises and cuts have no time to heal before he injures me again.

Tonight I begged him to refrain. Perhaps, instead, I could begin to teach him to read.

His anger frightened me as he asked if I dare to think I'm better than he. I told him, no, of course not. He was my husband, and I loved him. I merely hoped to help.

But he didn't believe me, and he hit me, and when he saw my tears, he laughed.

He <u>laughed</u>.

And then he hurt me in the conjugal way, this time on purpose, and when he saw my shock and pain, he laughed again. And he told me that he owns me.

I am numb.

May 7, 1895
Dear Diary,
He burned my books. We cannot take them with us to the little town where we are to live, and instead of giving them to Aunt E. or the local lending library, he burned them all.
I have married Satan himself.

Melody's entries grew more sparse through the end of 1895 and on into 1896, as she and her husband traveled across the country, going from town to town. There were only seven entries for the entire year of 1897. It was then that Alison realized that Melody never wrote out anyone's names. Instead, she used only their initials. She wrote about Aunt E. and S., although Alison wasn't sure if Melody was using S. for Silas or for Satan.

Still, all they'd need was a signature match, because the dates and locations lined up with Quinn's account of his travels.

Hope arrived for Melody at the end of 1897, in the form of a visit home to Dodge City.

Melody, having long reached the end of her rope, intended to go to her dear Aunt E. and ask for asylum from her abusive spouse.

But it was soon clear, upon arrival in Dodge, that help was not to come. Aunt E., her only living relative, had passed away in an outbreak of influenza three months earlier.

And Melody fell into a deep despair.

Her life was a repeated pattern of death threats, rapes, and beatings when she was at home with Quinn. Out in public, he paraded her on his arm like a trophy, always courteous and kind. She was, ironically, the envy of all women, wherever they traveled.

Alison read of her plan to escape from Quinn in New Mexico, read of its failure and the harsh violence that followed.

She read of Melody's arrival in Jubilation, read of her initial meetings with Jamie—J., she called him, or "my gambler." She read Melody's account of the shoot-out at the Red Rock Saloon, read of the welcoming ball. She read about Melody's loveless proposition to Jamie, and her subsequent discovery that hope did exist, even in her world. She read of their escape, of Melody's fears and doubts. She read of the long, painful road to trust, down which Jamie patiently guided her, and of the promise Melody made to him to never again let herself be helpless and afraid. She read of the rape in San Francisco, and of the child that resulted.

She read of the beginning of a town called Heaven, and of the love and laughter and pain that was shared there.

June 24, 1901
Dear Diary,
    Today we began building our cabin, our home. With four workers from Fairbanks—

men who owe J. the shirts off their backs from poker games, I think—we have begun construction.

Sunset lasts forever here. It's the most amazing thing. We sit together, J. and I, with the baby at my breast, just watching the colors in the sky. I never know if it's morning or evening or the middle of the night.

Heaven. J. calls it <u>Heaven</u>, and with his arms around me, it truly is.

And I should know, because I've spent plenty of time in Hell.

From 1905 on, the diary entries were limited mostly to those days that Melody and Jamie's children were born—and their life was far from sorrow free. There were a number of miscarriages and babies who didn't live past their first few weeks between Skyler and the twins. But now and again, Melody would take the time to recount a funny or sweet story or even just make notes about simple, ordinary events in their everyday lives.

And then her record was of graduations from school, of marriages and grandchildren, of holidays and celebrations.

But then came the final entry.

September 6, 1944
Dear Diary,
The days grow shorter again, the night is

upon us. I go into winter knowing I have seen my last spring.

My time has come. That is, if my gambler will let me go. While I sleep, and I sleep so often these days, he spends much of his time in the church downtown. The very one I never could convince him to attend. He claims he is praying, but I know that he is trying to strike a bargain with our Maker.

"One hand of Black Jack, God," I know he says. "Winner gets to keep the girl."

I know for sure, were J. granted that game of cards with the Almighty, he'd go into it with both an ace and a jack up his sleeve.

Cheating at cards never bothered him. It's always been just another part of the game. The best cheater wins.

When I was a young girl, I wouldn't have understood. He would have been a bad man, an outlaw, a liar and a cheat. He would have worn a black hat.

But I didn't know much of human nature back then. I married a man who wore a white hat, a man everyone adored, a hero, a legend. Look where it got me.

Look where it got me, indeed.

Black and white, white and black.

It took me fewer years than most to realize that all men's—and women's—hats are, in fact, decidedly gray.

My children were raised knowing this, and I see the fairness with which they treat all others, and I am proud.

I am proud, and so very tired.

This life was not an easy one, but I would not change it for all of the riches in the world. Even the time I spent with the monster— because look where it got me.

To Heaven.

Alison was crying again when I went up into the cabin to check on her.

She was reading Mel's diaries, and I read with her for a while, looking over her shoulder. I have to confess, if I could've cried, I would've been weeping at that last entry, too.

As she closed the book and carefully put it back into its plastic, the aircraft hit a patch of turbulence, and the plane bounced. I had to do a bit of dance to keep from bumping into her.

I may, in fact, have skimmed her, because she looked around as if suddenly aware that I might be there.

She held out her hand, and was probably on the verge of saying my name, when the airplane's phone rang.

She picked it up. "Hello?"

But then, looking around again, she put the thing on speaker, which was damned considerate. I'd heard too many one-sided phone conversations in the past few weeks. It was nice to be able to hear both ends.

"Thank God," came the voice of her redheaded friend Hugh from the slightly distorted speaker. "You're on the plane, you're in the air."

"Henry threatened to sue me," she told him, sounding none too happy.

"I know," Hugh said. "That was my idea. I know how freaked out you get when it comes to money."

"Well, fuck you," Alison said, her language proving how upset and angry she was.

"You're welcome," Hugh said, as if she'd used the word *thank* instead of the f-bomb. "I'm going to assume you haven't heard the latest in the A.J. Gallagher as America's Most Wanted episode. The man who sold him that submachine gun? Dead."

"What?" Alison said it in unison with me.

"Yup," Hugh confirmed. "He was bludgeoned to death, which I find a little ironic for a man who sold AK-47s as collector's items. He's a local guy and the Heaven sheriff's department found him in his kitchen with his head bashed in. Coroner says he was killed sometime between two and four A.M. The police think it's closer to two because that was when his security system was shut down. As in shut down because gun-collector guy knew whoever it was who was pounding on his back door in the middle of the night—A.J. Gallagher—

because he'd bought an MP5 submachine gun from him a few weeks earlier."

"A.J. was with me all night," Alison said. "I happen to know that at two A.M. we were . . . otherwise engaged."

"The gun guy's computer was on. Someone had tried to wipe clean his purchase order file. But they failed. A.J.'s purchase order for that gun was in the trash file."

"Did the computer experts who examined it make note of when the document was created or revised?" Alison asked.

"I don't know," Hugh admitted. "I assume so."

"Yeah, well, call me back when you find out for sure," she told him sharply. "Because I'll bet you next week's paycheck that A.J.'s alleged purchase order was either created or revised last night. And you know how certain I am that I'm right because you know how freaked out I get when it comes to money."

"Alison," Hugh said.

"He was with me," Alison repeated. "All night."

"So, what?" Hugh asked. "You didn't sleep? At all? Not even a little?"

"I did sleep," she told him. "But A.J. did, too."

"So then you can't be convinced—" he started.

"Actually," she said. "I can. We were . . ." She cleared her throat. "Still connected when we woke up. We were both so tired, neither one of us must've moved at all. You know. After."

And this was, as the kids say, TMI.

But Hugh didn't let it go. "And you don't think he could've sneaked out of bed, killed gun guy and come back with the intention of waking you up with a bang so that you'd think he'd been there the entire—"

Alison cut him. "But that's just it. He didn't have much of a . . . bang-maker. Not . . ." She cleared her throat again. "At first."

"That's dangerous, you know," Hugh pointed out. "Using a condom twice."

"We didn't," she said. "Use a condom. I'm on the pill and . . ."

"Holy crap, Alison!"

"No," she said. "Listen. Because A.J. had a record of risky behavior ten years ago, he's had himself tested, regularly. He's clean—it's been ten years. And we . . . kind of moved into a trust place where . . . It was my idea. I wanted to . . . give him something because . . ." She exhaled hard. "At the time, I didn't think I could give him more than just that night. Which he spent with me, Hughie. All of it. It was around five fifteen when we woke up. Six thirty before we were dozing off again."

"Hokay," Hugh said. "I don't suppose A.J. Gallagher has a non-crazy gay brother . . . ?"

"No," Alison said, "but he's got a really adorable cousin. . . ." She cut herself off. "Hugh, whoever killed the gun collector wasn't A.J." She

551

said it again, enunciating clearly. "He was with me. I think this man Brian, who Jamie saw outside the cabin after I was shot, I think he's the killer. Because he also killed this man named Wayne—just outside of Jubilation. I think he's also the man who ran you off the road."

"No, that was Genc," I said, but of course she couldn't hear me.

Hugh wasn't convinced. "The police have put out a BOLO for Gallagher," he told her. "If you have a way to reach him, Al, you might want to let him know that. They have him down as armed and dangerous. And with his history of mental illness? They're going to shoot first and ask questions later."

"Oh, my God," Alison breathed. "Hugh, you've got to tell Henry to tell them that he was with me."

"You need to tell A.J. to turn himself in," Hugh countered. "He should go, with his lawyer, to the police station and Jesus, I don't know, lie down on the floor with his hands on his head."

"Hugh—"

"I'll be at the airport tonight, to pick you up when the plane lands," he told her. "Your ETA is, like, three A.M., which is proof that I love you. And if you really want to, I'll go with you to the police, and you can tell them what you told me. And all about this Brian guy and Wayne and whoever else, too, okay?"

"Thank you," Alison said, and she pushed the button that hung up the phone.

And then she surprised me by saying aloud, "Jamie, if you're here, you need to go tell A.J. to turn himself in. He's being set up—the fact that the gun collector was murdered when A.J. was with me is proof of that. I'm going to help him, but the first thing he needs to do is not get killed. Go tell him that. Now."

And she picked up the phone and left the same message for A.J., who was, in fact, right down in the plane's cargo hold.

Chapter Twenty-three

Even Craig Lutz had called and left a message on A.J.'s cell phone, telling him to turn himself in.

Everyone was calling him, with the same message. Everyone but his mother, Tom, and Bev.

And as the jet landed in the heat of the Arizona night, as he heard—and Jamie verified—that Alison had disembarked, A.J. waited to find out whether or not his mother, with the best of intentions, had told the authorities where he was.

But a SWAT team didn't rush into the plane's luggage bay.

In fact, no one did. For a good long time.

And now he was getting antsy, knowing that Alison was already walking into possible danger.

He sent Jamie to follow her, as he played some of his messages on his phone.

Lutz's was one of the ones A.J. actually listened to, mostly because the former SEAL had texted him, too, saying *Listen to your fucking voicemail, bitch.*

A.J. had always found his friend's irreverence hard to resist.

"Hey, man," Lutz said in his recording. "Your mother called and told me what's going on, and I gotta agree. It's time to surrender. Don't let them kill you—and you know that they will. They are scared motherfuckers—undertrained, understaffed, and underpaid—and they will shoot you dead if you try to run. Lookit, I'm in San Diego. Me and Reilly and Bozo are already in my truck. We're heading out there, to Jubilation. We'll connect with Alison, and we *will* keep her safe. I promise you. I'll call you when we reach her—should be around eight A.M. At that time, you *will* turn yourself in. I'm going to tell you how to do it, too, okay? Don't just go walking up to some cop and expect not to get damaged. But we'll go through that when it's time. I'm here for you, bro. We're going to make this right—I'll make sure Alison doesn't get hurt. Count on it. And call me if you need me. For anything, all right?"

He was just about to call Lutz back, to ask him to connect with Alison in Tucson, and then to call Alison herself and tell her to find the nearest police station and not leave the lobby until Lutz and co. arrived.

But the door finally opened, and the labradoodle's owner—the co-pilot named Julio—came in to get him.

"Hey, buddy," Julio said to the dog as he opened the cage. "Hey, Dexter. What a good boy. I bet you need to pee, don't you? Yes, you do."

The dog wasn't the only one, but A.J. leaned back into the shadows, hoping that the friendly animal wouldn't take the opportunity to come over and say hello. But Dexter hurried for the open door, straining at his leash.

Julio didn't close the door behind him, and A.J. waited only a few seconds before creeping closer. He could have used Jamie's eyes and ears, but it didn't take him long to realize that there was no one around at that hour of the night. He slipped out onto the well-lit runway, trying to look as if he belonged there, aware as hell that a stranger in a restricted area of an airport was going to generate attention.

But he made it into the terminal using a truckload of packages from a FedEx plane as a shield, keeping the exhausted personnel and technicians from seeing him.

Once inside, he moved quickly through the shadows toward the openings where luggage from flights could be loaded onto a conveyor belt and sent out to waiting passengers. He went down the row toward the one at the very end, and peeked through its opening, pushing aside the straps that hung down to provide privacy for the workers— or maybe they were there to discourage irate passengers from going in search of their missing bags.

No one was in that part of the baggage claim area, so A.J. said a quick prayer and hopped out, turning so that he was facing the belt, as if waiting for his nonexistent luggage.

There was no shouting, no screaming, no questions, no nothing.

So he turned, and just like Dexter had done after the long flight, he took care of his first order of business by hurrying into the nearest men's room.

A.J. finally called Alison back.

Her cell phone rang while she and Hugh were talking to the police at a special security office right there in the airport.

There was no way she could answer his call, sitting there with a bored but heavily armed trooper named Richard Salazar, and she immediately silenced the ringer.

It was twice as frustrating, because it was clear that the Arizona state police, like their counterparts in Alaska, had already decided that A.J. was their one and only suspect.

She tried to explain about Wayne and Brian without mentioning Jamie, but all that did was convince Salazar that A.J. was involved in Wayne's death, too.

Apparently the name of the man who'd been found dead in a burning car north of Jubilation *had* been Wayne, which freaked her out a little bit.

Salazar wouldn't give her any additional information, even when she asked to see a picture of the deceased. She would have to contact the FBI, he told her. The case was theirs now.

"But it's possible that I know him," she told the trooper. "I may have seen him, right before his death, in the company of a man named Brian, who killed him."

But he was not impressed. A.J. Gallagher was, without a doubt, the only suspect they were looking for. They weren't interested in hearing about any other options or possibilities.

Her dear friend Hugh wasn't particularly impressed either. Not even when they were walking to the parking lot, when Alison listened to and relayed to him the gist of the message that A.J. had left.

"He wants us to stay here," she told Hugh, who was still peeling and itching from his bad sunburn. "His friend, Craig Lutz, is driving out from San Diego. He's going to meet us here, at which point A.J.'s going to turn himself in."

Alison really wanted A.J. to turn himself in. The fact that he was still out there, with both the police and now the FBI looking for him, scared the hell out of her.

"Alison, I love you," Hugh told her as he unlocked his Jeep, "you know that. But I am not going to deliver you into the hands of one of Gallagher's potentially equally crazy friends. We're going to Jubilation, where Henry is expecting us. This Lutz guy can connect with us there—when we're surrounded by security guards." And then he played his most convincing card. "Jubilation's closer to San Diego. If we meet Lutz there, A.J. will turn himself in that much sooner."

Alison dialed A.J.'s cell, and—of course—went right to his voicemail.

"Hi," she said, as she got into Hugh's Jeep, "I know you're not going to want to hear this, but . . . We're going to meet Craig Lutz in Jubilation. Tell him to go to the main production trailer. I'll be in there, with Henry and Hugh."

And about a dozen armed guards, but she didn't want to tell him that. Of course, he probably knew.

As redheaded Hugh's Jeep pulled out of the airport parking lot, a dark sedan with heavily tinted windows followed.

And okay, yeah. Maybe I was paranoid. Maybe I was seeing trouble where none existed.

Maybe Dolly Parton had just arrived in town and was being driven to her hotel.

I hovered close, closer, keeping up with the car as it followed the Jeep onto the road, heading for the same airport exit. There were only a few ways in or out, so it wasn't that alarming that both vehicles would be traveling in the same direction.

Still, there was something about the way that the sedan stayed slightly back from the Jeep that made me nervous.

So I stuck my head into the car and took a look-see.

There was no one in the back—not Dolly or anyone else. The car was empty save for the driver, whose back-of-the-head wasn't immediately familiar to me. He had short dark hair. No silver-dollar bald spot like Gene. And unlike Wayne, he still *had* a head. I maneuvered around to see the man's face, and would've crapped my pants in surprise, had I either the ability to crap or real pants.

It was Brian. He'd gotten his long hair cut, no doubt after A.J. had gone Rambo on his ass, up in Alaska. He had a few big scratches on his cheek, too, like he'd run face-first into a fir tree.

He must've gotten on a boat to Juneau directly after returning the Robinsons' SUV to their garage, then boarded a plane to Seattle and points south immediately after that.

I rode with him in his sedan while I tried to figure out my best move. Should I scramble over into Hugh's Jeep and try to warn Alison directly, or jump to A.J. and get him to call her and warn her?

I'd do both, I decided. I'd jump to A.J. first, though, and I went, closing my eyes and projecting myself . . .

Directly into Silas Quinn's old house in Jubilation.

I didn't recognize it at first, because it had changed a lot over the years. But then I saw the man I'd originally thought was Gene when he'd first arrived on set. His name was Neil Sylvester and he was Quinn's great-great-grandson. He was also as tightly wound and tense now as he'd been when I'd first seen him.

He was sitting at a table in what had long ago been Melody's kitchen, wearing a silk bathrobe with a green-and-brown paisley print that hung open to reveal his beer belly and a sagging tattoo of a tired-looking dragon on his man-boob.

It was not a pretty sight.

He had a can of beer open on the table in front of him, and he spun it around and around, making patterns with the condensation.

It wasn't until he spoke that I realized there was another man in the kitchen with him.

"Look, Skip," he said. "I think it's time to quit."

"You really want to spend the rest of your life in jail?" the other man asked, and I realized he was that actor Trace Marcus's assistant.

Neil shook his head. "I won't," he said. "I

borrowed some money—that's my only crime. I'm not involved—"

"Oh, you are," Skip said, and his phone rang, interrupting him. He answered it with words that chilled me. "Yeah, this is Loco."

Skip Smith was *Loco*—the man that tall Brian of the former ponytail had been talking to after Wayne's murder.

"Good," he said into his phone, telling Neil, "Brian is following them. They're heading back to Jubilation. He hasn't got them yet, but he will. Soon. He's calling us now because he's going to turn on the machine, which means he'll be out of touch, too."

The machine. Holy moley, he was talking about a TechWhiz 7842—I just knew it. It was, absolutely, his MO. And once Brian turned it on, A.J. wouldn't be able to reach Alison to warn her.

I closed my eyes and jumped, willing myself to wherever it was that A.J. was, but wound up back in Brian's car.

"*Son* of a bitch!" I said.

But maybe I was supposed to be there for a reason, because right when I popped in, Brian said into his cell phone, "I want you and Neil to meet me—where we talked about."

And wasn't *that* frustrating. "Come *on*," I said. "Give me more than that to work with."

But "Bring a shovel"—words I didn't want to

hear—and "I'll see you there," was all he said before he hung up.

And with that he reached over and flipped the switch on what was, indeed another of those deadly little cell phone jammers.

I closed my eyes and jumped, willing myself to A.J.—but again, I wound up in Mel's old kitchen, where Skip, aka Loco, was pocketing his cell phone. And okay. There was definitely a reason for my jumping here. Skip, after all, knew where he was supposed to meet Brian—although, by then it might well be too late for Alison and Hugh.

"Get dressed," Skip now told Neil.

But Neil shook his head. "I'm not going to do it," he said. "This deal isn't worth killing people over. It's just not."

"Too late," Skip said.

Neil disagreed. "No," he said as he stood up and went toward the phone that was hanging on the wall by the kitchen cabinets. "It's not too late. I'm done, man. I'm not going to be part of this any longer." He picked up the phone.

"What are you doing?" Skip asked.

"I'm calling your boss," Neil said, punching in a series of numbers. "I'm going to tell him what I just told you. I'll find some other way to pay back the money I borrowed. As of right now, I'm out."

It was then that Skip reached into his jacket and drew a semiautomatic handgun, one of those newfangled ones with a very large clip. None of this six-bullets-and-then-you-need-to-reload business that I'd dealt with my entire gunfighting career. If you could call that dark part of my life a career.

"Hang up the phone," Skip ordered Neil, who turned to look at that giant gun with what I thought of as somewhat foolish shock. You don't dance with—or borrow money from—the devil and then get to be all surprised when he reveals that he's evil. "You dumb piece of shit."

Neil hung up the phone. He used his hand to sweep off a film of sweat that had suddenly appeared on his wide forehead. He didn't say a word. He just stared at the gun pointing at him, and then he stared into Skip's eyes. And whatever he saw there made him turn and run.

But Skip shot him in the back. Twice. Neil hit the floor and skidded, leaving a gruesome trail of blood. Skip watched as Neil's legs twitched a few times and then finally stopped.

Skip then turned, and walked out the front door. He passed right through me, but he didn't even seem to notice the shock or chill.

We were in trouble here. We were in deep, *deep* trouble.

And this time, when I jumped to A.J., I reached him.

Jamie popped in just as A.J. was paying a parking fee, with a ticket that he'd found conveniently tucked into the sun visor of the truck.

The truck that he'd borrowed from the short-term lot.

He'd searched for one with a set of keys hidden up on the tire or inside the wheel well or under the front bumper.

It had taken him a while, but he'd finally hit pay dirt. And he now kept his face hidden in the shadows beneath the brim of the baseball cap he'd found in the truck's front seat, aware that there was a security camera behind the woman who was taking his money.

"Have a nice day," she said, as he pulled away, and he put the window back up and headed for the exit.

"Brian's here," Jamie told him, and A.J. nearly went off the road. "He got a haircut. He's following Alison and Hugh. Both cars—Hugh's Jeep and Brian's black sedan—are about forty-five minutes ahead of us."

"God damn it, she's supposed to be—"

"Well, she's not," Jamie cut him off. "Brian's got a cell jammer in his car, he's using it, but I think you should call Alison just in case they manage to pull out of range. Leave a message. They need to drive to the nearest police station, or at least go somewhere public, with a lot of people around."

A.J. immediately dialed his cell phone, but his call to Alison went right to her voicemail. He quickly left her a message, then called his mother.

As her phone was ringing, Jamie told him, "Skip Smith—Trace Marcus's assistant—is part of this. I just saw him kill Neil Sylvester."

"Jesus!"

"Yeah."

His mother picked up. And A.J. quickly told her what was happening, asked her to call the police and request that they stop Hugh's Jeep on the road between Tucson and Jubilation.

She hung up to do just that, but A.J. didn't have much faith that she'd get through—let alone convince anyone to take her seriously.

"Go to Alison," A.J. told Jamie. "Stay with her."

"I will," Jamie said. "What *you've* got to do is call the main production office for the movie, and ask them to connect you with two people who work in the mess tent. A man named Rob or a woman named Charlotte Lombardi."

"The FBI agents," A.J. said. "What makes you think they're going to believe me?"

"Because," Jamie said, "you're going to tell them the whole truth. You're going to tell them about me."

There was a car behind them.

Alison didn't know when she'd first noticed it—certainly not until they'd left the highway for the state road that took them up into Jubilation. For a long time, there'd been a car in front of them, its red taillights glowing in the darkness.

But sometime in the past few minutes, it had turned off, leaving them alone on the deserted stretch of road leading up into the hills.

Alone except for the headlights behind them.

Alison opened her phone—and got nothing. No reception.

Hugh'd put his own phone in the cupholder, and she opened that, too.

Again, nothing.

She searched the Jeep, looking under the seats and even crawling into the back to rummage through all of Hugh's stuff that was back there, wishing she had a flashlight.

"What are you looking for?" Hugh asked.

"What does a cell phone signal jammer look like?" she asked in response as she jarred her injured arm. "Ow!"

"Oh, come on," Hugh said, but then he looked at his lifeless phone, and then looked in the rearview mirror. "Oh, shit. Really?"

"Don't slow down," she warned him. "Don't speed up. Just tell me. If one were back here, would I know it?"

"Yeah, it's about the size of a cheap DVD player," he said, watching her in the rearview, his face lit from the dash. "It would either be plugged into the car or running off a battery—either way it would be warm to the touch."

Alison peeked out the back window at the lights. As far as she could tell, it was a car, not an

SUV or a truck. "Okay now, speed up," she told Hugh. "Haul ass. Get us away from him—as far as you can." As soon as she got a cell signal, she was going to dial 9-1-1. And hope that the state police would be able to trace her call.

Hugh NASCARed away, downshifting to give the Jeep's engine more power.

But the car behind them leapt to keep up.

If Hugh hadn't been fully convinced before, Alison knew that he was now certain they were in trouble. "In the back," he told her as he drove even faster, "in the black case. The combination is four-two-four-five. Open it, Alison."

He was talking about his gun case. It was perhaps the last remaining part of his summers-in-Montana childhood that he still always carried with him.

But Alison had never fired a weapon, and it seemed likely that if they started a gun battle, it would be one they wouldn't win.

So instead, she sat back in her seat and closed her eyes, lifting her face to the sky the way she'd seen A.J. do, and she said, "Jamie, I need you!"

"Are you kidding me?" Hugh said.

"Shhh," she said. "I need to concentrate. Jamie! Where *are* you? We're in trouble and we need your eyes!"

I was right in the middle of telling A.J. everything I knew about Rob and Charlotte, everything I'd overheard—including their conversation about Rob's brother John, and about Rob's dumbass suggestion that he hook Charlotte up with his friend whose name I couldn't remember. Danny maybe. No—Donny. That was it.

One minute I was telling A.J. about Charlotte's asking Rob to get her cell phone charger—another conversation to which no one else had been privy—and the next I was jumping to God knows where.

Except then I knew exactly where, because I heard Alison's voice, clear as day inside my head, shouting, "Jamie, I need you!"

And there I was, like a genie pulled from his bottle at my mistress's command.

It was kind of weird, because even when A.J. called for me, there was choice involved. I didn't *have* to go.

But maybe something or someone else was involved here, because I saw right away what was going on.

Brian's black sedan was racing up the hill after their Jeep, its front mere feet from their rear bumper. And every now and then it surged forward and gave them a little kiss.

So to speak.

"Jamie!" Alison shouted again, because of course she didn't realize I was there.

So I grabbed her and my arms passed through her, giving both of us that jolt.

She gasped. "Jamie?"

I knew that if we were going to attempt to communicate I had to set some parameters. So I touched her on the shoulder of her uninjured arm. That was going to be my way of saying *yes.*

"Oh, my God," she said. "Is that really you?"

I gave her another *yes,* hoping she was catching on.

"The car behind us," she said. "Who is it?" She reached out for me, but I shifted back, away from her.

"Come on, girl," I said, even though she couldn't hear me. "Use your brain. How can I possibly answer that question? Keep it simple."

She was flailing around, searching for me, looking for that electrically charged cold air. But I stayed carefully out of reach.

"Are you still here?" she asked.

I touched her shoulder.

"God," she said, "that's weird."

Yes.

"Are you . . ." she said, thinking hard. "Are you *agreeing* with me?"

Yes.

"Are you telling me *yes?*"

Yes, yes, yes.

"He's telling me yes," she told Hugh. "Oh, my God. Okay. Okay. Is it Brian or Gene behind us?" she asked. "Shit. Wait. Yes/no questions only. Okay, Jamie, it is Gene?"

I didn't move.

"Brian?"

Yes.

"Oh, God. Does he have one of those cell phone jammers?"

Yes.

"Will we make it to Jubilation?" Hugh asked. "Jesus, this is like using a freaking Ouija board."

"He didn't say yes," Alison reported when I didn't move. "Is he going to kill us?" she asked. "No, don't answer that. We can't let him stop us. Right?"

Yes, I agreed.

"Is A.J. safe?" she asked, her heart in her voice.

Yes, I told her, but then I touched her on the knee, too, simultaneously, hoping she'd notice the difference.

"Do you want me to . . . ask more questions about A.J.?" she asked.

How I loved smart women. Yes.

"Oh, my God," she said. "Is he here, in Arizona?"

Yes.

"Should we go off road?" Hugh asked from the front. "The car behind us won't get far if we do."

"He says yes," Alison reported, after I answered him.

"What the hell is that?" Hugh asked, and Alison looked out the front windshield.

The road we were on was relatively straight at this point, cutting through the darkness of the uninhabited rolling hillside. But way in the distance, as if farther down the road, were several very bright lights.

I elevated and dashed ahead to check, and found that it was a truck with some kind of searchlights attached. Not only was that truck completely blocking both lanes, its driver was none other than my old nemesis Gene of the bushy eyebrows and silver-dollar bald spot.

I zipped back into the car and told Alison, Yes, yes, yes yes yes.

She somehow understood that I was still answering Hugh's last question and she shouted at him. "Go off road! Now!"

And he turned the wheel hard. The Jeep bounced and the wheels spun and then caught and they half rolled, half slid through the darkness down the hill into a little valley.

Again, I soared up, high above both the Jeep and the sedan, who'd indeed tried to follow and was stopped, nearly up to its axles in sand.

With my unearthly ability both to judge distances and see in the dark, I saw Gene's truck leap forward, and I knew that Alison and Hugh had about three minutes to either get away or hide.

I could also see that the terrain was hellish in that spot—their best chance lay in their ability to conceal themselves in the vastness of this part of the desert.

Except there weren't that many places to hide, especially from a truck with a searchlight.

But I looked and immediately saw the entrance to an old mine, and I dove back down into the Jeep and closed my eyes and damn near sat on Alison until she said, "We're doing something wrong."

Yes.

"Are we trapped?" she asked, thinking fast. "If we stay in the Jeep?"

Yes, yes, yes.

"Should we get out—go on foot?"

Yes.

"Stop," she told Hugh, even as she scooped up a bottle of water and her cell phone, taking them with her.

Hugh hesitated, like he wanted to get his weapon from the back, but there was no time. Alison knew that and grabbed him and started to run up the hill. "Are we going the right way?" she asked me.

I passed straight through her, and she got my message and she changed direction, heading more west, stumbling slightly in the darkness. "This way?"

Yes. But then she went too far—this was frustrating for the both of us. Brian was surely on foot by now, and Gene's truck could handle this moonscape, no problem.

I walked through her again, and she said, "No, that means no, right?"

Yes.

"Do we go right?" she asked.

No.

"Left?" She was already moving, since she'd been heading forward and coming from the rear—it was the only direction to go.

But I told her yes anyway.

And then she saw it as her eyes adjusted more fully to the night—the mine. And she and Hugh ran for it, slipping into the cooler darkness of its entrance.

No one believed him.

A.J. didn't dare keep his cell line open for long for fear that they would track him, so he made a series of short calls. The first few times he was told that Rob and Charlotte were unavailable, could he hold please?

So he just kept hanging up and calling back.

And finally assuming that he was on some kind of speaker phone, he just started to talk, rattling off everything Jamie had told him about both Rob and Charlotte, hoping to get some sort of response.

And sure enough, there was a click, and Rob picked up. At least he said he was Rob. Without Jamie there to verify, A.J. couldn't know for sure.

"There's a man named Brian," A.J. told him, "and he's trying to kill Alison Carter. He's in a black sedan on the road between Tucson and

Jubilation. You need to send the police out there now. Brian killed Wayne. That's what this is all about. He thinks Alison knows something about that murder. There are at least two other men he's working with. A drug addict named Gene—bushy eyebrows, bald spot. And Skip Smith, who works on the movie set as Trace Marcus's—the actor's—assistant. I don't know if Marcus is involved, but Smith just shot and killed Neil Sylvester. You'll find him in the kitchen of his house in Jubilation."

"Lot of bodies showing up in kitchens when you're around," Rob said, and A.J. knew that the man didn't believe him. Not even a little bit.

"That's right," A.J. said, changing his voice, making it rougher, harsh, giving them what they wanted—someone who was, as Lutz would say, batshit crazy. "And you better find Alison first, motherfucker, or she's next." He switched back to his own voice, and it wasn't hard to sound frantic and upset. "Please," he begged, "find Alison. Don't let me hurt her."

And he hung up his phone, praying that the FBI agent had finally taken him seriously, even though it meant that when they found him, there was no longer any doubt that they would shoot to kill.

Chapter Twenty-four

The mine wasn't much of a hiding place.

There'd been a cave-in, probably years ago, and the entrance wasn't an entrance any longer. It was a dimple in the hillside. There was no shaft to escape down. No myriad tunnels to provide misdirection or confusion.

Just this shallow indentation.

"Have I mentioned," Hugh breathed into Alison's ear as they crouched in the darkness, "that I'm claustrophobic? And afraid of spiders?"

"Shh, just close your eyes," she said, because Brian was out there. God, her arm was throbbing with every accelerated beat of her heart.

Jamie had walked through her, telling her no over and over again when they'd first come in here and he'd realized that the cave was no kind of a real hiding place.

But it was better than being out there, exposed, kneeling behind some scrub brush.

Still, she'd asked him to go out and try to find them a better place to hide. And as she waited for him to return, she closed her eyes, too, and prayed that A.J. would appear out of the sky like some superhero, rushing yet once again to her rescue. She was foolish for doubting him, foolish for fearing Henry's threats of a lawsuit, foolish for getting on that plane.

She felt Jamie return, felt the now familiar buzz of cold energy as he passed completely through her. The buzz, oddly, made her injured arm feel better.

But what he was telling her was a great big no.

"No, there's nowhere else out here to hide?" she asked, and he touched her shoulder, yes.

"Jamie, tell A.J. that I'm sorry," she said, barely audibly, but he gave her another very definite no. Still, she wanted to say it. "Tell him I love him and that I'm sorry that . . . it turned out *I* was the one who couldn't give *him* a guarantee."

A.J. was still a good half an hour away.

"Drive faster," I told him, then went back to the hillside where Alison was hiding.

I arrived just in time to hear Brian whisper to Gene, "Change in plans. Keep 'em alive."

"What the hell . . . ?" Gene asked plaintively.

To which Brian replied, "The car's up to its fucking axles. We're not going to be able to get it out without their help. And if we can't, if it's stuck . . . ? You want their brains and blood in the back of your truck?"

Gene mumbled something in reply, but Brian's powerful flashlight swept across the hillside.

I jumped up to Alison and Hugh as that beam of light made another pass. We all ducked. Me, too—it was instinctive.

We held our breath, but the light swept back toward us yet one more time. And then stopped.

Brian had found the cave.

I heard Alison moving and I saw in the darkness that she was looking for a rock, small enough to conceal in her hand, but big enough to pack a wallop.

I told her no. This was not the time or place for this—A.J. was coming—but she ignored me as the light got closer and closer and closer.

And then it was shining right on Alison and Hugh. And Brian locked and loaded the rifle he must've gotten along with that flashlight from Gene, who did the same to his own weapon a few yards away from him.

"Hands up," Brian ordered. "Where we can see 'em. Move slowly!"

And slowly, obediently, Alison and Hugh both straightened to their feet, as I touched Alison's shoulder to let her know that I was still there.

"You!" Alison breathed as Gene moved closer and his flashlight illuminated Brian's face. "I saw you, outside my trailer—threatening Trace Marcus. With that other man, with the tattoos. Oh, my God, Jamie, was *that* Wayne?"

Yes, I told her. Yes. *Yes.*

I was right. I'd been right all along. Alison had seen something she wasn't supposed to see. She'd seen Brian and Wayne with Trace Marcus, moments before Brian had killed Wayne.

"No talking," Brian ordered. "Hands on your heads. Both of you. Move it. Now!"

• • •

The car was stuck in the sand.

The tall man that Jamie called Brian made both Alison and Hugh try to push it out as he sat behind the wheel and Gene stood guard.

But neither of them had the muscle or bulk—at least Alison didn't, especially with her injured arm—and it didn't take long before Brian realized it was hopeless.

She watched as he wiped the car down, presumably so as not to leave prints. And then he ordered the other man—Gene—to empty out the covered bed of his truck.

Yes, Jamie told her, but he kept his hand on her shoulder a long time, as if he were saying yeeeeeesssss, really slowly, and although she didn't know it for sure, she suspected he was trying to tell her what she'd already figured out.

Delay was a good thing.

Because A.J. was on his way.

Please, God, let A.J be on his way. . . .

But Gene's truck didn't have all that much in the back, and he quickly moved it into the cab, whereupon Brian marched her and Hugh over and ordered them into the truck bed.

"First give me the keys to your Jeep," he told Hugh, who immediately handed them over.

"I didn't see anything that day," Alison tried to tell Brian, and felt Jamie tell her no, even as the tall man hit her.

He backhanded her almost effortlessly, casually, and even though she saw it coming it still nearly knocked her off her feet as her brain clouded from both fear and the sudden burst of pain.

And she should have been terrified, and she certainly was, but a part of her seemed to separate and look down at herself with distance and analysis. And that part was thinking not of her own impending and likely death, or of her fear for Hugh and A.J.'s lives, but of Melody Thompson Quinn Gallagher, who had received blows *exactly* like that one, as a matter of course.

For scrambling Silas Quinn's eggs in the exact same way as she had the day before, when he'd told her he'd enjoyed them.

For speaking when not spoken to, or for not properly greeting her husband when he came into a room, even though she couldn't possibly do both.

There was no rhyme or reason, no pattern, no way to do anything but lose and continue to lose, day after day after horrible, hopeless day.

And Alison knew what that was like—it had been the same with her mother. Even though she'd never been hit, even though she'd never even really been screamed at or berated, there had been no pattern, no rhyme or reason to her mother's drinking.

Things would be going wonderfully well—and after months of sobriety, her mother would drink.

Things would be terrible, and she'd drink.

Things would be in between, they'd be average, moderate, uneventful, unimportant—and always and forever, Alison would never know whether or not her mother would come home sober or staggering and word-slurringly drunk.

You're not a kid anymore, A.J. had said when she'd told him about her mother, when he'd told her the truth about being an alcoholic himself. Recovering alcoholic. *You could walk away from me.*

Like Melody before her, Alison didn't quite believe how strong she could be.

But like Melody, she *could* walk away—if there were good reason to. But to walk away before that, from the most incredible man she'd ever known . . . ?

A.J. was not her mother, in the same way that, for Melody, Jamie hadn't been Silas Quinn.

It was then that her fog lifted and she was back. Hugh was helping her, pulling her with him into the grimy bed of Gene's truck. She hit her head again on the metal cover, which was much too low—just a few feet above the truck bed—and Hugh pulled her down again as she saw stars, holding her in his arms both to protect her and to keep her from bumping her head again as her ears continued to ring.

Gene or maybe Brian closed the tailgate first, then the cover's flap, plunging them into total darkness and heat. Unlike some truck bed covers, this one had no windows.

"Oh, my God," she heard Hugh breathe as someone outside—Brian or Gene—put a key in the cover and locked it shut with a clunk.

Alison was still carrying her cell phone—they hadn't taken it away from her, and she opened it, hoping . . .

But it was still useless. Maybe if they drove away from the sedan . . .

"Jamie," she said, aware that the inside of her cheek was bleeding from that blow—cut by her own teeth—and that beneath her bandage, her arm felt wet and warm, "are you still here?"

Yes.

It was hard not to cry when she felt that now reassuring buzz. "He's here," she told Hugh as she felt the truck jerk forward, but then stop. It jerked again, and again, tossing them about in the darkness. "What are they doing?" she asked, but then immediately rephrased. "Are they trying to tow the car out of the sand?"

Jamie's answer was both a yes and a no. Which meant . . .

"Are they towing something else?" she asked.

Yes.

"Hugh's Jeep?" she asked, and again he told her yes.

"Melody's diaries," she told him. "They're still in that Jeep. Tell A.J. . . . ."

"Tell A.J.," Hugh hissed in the darkness, "to call the fricking police and FBI and tell them that we're held hostage in the back of this truck!"

The police had set up an observation post out on the road into Jubilation, but Gene and Brian had already slipped past it before I saw what was going on.

There were three state cruisers and an unmarked car, probably FBI, hidden behind a hillside at a curve in the road, and none of them moved an inch as the truck and Hugh's Jeep went by.

They were, no doubt, watching for that black sedan that A.J. had described—which was now well off the road, mired in the sand.

I jumped to A.J. to tell him, and he immediately dialed his cell phone, muttering about how his battery was running low.

Whoever was on the other end of his call answered immediately, and A.J. said—as if they were good friends—"Rob, it's me. Call your boys who are sitting two miles outside of Jubilation. A truck and a Jeep just blew past them. Hugh Darcy and Alison Carter are locked in the bed of that truck."

He hung up before giving Rob time to respond, telling me, "He always says the same thing after I call. I think he might be reading off the turn-yourself-in page of the manual. How far am I behind them?"

He was going eighty-five, which was as fast as that truck he'd stolen could manage without shaking itself apart.

"Seventeen minutes," I told him, and he swore.

But then he said, "Go stay with Alison. If the cops stop them, she's going to need to know to kick and scream."

"She said to tell you that she loves you, kid," I told him, hoping it would help bring him hope.

But the look he shot me was black. "Don't tell me that," he said. "You go back to her and you tell her that I am *not* going to let her die."

"I've been trying to," I said, and I popped away, hoping to hear sirens as the cops chased after the two vehicles they'd let pass.

But there was only the sound of tires against the road as Alison again tried her cell phone, cursing softly as she snapped it shut. Hugh, meanwhile, was feeling his way along the bed of the truck, looking for a way out and finding none.

I touched Alison, and she bumped her head on the cover again. "Ow! Jamie?" She didn't wait for me to say yes, she asked, "The cell phone jammer. Did Brian or Gene take it out of the car and bring it with them?"

I did a quick check and sure enough, it was in the front seat of Gene's truck. I also verified visually that none of the state troopers or even the unmarked car had followed the truck and the Jeep.

I took a few extra seconds and zoomed down

the road, where—God damn it—they'd moved all right, but only to create a road block, with their lights flashing. No doubt they'd interpreted that phone call from A.J. to mean that he was nearby.

It was an impressive show of power and force, and A.J. was maybe twelve minutes from running right into it.

I dropped back in and told Alison, yes, then tried to figure out the best way to tell her that I had to leave, I tapped her on the head, once, and then ten times in a row. Tap, tap, tap, tap, tap, tap, tap, tap, tap, tap.

"What are you telling me?" she asked.

I did it again. One tap, then ten.

She was silent, thinking hard.

"Come on, girl," I said. And I did it again, but this time, around tap four, she said, in a rush, "A, b, c, d, e, f, g, h, i, j—A.J.?"

Yes, I told her. Yes.

And then I left, because right at that moment, he needed me more than she did.

But before I popped back to him, the truck jostled as it took a turn, and the engine dropped into a lower, louder gear as it started up a hill.

And I went out into the night to see what the hell, and discovered that Brian in Hugh's Jeep was leading Gene in his truck up the road that led to that silver mine that used to belong to me. The one I'd won in that poker game all those years ago.

They were going to Gallagher's Claim.

• • •

A.J. stopped his truck at a place where an arroyo had completely washed out the road.

If you could even call something that had never been paved a road.

Still, this two-rut pathway was—according to Jamie—a shortcut up to the mine where his great-grandfather's ghost said Alison and Hugh were being taken by their captors.

Short cut in that the distance between here and the mine was less than the main road. And *short cut,* too, in that A.J. didn't have to crash his way through a police road block to get there.

But not *short cut* in the sense that it would take him less time to arrive.

He was about to put the truck into reverse to try going off road to work his way over to the remaining trail farther up the hill, but Jamie popped back in, shaking his head. "It's washed out in other places, too," he told A.J. "All the way up to the mine."

Which meant there was only one thing to do.

A.J. took his cell phone and his borrowed baseball cap, and he got out of the truck and started to run.

I returned to Alison and Hugh just as Brian pulled the Jeep up in front of the mine.

He'd made it all the way up the trail that the movie crew had designated for pedestrians only—as had Gene behind him in his truck.

There was a third vehicle waiting for them there—another truck—and as they shut off their engines, Skip Smith, whom I'd seen murder Neil Sylvester, climbed out.

He was smoking a cigarette, and he dropped it in the dust, grinding it out beneath his boot. "About time you got here," he said. "I brought the dynamite into the mine all by myself. It's all ready to go." He looked around. "Where the hell are they?"

"In the truck," Brian told him.

"They dead?"

"No, asshole," Gene said in his thick accent, as he unlocked the cover and opened it and the tailgate. "You think I want to have to burn bloodstains and other DNA shit offa my truck bed?"

Brian was carrying that rifle again, and as he'd done before for emphasis, he cocked the thing. *Cha-chunk.* "Get out," he ordered.

A.J., on foot, was still a mile and a half away, and most of that was uphill. I dove into the truck bed and let Alison know that I was there.

"Is A.J. close?" she whispered, and I backed away, because he wasn't.

She took a deep breath and exhaled hard at that lack of news, then took her sweet time getting out.

Of course, I stood there praying that Brian wouldn't get mad at her and hit her again.

But he didn't, even when she pretended that her knees were weak upon exiting the truck. She sank to the ground, and Hugh tried to help her. I wanted to grab him and tell him to back away, because we needed to stall.

Although what A.J. was going to do when he got here—unarmed—was something I hadn't yet figured out. I supposed he could start by throwing his cell phone at Brian and hopefully hitting him in the head and knocking him out.

But that left Skip, who also had his gun drawn as he stood several paces back from Brian. Gene, lazy as always, no doubt figured that was enough firepower, and he kept the weapon that he wore in its holster. Still, I knew that if A.J. appeared, even with Gene's fumbled draw, he'd get his piece out and firing faster than A.J. could overpower him from a dozen or so paces away.

I elevated straight up to scan the surrounding countryside, but saw no sign of A.J. The sky to the east was slowly getting lighter. Dawn was on its way.

Brian turned to Skip and asked, "Did you bring the shovel?"

"You know it," Skip said.

"Then get it," Brian said.

And Skip tucked his sidearm into his pants as he turned to head toward his truck.

Which was when Brian surprised me—although it really shouldn't have. If he was so intent on cleaning up after Wayne's murder, it made sense that he would be thorough.

But he took that rifle of his and pointed it at Skip and neatly blew a hole in the back of his head. The dead man crumpled to the ground.

Gene was frozen. He was possibly even more stunned than Alison and Hugh, who'd nearly flattened at the sound of that gunshot and were now clinging to each other, wide-eyed in shock.

As we all watched, Brian swung that weapon around and drilled Gene, too, right between the eyes.

He also fell in the way of the instantly dead. It wasn't like in the movies—no staggering, no flailing. One minute Gene was standing and the next he was in the dirt.

Brian quickly took the weapons from both of his former cohorts' bodies, making sure the safeties were on before he tucked them into his pants.

"Another fine weapon that crazy bastard A.J. Gallagher purchased at a gun show, this time here in Arizona," Brian told Alison and Hugh, as he admired the rifle in his hands.

They thought they were next, and I did, too. And I could see from both Alison's and Hugh's eyes that they were well aware that the odds had just changed from three against two, to two against one.

Except it was really three against one. And Alison knew that, too.

"Now, Jamie, now!" Alison shouted, and I launched myself at Brian, hoping he'd be stunned like the snake that he was, and would fumble that gun.

It all happened so fast.

Alison leapt forward, too, even as Jamie ran into Brian's personal space and stayed there, lighting him up with that electrical buzz.

It wasn't really that painful, but it was startling, and she was counting on that.

Hugh was right beside her, fighting for their lives as together they took Brian down into the dirt, his rifle skittering away.

But he was bigger and stronger than he looked—most of his bulk was muscle, and even as Hugh scrambled after that rifle, Brian twisted and managed to kick him in the jaw. Hugh's head snapped back and his eyes rolled up, and Alison knew that her friend was either dead or unconscious. But she grabbed for the butt of Skip Smith's gun that was there at the top of Brian's pants.

Her arm hurt like hell, but she grabbed it and got it, and scooted away from Brian, pushing herself back on the seat of her jeans as she held it—God, it was heavy—in both hands. She aimed it at the biggest part of Brian—his chest.

"Freeze," she shouted.

And he froze, one hand outstretched, still

reaching for the rifle that was half under Hugh's limp body.

One second passed, then two, and she felt Jamie's now familiar presence telling her what sure as hell felt like both yes and no.

And Brian smiled and in that instant, she knew he was going to do it—he was going to go for that rifle, so she pulled the trigger.

And nothing happened.

Brian laughed and she pulled it again, and he moved and she knew there was something called a safety, but she had no clue how to remove it so that the gun would fire, so she did the only thing she could do. She dropped the weapon and she ran, slipping and scrambling her way into the darkness of the mine.

A.J. was almost there.

He could see lights blazing—probably headlights—at the entrance to the mine.

He'd heard the gunshots—two of them, God help him. Then he heard another, and he ran even faster.

I followed Alison into the mine, wishing she hadn't dropped that weapon, but knowing that my priority now was to help her hide from Brian, who was coming after her, not try to show her how to remove the safety on an unfamiliar gun using taps and other signals.

She stumbled in the darkness over a pile of rocks, and I realized that I could see what she couldn't, so I positioned myself in front of her and waited until she bumped into me with her outstretched hands.

"Jamie," she whispered, and we moved slowly forward, shuffling along, the dead leading the blind.

I'd been in that mine only a few times, and I struggled to remember where the tunnel split. I knew there was a fork up ahead, but just how far?

And then the question became moot, because Brian had returned to Gene's truck to get a flashlight, and its beam bounced along the rock and dirt walls that were barely shored up by a series of rotting timbers.

Alison saw the light, too, and tried to move faster now that she could see.

But we were in a stretch of the tunnel that had nowhere to hide, no cover save an ancient wooden cart.

In seconds, Brian would round the corner that was keeping Alison concealed from him, and she was going to die.

And I couldn't do a goddamned thing about it.

Never had I felt so utterly impotent and useless.

Never had I wanted anyone to see and hear me as badly as I did right at that moment. Never had

I wanted so badly to be flesh and blood again, and for the gun belt that I wore on my hips to be real leather and steel.

Brian rounded that corner and saw Alison and raised his rifle.

With a shout, I drew my own gun and fired.

Bullets were flying in what seemed like every direction, the sound of the gunshots deafening in the mine.

Alison dropped to the ground, uncertain where to go for cover, where to hide.

Brian must've had yet another helper, because there were two gunmen—one of them firing from the darkness behind a flashlight. The other—in a cowboy hat—was only a few feet away from her. But he wasn't shooting at her, he was shooting at . . . Brian?

"Stay down, get behind that cart!" that second man was shouting at her, riding the hammer of what looked to be an authentic antique Colt 45.

Bullets from the other gun cut through him, but he didn't fall. It was as if he were insubstantial. But Brian didn't seem to realize that, he just kept shooting at him.

Around her, bits and pieces of the mine's walls and ceiling shook loose from the noise.

"Come on, Alison," this new man shouted. "Move!"

He turned and looked directly at her from under

the brim of his black hat, his eyes a sharp blue, his lean face intense.

It was Jamie Gallagher. The ghost of A.J.'s great-grandfather.

And Alison moved, scrambling back behind that cart for cover, even as she saw Brian fall, his flashlight hitting the mine floor and rolling down the slight incline, toward her.

Had Jamie really managed to kill him? It didn't seem possible, but then in the sudden silence, she heard a voice from the entrance of the mine. "Alison?"

"It's A.J.," Jamie told her. "Hallelujah!"

But then, with a rush and a roar, the sky fell.

Chapter Twenty-five

The mine was caving in.

A.J. stumbled back, diving and scrambling out as dirt and rocks rained down upon him, coughing and gasping for air as he pushed himself up onto his hands and knees.

And the panic and the bile that he'd felt when he'd first arrived at the mine and saw the bodies and the blood was back with a vengeance and it was all he could do not to throw up, right there in the still swirling dust.

But he'd shot Brian. Shot and hit him—as Brian was aiming that rifle to take another shot at Alison.

Which meant that—at that moment, at least—she'd still been alive.

"Jamie, where are you?" A.J. said, but Jamie didn't appear.

As the dust began to settle, I found Alison.

Brian's flashlight had rolled down next to her, and in its light I could see that she was lying facedown. She was half-buried by dirt and debris, but she was stirring and still alive, thank God.

A quick look around told me that, had A.J. not already killed Brian, he would've been good and dead, crushed beneath the pile of rocks and earth that now blocked our way out of the mine.

Well, it didn't block *my* way out. I could walk through anything. But Alison had to use a more conventional form of exit, and it wasn't going to be the way she'd gotten in.

Farther down the shaft, though, another cave-in had occurred. She was lying in a very small open area. Several feet in any direction, and she would have been crushed—which made me think about divine intervention and miracles.

Although I have to confess, I also spent a second or two considering that a pocket this small had to have a limited amount of air.

Alison lifted her head and looked directly at me.

"A.J.," she said, and for a moment I thought she mistook me for him. But then she added, "Is he all right?"

I nodded, because I could feel him out there, calling me. "He made it out," I told her.

"Thank God," she said, trying not to cry. As she composed herself, she looked around, picking up that flashlight to shine it on the walls and ceilings and fresh new piles of earth and rocks. Her mouth tightened as she no doubt came to the same conclusions about the air supply that I had.

She pulled herself up so that she was sitting, wincing at the bruises she'd collected. She brushed as much of the dirt and dust as she could from her clothes and hair, making note of the fact that her injured arm had bled through its bandage and her shirt sleeve.

"I doubt I'm dead," she finally said. "Or I wouldn't feel so awful. But . . . how come I can see you?"

I didn't have a good answer. So I shrugged. "I don't know," I said. "You're not supposed to be able to."

"But Brian saw you, too," Alison pointed out. "He shot at you instead of me because he saw your gun."

I shrugged again. "I guess I fooled him into thinking I was real."

"You are real," she said. She laughed as she shook her head. "I still don't completely believe it, but you're really real, aren't you?"

It felt odd. I'd studied Alison's face well over a

hundred times, but I'd never before seen her looking directly back at me.

A.J. was right. She did have beautiful eyes.

"I don't suppose this part of the mine has a secret back door," she said, pushing herself to her feet and wincing as she put weight on her right leg.

I shook my head. "Why don't you sit tight?" I suggested. "I'll go tell A.J. you're alive, and trapped in here. I'm sure he's fretting about that."

She flashed that light around us again, limping as she moved about the space, and I knew that she was trying to calculate how long it would take to dig her out—if digging her out were even possible—and how much air she had left.

I'm not real good at mathematical equations, but like I already said, the odds didn't appear to be in her favor. Unless we could get her an outside source of air, she was going to run out of oxygen long before she was unburied.

"If I don't make it out of here, I need you to tell A.J. something for me," she said, turning to look at me.

"You'll get out," I told her. "Even if the kid has to dig with his bare hands."

She nodded, and I knew she didn't believe me. "But if I don't, I need you to tell him something for me," she said again. "Promise me you will?"

"I promise," I said. "And I know the drill, dear. You've already said it. You love him, you're sorry. I got it. You're going to be able to tell him that yourself. Hang tight, I'll be right back."

And with that, I popped away, because it had been awhile since I'd played a hand of poker and my ability to bluff wasn't what it had once been. I could tell that Alison wasn't fooled by my bravado, because this time I wasn't even able to fool myself.

"Come on, Jamie," A.J. said. "Damn it!"

There was only one reason A.J. could think of why Jamie wasn't answering him, and it was because the ghost couldn't face him. And if Jamie couldn't face him, it was because Alison was dead.

But then, from behind him, he heard a voice— "Gallagher?"—and A.J. spun around, raising the handgun he'd found just lying in the dust.

His first thought was that now he truly did see dead people and that Hugh Darcy's ghost was approaching him.

But the man staggered slightly, his hand against a gash in his head that was still bleeding, his other hand out and up to show he was unarmed. A.J. lowered his weapon, and moved to help the other man. Who was solid and living, thank you, Jesus.

"What happened?" Hugh asked as A.J. helped him sit on the ground. "Alison and Jamie and I— we jumped that man, Brian. He'd just killed Skip and that other guy Gene, and . . ."

"Alison must've gone into the mine to try to get away from him," A.J. told him, unable to keep the anguish from his voice, "but there was a cave-in."

"Oh, God," Hugh said. He pointed back at one of the trucks. "There's a shovel. . . ."

"We're going to need more than a shovel," A.J. said, although it was definitely a start. He strode toward the truck, trying not to look at the bodies on the ground, and there absolutely was a shovel in the back. He grabbed it, but then looked at the hillside, uncertain as to where to start digging.

But then Hugh said, "What about dynamite?"

And A.J. turned to look at him.

"Skip said he put some at the entrance to the mine," Hugh told him. "I think they were going to kill us in there, and then blow the mine shut."

A.J. looked, and there it was—half-buried in the dirt—what looked like a full case of explosives.

"At least that was Skip's plan," Hugh said. "Brian had a different agenda. I think his plan was to kill everyone. You know, maybe we should call for help."

Call. Yes.

A.J. pulled his cell phone out of his pocket, but he had no reception, no ability to call anyone. Except what was it that Jamie had told him? Brian was using another jammer, and he strode over to Hugh's Jeep, and then the other truck, the one with the cover on the bed, and yes, there it was, sitting right on the front seat.

He pulled the gizmo out of the truck and threw it on the ground and hit it again and again with that shovel until it was a pile of circuit plates, and wires, and smashed metal casing.

And this time? When he opened the cell phone his mother had given him, he had service. So he used it—to call Alison, praying that she'd pick up.

But he was sent straight to her voicemail.

And enough was enough. "Jamie," A.J. said. "Where the *hell* are you?"

"I'm *right* here," I said. "Jeez, kid, don't you see me?"

But he didn't. A.J. didn't see me. Or rather, he *couldn't* see me. This was one hell of a time for the rules of the spirit game to start changing. But then I realized that I'd probably changed the rules myself back in the mine, when I'd somehow managed to appear to both Brian and Alison.

I tried shouting in his ear. "I'm right here, A.J.!"

He didn't even flinch.

I snapped my fingers in front of redheaded Hugh's face, too. He was trying to convince A.J. that it was time to call the local authorities for help—or at least to call his uncle Henry.

But Hugh didn't see me either, so my theory that everyone *except* A.J. could see and hear me wasn't a viable one.

A.J., meanwhile, scrambled around, looking at the mine entrance from all angles. I followed him as he went to the other side of the hill. What was he looking for?

He went back to the entrance and began moving the rocks and rubble with that shovel he must've gotten from one of the trucks.

"Come on, Jamie," he muttered. "Please tell me she's still alive."

"She's still alive," I said, but he couldn't hear me.

He couldn't see me, he couldn't hear me, but he *could* feel me. I closed my eyes and walked into him, praying he'd remember what I'd told him about my method of communicating with Alison.

He straightened up, and swept the air around him with his arms. "Jamie?" he said. I didn't move and he found me. "What happened?" he asked. "Why can't I see you?"

He realized instantly that I couldn't answer those questions. "Okay," he said, holding out both of his hands, palms up, about two feet apart. "My right hand is *yes,* my left hand is *no.* Okay?"

I touched his right hand.

"Is Alison . . . ?" He closed his eyes and took a deep breath, afraid of the answer. "Is she alive, Gramps?"

Yes.

"Thank you, God." A.J. took another deep breath, but he wasn't able to stop the flood of emotion that filled his eyes with tears. "Thank you."

I touched his right hand again. Thank you, indeed.

"Is she hurt?" he asked me.

Yes.

His shoulders tightened as he braced himself. "Badly?"

No.

He started breathing again. "Have you been able to find any access to fresh air?"

No.

"Have you looked?"

Yes.

"Shit."

Yes, sir. Big shit.

"Where is she?" he asked me. "How far from the entrance? And yeah, I know you can't answer that with a yes or a no. But Alison told me that the mine runs relatively close to the surface of the hill line for about an eighth of a mile before angling down, and that there's a second entrance not too far from here. What I want you to do is go find her—" He stopped himself. "Can you still walk through walls?"

Yes.

"Rock walls?"

Yes. That was not a problem. Besides, the walls of this mine were mostly rubble and dirt.

"Can he?" Hugh asked, and A.J. nodded.

"Okay, Gramps," he said. "Find Alison and take the shortest distance from her up to the surface and make note of where you end up. Then come

601

back to me and we're going to use yes and no until I reach that same spot. Got it?"

Yes.

"Tell him to take a measurement while he's at it," Hugh suggested. "Let us know how many feet or yards we're going to have to dig through to reach her."

"Blast," A.J. said. "Not dig. We've got dynamite, we're going to use it. Got that, Gramps?"

Yes. Dynamite? For the first time, I actually had hope. Provided, of course, that we did it right, and didn't bring Alison's part of the mine down on top of her. But A.J. was clearly aware of that danger.

"I also need to know the exact size and location of the area where she's trapped," A.J. told me, "so while you're down there, walk it with your feet, okay?"

Yes.

I popped away, but quickly came back and we went through some speed rounds of both the hot-and-cold game and Twenty Questions. It was tiresome and frustrating, and all the time we were doing this, I knew Alison was down there alone, thinking she'd been buried alive. But after we were done, A.J. was able to estimate accurately where in the mine Alison was, and how much time she'd have before the air ran out.

We didn't have an awful lot of time.

Whenever A.J. stopped to think, he shoveled and moved rocks and earth from the hillside beneath which Alison was buried. By the time he finished with his calculations, his hands were raw and bleeding.

But I knew he wasn't going to stop until he got his woman out of there.

A.J. turned back to where he'd last felt my presence. "Okay, Gramps," he said, wiping the sweat from his forehead with the sleeve of his T-shirt. "Here's what we're going to do."

"Come on, woman," Jamie said, popping back in and nearly scaring Alison to death. "I need you to move over this way, as far as you can. You have to take cover. A.J.'s gonna blast you out of here."

She pushed herself up on her hands and knees—that was the best she could manage with her twisted ankle—and crawled toward the ghost. "Blast?" she repeated.

"With dynamite." Jamie flashed her a grin that made her understand Melody Quinn's description of him as *pretty*. With his sparkling blue eyes, and his twenty-something appearance, he was a remarkably handsome man. Almost as handsome as his great-grandson. "He's calling his buddy Lutz right now to make sure he did the math right."

"What does A.J. know about dynamite?" Alison had to ask.

"Apparently," Jamie told her, "when you hang around with Navy SEALs, you learn a lot when you, and I quote, *blow shit up for fun*."

"The war," Alison said.

"Yeah," Jamie told her, his expression somber. "It's a case of good coming from bad. A.J. went through hell, but he spent all that time with Craig Lutz. And now he's going to use what he learned to save your life."

"May I ask you something?"

"You can ask," he told her. "I may not be able to answer."

"Have you seen God?"

He shot her a smile that was loaded with mischief. "I certainly have. Every single time I made love to my beautiful wife."

"That's not what I meant," she said with a laugh, but it made her cough—it was getting harder to breathe in there.

And Jamie knew it. "I'm going to go check on the kid," he told her. "Sit tight."

"I'm not going anywhere," Alison said, but before he popped away, she stopped him, even though her hand passed right through his arm. "Everyone in your family loved you so much. They still love you," she told him. "A.J. most of all. I'm glad you came back for him."

"He deserves some happiness," Jamie told her, "which is why *I'm* so glad that he met *you*."

"Jesus," Lutz said, on the other end of A.J.'s cell phone. "You don't do anything halfway, do you?"

604

"Yes or no," A.J. said. "I don't have a lot of time here. Did I use too much, too little . . . ? The fuse is really short, I know I'm going to have to run like hell, but I don't have a choice about that."

"A.J.," Lutz said. "Man, you're talking about using explosives that are old and unstable. There's no way that I can—"

"Guess," A.J. said. "That's all I really want, Craig. Just please, God, give me your best guess."

There was silence on the other end of the phone.

And then Lutz sighed. "A.J., if I tell you and I'm wrong, and you kill her—"

"She's dying," A.J. said. "Right now. Jamie was just with her and she's running out of air." His great-grandfather was walking through him repeatedly. Over and over and over again, in a signal that was impossible to misunderstand. "It's now or never."

"Then do it," Lutz said. "Yes. If I were there, I'd've set up the blast exactly as you did. Exactly."

"Thank you," A.J. said. He closed his cell phone and turned. "Hugh, I need a match!"

But it wasn't Hugh behind him. In fact, Hugh was nowhere in sight. Instead, Rob from catering, aka Rob the FBI agent, was standing there, along with a red-haired woman who had to be his partner Charlotte. They both had their weapons drawn and aimed at A.J.

They both looked a little pale—no doubt from

seeing the gruesomely murdered bodies of Skip Smith and the man Jamie had known as Gene, that were still lying in the dirt near the trucks.

"I need you to move slowly, Mr. Gallagher," Rob told him, in that voice A.J. recognized from all those phone calls. "Hands on your head, then lie on the ground."

Alison was light-headed and dizzy, and she knew that she was out of time and out of air.

God, she was so tired. . . .

"Don't you dare go to sleep!"

She opened her eyes to see Jamie standing over her, frowning. For a man who, like A.J., had angelic good looks, he had an impressively dark scowl.

"A.J.'s outside," he said. "He's going to get you out of here. Don't you give up, girl."

"My mother and my grandmother both," she told him. "They died of breast cancer. A.J. was right—there're no guarantees. Not for anyone. I don't know why I was so afraid. . . ."

"Good," Jamie said. "You're not afraid anymore. That's great. I want great-great-grandchildren and I want 'em soon. You're no spring chicken, dear, and A.J.'s not either. After you get out of here, you and the kid should get to it, fast."

"Tell him," Alison said as she settled back against a pile of dirt and rocks, "to hurry. And to not blow anything important off with that dynamite."

It was supposed to be a joke, upbeat and positive—see? She really did think A.J. was going to get her out. But God, it was so hard to breathe, so very hard.

And she had to close her eyes.

"Hold on, Alison," Jamie said, jolting her awake. "You *hold* on!"

When I popped back outside, A.J. was in the middle of a standoff, because Rob and Charlotte from the FBI had appeared.

Hugh was talking a blue streak, trying to explain that A.J. had *saved* him and Alison from the man who'd done the killing—including that of not just the hapless gun collector up in Alaska, but a second firearms "collector" here in Arizona, too. Meanwhile, the red-haired kid was inching forward, toward the fuse, matchbook hidden in his hand.

A.J., though, had had enough. He held out his hand to Hugh, gesturing for the matches, which made both Rob and Charlotte refresh their grips on their weapons.

"On the ground *now*," Rob ordered in a voice that meant business.

"You're just going to have to shoot me," A.J. said, as he took the matchbook from Hugh.

And—damn! Rob did just that, or at least I

thought he did. It scared the hell out of me, but he'd only discharged his weapon into the ground at A.J.'s feet.

But A.J. didn't flinch. He just looked at Rob. "I love her," he said. "The way I know you love Charlotte. I can't let her die, so shoot me if you have to, but shoot me dead, because I'm gonna keep going until I light this fuse."

And he turned, and I confess I may have done some heavy-duty praying right about then, because Rob didn't look happy.

It was Charlotte, though, who spoke up. "Hold your fire," she told her partner as A.J. sprinted toward the fuse. "Everyone get back and get down," he told them as he lit it and he, too, ran for cover.

Boom!

It was a magnificent blast, spraying them all with dirt and little pieces of rock.

But A.J. was back at the side of the hill, using Skip's shovel to dig farther into that crater he'd just made, even before the smoke had cleared.

It would have been a lot easier simply to close her eyes.

Her death would be painless that way—she'd just go to sleep.

This way was torture—forcing her eyes to stay open, forcing air that was much too thin or too poisonous into her lungs, her head pounding with each labored beat of her heart.

Alison heard the explosion and turned off the flashlight, waiting for a stream of sunlight to guide her to the fresh air. But there was no sunlight.

And no fresh air.

The disappointment hurt more than her lungs or her head. She tried to turn the flashlight back on, but it had rolled away, out of her reach, and she couldn't find it.

She was going to die, alone and in the dark.

But then she *could* hear something. Digging. Someone was digging. Somewhere. Calling her: *Alison!*

It was A.J. She couldn't call back to him, she couldn't even tell which way the sound was coming from.

But then Jamie was there, glowing like an angel in the dark, imploring her, calling to her: *This way! Come on, Alison. This way . . .*

Slowly, painfully, she began to crawl toward his light.

A.J. was a machine. He was digging. Only digging. The shovel was an extension of his arms, and when it was no longer useful, he threw it down and used his bare hands.

He was going to get Alison out of that mine. Or die trying.

Hugh was beside him. Rob and Charlotte, too— helping him.

Finally, *finally* his hand broke free to the other side of the wall of earth. Sand and dirt rained down on him, but he had what he hoped was a clear hole. He worked to make it larger, even larger, and he tried to look inside, but the mine was so dark, he couldn't see a thing.

"I need a flashlight!" he shouted.

As Hugh scrambled to get him that, A.J. reached his hand and then his arm into the darkness, praying he wouldn't hit another wall of solid rock.

But he didn't touch rock or dirt or sand.

He touched human flesh, another hand, grasping, reaching for him.

Alison. It was Alison!

"She's alive!"

Her fingers encircled his wrist and he grabbed her arm, pulling her closer and using his other hand and arm to widen the hole.

With a superhuman heave, he pulled her up and out of the mine and into his arms.

Her lips were dry and tinged with blue from lack of oxygen and she was covered with dirt and dust and gasping for air. Her injured arm, where she'd been shot yesterday, was bleeding again— the stitches had opened. But she was alive, and to A.J., she had never looked so good.

"We need an ambulance," A.J. told Rob, but Charlotte was ahead of the game.

"I've already called for a Medevac," she told

them. "And the paramedics from Jubilation. They'll get here soon with oxygen."

"A.J.," Alison whispered. "I'm so sorry that I didn't believe you."

"Shhh." He smiled down at her as he held her there in the hot morning sun. "You made one little mistake. Big deal."

"I nearly got you killed," she breathed, as she started to cry.

"That was yesterday," he told her. "This is today. One day at a time, remember?"

She laughed through her tears at that. "I don't think that applies to something like this."

"Sure it does," he said. "Trust me on this. It applies to everything."

"I *do* trust you," she whispered.

And then Hugh was there, with a golf umbrella that he must've had in the back of his Jeep, providing them with a little shade, which was nice. He shifted slightly so that Rob was protected from the sun, too.

Poor Rob looked shell-shocked, particularly when Alison turned to him and said, "Jamie wants me to tell you to man up and give Charlotte the ring."

"Jamie," Rob repeated. "The ghost."

They all nodded—A.J. and Alison and Hugh.

"He's absolutely real," Hugh told him. "Jamie, go ahead and do your crazy thing to Rob."

"Holy *shit,*" Rob said after Jamie must've done just that.

In the distance, A.J. could hear sirens—ambulances and a fire engine and probably state police cars and the sheriff's vehicles, as well as security details from the movie set.

"I don't know what they're going to do to me," he told Alison, whose breathing was getting a little easier, thank God. "Where they're going to take me. But I'll make sure Jamie stays close to you, okay?" He lifted his head. "Jamie, you hear that?"

Jamie told him yes.

Alison nodded, worry in her eyes. "Why would they take you away?" she whispered. "You haven't done anything wrong."

"Sometimes it takes awhile for the truth to catch up," he told her. "I'm a veteran with a mental health discharge. People are always going to look at me sideways and assume that I'm maybe a little dangerous."

"Not while I'm around," Alison said.

"And not while I'm around either," Rob chimed in. "You'll be going to the hospital along with Dr. Carter. I'll make sure of it."

Rob—good man—held to his promise to not let anyone take A.J. away. He even got into a shouting match with a pair of state troopers over it, but he didn't back down.

He was helped when A.J.'s friend Craig Lutz and his SUV filled with other former SEALs made the scene. They were a convincing bunch, that's for sure, each one bigger than the last. Lutz hugged A.J. and kissed Alison and made damn sure that when Alison—oxygen mask on her face, blood pressure cuff on her arm—was whisked aboard that medical chopper, A.J. was right there, by her side.

Promising to be in touch, he and his team went zooming back to San Diego, where duty called.

Hugh, meanwhile, was busy recounting the horrific events of the past night, giving a statement to Charlotte, who, it turns out, was the highest-ranking FBI official on the scene.

Which made her Rob's boss, which I found interesting.

The bodies were bagged, the remainder of the dynamite was contained, the trucks impounded, and the place where Brian's body was buried in the rubble was clearly marked.

Excavation equipment would be brought in over the next few days so that his remains would be recovered.

He was identified as one Stewart Brian Bacca from his truck registration—can you imagine going through childhood as Stew Bacca?

Still, I'm not sure it's enough to excuse his choice to live a soulless existence as a hired killer.

I still didn't understand exactly what had happened, but I *did* know that both Rob and

Charlotte were supremely satisfied with the outcome.

Apparently, there was a very, very bad man by the name of Stanley Parker, whose home in L.A. was being surrounded by a SWAT team at that very moment.

"We'll get a call," Charlotte told Rob, "when it's over."

One by one, the emergency vehicles had left the entrance to the mine that I'd won in a poker game over a hundred years earlier.

My FBI friends, Charlotte and Rob, were alone, walking back down the trail to where they'd left their car when they'd decided to check out the gunshots Charlotte had heard coming from these hills, early in the morning.

They silently climbed into their car, and Rob—who was behind the wheel—started the engine and blasted the air-conditioning. I joined them, in the backseat, mostly because I didn't have anywhere pressing to go. I wanted to give Alison and A.J. a little alone time.

I was also curious, I admit.

"That," Rob said, "was weird." He turned his head to look at Charlotte, who looked like she needed a long, quiet nap. She nodded.

"It was," she said. "I know most people are a little crazy—who's not? And don't get me wrong, I love that we helped catch Stanley Parker. But a ghost? Come on."

Rob chuckled and looked a little embarrassed as he said, "I think the ghost is real. It walked through me. It was . . . kind of cool."

She looked at him, and he shrugged.

"I don't know," he said. "A.J. knew all that stuff about us that . . . He knew it, even though I swept our trailer with a bug detector twice a day. I don't know how—"

"Long-range listening device," Charlotte suggested.

But Rob shook his head. "No," he said. "There were things he knew—that Alison knew, too—that I didn't talk about."

"Like what?" Charlotte asked.

And Rob—good man—did it. He dug into his pocket and pulled out that little jeweler's box. "Like this," he said as he handed it to her. "They knew about this. They knew that I've been carrying it around. For you."

Her eyes were wide as she looked from it—it was undeniably a ring box—to him.

"After the ghost walked through me," Rob told her, "Alison—she can see him and hear him. He told her to tell me to, um, man up, I think is what he said. And to give this to you. Along with, I assume, the right words, which would be . . . Marry me."

Charlotte swallowed and opened the box, and exhaled her surprise.

I leaned over to get another look. "Nice choice,

Rob," I told him, even though he couldn't hear me. It was a decent-sized diamond in a simple solitaire setting—a serious investment for a government employee.

And Rob, probably realizing that the words may not have come out exactly right, rephrased. "Will you marry me?" he whispered. "God, I love you so much, Charlie. I want to spend my life with you. Please say yes."

"Yes," Charlotte said as she slipped that ring on her finger, and hauled old Rob in for a kiss.

Which, of course, is when I popped out.

Chapter Twenty-six

Alison was allowed to shower before the cast was put on her ankle.

It was broken—just a hairline fracture that would heal quickly, if she took care of it properly.

The application of the cast was quick enough— it was the trip through the hospital hallways via wheelchair that seemed to take forever. But finally Alison was returned to the private room where she would spend the night, as the doctors monitored a bump she'd gotten on her head when the mine caved in.

There was very slight swelling, and it was probably nothing, but overnight observation was recommended.

A.J. wasn't happy about that—his worry for her

was all over his face. He'd showered and shaved while she was gone, and someone from the set had brought him his backpack, so his clothes were clean, but he still looked considerably worse for the wear. His hands were a mess—he'd actually needed a few stitches from clawing at the earth, trying to reach her before her air ran out.

He'd saved her life today—this man she'd been afraid to take a chance on.

"Hey," she said, because the alternative was to burst into tears at the sight of him. "Good news—nothing else is broken. Just bruised."

A.J. smiled as he got to his feet and helped the nurse assist Alison into the hospital bed. "Yeah, the doctor already came and told me. That's great."

He waited until the woman was gone and the door shut before he leaned over and kissed Alison soundly. She closed her eyes and kissed him back, and she couldn't help but think of Melody's description of Jamie's sweet kisses, from her diaries. Melody, too, had been rescued from certain death in a dark, airless prison by a man who loved her more than life itself.

And when A.J. would have pulled back, Alison clung to him, unwilling to let him go. So he sat down on the edge of her bed, and just held her in his arms.

"I was sure I was going to die," she admitted into the soft cotton of his shoulder, as he stroked her back, her hair.

She felt him breathing, felt the solid beat of his heart as he didn't respond with false bravado, with *I'd never let that happen.* . . . Instead he nodded, as always, quietly honest. "I was terrified, too." He laughed. "Thank God for Jamie. And Hugh."

Alison pulled back to look at him. "Thank God for you."

"It was a team effort," he told her.

But she wasn't fooled. "Jamie said . . . Did you really tell the FBI to shoot you?"

A.J. made a face, a little embarrassed. "I might've said . . . something like that."

"While proclaiming your undying love for me," she said, and she couldn't help it, she teared up again. "Which I almost walked away from."

"Hey," he said, kissing her. "The important word there is *almost*. Right?"

"I also almost got you killed, all because I saw some stupid guy with some other stupid guy before the first stupid guy killed him." Alison shook her head. "God, it doesn't make any sense."

"No," he agreed as he intertwined their fingers. "It doesn't. Someone from the FBI was here while you were upstairs. He couldn't stay and I tried to ask him all the questions I thought you might have, but . . ."

Alison laughed. "You mean there're actually answers?"

A.J. shrugged. "I think it depends on the question."

"The first one," Alison said, "obviously, is *what the what . . . ?*"

A.J. laughed, which was nice, because even though she was going to be okay, the lines of worry on his face were still much too deep.

"Okay," he said. "Let me give it a try. Ready?"

"Very," she told him.

"Once upon a time, there was a crime lord who lived in Los Angeles," he started, and Alison laughed. And complained.

"I don't want the fairytale version," she said. "I want facts—oh, my *God!*"

Jamie had popped in—just appearing over by the window, in his full gunfighter's garb.

"That's so freaky when you do that," she told him. "You really need to learn to knock, sir."

"Jamie?" A.J. asked, and Alison nodded.

Jamie meanwhile was demonstrating his lack of ability when it came to knocking, showing her that his fist went right through the wall.

"How about this?" Alison suggested. *"Knock knock!"*

"I could do that," Jamie agreed. "Although, to be honest, I don't know how much longer I'm going to be around. Especially with all the new evidence."

"What new evidence?" she asked, but then looked at A.J., who was sitting there patiently while she had a conversation with the thin air. "Sorry."

"No," he said. "And I totally get it now—how strange it looks. But it's okay. What new evidence?"

"Joey's flying down," Jamie told them both, with Alison relaying his words to A.J. "He tracked down a whole pile of birth and death certificates. Oh, and Rose found the title to the house. Both mine and Mel's names were on that."

"That's great," Alison said. "But we were both thinking about evidence having to do with me nearly getting A.J.'s entire family killed up in Alaska."

"If you're going to take the blame," Jamie told her tartly, "you better be ready to share. Because it was *my* fault, completely, that Brian Bacca came after you. If I'd just walked away from Wayne's motor vehicle funeral pyre, none of this would've happened."

Again, Alison repeated his words.

"Not true," A.J. said. "At least not according to what I've been told. Brian Bacca—the man who killed Wayne and shot Alison—he was cleaning up. Anyone who was a potential witness, even fellow thugs like Skip and Gene, were being removed from the maybe-they'll-turn-state's-evidence list. Apparently, Brian was methodical. After he was done here, he was going to go after Skip and Gene's girlfriends, silence them, too. Just in case they knew anything remotely incriminating. I was probably on his list, too."

"That's crazy," Alison said. "And it all started with Brian killing Wayne—why? When I saw them, they were working together to shake down Trace Marcus. Oh, my God—is Trace dead, too?"

A.J. was shaking his head. "I don't know," he said.

"I do." Jamie came up large. "Shh, tell A.J. we need to keep this quiet, but Trace Marcus is in an FBI safe house. He's the prime witness in the case against Stanley Parker."

Alison whispered Jamie's words to A.J., but then asked, "Who's Stanley Parker?"

"He's the crime lord," A.J. told her. "The one who lives in L.A.? Brian Bacca worked for him. He was his right-hand man for over ten years."

"Seriously?" she said, dismayed. "I was nearly killed on the orders of a *Stanley?*"

A.J. laughed again, and a little more of the strain from the past few days left his eyes.

"Apparently, he's a badass," A.J. told her, "despite his non-badass name. Brian's not the only one who worked for him. Skip Smith and Gene Solomon both did, too. Along with the original murder victim, Wayne Cortez."

"Trace Marcus was connected to Stanley Parker, too," Jamie chimed in. "Trace owed him a lot of money—to the point that Stanley owned him. It was a symbiotic relationship, though. Stanley provided drugs for him as well as—"

"No, Skip said he was clean," Alison said. But

as soon as the words left her mouth, she realized how stupid she was to believe anything that Skip Smith had told her.

"Stanley also provided Skip to wrangle Trace," Jamie told her, "as well as keep him supplied with, yes, both drugs *and* a way to cheat the system when it came to drug tests."

"Okay," Alison said, after relaying Jamie's words to A.J. "Wait. Rewind. I saw Brian and Wayne shaking down Trace, outside of my trailer. And it's *Wayne* who was killed? Not Trace? I don't understand."

"Stanley thought he owned Trace's soul, but it turns out he misjudged the actor's malleability," Jamie said. "The way I understand it is, Trace was supposed to give Stanley a percentage of his paycheck every week, and he'd missed several weeks running. Now, in truth that payment was peanuts compared to how much Trace owed. But the payment was symbolic—a constant reminder to Trace that Stanley was his lord and master. So Stanley had Brian and Wayne come out to Jubilation, to remind Trace who was really in control."

"But it was a two-birds-with-one-stone thing," A.J. said after Alison relayed Jamie's information to him. "Because Wayne Cortez—the man with all the tattoos—had just gotten out of jail, and Stanley apparently believed—correctly—that he'd cut a deal with the feds, and that he was working to help solidify a case against Stanley."

"That's right," Jamie said. "So our buddy Brian Bacca killed old Wayne in front of Trace for two reasons. One, because he wanted to scare the hell out of Trace, and two, because according to Stanley, Wayne needed to be killed."

"After I saw them with Trace," Alison remembered, "I heard a car backfire."

"That would've been the gunshot," A.J. told her.

"With Wayne sans head and Trace properly terrorized, Brian drove his rental car into the desert, where he torched it," Jamie said. "Wayne wouldn't have been identified if I hadn't stumbled onto the fire. But together A.J. and I reported both the fire and the murder, and suddenly you were a potential witness, who could put Stanley Parker's right-hand man with a deceased federal informant on the day of that informant's death.

"But worse than that," he continued, "you could put the two of them with Trace Marcus, who'd actually witnessed the murder. Stanley believed they could control Trace with drugs and the promise of more drugs, but he knew that if the FBI picked him up for questioning, all bets were off. So you became the target, Alison. And toward the end, when things were getting wildly out of control—you're a hard woman to kill—Brian was desperately trying to clean up all the loose ends, including Skip and Gene. What he didn't know, though, was that Trace Marcus had already gone to the FBI, asking for protection in return for information about Stanley Parker."

"So no hospital visit for an appendectomy," Alison said.

"Nope," Jamie said. "But Trace did spend several key days negotiating his immunity before giving the feds the information that would have helped them take the threat against you seriously. If we're still laying blame, Trace should get a stinking bucket of it thrown in his face."

This was crazy. "Hugh told me Neil Sylvester is dead, too," Alison said. "That Skip killed him?"

A.J. nodded. "Neil was involved, too. Stanley loaned him several million dollars that he was going to use to turn Jubilation into a tourist mecca. In return, aside from the low interest rate, Neil was responsible for getting Trace Marcus the role of Silas Quinn. He gave the production company permission to film in Jubilation, provided they cast Stanley's property, Trace."

"Neil tried to get out," Jamie told her, "when the body count started. In fact, the last thing he did before he died was put in a call to Stanley's private phone number—which is going to be used as evidence in the case. Hey, you know those letters you were waiting for?"

"The ones written by Penelope Eversfield?" Alison asked.

Jamie nodded. "The FBI was going through

Neil's house, and they found them, along with an entire vault of documents that had belonged to Silas Quinn. A marriage certificate that Mel had signed and, drumroll, please . . . The missing locket, with that curl of Mel's hair."

"DNA evidence," Alison said.

Jamie nodded. "There's also information about Quinn's second wife, Agatha, who was nicknamed Annie. She was only fifteen when the scumbag married her. She was Dick Eversfield's youngest daughter. And I was right about Quinn being poisoned. Annie and her stepmother, Penelope, did the deed. It's in the letters. Which Neil was trying to keep from you, along with all of the other stuff, because he didn't want his great-great-grandfather's good name ruined."

"I've got to get my hands on those letters," Alison said, after repeating that information for A.J.

He squeezed her hand. "I'll help you."

"I also need your DNA," she told him.

He smiled at that.

"Not that way," she said. "I mean, *yes,* that way, but also . . ."

"I know," he said.

They all sat there in silence for a moment, but then Jamie cleared his throat. "Rose, um, asked me to give you a message."

"Me?" Alison asked. "Or . . . ?"

"You," Jamie said.

"Can she see you?" Alison asked.

"No," the ghost said. "But she's inclined to take it seriously now when Tom tells her I'm in the room."

"What's the message?"

"She said she's going to email you with a whole long list of books and Internet loops and support groups. Both for Al-Anon and family members of Gulf War vets."

When Alison relayed that to A.J., he was embarrassed. "I'm sorry that she's so pushy. God," he said, "we come at you from all sides, don't we? My mother and . . . Now I can't even filter Jamie. God only knows what else he's been saying to you."

"He's not saying anything terrible," Alison said. "Although he did tell me that story about when you were little and you forgot to do your homework, so you thought if you went into math class and burst into song, like in a musical, everything would turn out okay."

"Oh," A.J. said. "Good. Great."

"He also told me about the time that mean boy at school fell through the ice, and you were the only one who risked falling in yourself, to save him."

"It wasn't that big a deal," he said.

"As for your mother," Alison told him, "I asked her for that information. I asked her to . . . help. Me. It's been a really long time since I've had any kind of a real family to lean on, for anything, and . . . I think it's really nice."

He was surprised—pleasantly. She could see his hope in his eyes.

From over by the window, Jamie spoke up. "Speaking of family, when we were in the mine," he said, "you promised me great-great-grandchildren."

Alison looked at him. "I don't remember saying that."

"A promise is a promise," he pointed out.

"But not if it's made when you're high from lack of oxygen, mixed with, I don't know, sheer terror?"

"Fear makes people honest," he countered.

"Not everyone wants children," she said.

"But you do." He was absolute in his conviction.

He was also right.

A.J. was clearly puzzled as he followed only her side of the conversation. Thank God.

But then the nurse was back, knocking on the door as she opened it, saving Alison from an embarrassing explanation.

"Sorry to interrupt," the nurse said. "I just wanted to give you fair warning. We'll have a wheelchair in here in about five minutes."

A.J. frowned. "Where are they taking you now?"

"Back into the labyrinth of doom," Alison told

him. "For another CAT scan. And hey, while I'm gone—I meant to tell you this before—Melody's diaries. A.J., you need to read them. They're both heartbreaking and . . . *so* inspiring. You were right when you said that the truth was better than the legend. Melody Gallagher's my hero, and I'm going to try, every day of my life, to make choices and decisions that she would've been proud of. You know, after what she went through with Quinn, she had every reason never to trust another man. Ever. But she did and . . ." She broke off, shaking her head. "They're in my lockup. I'll tell the nurse to give you the key. There's one entry in particular that . . . Well, I just think you need to read them all to understand what I've . . . been thinking about."

"Okay," he said. But then he asked, "Why do you need another CAT scan?"

"They just want to make sure the swelling is getting better not worse," she told him. "It's nothing to worry about."

A.J. nodded. "And me being worried about you is nothing for *you* to worry about," he told her quietly.

She took his hand, lifting his poor, battered fingers to her mouth, where she kissed him. "You're going to have to give me time," she told him.

"I love you," A.J. said. "I'll give you all the time you need."

● ● ●

"Mr. Gallagher?"

The nurse's voice woke A.J. from a deep, dreamless sleep.

He was out on the couch in the hospital waiting room. He'd come out here to give Alison privacy when Hugh had visited, and damn, he'd fallen asleep.

It was stupid, because he'd just finished reading Melody's diaries and he knew exactly what had affected Alison so intensely. He was dying to talk to her about it, but then Hugh had appeared, so A.J. had stepped outside, because it was clear that Hugh wanted to talk to Alison privately. He was, no doubt, making sure that Alison really wanted crazy A.J. hanging around.

A.J. was glad that Alison had friends like Hugh, so he'd gone out into the little waiting area and he'd sat down and made the mistake of closing his eyes. And instead of sleeping for five minutes— he checked the clock on the wall—he'd been unconscious for closer to five *hours* . . . ? He sat up and ran his hands down his face, still groggy. "Hugh was supposed to wake me when he left," he said.

"We all thought it was best to let you sleep," the nurse told him. "Although you *do* know that you can use the futon in Alison's room . . . ?"

"I didn't," he said. "Thank you. That's . . . Thank you very much."

"She's asking for you," the nurse told him. "Alison."

He was instantly awake, standing up and already moving down the hall toward her room. "Is she okay?"

"She seems fine," the nurse said. "But she says that it's urgent that you come into her room."

A.J. quickly ran his fingers through his hair and tucked his T-shirt into his jeans.

The light was on in Alison's room, and the door was ajar, but still he knocked lightly as he pushed it open.

"A.J.?" she called.

"You all right?" he asked, closing the door behind him.

She was sitting up in bed. Her hair was mussed as if she'd been sleeping, too, but her eyes were bright and clear.

She looked wonderful.

"Yeah," she said. "I'm fine. But Jamie's here and . . . A.J., he says it's time to go. He wanted to say good-bye."

A.J. looked around the otherwise empty room. "You can still see him?" he asked.

Alison nodded. "He's over by the window," she said. "But he's starting to fade. He says it's probably got something to do with his breaking the rules. He's got to go back—wherever back is. He won't tell me." She smiled then. "But he says he's not too disappointed about leaving—he's

630

missed Melody. He says he wanted to give you his congratulations on our impending nuptials. Even though I've told him that we're going to take it slowly. One day at a time." She laughed suddenly then. "I will *not* tell him that," she said to Jamie.

A.J. sat down next to her on the bed. "What'd he say?" He smiled, imagining just what Jamie might've said to make Alison blush that way.

Alison looked toward the window, toward Jamie, and made a face. "Oh, all right," she grumbled. "But I'm going to paraphrase." She looked back at A.J. "Jamie claims that I promised we'd give him a great-great-grandchild, while I was in the mine. He suggests that we don't take more than a year or two to 'practice,' but then we need to get busy. His words. He wants us to name the first baby after him. He says Jamie works for either a boy or a girl." She laughed. "I can't believe I'm having this conversation. I mean, we haven't even talked about anything permanent. And God, babies? It's too soon even to talk about . . ." She broke off, and when A.J. started to speak, she held up her hand, telling him to wait, and he knew she was listening to Jamie.

God, babies, indeed. Babies meant diapers and new clothes and new shoes and college educations and one hell of a lot of responsibilities. But somehow that thought wasn't frightening, not even a little. In fact, it made A.J. feel warm inside—so warm that he didn't think he'd ever feel cold again.

He took Alison's hand, and even though she was quiet, listening to Jamie, she squeezed his fingers. When she turned back to A.J., her eyes were glistening with unshed tears. Still, she smiled.

"Jamie said to tell you," she said, in a voice that she was trying to keep from wobbling, "that he wishes upon you, upon *us,* the same joy that he received from his own children. He says that each one of his kids, from Jim to Adam, brought him great joy. And each of his children gave him grandchildren that he adored, and each of those grandchildren gave him still more children to love." She stopped, taking a deep breath. Still, when she spoke again, her voice shook with emotion. "But out of all of those wonderful kids, there was one more special than the rest." She reached up and touched A.J.'s face. "I think he's special, too, Jamie," she murmured.

A.J. gazed into Alison's eyes, letting himself drown in the love that he saw there.

"Tell Jamie," he started to say, but Alison shook her head.

"There's more," she said, and a tear escaped, sliding down her face. "He wants me to tell you that the great-grandchild he loved so dearly grew into a boy that any man would've been proud to call son, and that boy grew into a man capable of breaking free from the darkest reaches of hell, a true man among men."

A.J. had to swallow. "Thanks, Gramps," he whispered. "I had one hell of a teacher."

"I wish I could've been there for you longer, kid," Jamie said.

A.J. could see him!

Jamie was fuzzy, almost transparent, and his voice sounded as if it were coming from way, way off. One glance at Alison told A.J. that she could still see the spirit, too.

Jamie was wearing his favorite horseman's duster over his jacket. It was a well-worn shade of tan and quite long—it went nearly all the way to his ankles, with a deep split up the back. Even if he were on horseback, the duster would protect his legs from the elements. On his head, he wore his black cowboy hat.

Back when A.J. was a boy, Jamie had called his duster and that particular hat his traveling clothes. Tonight, it was clear, Jamie was intending to do some traveling.

"Write a good book about me," he told Alison. "Make sure you let folks know I was human and that I made mistakes—plenty of 'em."

"I will," she said. "And they're going to love you as much as I do."

"Kids, I've got to go."

"I'm going to miss you, Gramps," A.J. said, looking into Jamie's familiar blue eyes.

"Likewise." Jamie smiled. "But you should know, always and forever—I'm not far away. I'll never be too far away." He flickered once. "I love you, kid," he said. "I always will."

And then he was gone.

A.J. looked at Alison. "Ah, shit," he said. "Is it okay if I cry a little?"

She was crying, too, and she pulled him close to kiss him. "Always," she said. "And forever."

He kissed her again, because kissing wasn't as scary as sitting there and letting her see the tears on his face. And she was okay with that, too, just kissing him back so sweetly and holding him close, until he wiped his face on her sheet.

"Sorry," he said. "I was suddenly ten again and . . ."

"I know," she said. "God, it's going to be quiet without him, isn't it?"

"A little." A.J. pushed her hair back from her forehead as he gazed down at her. "I read the diaries," he told her. "And I . . . Well, I want to read something to you. I think it's the part that you wanted me to read and . . ."

She had the leather bag that held the diaries on the chair next to her bed, and he unwrapped them from their plastic and found the piece of paper that he'd stuck inside to mark the entry.

"Ready?" he said as he angled the book toward the bed's light.

Alison nodded.

He cleared his throat and began to read his great-grandmother's words.

Never, he told me, <u>never</u> would he strike me. If there was only one thing in life I could count on, it was that—because he truly loved me.

I would try to remember, I told him. I didn't mean to mistrust him.

He'd earn my trust, he said, through time, if nothing else.

I have never seen a man cry before. It touches my heart that my gambler should have tears so like mine.

But one thing he said rings in my mind, louder and stronger than all of his vows and words of love. It was a promise that he made me give to him.

"If ever I hit you," he told me with those tears in his beautiful eyes, "you <u>will</u> leave me. You'll walk away. Or hell, you'll pick up a gun and order me out of our house, if we ever have a house. Promise me right now that you won't take that abuse from me or from any other man, God forbid something happens to me."

"I promise," I whispered, and he kissed me so gently.

A.J. looked up at Alison, who had tears again in *her* beautiful eyes. She nodded. "That was the entry."

"I can't give you guarantees," he told her. "I can't promise that I'll never slip or even fall. But I *do* know this. You must promise me, that if I ever drink again the way your mother did, if I ever throw away my sobriety for more than one brief moment, if I leave you frightened and guessing and uncertain, you *will* leave me. You'll walk away. Or you'll pick up a gun— after I show you how to use one—and you'll order me out of our house. Promise me right now that you won't take that abuse from me or from any other man, God forbid something happens to me."

Alison nodded. "I promise," she told him, as she watched him carefully put that diary back.

Then A.J. kissed her, and then he kissed her again and again, each kiss longer, slower, sweeter than the last.

He held her close, turning off the light and lying back with her on her narrow hospital bed, feeling the heaven of their two hearts beating together.

"I love you," Alison whispered. "And I'm a lot less scared now than I was before."

"One day at a time," he reminded her. "I love you, too."

"I'll be even less scared tomorrow," she said. "And the day after that . . . Maybe, in a year or so, we *could* start thinking about having, you know, a baby. If you want. . . ."

A.J. kissed the top of her head and smiled into the darkness.

And somewhere, not far away, never too far away, Jamie smiled back.

Epilogue

Two years later

". . . And the Oscar goes to . . . Jonathan White as Jamie Gallagher in *Gallagher*."

The theme music for the movie swelled for the eleventh time that evening, and the crowd roared its approval as young Jon White climbed the steps to the stage.

"Wow," he said as he hefted the golden and gleaming Academy Award, his face shining with his excitement. "Guess I finally made it, Mom."

The audience laughed.

Jon looked directly into the TV camera. "I'd be lying if I said that I didn't expect this, because, honestly? I did. You don't participate in a Henry Logan film without expecting greatness all around." He hefted the Oscar again. "Part of this belongs to Henry, part of it to the terrific team he hired to write the script that became *Gallagher*, and part of it belongs to my wife, Michelle, for not getting too upset when I filmed those steamy love scenes with the talented Winter Baxter."

The audience laughed again.

"But the biggest part of this award belongs to my good friend Dr. Alison Carter. I saw Henry in the lobby earlier this evening, and he told me that Alison is in the hospital tonight, up where she and her husband live in Heaven, Alaska. She and A.J. are the proud new parents of a nine-pound, twelve-ounce baby boy. Believe it or not, this kid's name is Jamie Gallagher."

The audience erupted in applause.

"Alison Carter is this movie's historical consultant," Jon continued, refusing to give up the microphone, even though the band was getting ready to play him off the stage, "and this Oscar is as much hers as it is mine. She provided me with an incredible wealth of information about the character I played. And she wouldn't take no for an answer when I told her I had it handled. Her notes and recently released book about Jamie Gallagher were so complete and so compelling— you could have sworn she actually knew the man.

"So this one's for you, Alison—and A.J. and little Jamie, too. And Henry, if you're listening, and I know you are, Alison recently emailed me with an early draft of her newest book—about the life of World War Two hero, George Gallagher. If I were you, my friend, I'd be thinking option, and I'd start my bidding high. And, by the way, I happen to be looking for a new project.

"Thanks again, Academy! Good night!"

Center Point Publishing
600 Brooks Road ● PO Box 1
Thorndike ME 04986-0001 USA

(207) 568-3717

US & Canada:
1 800 929-9108
www.centerpointlargeprint.com